THE SECRET OF VILLA SERENA

... started her career working at the *Bookseller*, ... on to work in children's publishing, in publicity and in editorial. Under the name Elly Griffiths she is the author of the acclaimed and bestselling Dr Ruth Galloway series of mysteries, and the Stephens and Mephisto mysteries. Domenica is half-Italian and loves the Tuscan coast, although she mainly settles for Brighton, where she lives with her husband, their twins and their cat, Gus.

Domenica De Rosa

THE SECRET OF VILLA SERENA

Quercus

First published in Great Britain in 2007 by
Headline Review as *Villa Serena*

This paperback edition published in 2018 by

Quercus Editions Ltd
Carmelite House
50 Victoria Embankment
London EC4Y 0DZ

An Hachette UK company

A CIP catalogue record for this book is available
from the British Library

PB ISBN 978 1 78648 436 9

10 9 8 7 6 5 4 3 2 1

Typeset by CC Book Production

Printed and bound in Great Britain by Clays Ltd, Elcograf S.p.A.

For my mother, and for my sisters, Giulia and Sheila

PART 1

Summer

CHAPTER 1

Thoughts from Tuscany
By Emily Robertson

Today, I have been thinking about the rush hour. About my journey to work in London: the brisk walk through petrol fumes and flapping bin bags, the brief but violent struggle to board the tube, the journey spent snugly wedged under somebody's armpit, apologising whenever people tread on me, the surge up the escalator, and finally the arrival, exhausted, at my desk.

My journey to work now is as follows: awake to the operatic sound of my neighbours' new cockerel, throw open the heavy wooden shutters and allow the morning sun to infiltrate every wood-beamed, stone-floored inch of the bedroom, go downstairs to a cup of espresso, a slice of ripe *melone* and a handful of figs, shower in the bathroom which looks out onto four uninterrupted acres of breathtaking Tuscan hillside, dress in a thin cotton skirt and T-shirt, then walk slowly to my table on the *terrazzo* under the olive trees. Sit. Think. Breathe.

On days like this I don't worry about Spouse's latest idea to buy a pig and set up as a truffle hunter. I don't worry about Eldest Daughter's predilection for sitting in the piazza eyeing up passing Italian youths, or Younger Daughter's refusal to eat anything other than peeled grapes and Mars bars. I don't worry that dear old Romano has told us that we must start the olive oil harvest when the moon is in Taurus. Or that the *acqua minerale* which flows, amazingly, from our very own well has slowed to a sulky trickle. No, I don't worry about anything. I sit and I think.

And, when I think of the rush hour, I smile.

'Mum. The water's gone off again.'

Emily Robertson looks at her elder daughter who is standing in a patch of golden sunlight. Behind her the silvery olive grove merges with the pale yellow hills, deepening to ochre where they meet the sky, the pine trees are almost mesmerisingly dark and the house itself, terracotta in the evening light, is now bleached to the palest pink. It is all relentlessly beautiful and it gives Emily no pleasure at all.

'Oh dear,' she says weakly. On the table in front of her the laptop glints and she presses 'send'. Another 'Thoughts from Tuscany' is dispatched.

'Oh dear? Is that it? Oh dear? Is that all you can say?' Siena's righteous fury threatens to catapult her into the air,

4

like a modern-day Assumption of the Virgin. 'I've got to meet Giancarlo in an hour and I can't finish washing my hair. There's no water anywhere in this stupid house. Christ! No wonder Dad doesn't spend any time here.'

'He's coming home tomorrow,' says Emily, assailed by a tiny, a very tiny twinge of fear.

Siena ignores this. 'What about my hair?'

'There's some water in the kettle,' says Emily. 'I'll get that.'

Emily rises from the table and winces as she steps out from the shade of the terrace. It is nearly midday and the sun is at its hottest. Emily feels it pounding on her head as she crosses the parched grass and climbs the shallow stone steps to the kitchen door. Siena follows her, silent and watchful, refusing to be placated.

The kitchen is dark and cool. Emily's bare feet shrink with delight as they touch the cold, stone floor. The remains of breakfast – cornflakes, Marmite, Coco Pops, all brought from England – are still on the table. The kettle on the gas hob (impossible to find electric kettles in Italy) is still half full of water. Emily offers this humbly to Siena.

Siena mutters grudging thanks and makes her way out of the kitchen towards the narrow staircase that leads to the bedrooms. In the doorway she stops. Parting shots are her speciality.

'By the way, Mum,' she says. 'Your skirt's ripped at the back. Did you notice?'

*

Emily's younger daughter, Paris, writes in her diary. *O dark, dark, dark, amid the blaze of noon.* She pauses for a moment to look at the words, satisfyingly black against the empty page, and to think that there is probably no other thirteen year old in the world who could quote *Samson Agonistes* in such an offhand yet utterly relevant way. After all, here she is, with the horrible, white-hot Italian sun blazing in through her window (not quite noon, true, but all great writers take liberties with the facts) and she is, quite simply, in *black despair.*

Slightly comforted at the thought of the blackness of her despair, Paris rolls over onto her back and stares at the ceiling. She is wearing just a white vest and football shorts but she is boiling; limp and exhausted from the heat. Her mother has given her a fan for her bedroom but all it seems to do is move the hot air to different places. The ceilings of the house are Emily's pride and joy, dark beams arching across authentic brickwork, like a cathedral, Emily says. But, to Paris, looking up, it feels more like being inside the ribcage of some prehistoric monster. Unspoilt, Mum says, like going back in time. That's just it: going back and back until, in the end, you are just nothingness, just floating in some awful dark matter. The sun shines and the crickets sing and nothing ever happens, except that she, Paris, gets more and more unhappy and nobody ever notices.

I hate this house, she writes for what feels like the fifty millionth time. *I hate Tuscany and I hate Italy and I hate having no friends and nothing to do and just lying on my bed waiting for it to* get cooler so that I might, perhaps, go out for a walk. She pauses, thinking how much she hates the phrase 'go out for a walk'. Her mum used to use it when they still lived in London: Sunday afternoons, too much lunch, football on the telly, 'Let's go out for a walk.' Dad was always too tired after a week at work, Charlie was too little and it was no good even asking Siena to do anything that sounded like exercise so it was always just her and Mum. The long, tedious slog past the shuttered shops, up to the common where families tried to fly kites in the windless air and small, shaven-headed boys played football with what looked like random violence. If they had had a dog, it might have been different, a dog would give purpose to a walk but Charlie (of course!) had asthma. 'Another reason to move to a warmer climate,' Mum had trilled. Another reason to hate Charlie.

A walk, she writes. *You can't even walk in these stupid hills because they're full of horrible loose stones and bits of tree roots and, just as soon as you get to the bottom of one hill, there's another one right there in front of you. There's not one flat bit of land in the whole of Tuscany and, if there was, the boys at school would build a football pitch on it because football is literally all they ever think about.*

She lies back, exhausted with hatred, and the door opens (no knock, of course) and Siena drifts in, wet hair plastered against her shoulders.

'Paris, can I borrow your red scrunchy?'

'No,' answers Paris, eyes closed.

'Oh, for God's sake!' Siena is furious though not, deep down, actually surprised. 'What do you need it for anyway? You can't use it now that your hair's so short.'

'I'm keeping it as an ornament,' says Paris, eyes still closed.

'Christ, you're pathetic,' Siena retreats to the door where she tries one last, desperate parting shot. 'I'll tell Mum.'

Paris lets out a snort of contemptuous laughter. It is meant to silence Siena once and for all – and it does.

Olimpia, Emily's cleaner and part-time childminder, parks her wheezing, three-wheeled van outside the open door of the kitchen. Then she tenderly lifts down three-year-old Charlie who fell asleep on the drive home from his nursery school, where he goes three mornings a week to sing Italian songs and create pictures out of dried pasta and glittery glue.

'*Carissimo*,' Olimpia drops a kiss on his tousled, blond head. Charlie wakes up and pulls away irritably. Sometimes, when he is in a good mood or wants to annoy his mother, he will sit on Olimpia's lap and let her sing to him about a cricket and a grasshopper who are getting married. At other times he is cold and distant to his mother and to Olimpia, who both continue to adore him unreservedly.

'It's not even as if he was especially interesting,' wail Siena and Paris, united on this subject as on no other.

'He's nothing special,' Paris points out. 'He's just small. Midgets are small.'

'He's a boy,' replies Siena darkly.

In the kitchen, Emily is dispiritedly repairing her dress. She can't be bothered to take it off so she has twisted it round and is sewing up the spilt with large, untidy stitches. Olimpia, Charlie in her arms, watches critically.

'*Uno strappo*,' explains Emily apologetically. She feels that Italian women would never tear their clothes and, if they did, they would have little women (probably Albanians) to mend them. Anyway, no Italian woman would be seen dead in ankle-length floral cotton.

'*Carlito é stanco*,' counters Olimpia. Sometimes, she will only speak to Emily in Italian, at other times she demonstrates considerable, though colloquial, fluency in English.

'Charlie! Baby!' Emily's face changes completely. Paris, watching from the doorway, thinks that her mother's face goes slack and pouchy whenever she looks at her youngest child. She prefers Emily's face tight and animated, every emotion signalled in advance, as it had been in the golden days before Charlie's birth. When they had lived in London.

'Want chocolate,' demands Charlie, in the whine he has developed since discovering that it works in two languages.

'Baby,' says Emily, 'we agreed. Only a tiny piece after your lunch. Now what have we got for lunch? Pasta? Eggy?'

It is no good. Charlie's mouth goes square and he howls to the newly restored ceiling that he wants chocolate and he wants it now, he does, he does, he does. Neither he nor Olimpia think it worth mentioning that he had two fingers of a Kit-Kat in the car.

Paris glides from the room like a ghost. When she was a

9

child they had only had chocolate for a treat, at birthdays or at Christmas. She still remembers the taste of the chocolate money that they had in their stockings at Christmas, milky and foreign, not like proper chocolate at all. Come to think of it, not unlike Italian chocolate. Mum says that Italian chocolate is better than English because it contains fewer additives. It has become obvious to Paris that it is the additives that make it nice. She thinks of Italian chocolate, ponced up in blue and silver bags and tied with bows; and she thinks of Mars bars, as solid and vivid in their black and red livery as the God of War himself. Her mouth waters. It seems a long time since breakfast (three perfectly peeled grapes and a breadstick) but she has promised herself not to eat anything else. More than that, it's a kind of deal. If she doesn't eat, things will get better: Mum will stop mooning over Charlie and ignoring everyone else, Dad will come home more, and Siena will just simply go away. It's all linked, in some complicated way that she doesn't quite understand, to the gnawing feeling in her stomach. A feeling which, uncomfortable though it might be, has become almost company, almost a friend.

As Paris reaches the kitchen door, the mosquito-whine of a Vespa announces the arrival of Giancarlo. Thin and almost frighteningly dark, he grins at Paris before calling loudly for Siena. Don't come running, Paris silently urges her sister, make him get off his bloody bike at least. But an ecstatic cry of 'Pronta' floats down through the house and, in a cloud of Mum's best perfume, Siena appears. As the Vespa squeals its way back down the drive, Paris gets a glimpse of the stolen scrunchy.

In the kitchen, Charlie sits happily at the table eating a bar of chocolate. Emily is sitting opposite, chopping tomatoes. Olimpia is noisily sweeping the hall.

'What shall we have for lunch, Paris? What about a lovely salad?'

'I loathe salad.'

'Oh darling.' That face again. 'You used to love it so. Remember when you went to Rebecca's for tea and asked for salad? I was so proud of you.'

'Mum, I was five.'

'That's what made it so unusual,' says Emily earnestly. 'When you think what most five-year-olds eat.'

'I'm trying not to,' says Paris, staring pointedly at Charlie's chocolate-smeared face.

'What about a pizza then?' persists her mother, not getting it at all.

'Mum, I'm just not hungry. It's too hot to eat.'

'At least have a cold drink.'

To shut her up, Paris goes to the tap over the authentic farmhouse sink (designed in Milan and ordered on the internet). A sad trickle of brown water splutters out.

'Mum! The water's gone off again.'

Far away, though not perhaps quite as far away as it feels, Petra McAllister sits in the basement kitchen of her Brighton home and reads the paper. Outside, horizontal grey rain lashes the deserted seafront. The few holidaymakers who have braved the pier huddle under its curly Victorian awnings, the lights from the rides barely visible in the fog, and the all-pervading music from the pier's very own DJ giving the whole scene a strange, surreal feel. The loudspeakers blare a jolly, summer song about fun and laughter and free drinks. Meanwhile the rain falls relentlessly from the lowering skies.

Petra hardly notices the rain, or the pier or the sodden tourists. She is used to Brighton in the summer. Besides, from her subterranean window, all she can see are feet hurrying past. Wet, cold feet in unsuitable sandals, smug feet in wellingtons and, occasionally, the bare feet of the army of homeless people who sleep in the nearby square.

Petra pours herself another cup of coffee and spreads the paper out on the table. She can hear the boys in the playroom upstairs and, although there are raised voices, she judges these to be assumed for the purposes of play. 'How dare you break my track,' Jake is yelling, but Harry's nasal rendition of the *Thomas the Tank Engine* theme tune does not falter. That's all right then.

From habit, she flicks straight to the 'Thoughts from Tuscany' column. Next to it is a tasteful pencil drawing of a Tuscan villa, stark against the hillside, with one perfect olive tree growing beside it. Petra puts her coffee mug on top of the Tuscan house, noticing with satisfaction that some liquid has spilled over onto its picturesquely sloping gables.

'Summer in the Villa Serena has a rhythm of its own,'

she reads. 'I wake at six in the shimmering beauty of the dawn, eat a slice of cool watermelon, do as many chores as I feel like and, by midday, I am ready for a siesta. I am convinced that I sleep better in those few hours than I ever did in London. Heavy, scented sleep, lulled by the crickets outside and the tinny whirr of my bedroom fan. I wake in the long afternoon and, finally, as night falls, we eat our first meal of the day, sitting out on the *terrazzo* as the stars come out.'

Petra sighs. She can't remember when she last had a good night's sleep, scented or not. She thinks of Emily Robertson, who has been her friend since university. On the one hand, she is happy that Emily is having such a wonderful time in Italy, on the other, she wants to slap her sun-kissed face very hard indeed. She also misses her very much.

Idly, Petra turns the pages. It is the Sunday paper (though today is Tuesday) and the pages are huge and unwieldy. Her cat, named Thomas by Harry but called the Fat Controller by the rest of the family, jumps heavily on the paper. Petra pushes him out of the way and begins to read an article about the dangers of drinking too much coffee. Then she stops. She pushes Thomas's fluffy bulk further and sees, under his left paw, a picture of a man, in his forties, good looking, half smiling. 'Dr Michael Bartnicki,' she reads, 'Consultant in Neurology at King's College, London . . .' Then she reads it again.

'Michael,' she says aloud. 'So that's where you got to.'

*

In Tuscany, Emily is having a frustrating few hours trying to sort out the water situation. First she rings the Idraulica, the water company, situated in futuristic splendour a mere few hills away. However, though she has carefully composed a few Italian phrases in her head (*'non abbiamo acqua'*), the woman at the other end of the phone seems to have no idea what she is saying and preserves an incredulous electronic silence. Eventually, Emily scoops Charlie up (Olimpia has gone home) and trudges out to her tiny Fiat. 'Paris!' she calls. 'Do you want to come for a drive?' Another incredulous silence followed by a snort, which Emily takes (rightly) for an answer in the negative.

The car is boiling. Charlie shrieks when his bare legs make contact with the seat. Frantically, Emily winds down the windows. 'It'll be better when we get going,' she promises. Charlie looks at her sulkily beneath lowered eyelashes. Paul's car has air conditioning but it is at Pisa airport, awaiting its master's return. 'Be sensible, darling,' Paul said. 'You can't expect me to meet clients in a Fiat Panda.' Emily gave in immediately. He had invoked the C word; clients are sacred in their family.

Now, as they wind their way down the drive, hot air blows in through the windows as if a giant hairdryer were pointing at them. At least Charlie cheers up, especially when Emily puts on his favourite tape, nursery rhymes sung by a relentlessly cheery trio with comforting northern accents. At home, Charlie had condemned this tape as hopelessly babyish but here he clings to it like the aural equivalent of a security blanket. Perhaps it is the voices, so cheerfully English with their flat vowel sounds and breathless intonation. Emily doesn't like to admit that she, too, finds the voices obscurely comforting.

The Idraulica is only a few miles away but because it, like the Villa Serena, is built on top of a hill, this means going down one hill and up at least three others. The Mountains of the Moon, this area is called, the Alpe della Luna. It's a place of densely wooded hills, with an occasional gleam of white stone, startlingly flat plains and scattered hilltop towns, walled like fortresses. The nearest town to the Villa Serena is Monte Albano, a medieval citadel built around a square tower and a picturesque, cobbled piazza. Emily laboriously negotiates its narrow streets, entering through a low, stone archway and scattering tourists as she bumps the wrong way down several streets marked *senso unico* (she has been in Italy long enough to know that this is allowable, if not essential). Out the other side through another archway, down the hill through a succession of dusty hairpin bends, each one offering a brief, terrifying view of spectacular beauty. On the tape, jolly voices sing about double-decker buses. It all seems a million miles away.

Hands sweating on the wheel, she drives on through several equally beautiful hill towns, each with its Biblical backdrop of cypresses and mountains, past countless churches and wayside grottos (grotti?), on and on past perfect view after perfect view. When they had first arrived in Tuscany, Emily used to exclaim at each crumbling archway or lapis blue Madonna, until Siena and Paris began to mimic her savagely, 'Oh look! A dustbin. How charming! Oh look, a typical Italian drug addict. *Che carina!*' Paul had laughed and Emily lapsed into hurt silence.

She still does think it all beautiful, really, but she has to admit that you can get used to beauty so that it becomes just another daily duty: make beds, cook lunch, sweep floors, admire view.

Like a modern castle, the Idraulica is visible for miles around, its new white walls shining painfully in the sun. 'Azienda Idraulica Comunale' reads the sign in small, unfriendly letters. Emily drives past rows of tankers and parks her car in front of the grandiose marble entrance. As she lifts Charlie out, he looks up in awe. 'Is this a palace?' he asks.

After the heat of the afternoon, the Idraulica's reception area is freezing. Weird, thinks Emily, shivering, how in a second your body can forget that it was ever hot. They cross what feels like acres of orange marble and stop in front of a desk grotesquely decorated with bronze snakes. The ornate furnishings and the icy cold are beginning to make Emily feel as if she is inside a tomb. A glamorous receptionist, barricaded behind the snakes, eyes them without interest.

Emily begins hesitantly, '*Scusi. Abito a Villa Serena. Non abbiamo acqua.*'

'Have you paid the bill?' asks the receptionist in perfect English, drumming her elegant nails.

'Yes,' says Emily lapsing meekly into English, 'we pay by direct—'

The receptionist taps her details into the computer. 'Last month's payment is overdue,' she says, unsmiling.

'Is it? But the bank—'

'Better you pay me now,' says the receptionist flatly, 'and take it up with the bank.'

Emily empties her battered handbag (she can feel the receptionist looking at it with horror, she probably favours a minimalist Gucci number made from an endangered species) and finally unearths her chequebook. She writes a cheque for a dizzying amount of money and hands it over. Throughout all this, Charlie looks on, open-mouthed.

The receptionist prints out a receipt. '*Carino*,' she says, pointing to Charlie, and then turns back to her computer. There seems nothing more to say.

Back at the Villa Serena, the water gushes triumphantly from the taps. In delight, Emily has a shower and bathes Charlie. Afterwards she sits outside on the terrace and watches Charlie play in the dusty earth under the olive trees. The faintest shiver of a breeze lifts her wet hair. She closes her eyes and feels that perhaps, somehow, maybe this is paradise after all. It is a few seconds before she realises that Paris is speaking to her.

'Mum? Your mobile was bleeping. You've got a message.'

Emily reaches out a hand for her phone. It must be Paul, she thinks, he is addicted to texting and, indeed, to all forms of electronic communication. She hopes he isn't bringing clients home with him tomorrow. She doesn't think she can face hours of making crostini and saltimbocca while German businessmen drink Montepulciano and talk about motorways. I must be a better wife, she tells herself. I must welcome people into my gracious home, warm with home cooking and family life. Nobody minds a bit of untidiness. I must not be neurotic.

She clicks on the message icon. The text is brief: *sorry darling, not coming home, am leaving you. p.*

CHAPTER 2

Thoughts from Tuscany
By Emily Robertson

Friday night is pasta e fagioli night. In Italy, the custom of no meat on Fridays is still strong. The local *pescivendolo* does a roaring trade in gamberetti, scallops and little grey fish like sardines. Even some restaurants refuse to serve meat, which, admittedly, is no sacrifice in a country so rich in other culinary delights. Italy really is paradise for the vegetarian. Even Daughter Number 2 who, in England, dined sullenly on congealed baked beans and beige toast, is suddenly devouring pizza napolitana and spaghetti con aglio.

Pasta e fagioli is a traditional Tuscan dish (the Tuscans are known in Italy as 'the bean eaters') which comes to us courtesy of Olimpia, our Treasure. Olimpia is an angel in a headscarf and pinny who came on our first day to 'help us out' and has become a member of the family. She cooks for us, cleans for us and scolds us constantly but we couldn't live without her. She has enriched our lives in so many ways but in no way more than in bequeathing us the recipe for pasta e fagioli, a heady fusion of borlotti beans, tomatoes, garlic and herbs. The recipe is actually meant to include bacon, which Olimpia devoutly omits on a Friday, but sometimes I surreptitiously add a dash of pancetta fat and don't tell Number 2.

So, on Friday night, the pasta e fagioli is simmering on the stove. An earthenware pitcher of the local Chianti stands on the scrubbed, wooden table. Crusty ciabatte (the Italian word, incidentally, for slippers), fresh out of the oven, sit steaming in their plaited basket. Spouse, who has been away for a week on business, stands in the doorway and sniffs appreciatively. 'Now I know I'm home,' he says.

To: Petra McAllister
From: Emily Robertson
Subject: None

Paul has left me. Bugger.

To: Petra McAllister
From: Emily Robertson
Subject: Thank you

Thank you so much for ringing last night. It meant so much just to hear another human voice. I mean, I know the kids are human but I can't really talk about it to them. I've just told them that Dad has been delayed at work and, God knows, they're used to that. I think Siena knows that something's up. She keeps asking questions, which is really unlike her. Usually she's totally absorbed in her own life: Giancarlo, school, clothes, etc. But now she keeps asking when Dad will be back, why hasn't he rung, what's this important meeting he had to go to. On and on. It's driving me mad. Paris says nothing but then she never does.

You asked if this was a surprise and I said, yes, of course it was. I was even quite cross with you for asking. But actually I don't think it was really. I mean, I didn't think Paul would leave me like that, without any warning, but I've known for ages that something was up. Last night, I couldn't sleep so I just sat outside on the terrace all night thinking and thinking. Once I heard this howl quite near me (do you know they still have wolves in Italy?) and I thought, serve Paul right if I get eaten by a wolf and it's all his fault. But actually it wouldn't serve him right at all, only make it easier for him to start a new life with whoever she is. And yes, I am sure there is a whoever she is. I just know him so well. He might be fed up with me but he'd never go to all the trouble of leaving me if there wasn't something better on offer. I remember, when we first met, he always had something lined up for Saturday night. If something better came along, he'd cancel the first date but he'd never do that unless he had a better offer.

So I'm sure he wouldn't walk out on one woman unless he had a better one lined up.

Oh God, Pete, what a long, depressing email. I'd press delete if I were you. Wish I could press delete on the whole of yesterday, on the whole of the last five years if that wouldn't mean losing my darling Charlie. Life's a bitch, as they say. Remember: Michael used to say 'Life's a beach and then you fry'? Sometimes nostalgia hurts more than anything.

Take care

Em

xxxx

On Monday morning, Emily sits on her terrace trying to ignore Olimpia who is inside muttering about the dirty habits of the English ('What is a bidet?' she mimics in a vicious falsetto). Emily is staring at her laptop. The file at the top of the screen reads 'ThoughtsfromTuscany50'. Her fiftieth column about the delights of Tuscan life. Dispiritedly she types in a title, 'Summer nights at the Villa Serena', then clicks on the icon to underline it. She sighs. She can't think of a single thing to say about summer nights at the Villa Serena. Olimpia's Hoover whines from inside the house. The Microsoft flag waves at her jauntily from the bottom of the screen.

Siena and Paris have gone to the local swimming pool (Paris making up a threesome with Giancarlo, under protest). Charlie is having his siesta. Emily's copy is due tomorrow yet her mind seems vast and empty, filled just with one tiny scrabbling gerbil of a thought: *Paul has left me, Paul has left me*. Because she is so used to being without Paul, his absence doesn't impinge on her everyday routine: it is not as if she misses his shoes under the bed, his body in the shower, his whisper in the night. It is as if she needs this ridiculous gerbil thought, just to remind her of how serious things are. *Paul has left me, he has left me*.

In desperation, Emily types a string of keywords about Tuscany: light, heat, olive oil, sun-dried, wine, terracotta, hills, vines, piazza, antipasti, rustic, unspoilt, cappuccino. Then she tries to form these into elegant, elegiac sentences: 'We ate antipasti under the vines in the rustic piazza', 'Sun-dried tomatoes, sprinkled with a little virgin oil make the perfect antipasto', 'Cappuccino drunk in the heat of the morning in the beautiful local piazza'. She groans and presses delete, delete, delete. Then she types another list of words: shit, fuck, bugger, bastard, wanker.

The sun is hot on the back of her neck so she shifts round until she is in the shade of the beautiful, rustic, etc., etc., vine. Bunches of grapes dangle in front of her like some illustration of plenty (though she knows that, in fact, they are not yet good to eat, being sour and hard). Two hunting dogs with bells round their necks crash through the undergrowth and disappear around the side of the house, intent on business of their own. A lizard suns itself on the baking stones, shutting its eyes with prehistoric calm. Emily, too, shuts her eyes and thinks about her husband. *He's left me, he's left me*.

'I'm not leaving the kids,' Paul explained kindly when she finally reached him on the phone late on Friday night. 'I'm leaving you.'

'But why?' Emily asked for the hundredth time.

'Our marriage is over,' pronounced Paul as if this was an indisputable fact, one which Emily had been wilfully denying for some time.

'How can you say that? We've never even talked.'

'Emily,' said Paul, with awful heaviness, 'I don't want to discuss this any more.'

'Don't you? Well I do! After all, you've just told me that our seventeen-year marriage is over. Don't you think I deserve an explanation?'

'Don't get hysterical, Emily.'

'I'm not hysterical,' said Emily. 'I'm fucking furious.'

Then she had slammed down the phone and spent the next two hours trying to ring him back. His phone was switched off. Panicking, she phoned his parents in Portsmouth – 'Neither Derek nor Anthea is able to take your call right now' – then his brother in Gravesend.

'But it's the middle of the night, Emily,' Anthony kept saying.

'I know. Your brother's just left me. I need to talk to him. Do you know where he is?'

'But it's the middle of the—'

She had hung up on him and sat in the dark sitting room of the Villa Serena (all exposed beams and giant fireplace), trying to breathe calmly. Then she texted Paul (*bastard!*) and wrote him an email. Then she deleted the email and sent one to Petra instead. She went into the kitchen and poured herself a large glass of wine. Drinking was difficult because her throat seemed to have closed up but she persevered, sip by sip. Why had Paul left her? They had been happy, hadn't they? Of course it had been a strain coming to live in a new country but, she told herself, that was only to be expected. OK, Italy was her idea but Paul owed her that much surely, after the Affair? And Paul had seemed happy enough; it had fitted in with his idea of his own lifestyle (villa in Tuscany, skiing in Klosters, Christmas shopping in New York). He had even set up his own company, selling Italian property to starry-eyed English families. And she had got a job writing about how wonderful it all was. Paul was lucky to have her. She had looked after the children, made the house look lovely, she was the one stuck here all the bloody time. Self-pity was dangerous. She took another deep breath. What was going to happen to her now?

The phone rang and she raced across the hallway to answer it. In those few seconds she lived through the entire reconciliation: Paul's tearful apologies, her own gracious understanding, their ecstatic reunion. A second (or third) honeymoon, somewhere exotic (not Italy), away from the children. A new start. Perhaps even a fourth baby.

But it wasn't Paul, it was Petra.

Now she sits frozen in the sun and thinks, I might never see Paul again.

She will, of course. Paul finally rang back on Saturday night and proposed flying to Italy the next weekend so they could 'discuss things more sensibly'.

'Discuss what?'

'Well, access, solicitors, that sort of thing.'

Emily had been dumbstruck. 'Access' had such a worn, legalistic ring. How could Paul, who had once, in a Siena hotel room, compared her to Botticelli's Venus, be talking to her about *access*?

'Emily? Are you there?'

'Yes. Don't you think you're moving rather fast? Yesterday I had no idea that anything was wrong and now you're talking to me about access and solicitors.'

'Emily.' Deep sigh. 'You must have known for years that something was wrong.'

'Well, I didn't.'

Emily traces her name in the dust on the terrace wall and thinks: did she really know all along? All right, they had had what they always referred to as their 'rough patch'. Siena had been twelve and Paris ten and Emily was just resigning herself to the fact that she wouldn't have any more children. Paul was working all hours starting a new company and Emily felt lonely and neglected. Siena was at secondary school, Paris would follow next year. She remembers how much she dreaded losing the comforting routine of the school gates. But then it turned out that Paul would miss it even more as he was having an affair with one of the teachers, a woman he had actually met during a parent–teacher consultation. Emily had left him, gone to Brighton, asked for a divorce. But then they had got back together. It had been Paul who wanted the reconciliation, she thinks sourly; he had come racing after her, begged her to go back to him. She remembers, at the time, feeling quite strong and determined about the whole thing. She was going to divorce Paul and start a new life with the girls.

But Paul had arrived, begging her for a second chance, and she had relented. This time it must work, she had told herself. And, for a while, it had. Paul had been lovely to her, wooing her all over again, and eventually she had begun to love him again. She suddenly became consumed with desire for a third child and Paul had agreed, with hardly any persuasion. They had had darling Charlie and they were both besotted with him. Then Emily had her big idea. They should go to Italy, start a new life, just the five of them. A perfect new life in the sun. She remembers how the vision of this perfect new life, the children playing under the olive trees, tranquil evenings in the cool of the terrace, the view of the hills at sunrise, had sustained her for months, had carried her through all the actual horrors of moving, the children's hysterics, Paul's boredom, her own suppressed feelings of panic and inadequacy. It is only now that she wonders if this vision was ever really shared by her husband.

He had loved the house, though. They had fallen in love with it together, during that magical holiday in Siena. Leaving the children with Emily's parents, they had embarked on a second honeymoon: visiting crumbling properties by day, eating in the famous piazza in the evening, making love all night to the sounds of Tuscany (church bells, scooters whizzing past, the cries of Italian youth at play). One evening they had seen the Villa Serena, dusky pink in the evening sun, and they knew they had come home. But then they actually moved to Tuscany and their idyllic tourist days were over. Emily had thrown herself into the renovations but she knew that Paul was bored and irritated by the mess and chaos involved making the Villa Serena a Tuscan paradise. He spent more and more time away, returning only to complain about the workmen and, increasingly, about Tuscany itself. Too late Emily realised that Paul, the urban wheeler-dealer, was never at his best in the country.

Yes, of course she knew.

Emily sighs again and turns her laptop away from the sun. She opens 'ThoughtsfromTuscany50' once more and types: 'Summer evenings in Tuscany, drinking cold white wine and watching the stars appear over the distant hills . . .'

Paris sits by the side of the swimming pool, in the only available shade (half an umbrella). She adjusts her peaked cap and pulls her T-shirt down over her knees. She is not going to get skin cancer, thank you very much, not like that idiot Siena, sitting on the baked concrete in the full glare of the sun, pulling her bikini straps down over her shoulders. Just asking for melanomas, thinks Paris sourly; she is sure that mole wasn't there last week. A beauty spot, Siena calls it. The Lake District is a beauty spot, mocks the running commentary in Paris's head, *that* is the grim reaper, my sweet. The Lake District sounds so wonderfully cold and English that she has to close her eyes for a moment to stop herself feeling dizzy with homesickness.

Siena saunters over, her blue bikini now just clinging to the bottom half of her breasts. Paris had never realised before just how *fat* Siena was getting. Her boobs are huge, all sweaty and glistening with suntan oil, and there is a definite roll above her bikini bottoms. Not a roll, almost a *tyre*. Paris shuts her eyes.

'Paris! Do you want an ice cream?'

'No thanks,' says Paris, eyes shut.

'A drink then. You ought to, it's so hot.'

'No thanks.'

'You ought to,' Siena persists.

'OK,' says Paris, to get rid of her. 'Water.'

'*Con gas?*' asks Siena with an affected Italian accent.

'Still,' says Paris, through gritted teeth.

Siena wanders over to the café where she is joined by Giancarlo and his friends. Then they start that whole loud, horseplay thing that Italians seem to do at the drop of a hat: throaty cries ('*Aiee! Hai!*'), extravagant hand gestures, lots of pushing and shoving and laughter. What in God's name, thinks Paris, have they got to laugh at? Giancarlo, the pastry chef's son, doomed to a lifetime of cooking biscotti in ninety-degree heat. Massimo, the farmer's son, whose parents have never travelled outside Tuscany. Pretty Francesca, already engaged to sullen Mauro, the mechanic. Clever Andrea, who will probably never get to Pisa University to study medicine. Why the hell do they look so pleased with themselves, wrestling with each other at the pool's edge, drops of water like jewels shining on their brown legs and arms? OK, they're good looking, if you like that smug, well-fed look, which Paris doesn't. But is that everything? Is that *enough*?

If they were English, she would think they were drunk, the way Dad and his friends sometimes got on a Sunday afternoon after watching the rugby. But Italians didn't seem to drink, alcohol that is. She'd heard Mum saying that it was impossible for a woman to get a second glass of wine in Italy. Well, that was OK. She hated Mum to drink wine. It made her face softer and vaguer than ever. When Mum and Dad both drank wine it was unbearable. They'd either argue or get all kissy and stupid. But Giancarlo and his friends were all kissy and stupid on two cans of lemon soda and an *acqua minerale*. Weird.

Siena hands her a bottle of mineral water, still sweating from the freezer. Paris opens it and takes a tiny sip. She is experimenting with taking smaller and smaller amounts of food and liquid. She can almost feel the water trickling slowly past her larynx and sliding gently down her throat, drop by drop.

'Hey, Parigi!' This is Giancarlo, using a version of her name that she hates. She ignores him. 'You want to swim?'

He stands in front of her, all skinny brown body, baggy swimming trunks and beaded necklace. How *can* Siena find him attractive?

'No thanks,' she says.

Giancarlo lifts both hands in an operatic gesture of

acceptance. He turns back to Siena and Paris hears him say, 'Your sister. She hates me.'

She cannot hear Siena's reply but there is a lot of giggling and head-tossing. Paris lies down in the shade of the umbrella and closes her eyes.

At the Villa Serena, Emily makes scrambled eggs and attempts to arrange her thoughts. Paul has left me, she begins briskly. Things to do:

1. Sell house
2. Move back to England
3. Get a proper job
4. Organise childcare
5. Get a divorce

She stops because she is crying. Charlie, sitting stolidly at the table waiting for his eggs, says, 'Mummy's face is wet.'

'It's the cooking,' says Emily. Charlie stares at her as if this answer is beneath his contempt. Emily stirs the eggs with a wooden spoon and adds salt and pepper.

'No black bits,' says Charlie sharply.

Emily starts to pick out the pieces of pepper. Paul has left me, she begins again. I have three children without a father. No great change there, she thinks. Paul was away most weeks, travelling to London or Frankfurt on business. She is used to living without him, she tells herself, she'll hardly miss him at all.

But then she stops herself, staring at the congealing egg, pale yellow against the heavy iron frying pan. There is a big difference between your husband being away on business and your husband leaving you. A vast, yawning gulf of a difference. Paul may not have been with her physically during those long, hot afternoons when the washing machine broke down and Paris broke her arm jumping from the terrace, but he had been there somewhere, in the background, a phone call away. Someone to moan to about the kids, safe because he was the only other person in the world who loved them as much as she did.

Dispiritedly, Emily spoons the scrambled egg onto a Postman Pat plate. It looks disgusting, she thinks, but Charlie, watching her through narrowed eyes, consents to eat a spoonful. She does not feel like eating. In fact, she feels as if she will never eat again. At least then she will lose some weight. She just *knows*, somewhere deep in her heart, that Paul has left her for someone slimmer.

She is sure that he has another woman, just as she is sure, even deeper in her heart, that the Affair with the teacher was not the only one. Paul is attractive to women, with his mesmeric blue eyes and his habit of sitting just a little bit too close. She has seen it so often, with strangers, colleagues, even with friends, women who criticised Paul behind his back ('He doesn't *deserve* you, Emily') but became curiously skittish and playful in his presence.

Slowly, deliberately, Charlie tips his drink over. Bending

down to clear it up, Emily says brightly, 'What shall we do this afternoon, Charlie Bear? Shall we play with your train track?'

'No train track.'

'What about a lovely walk? We could go and look at Anna-Luisa's hens.'

'No walk. Horrible hens.'

Afternoons in Italy, with no parks, no soft play areas and no children's television have begun to assume monstrous proportions in Emily's mind. Hour after hour of hot walks to see the hens or endless games running wooden cars along stone floors. All the thousands of times she has looked at her watch to find that only ten minutes has passed. All the tears, tantrums and capitulations. Emily sighs.

'What about a video?'

Ten minutes later they are sitting in the cool, high-ceilinged sitting room watching *The Jungle Book*. Charlie looks up from the screen as Mowgli is adopted by the wolf family. The Father Wolf is standing on a rock laying down the law about something, the Mother Wolf is looking at him apprehensively.

'When's Daddy coming home?' asks Charlie.

CHAPTER 3

Thoughts from Tuscany
By Emily Robertson

Summer evenings in Tuscany, drinking cold white wine and watching the stars appear over the distant hills, are what makes it all worthwhile. Summer days can be hot and quarrelsome; the children arguing, Spouse full of some madcap scheme to create a water meadow in the bottom field (in an area where the summer rainfall is approximately an eggcup-full), the *supermercato* full of tourists buying the wrong sort of sausages for the ubiquitous barbeque. The afternoons can be slow and oppressive, heavy with regret for that extra glass of wine at lunchtimes, but the evenings, the evenings are perfection. The smell of lemons floating up from the citrus grove, the tang of grilled rosemary, the death-defying swoops of the birds coming home to roost in the Torre Albano. This is what we came to Italy for.

Emily, a glass of warm, flat beer in her hand, sits on the terrace and thinks about the fact that she is stuck in a foreign country with three children, no husband, no money and a psychotic cleaner. The smell of lemons from the citrus grove gives her no comfort whatsoever.

The Tuscan night is dark, a heavy pulsating blackness that has nothing to do with lack of light, more a presence of dark. The throaty buzz of the crickets sounds like deep breathing, hoarse and regular. Through the olive trees, Emily can see the white gleam of stones where the swimming pool is being built. What will happen to it now, Paul's beloved symbol of expatriate life? The workmen seem to have downed tools for the summer but what will happen when they come back in the autumn? Emily does not feel equal to the task of supervising the construction of a Roman-style pool complete with mosaic tiles and terracotta surrounds. And have they even got enough money to pay for it? She *must* talk to Paul about money.

A faint breeze whispers through the vines on the slope below. Emily shivers but does not go back into the house. After the heat of the day, the cold is invigorating. She finds it hard to think during the day, her brain is sluggish and lethargic, dragging itself round the same tired loop of ideas, as she drags her body round the house and garden, moving from shade to shade. Now, she can almost feel her mind tingling with life.

What is she going to do? Is she really going to sell up and go back to England? For a moment, she allows herself to think of it. A flat in Brighton, all blond wood floors and gleaming surfaces. Herself, striding out every day to a demanding yet really *creative* job. The children, happy and secure, trotting off to a wonderful English comprehensive (the kind that really nurtures the inner child whilst remaining true to its socialist principles; the kind that doesn't exist). She can even see the flat, fair face of their Danish au pair, her capable, freckled hand holding Charlie's as she takes him to the beach after nursery school. They will collect pebbles and bring them back to paint them, the *Guardian* spread out on Emily's scrubbed pine kitchen table. God, how she misses English newspapers.

There is no man in this colour supplement fantasy. Does she really think then that Paul has left her forever? The other time, the time when he had the Affair, she *had* escaped to Brighton but he had come after her. He had begged her to go back to him. She remembers the tears, so surprising in his bold blue eyes. She remembers walking on the beach with him, battered backwards by the wind and Paul saying, 'I'd be nothing without you. You're everything to me. If you leave me, I don't know how I can go on.' She remembers the exact soapy taste of the coffee they drank in the seaside café, the thick china cup with its faint residue of lipstick, the tramp at the next table slowly unwrapping his newspaper parcels of possessions. She remembers the curious sigh that had escaped Paul when she said, 'Well, all right, maybe we can give it another go . . .'

She can see all these things, sitting on the terrace with the alien countryside all around her, but she cannot see Paul. She can hear his voice saying, 'Our marriage is over,' but she cannot conjure up his face. The man she was married to for seventeen years (already it is in the past tense), who gave her three children, who loved and made love to her – she cannot see him at all. Dimly she remembers dark hair, a spreading waistline, white teeth, gritty early-morning stubble. She can feel his face pressed against hers when they last said goodbye. 'Don't forget to phone Romano about the driveway.' Would he have said that if he had been planning to leave her? Would his ongoing squabble with the neighbouring farmer about access rights still have loomed so large in his mind? There had been no clue, no hint that this was the last time they could hold each other like this, with such casual intimacy, a mere touch of the cheek, a pat, hardly registering at the time. If she had known, she could have done something, reinvented herself, tried to be more efficient, less dreamy. Of course, she had not rung Romano about the driveway.

Can it really be over? Is this how things end? She remembers, when she split up with Michael, the great love of her university years, the sense of utter desolation. How would she ever meet anyone else who was so nearly perfect? And she had been only twenty-two, for God's sake. Now she is forty-one and, if Paul has left her, she can't imagine ever meeting another man. Not that she wants to, really. The past, where she is forever young, running across the quad to met Michael, her long hair flying out behind her, slim legs in faded jeans hardly touching the grass, the past is far more attractive. She wishes she could open the computer and just step back into her youth. One click and she could be there. Facebook. She could look for Michael's name and, just in that familiar combination of letters, she would be back.

She must go to bed or she will be even more stupid tomorrow. Just one last email to Petra? Maybe just one look at Facebook? She is so near him, a mere click away. But she hesitates, she won't conjure him up. Not yet.

Upstairs, under the high authentic ceiling, Paris, too, is conjuring the past. Carphone Warehouse, she thinks, the Bedford Arms, Bilal's Burgers, Tesco Metro, Sinatra's Wine Bar, HSBC Bank. Slowly, store by store, she re-creates the walk from their London house to the tube station. If she concentrates hard she can see the Styrofoam burger boxes in the street, the thrown-away leaflets (Lose weight in two weeks! Ask me how!), the chrome tables outside the restaurants waiting for that mythical sunny day. She sees the dusty plane trees of the common and the boarded-up windows of the minicab office. She sees the café where she and Cassie once saw someone who had been in *EastEnders*. She sees the shop where she bought her first bike, riding home in triumph through the dog shit and broken glass. Finally she sees the tube station, with its familiar red and blue sign like an arrow through her heart. Clapham Common.

And she lies in bed and weeps, silently, for the Northern Line.

*

Further along the Northern Line, in Kennington, Michael Bartnicki dresses quickly to go to work. In less than an hour he will be performing emergency surgery on an eighteen-year-old girl who has been involved in a car crash. He knows this but it does not trouble him unduly as he pulls on a thick sweater (the summer night is cold) and bends down to do up his shoelaces. Such late-night summonses are commonplace. Besides, a doctor can't afford to think like that (the young life, the terrified parents, the nightmarish blood on the road), he can only think of the procedure, of the surgical incision, the operating table in its blaze of artificial light. Michael hums quietly as he picks up his phone and car keys from the bedside table.

As he puts on his watch, he looks at his wife who is sleeping deeply. Should he wake her to remind her about Jessica's appointment tomorrow? He decides against it, she will only become hysterical and say that he doesn't trust her. Jessica will remember. Michael checks his watch. Three forty-five a.m. The low point of the night. The hour most doctors dread; the hour most patients die.

The kitchen is dark, appliances whirring silently. Michael gets a bottle of mineral water from the fridge and swigs deeply. No time for anything to eat. The green lights on the microwave say 03:55. For a moment he sits completely still in the darkness, staring straight in front of him.

And in Tuscany, only a few miles from the Villa Serena, a man called Raffaello looks into a grave and smiles.

CHAPTER 4

Thoughts from Tuscany
By Emily Robertson

At last I have my own herb garden. In London, I used to be an enthusiastic purchaser of those little pots of basil from the supermarket. For about a week, they would add a genuine Italian flavour to my salads and then, inevitably, they would wither and die. It was as if the little plants were saying to me: 'Who are you trying to kid? This is Clapham not Chianti.'

Well, now I have my own basil. It grows plentifully just outside my kitchen door. When making a salad, I just need to reach out a hand and crush those aromatic leaves between my fingers. I have become profligate. I scatter chopped basil on soups, on new potatoes, on bruschette, on freshly picked tomatoes. Spouse says that he lives in dread of being given basil in his beer. But I will never grow tired of it. For me it is the essence of Italy.

Emily is dispiritedly weeding the vegetable patch when she hears the buzz of a Vespa coming up the drive. Romano, the neighbouring farmer, has told her that dry weeds must be cut down in case of fire. The whole countryside is dry, with ash-white grass that shrivels in your hand. Emily imagines the whole thing flaring up in a single sheet of flame, engulfing the Villa Serena like a medieval picture of hell. Dutifully, she drags the hoe across the stony ground, her T-shirt sticking to her back.

Paul was determined that they should grow their own vegetables. At the back of the house, next to the kitchen, is the perfect place, sunny and flat, shaded by elaborately gnarled fig trees. Romano says it was once a herb garden and certainly it is overgrown with rosemary and thyme, huge, grey-green scented monsters. But Paul pulled up the rosemary and thyme and planted lettuces and tomatoes, like a south London allotment. The lettuces grew to an immense size but, since none of the children like salad and Paul preferred more interesting versions bought in tubs from the Co-op, they were soon eaten by caterpillars. The tomatoes were beautiful, small and firm with fragrant leaves, but Emily soon gave up picking and preserving and bottling. They, too, were eaten by the birds.

Now Emily pulls up another rotten lettuce and throws it onto the bonfire pile. Behind her, she hears a voice, elderly but surprisingly resonant, a voice used to being heard.

'*Basilico*,' it says. Then, in English, 'You need basil by your kitchen door. To keep away the flies.'

Emily straightens and looks round. She finds herself looking at a priest, in black shirt, dog collar, and dirty white plimsolls, sitting astride a Vespa. He is old, with thick white hair like a judge's wig and a heavily lined face but, as he leaps nimbly from the motorcycle and comes forward to greet her, his movements are that of a much younger man. And his handshake, as he introduces himself, is strong enough to make her wince.

'Don Angelo,' he says.

'Emily Robertson,' mumbles Emily, wiping a sweaty hand on her shorts.

'It is too hot to work,' says Don Angelo sternly. 'You need a rest and a cold drink.'

'Would you like a cup of tea?' asks Emily. She knows nothing about Catholic priests but surely tea is an essential part of any clerical visit?

'Tea? Never!' Don Angelo shudders violently. '*Acqua minerale*, yes.'

'Would you like a glass of *acqua minerale*?' asks Emily obediently.

'*Grazie*,' says Don Angelo sweetly, as if it was not his own idea.

They sit on the terrace, by the side of the overgrown kitchen garden. Father Angelo sips his water and casually reaches out to pick a white peach from one of the overhanging trees.

'You'd like?' he asks politely.

'Oh, no . . . thank you. You have it.'

He requests a knife and proceeds to cut the peach into

41

perfect segments, like little gleaming half moons. He throws the stone into the undergrowth. 'Now you'll have another tree. Yes?'

'In a few hundred years' time.'

'A few hundred years?' The priest shrugs eloquently. 'Is nothing.'

'Not to God, maybe,' says Emily, rather daring.

The priest laughs heartily. 'No! Not to God.' He has excellent teeth, she notices.

'So.' The peach finished, Don Angelo fixes his rather deep-set brown eyes on her. 'You are not a Catholic, I think.'

'No,' says Emily, apologetically. 'We don't really go to church, I'm afraid.'

'No,' agrees Don Angelo. 'I have not seen you in the church.' The church in Monte Albano is supposed to be a rather fine example of medieval architecture. It dates, Emily seems to remember, from the twelfth century and is said to be built on Etruscan foundations.

'I believe it has a beautiful fresco of the Annunciation . . .'

But Don Angelo shrugs off any discussion of its attractions. 'Yes. Beautiful. Yes. You never come to the town?'

'Oh, yes, I do,' says Emily eagerly. 'I come every Tuesday for the market—'

'The market!' says Don Angelo contemptuously. 'That is for tourists. Go to the Co-op. Much cheaper. No, you never come to the town. In the evening. For a *passeggiata*.'

The *passeggiata* is an Italian ritual. Every evening, as the day starts to cool, the Italians emerge from their shuttered houses to walk up and down the village square, admiring and being admired. Emily loves the way that the old people sit on kitchen chairs outside their front doors and just, unashamedly, stare. Even so, she has never thought of trying it herself.

'Well, it's a bit difficult in the evenings, with the children.'

'The children! Bring the children. We love children.'

Emily does not add that Charlie goes to bed at seven, as Italian children usually stay up until midnight.

'I see your daughter in the piazza,' continues the priest.

'Siena?' says Emily, her heart sinking. 'Yes. I expect so.'

'She is a very beautiful girl,' says Don Angelo, with much more enthusiasm than he showed for the fresco. 'She courts Giancarlo from the *pasticceria*. Yes?'

'Courts? Oh yes, I suppose she does.'

'He's a good boy. A bit wild but a good boy.'

'Yes,' says Emily, unenthusiastically.

'So. You come to the town for *Ferragosto*. Yes?'

Ferragosto. The feast of the Assumption on the fifteenth of August is celebrated in Italy with a fervency that has nothing to do with religion. It is a joyous, anarchic carnival of unlicensed enjoyment, a sort of summer Twelfth Night. Emily wrote a two-page special about it last year.

'You never come to *Ferragosto*?'

'Oh yes,' says Emily, rather hurt by now. 'We came last year.' She remembers. They had visitors, clients of Paul's, and they took them into the town to see the fireworks. Helmut, from

Germany, shot two hours of video footage with which he is doubtless still entertaining the inhabitants of Wiesbaden.

'Not just for a few hours. With some *stranieri*,' snorts Don Angelo.

Emily is amazed. How could the priest know how they spent the *Ferragosto*? Was he disguised as one of the revellers, capering about under a medieval banner? And the word he uses, *stranieri*, literally foreigners, sounds hostile. It sounds more like strangers. If the Germans were strangers, what does that make them? She begins to revise the article she is writing in her head ('Don Angelo, an unlikely angel in dirty white plimsolls') and looks at her visitor with something approaching fear.

'*Ferragosto* goes on for two days,' continues the priest. 'You should be there. Cooking the food with the others.'

Emily looks at him doubtfully. She remembers the giant barbeque in the piazza, big enough to roast an entire pig. She remembers the women cooking the porchetta steaks with such casual expertise. She feels both honoured and slightly insulted to be invited to join them.

'I . . . I wouldn't know how,' she says at last. 'I'm a . . . I'm a sort of writer—'

Emily's explanation is cut off by a howl from the front of the house.

'Charlie!' She leaps to her feet. Siena, who has been reluctantly minding her brother, bursts into view, holding Charlie on her hip. He is screaming, his face scarlet. 'Charlie! Baby! What's the matter?'

'He got stung by something,' says Siena breathlessly. 'I don't know what.'

Dimly, Emily notices Don Angelo running down the terrace steps and fighting his way through the overgrown herb garden. In a few minutes he is back, some leaves in his hand. Roughly, he grasps Charlie's leg and rubs the leaves into his skin.

There is a second's stunned silence. A pungent smell rises into the air. Charlie, halfway between his mother and his sister, his leg held by a black-suited stranger, stops crying.

'*Basilico*,' explains Don Angelo. 'Also good for stings.'

'I met the priest today,' Emily tells Paris at supper time.

'I know,' says Paris. 'I saw him from the window.' She takes a tiny square of bread and cuts it into triangles.

It takes Emily a moment to realise what she has said. 'What? You saw Charlie getting hurt and didn't come down?'

Paris sighs, cutting the bread into a tangram. 'He wasn't hurt. It was a sting. Anyhow, the witch doctor cured him.'

Emily laughs but says seriously, 'He's not a witch doctor but he was rather scary. He seems to know everything about us.'

'Like what?' asks Siena, who is texting with one hand and eating with the other.

'Well, he knew you were going out with Giancarlo, for one thing. He seems to approve.'

'Cool.' Siena looks pleased. 'Perhaps he'll tell Gianni's mother. I'm sure she's putting the evil eye on me.'

'Oh, well. Mothers and sons,' says Emily vaguely. 'I'm sure I'll be the same about Charlie.'

Siena and Paris exchange glances. Charlie has only just been banished to bed, hours after he should have been, hours after *they* used to be sent to bed.

But Emily's mind is still on the priest. 'He was quite a funny-looking little man,' she says. 'But there was something about him. He had these really dark eyes. As if he could see right into your soul.'

'Did he try to make you go to church?' asks Siena.

'No. Not really. He seemed more concerned that we didn't go into town in the evenings.'

'I do.'

'Yes, I know. So did he. He wants us to go for *Ferragosto*. He wants me to help with the cooking.'

Both Siena and Paris laugh rudely. Emily's efforts at rustic Italian cuisine are not always appreciated by the family. Tonight they are eating pizza from the Co-op. Emily, rather defiantly, is eating salad, featuring their own caterpillar-ravaged lettuce.

'I'm going for *Ferragosto*,' says Siena. 'Gianni's band is playing.'

To add to his other failings, Giancarlo is the drummer in a loud yet almost entirely talent-free rock band. Emily groans. 'Why can't we have lovely, traditional Italian music?' she asks.

Siena sighs. 'Because it's boring and sad, Mum.' She gets up, snapping shut her mobile phone. 'I'm going to watch TV.'

'Me too,' says Paris immediately.

'You haven't finished your pizza,' says Emily.

'It's got bits in it.'

'They're herbs.'

When the girls have gone, Emily picks up Paris's pizza and eats it. She really must stop eating so much. And drinking too, she thinks, as she pours herself another glass of red. At this rate she'll be as fat as a house when she sees Paul on Saturday. She must impress him with her slim figure and her complete refusal to blame anyone for the crisis in their marriage. She will be understanding, wise and just a little bit sexy. She takes another bite of pizza.

When she first met Paul, he took her to all the best restaurants but she'd always be too excited to eat anything. That's how she was in those days: tense, living on her nerves, always with a knot, like seasickness, in her stomach. She was working so hard at the paper that she usually didn't have time for lunch. She'd drink Coke at her desk and eat weird things like olives or green chillies out of paper bags. And she smoked, twenty a day at least. She'd only stopped when she was expecting Siena.

She met Paul in Brighton. She had moved there when she split up with Michael, partly because Petra, her best friend from university, was living there and partly because she'd always loved the place. As students they had sometimes driven down after a party in Petra's ancient car, arriving over the Downs just as the sun rose, sitting on the beach at dawn, drinking mugs of tea from the all-night café. Brighton seemed optimistic, full of seedy charm and brash certainties. After the shock of losing the man she had thought she would spend her life with, she felt she could do with some optimism.

Emily and Petra had rented a ramshackle flat on the seafront, where the seagulls flew below their attic windows and the sound of the sea sent them to sleep at night. Even now, Emily sometimes tries to make herself sleep by imagining that soft, hissing rustle of water against stone. If someone could patent it, they would make a fortune. She had got a job on the local paper, made new friends, gone out to parties, had barbeques on the beach. It had been a strange, wonderful, terrible time. Emily still cried whenever she saw the name Michael, but she was also the girl who danced on the beach in her underwear and swam naked in the sea. She was the girl who worked hard at becoming a reporter but who sometimes turned up at work wearing her clothes from the night before. She was the girl who had five Valentines and joined the Labour Party but who still dreamt, obsessively, of becoming Mrs Michael Bartnicki.

She met Paul when she was sent to interview him for the paper. Paul was a local businessman with a rather shady reputation. His latest venture had been to buy up some listed 1930s buildings, fill them with student tenants, and leave them to rot quietly into the sea. This strategy had been shown up when one of the flats had nearly burnt down in an accident involving a faulty gas boiler. The students' families were threatening to sue.

Emily arrived at the interview late and flustered. On the way from the bus stop, the heel had come off her shoe and she was forced to hobble. A force ten gale along the seafront had blown her hair into wild corkscrews and she was tired from three nights' constant partying. Paul was living in a grand, but rather depressing, block of flats in Hove and, as Emily pressed the entry phone buzzer, she had a vision of being denied entrance because of her disreputable appearance. She was not to know that Paul liked wild-haired women. He also liked them young.

And he had been charm itself. He had fixed her shoe with some superglue and the sight of him, bent intently over the scuffed brown leather, filled her with an inexplicable tenderness. He had given her coffee and fed her with croissants. Afterwards they had walked along the seafront and thrown croissant crumbs to the birds. Paul took her to lunch and out to dinner and, in the middle, took her to bed.

Sex with Paul was a revelation. After Michael, Emily had thought that she could never make love to another man. Well, she had, with varying degrees of success, but afterwards she had always felt, more strongly than ever, that she would never be happy in bed with anyone except Michael. But Paul was . . . well, there was no other way to put it, Paul was better than Michael. She hadn't always had orgasms with Michael but, with Paul, they came with the same prompt reliability that Paul required in all areas of his life. Afterwards, she wondered if she had orgasms precisely because she didn't love Paul as much as she had loved Michael.

But she did love him. He was exciting, he made things happen, the seagulls wheeled out of the sea for him, waiters jumped at the sound of his voice, he could transform a dull afternoon into a dizzying array of possibilities. He took her to France, flying from Shoreham Airport in a friend's plane, he took her to elegant hotels in the countryside, he took her go-karting, he won her a fluffy toy on Brighton pier.

When Paul asked her to marry him, she didn't hesitate. 'Are you sure?' Petra had asked tearfully, the night before the register office wedding. 'Oh yes,' Emily had said, dreamily. Of course she was sure, that was what Paul was all about. He thought she should marry him and she did.

Emily finishes her wine with a hefty slug. Then she clears the table and loads the dishwasher (even rustic Italian houses have dishwashers). From the sitting room, she can hear Siena and Paris watching *Dad's Army*. The Villa Serena is too remote for satellite or cable so they have to rely on DVDs from England and, oddly enough, it is the old ones that they like best. *Dad's Army*, *The Likely Lads*, *Fawlty Towers*, *Are You Being Served*? Oh, the comforting sound of the studio laughter, the plodding approach of the punchline, Pike's eternal idiocy, Mainwaring's endless self-importance. Emily finds herself smiling in sympathy as she throws the stale bread out of the back door. She feels she would give anything, anything, for the sight of one seagull, swooping down on the crumbs with that familiar raucous cry of greed.

Emily goes up to check on Charlie, who is sleeping peacefully. Somehow the smell of basil seems still to linger in the air. Emily thinks about the priest. Why did he come to visit after all this time? After all, they have been in the house almost two years. Had he heard rumours that Paul had left? She is sure that Olimpia will have told the world. Her cleaner's antipathy seems to have reached new heights recently. Olimpia liked Paul; he flattered her and called her *signorina*. Had Olimpia told Don Angelo that Emily was an evil marriage breaker? Had he come to see what the scarlet woman looked like (she had been red-faced enough after all that digging)? Did he really just want to tempt her down from her isolated villa into the warmth of the piazza? Or did he just need another pair of hands to cook the porchetta?

She goes back downstairs but, instead of joining her daughters in the sitting room, she steps out onto the terrace and breathes in the night air. And she thinks of the first time that Michael took her to Vittorio's and the moment that she fell, fatally, in love with Italy.

CHAPTER 5

Thoughts from Tuscany
By Emily Robertson

Visiting a restaurant in Italy is a humbling business. For a start, in Tuscany it is the custom of restaurants to have their kitchen at the front, so that you actually have to walk through it to reach your table. The cleanliness and shiny order of these kitchens is enough to induce a serious fit of inadequacy. Pizzas slide in and out of the glowing, dome-shaped ovens, pasta is cooked to the perfect consistency (al dente, meaning to have bite), herbs are sprinkled, oil is drizzled, meat is rolled and secured with sage leaves. Everything is done at top speed but nothing is rushed.

Then, when you reach your table, you are greeted like a much-loved member of the family. Wine is opened and bruschette laid before you as if you were the prodigal son himself. And the welcome given to children! Coming from England, a country where being seen in public in the company of someone under three foot tall is almost a hanging offence, the Italian attitude to children is like balm from the heavens. A high chair? No problem. Pasta without sauce? A pleasure. Want to draw on the table cloth? Go right ahead. And what about some of chef's special antipasti to tempt the little *bimba*?

'When are you seeing your ex-husband?' asks Petra.

'He isn't my ex-husband.'

'Not yet,' says Petra bluntly.

'Saturday. He's coming to talk things over, he says.'

'Well, just don't give in too easily.'

'What do you mean?' asks Emily, nettled.

'I know you, Em. You'll go into one of your dreamy "whatever you say" states. Paul left you, remember. He's got some explaining to do. Don't let him just come swanning back like last time.'

'Do you think he wants to come back to me?'

'Christ, I don't know. Do you want him back?'

'Yes. No. I don't know.'

'Well, like I said, don't let him call all the shots. I know what he's like. I'll never forget him evicting all those tenants so that he could sell their flats to build a shopping centre.'

'He is ruthless. I used to find that quite attractive.'

'Heaven help you.'

There is a hum over the phone line as Petra is silent for a moment. Emily can hear a long, indrawn breath.

'Are you smoking?' she asks.

'Oh, for God's sake, Em. Just one or two a day. After meals.'

'It's ten o'clock at night.'

'I ate late.'

'What's brought this on?' asks Emily.

'Oh, I don't know. Worry about the kids, about work, about money.'

'Doesn't Ed help?'

'I don't even know where Ed is. Last communication was a card for Jake's birthday. Two months too late.' Another drag on the cigarette. Then Petra says, suddenly, 'I've got a photo of Michael.'

Emily finds herself holding her breath as if she had been expecting this, as if, somehow, all the events of the past week had been leading up to this. Michael. Her first love.

'A photo?' she whispers.

'Yes. It was in the paper. Something about some mega brilliant brain surgery he's done. Do you want me to send you the article?'

Emily finds her heart beating so fast that she is surprised that Petra can't hear it, all those miles away in Brighton. 'Yes,' she says. 'Yes please.'

She met Michael in London, at university. She was reading English at UCL, Michael was a medical student. It was a summer's evening and she was acting in an incredibly pretentious production of *The Tempest*, staged in Gordon Square, one of those secretive little London squares surrounded by looming university buildings. If she closes her eyes, she can still smell the dusty plane trees and hear the gentle roar of the London traffic. She can see the exact metallic gleam of Michael's blond hair as he turned to her and said, 'Are you involved in this shit?' As she had, at that moment, been wearing a rather unsuccessful Elizabethan dress and was offering him a symbolic bowl of water to 'purify' himself, this was rather a redundant question. But how well she remembers her pathetic eagerness to disassociate herself from the production.

'Oh, sort of,' she said, standing on one leg under the heavy skirts. The part of Miranda, fought for against stiff opposition from a dozen prettier, more confident girls, was suddenly unimportant, embarrassing even. 'Oh, brave new world! That has such people in it.'

After the performance (the director had denied them a curtain call, claiming that it would 'detract from the spell of the language') Emily saw Michael again. The audience were leaving, throwing cigarette butts into the purifying bowl, but Michael was still there, sitting alone in the second row, smiling in a way that was to become very familiar to her, half irony, half genuine sweetness.

'Congratulations,' he said solemnly.

'I was dreadful.'

'You were wonderful. Ferdinand was dreadful.'

'He couldn't help forgetting his lines.'

'No, but he could help being more interested in Ariel than in you.' Ariel had been played ('against type' explained the director) by a burly rugby player from Salford. Michael had been quite right about Ferdinand's inclinations.

Emily remembers standing in the shadowy garden, feeling the last of the sun upon her face and listening to the voices of the rest of the audience getting further and further away until they were nothing but a gentle chorus to the main action. She remembers standing there in her ludicrous brocade dress (where would Miranda have found a dress like that?) and feeling ridiculously, dizzyingly happy. She said nothing because she knew that Michael was about to take over her life completely. It was a wonderfully restful feeling.

Michael stood up and, leaning towards her, gently brushed a strand of hair from her forehead.

'May I?' he asked politely.

What would have happened, she thinks, if she had said no? If she had said no, she had a sixteen-stone boyfriend waiting for her back in Halls? If she had said no, she had taken a vow of pre-marital celibacy? If she had run screaming back to the post-performance party to hear the director reading aloud from his experimental poems? But, of course, she had done none of these things.

When Paul arrives at the Villa Serena on Saturday, he is, at first, an anticlimax. As he walks from the car, neatly dressed in polo shirt and chinos (Paul is one of those men who is only really comfortable in a suit), he looks like any one of hundreds of middle-aged men, hair greying, waistline only just kept in check, that can be seen at any fitness club, at any railway station, queuing at any departures desk. How can he have caused her so much unhappiness? But then he smiles, the old white-toothed, vulpine Paul smile, and her heart contracts. She knows him, she knows him so well; she knows that he is allergic to honey, that *The Railway Children* makes him cry, that he thinks Luigi Riva was a better player than Pelé. How can he be about to leave her? It must be a mistake, it must be.

He walks up to the front door, crushing pine nuts beneath his feet. Visitors to the Villa Serena usually come to the kitchen door, which is actually nearer the driveway, but this visit somehow needs the formality of the front door. Emily stands in the hallway wearing a white, floaty dress. She has done her hair and has taken an hour on her face. Even her toes are varnished (though she has forgotten to put her shoes on).

'Hello, Paul.'

'Emily.' He goes to kiss her but obviously thinks better of it. He puts his case down on the stone floor.

'Have you come to stay?' asks Emily, indicating the bag and half knowing that her words are ambiguous.

'It's empty,' says Paul. He feels tense and uncomfortable. Why is Emily wearing that ridiculous white dress and why the hell can't she put shoes on?

'Where are the kids?' he says, after a pause.

'They've gone down to the farm. They'll be back in a minute.'

'Good,' he says heavily. 'I've missed them.'

Emily is silent. She is damned if she's going to say that they've missed him too.

They go into the sitting room. Usually they sit in the kitchen which is cosy and comfortable with a scrubbed wooden table and squashy chairs but Emily feels the need for discomfort just now. She sits on one sofa; Paul sits on the other, separated by the monstrous fireplace. A giant grandfather clock ticks in the hallway

'Well,' says Emily, unhelpfully. 'What did you want to talk about?'

Paul tries an understanding voice. 'Emily, you know what we've got to talk about.'

'No I don't. What?'

'Don't make this harder than it has to be.'

'Why the fuck shouldn't I?'

There is a long silence. Outside, the crickets chirp and bees fly loudly through the overgrown herb garden. The clock ticks ponderously.

'Emily,' says Paul at last, 'you know our marriage hasn't worked for a long time.'

'No I don't,' says Emily promptly.

'Well, you know, ever since . . . ever since—'

'Ever since you had an affair.'

Paul looks hurt. 'Well, if you want to put it like that.'

'I do.'

'Ever since we . . . grew apart . . . you must have known something wasn't right.'

'But we got back together!' It comes out almost as a wail. 'We got back together and we had Charlie and we moved here and—' Emily is crying now, great, unromantic tears that make her gulp and sniff. She wipes her eyes on the hem of the floaty skirt.

Paul spreads out his hands helplessly but does not come to comfort her. He seems rooted to the other side of the room, across acres of unspoilt Tuscan tiling.

'I'm sorry,' he says at last.

'You're sorry,' says Emily, sniffing and gulping. 'You're sorry, Christ!'

At this moment, the children come rushing in. Blinking in the dark of the sitting room, they suddenly register their father's presence and fling themselves on him. Emily, marooned on her sofa, wipes her eyes again. If only the kids didn't love him, she thinks.

'Daddy! Have you come for the weekend?' asks Siena.

'Are you coming with us to *Ferragosto*?' asks Paris. 'I don't mind if there are clients,' she adds bravely.

'Present,' demands Charlie, climbing onto Paul's lap. 'Present for Charlie.'

'Actually,' says Emily in a hard voice, 'Daddy isn't staying long.' She looks at Paul and he looks away.

'The thing is . . .' begins Paul, uncomfortably. 'You know Daddy will always love you . . .'

He's actually going to say it, thinks Emily. Right up until this moment, she has thought that perhaps it isn't true, that it's an elaborate joke or a punishment to her for being too preoccupied with the kids and the house. She still can't believe that Paul is actually about to tell the children that their parents are getting divorced. But, when he says those words, the words that have hovered unsaid on the outskirts of so many marital quarrels, then that will be it. Her marriage will be over.

But before Paul can go on, Siena breaks away from him with an expression of disgust. 'Oh God,' she says. 'Is this one of those "Mummy and Daddy still love each other but they're going to live in different houses" conversations?'

Emily and Paul look at each other. Suddenly all the anger seeps out of Emily, leaving her simply feeling sad and very tired. 'I suppose so,' she says at last.

Paris looks at her parents in horror. 'No,' she says. 'No! No! No.'

'Paris. Sweetheart.' Emily takes a step towards her.

'Don't touch me!' shrieks Paris and runs from the room. After a second, Siena follows her.

'Daddy,' says Charlie. 'Where's my present?'

Emily's first experience of Italy was in a London restaurant. She had been going out with Michael for six heady weeks and was still at the stage when she had to touch him all the time, just to prove he was real. They were walking entwined along Charlotte Street, dodging the packs of foreign students and the old men with placards wanting to save their souls, when Michael said, 'Let's go to Vittorio's for lunch.'

'Vittorio's?'

'You know Vittorio's. Everyone knows Vittorio's.' Emily said nothing. Already in her relationship with Michael, she had come across several things that 'everyone knows' but she didn't. She didn't want Michael to think that she was a complete fool.

Michael swerved suddenly into a side street and there, tables spread out on the pavement, Italian tricolour hanging limply in the still air, was Vittorio's.

'We can't go in there,' Emily said. She had seen the menu, enshrined like an icon behind glass, and knew that she would not be able to afford even a breadstick.

'Course we can,' said Michael, pushing her through the heavy glass doors. 'It won't cost a thing.'

She remembers standing in the sudden dark of the restaurant, beside the curly Victorian hatstand, and hearing Michael shout, 'Mum! Mama! Your favourite son is here.'

Mum?

A figure emerged from the gloom. It had bright red hair, a large, white apron and a smile of ferocious welcome.

'Michele! My angel! What took you so long?'

Michael disengaged himself from the red-haired woman's embrace and dragged Emily forward.

'Mum, meet Emily. My girlfriend.'

Gina looked at Emily, a slow smile spreading over her dark face. 'Lovely,' she said at last. 'She's lovely, Michele. Well done.'

Well done? Emily thought as they sat down at a corner table

and Gina snapped her fingers for a waiter. What did that mean? She knew that she, with her untidy hair and scruffy clothes, was no catch at all for the glamorous Michael. His previous girlfriend, a titled classics student from King's, now she was a prize worth bringing home to Vittorio's. *Had* he brought her here? Was it some sort of rite of passage, a sort of trial by risotto?

'Do you bring all your girlfriends here?' she asked as they ate bread dipped in green olive oil and drank glasses of cold Prosecco.

'Of course not,' said Michael. 'You're the first.'

'Why?'

'Because I knew my mum would like you,' he said, draining his glass and holding it out to a passing waiter.

'Bugger off,' said the waiter. 'Get it yourself.'

Grinning and muttering something in Italian, Michael wandered over to the bar and came back with the bottle.

'I can't,' said Emily 'I've got a tutorial at two.'

'Skip it,' said Michael. 'You can't rush a meal at Vittorio's.'

'Does your mother own this restaurant?'

'She manages it. It belongs to my grandfather, Nonno Vittorio. He has another one in London.'

'But I thought you were Polish.'

'My dad's Polish. My mum's Italian. Her parents came over here before the war. She was born in London.'

'So she's really English.'

'Emily,' said Michael seriously, filling up her glass, 'never, ever say that to my mother.'

Afterwards, she could never remember exactly what she ate at that first meal. The courses seemed to come in bewildering profusion but in no particular order. A few grains of black risotto, three pieces of stuffed pasta in a delicious creamy sauce, meat rolled around herbs and garlic, bread with glistening slices of liver, a rich tender chop which Michael told her was rabbit, olives stuffed with anchovies, tomatoes stuffed with capers, ravioli stuffed with truffles.

'I can't eat all this,' Emily kept saying.

'Of course you can,' Michael said, his eyes bright in the candlelight. 'Just pace yourself.' He reached over and filled up her glass again.

Two o'clock passed. Three o'clock, four o'clock, five o'clock. Eventually, Gina came and sat with them as they drank bitter black coffee from tiny, gold cups. Michael lit Emily's amaretto paper and watched it rise up to the ceiling, scattering flakes of ash. 'It's lucky if it falls on you,' he said and Emily remembers feeling slightly aggrieved that the cindery strands fell not on her but on Gina, her glowing hair and her jewel-encrusted hands. Gina was pouring them rich, red liquor from a dusty bottle. It was like an enchanter's drink and, by now, Emily was thoroughly enchanted.

'So you love my son?' asked Gina, ruffling Michael's hair.

'Oh yes,' said Emily happily. 'I really love him.'

'That's good,' said Gina, 'because that means I will love you.'

CHAPTER 6

Thoughts from Tuscany
By Emily Robertson

There is no English word for *feste*. It is a peculiarly Italian invention; a sort of cross between a religious feast day and an all-night party. Sometimes, in Tuscany, they also use the word *sagra*. The *sagra della bistecca*, the feast of beefsteaks, the *sagra della lumaca*, the feast of snails. Only in Italy would food have its own feast day.

Ferragosto, in August, is the *festa* to end all *festas*. It is meant to celebrate the feast of the Assumption, on the fifteenth of August, but in reality it takes up almost the whole of August. All of Italy is on holiday in August and the whole country gives itself up to enjoyment for day after joyous day.

This year, I have been asked to help with the cooking for our little town's *Ferragosto* celebrations. And, as I stand by the giant grill in the baking heat, I realise that at last I am truly one of the family.

'*Porchetta per favore.*'

'*Aspetta uno momentino.*'

Emily, her hair dripping with sweat, is attempting to manoeuvre porchetta steaks onto a giant bap. They fall back onto the grill, hissing on the coals. Her neighbour, a black-haired woman who has not yet exchanged one word with Emily, expertly flips the steaks onto the bread, grinds salt and pepper and plonks the sandwich onto the waiting plate.

'*Grazie,*' says Emily weakly. The woman ignores her.

It is ten o'clock on the evening of *Ferragosto* and still people are eating. Tables have been put out in the piazza under a giant awning and families are laughing, talking and eating in the light of hundreds of lanterns rigged up around the square. Emily's family, though, is scattered. Charlie is with Olimpia, sitting on her lap and eating hazelnut ice cream. Siena is presumably somewhere with Giancarlo. 'I'm with the band,' she announced earlier, only half ironically. And Paris? Emily hasn't seen Paris since she refused the porchetta with a shudder and disappeared off into the noisy smoke-filled night.

Emily, hot, bored and smelling of pork fat, is fed up. She is just about to take off her apron and go in search of Paris when a voice says, '*Brava*, Mrs Robertson. Thank you for joining us.' It is Don Angelo. He is holding a bottle of wine (no label, obviously not shop bought) and a dozen plastic glasses. Emily's black-haired neighbour starts to bridle and flick her hair about like a teenager. '*Don Angelo! Troppo gentile.*'

Don Angelo pours wine into two glasses and hands them to

Emily and her neighbour. Emily takes a cautious sip. It is a red wine, young and slightly fizzy.

'*É buono*,' she says.

'Is my own,' says the priest complacently.

'*Buonissimo*,' says her neighbour, not to be outdone.

Another woman claims Don Angelo's attention and, for a minute, Emily just stands there, sipping the cool wine and letting the talk flow over her. The queue has disappeared; most families seem to be sitting in the square, drinking wine while the children run about madly. Emily can see Charlie chasing a little girl with plaits and has to physically hold on to the side of the barbeque to stop herself from reaching out and grabbing him. She knows Olimpia is taking good care of him (she can hear constant cries of '*Carlito! Fai attenzione!*'); this is what she finds hard to bear.

Then she hears the words 'Villa Serena' and turns to Don Angelo's conversation. Another woman has joined him and they are all talking animatedly, Don Angelo spilling wine as he gestures wildly.

'*Scusi*,' says Emily. They ignore her.

'Excuse me,' she says in English. Father Angelo turns to look at her.

'Were you talking about my house?' asks Emily.

'Your house? Oh yes. We are talking about the digging.'

'Digging?'

'The . . . what is the word? . . . the archaeology.'

'Archaeology?'

'Yes, they are digging in the fields behind your house. They think there is an Etruscan *campo santo* . . . burial ground.'

'Really? How exciting!'

Don Angelo looks at her quizzically. 'Some of us do not find it exciting, Mrs Robertson. The dead, they should be left in peace.'

'But if it's important historically?'

'Historically!' Don Angelo spreads his arms out wide in a gesture of complete contempt. 'What use is history?'

Emily does not know how to answer this. Fortunately one of the other women leans over and diverts the priest's attention. Emily just catches the name 'Raffaello'.

Thinking of the artist, she says excitedly, 'Raffaello? Have they discovered a Raffaello?'

Don Angelo turns back to her with a grim smile. 'We are talking of the archaeologist, Raffaello Murello. He is a man well known in these parts.'

'He is a devil,' says the black-haired woman, lapsing disconcertingly into English.

Paris is beyond fed up. She is literally *stiff* with boredom. She sits at a table at the far end of the piazza near a family stuffing themselves with food and thinks dark thoughts. Mum is still cooking that disgusting meat, all bloody with globules of fat and nasty white sinewy bits. Paris would not eat it if you paid her a million pounds, though the next-door family seem to be enjoying it no end, revolting drops of sauce falling on the tablecloth as they stuff more and more into their fat faces. Paris gives them a killer death-ray stare.

Siena is off somewhere with stupid Giancarlo, poncing about talking about sound checks and drum solos as if he's Bruce Springsteen or someone. Charlie is being spoilt rotten by Olimpia; she can hear him from the other side of the square, demanding ice cream in a high-pitched bilingual whine. She is the only one who is tired, hungry and on her own. She takes a Mars bar from her pocket and begins to eat it slowly. She can make it last an hour if she tries. She thinks, I have measured out my life in Mars bars. God! She is wasted on this place. Who else reads T. S. Eliot just for fun, like she does? Siena was only interested when she told her that his name was an anagram of toilets. God! The ignorance of her family!

'*Ciao*, Paris.' She looks up, scowling. It is Andrea, the teacher's son, the one who wants to go to Pisa University. She has always liked Andrea best of Giancarlo's friends. He is blond and rather quiet. He also has the distinction of coming from a single-parent family, which makes him both unusual in Tuscany and comfortingly like her friends in London.

'*Ciao*,' says Paris, almost smiling.

'Why are you sitting here on your own?' asks Andrea, in Italian.

Paris, whose Italian is a lot better than Emily's, answers, 'I'm bored.'

'Bored? Why?'

'I don't know. I just am.' And to her horror, Paris feels tears beginning to sting behind her eyes. She ducks her head so that Andrea won't see.

Andrea looks at her for a moment and then puts his hand on her arm. 'Would you like me to take you home?'

'Yes,' says Paris. 'Yes please.'

She almost leaves without telling Emily, just to serve her right. She can see her mother by the barbeque, laughing and talking with the priest. He is drinking wine and waving his arms about. Honestly! You would never find an English vicar behaving like that. It would serve her mum right if she just disappeared into the night. But then she relents. Seeing Olimpia nearby, holding a now sleepy Charlie tenderly in her arms, she leaves a message for Emily. Could Olimpia tell her mum that she was feeling tired and had gone home? A friend will give her a lift. *Grazie.*

The ride home, on the back of Andrea's motorbike, is quite exciting. The night air is cool against her face and, pressed against Andrea's leather jacket, she does not need to talk. As they reach the Villa Serena, the sky explodes with fireworks. They stand for a second, on the terrace steps, watching them.

'Beautiful,' says Andrea.

'The ones on Clapham Common are better,' says Paris. She remembers Bonfire Night on the common, wearing one of those stupid fluorescent necklaces and frightening Charlie with a sparkler. She can almost smell the frying onions. In those days, food didn't make her feel so sick.

'Will you be all right on your own?' asks Andrea as Paris pushes open the (unlocked) front door.

For a second Paris considers asking him to stay. The house looks very dark and the clock is ticking portentously, like the soundtrack to a horror film. But he might think that she fancies him, might (horrific thought) jump on her and try to kiss her. She looks at his solid body in its biker's jacket and imagines it pinning her to the floor, her screams as she tries to escape. She imagines his pale, clever face turned livid with that awful intensity that she sometimes sees in Giancarlo when he kisses Siena. Never, never, never. She would rather take her chances with the wolves.

'I'll be OK,' she says.

'*Va bene*,' says Andrea equably. He is not the type of boy to argue. She watches him running down the steps and hears the roar of his motorbike. Briefly, headlights illuminate the fig trees and then all is darkness.

Paris shuts the door. Then something makes her take the heavy iron key and turn it carefully in the lock. Instead of making her feel more secure, however, she finds this makes her feel more frightened than ever. Isn't this what happens in every horror film? The girl left on her own in the big house locks herself in and turns round to find the hooded madman standing right behind her. Paris swings round. There is nobody there, just the looming clock with its spectral tick and the hatstand with its headless coats hanging gruesomely on their hooks. She remembers an apocryphal story that was very popular at her old school in Clapham. Babysitter on her own in the house, picking up the phone to hear the madman saying that he is going to kill her and realising that it is an *internal line.* The horror is within the house. The madman in the attic. Stop it, she tells herself, you scored top marks in the logic paper we did in Mr Dixon's class, you do not believe that there is a mad axeman waiting upstairs. You are perfectly calm and completely in control.

With an effort, she turns her back on the front door and walks purposefully into the sitting room. Here it is better. One of the sofas has been pushed towards the television set. Paris turns on all the lights and selects *Dad's Army.* Then she sits on the floor and takes out her half-eaten Mars bar, shaving off a thin layer of chocolate with her front teeth. The next moment, the cosy quavering voice asks, 'Who Do You Think You Are Kidding, Mr Hitler,' and she is transported to Walmington-on-Sea, to the wonderful world of Jones's butcher's van and Pike's scarf and Godfrey's need for the lavatory. Paris stretches out full length on the stone floor, a cushion under her head, nibbling smaller and smaller pieces of chocolate. Then, without warning, Fraser, Jones and Godfrey decide that they look too old for the Home Guard and Fraser takes them to his undertaker's lair to rejuvenate them. Fraser's spooky Scots whisper invites them to climb onto the slab. Paris shudders then presses stop.

She shifts through the other DVDs. She must find something that is a million miles away from Tuscany, deserted houses and mad axemen lying in wait upstairs. She picks another disc and lies down on the floor again. A mad, moustachioed man prances across the screen kicking up his legs and screeching hysterically about the Germans.

Paris relaxes, soothed by the anger and prejudice of Basil Fawlty.

Emily is searching, with increasing panic, for Paris. She locates Siena, dancing like a zombie in front of the band, her blonde hair a curtain over her face.

Emily grabs her arm. 'Have you seen Paris?'

Siena points vaguely. 'She's over there. At one of the tables. Sulking.'

'Where?'

But Siena just continues to dance, her hair spinning out around her. On stage, Giancarlo, too, is tossing his hair in a frenzy, drumsticks a blur. Emily retreats, her ears ringing.

She circles the tables, asking again and again for her daughter. People point out Siena (she is all too noticeable, dancing on her own in front of the stage) and Charlie, asleep in Olimpia's arms. But no one seems to have seen Paris. One woman even seems surprised that she has another daughter. '*Una tipa differente*,' someone else explains, nodding at Siena. But Emily has already run on to the next table. Her heart is pounding, this is her very worst nightmare come crashingly true. *She has lost one of her children.* She is a terrible, terrible mother. Paul will never forgive her if anything happens to Paris (his fellow football fan, his beloved tomboy), she will never forgive herself. The world becomes a nightmarish kaleidoscope of images: Paris dead, her small white coffin, her empty bedroom, her own scream of horror, Paul's cold-eyed hatred. Oh God, please let her find Paris.

Eventually she arrives at Olimpia's table. Olimpia looks at her impassively, arms folded across her chest. She must have seen Emily's frantic questioning of the other tables but makes no move to reassure her. She hates me, she absolutely hates me, thinks Emily.

'Olimpia,' she begins pleadingly, 'have you seen Paris? I can't find her anywhere. I think she's lost.' Her voice breaks and she has to hold on to the table to stop herself shaking.

'Oh, Paris,' says Olimpia placidly, in Italian, taking a sip of wine. 'She left a while ago. With Andrea.'

'Andrea?'

'Yes, the teacher's son. He's a nice boy but his mother, well, I remember her as a child. Pretty but wayward. There's no father, you know.'

'Where did they go?' interrupts Emily.

Olimpia shrugs. 'Back to your house, I think.'

Wordlessly, Emily snatches up the sleeping Charlie and runs, with his head lolling against her shoulder, over to Siena.

'We're going home,' she pants.

'I'm not,' says Siena calmly, swaying and tossing. 'Gianni'll bring me later.'

Emily has to give in. She can't argue with Siena in her tranced state, not with Charlie a dead weight in her arms and Paris lost, vanished into the night with the mysterious Andrea. She exhorts a promise from Siena to be home by midnight and jogs away heading for her car.

The town is so full for *Ferragosto* that she has had to park outside the walls, halfway up the next hill. By the time she reaches the Fiat Panda her arms are killing her and her breath is coming in ragged gasps. She puts Charlie in the back, climbs into the driver's seat and turns the ignition. 'Please start,' she prays. The god of Fiats is on her side and the engine purrs smugly. As she performs a fifteen-point turn in the road, the fireworks start, lighting up the sky with red and gold. The noise is unbelievable, Emily imagines this is what it must have been like living through the Blitz.

Disorientated and panicking, she pushes in a CD. The friendly northern voice sings about the wheels on the bus. Emily breathes deeply. She must concentrate, she mustn't have a crash.

Three nursery rhymes later, she screeches in through the rusty gates of the Villa Serena. Thank God there is a light on. Lifting the still sleeping Charlie, she stumbles up the drive. The door is locked. Oh Christ, has she got a key? Balancing Charlie on her hip, she feels in her bag. Tampax, money and lipstick fall to the ground but Emily doesn't notice. She has found the key still with the estate agent's label attached: 'Villa Serena, near Sansepolcro'.

Inside, she can hear a man's voice raised in anger. For an instant she stiffens, then she recognises the voice and relaxes. Entering the sitting room, she finds Paris asleep on the floor and Basil Fawlty ranting on the television. Laying Charlie on the sofa, she sinks to the floor and takes her daughter's bony body in her arms. 'Oh my sweetheart,' she says. 'Thank God you're safe.'

While Basil Fawlty dismantles a trifle in search of roast duck, Emily rocks her daughter in her arms.

CHAPTER 7

**Thoughts from Tuscany
By Emily Robertson**

It is very hard to describe the English seaside experience to an Italian. Why, an Italian acquaintance asked recently, do the English take flasks to the beach? So they can have a hot drink (preferably Bovril) after swimming, I explained. *É vero?* Why would they want a hot drink on a hot day? I broke it to him gently. The English seaside is not necessarily hot. Getting into the freezing sea requires Olympic levels of stoicism. Staggering out over tiny, sharp stones requires the mind-over-matter abilities of an Indian fakir. And, when sitting afterwards in a howling gale, with a wet towel wrapped round your shoulders, you need to force some hot liquid between your chattering lips. What is this Bovril? he asked. Don't even get me started, I said.

Paris's diary

I am writing this in England. In Brighton, to be precise. I am
sitting in Petra's attic bedroom, watching the man in the attic
bedroom across the street practise juggling. It is so BRILLIANT
to be here. When the plane flew over England I cried. Honestly.
I really did. It just looked so beautiful, so incredibly green, with
all the little houses surrounded by fields – proper, flat fields, not
stupid terraces up the side of a mountain. OK, OK, I know it's
green because it rains all the time, Siena has told me that at
least a million times. But I like the rain. I like wearing a fleece
and feeling cosy instead of boiling hot all the time. I like not
having to put on sunblock. I like cuddling under my duvet at
night with my ears cold and my body warm. I like the mornings
when everything looks washed clean by the rain. I love speaking
English all the time.

Siena doesn't like it though. She's in a mega sulk because of
leaving Gian-bloody-carlo. She cried all the way to the airport.
So pathetic! After all, she'll be seeing him again in a week. But
she kept going on about how there were only two weeks left of
the holidays and how G was going to take her to his apartment
in Forte dei Marmi. Mum pounced on that pretty quickly.
'There's no way I would have let you go anyway,' she said. I've
noticed that Mum seems to have gone off G a bit. Also, she's
a lot snappier with everyone. Even with Dear Little Charlie.
Hooray!

Anyway, Petra met us at Gatwick and Mum sort of fell

*into her arms and cried and cried. Siena and me were really
embarrassed. Petra (I really like her) calmed Mum down and
sorted out all our bags and stuff. She had her children with
her. Jake, who I sort of remember, and Harry, who's Dear Little
Charlie's age. Mum has been saying that Harry and DLC can
play together, it'll be so good for him to have another child to
play with etc. etc. Anyway, the first thing Harry did was kick
Charlie and the second thing he did was bite his leg. I think I'm
going to like Harry.*

*The first evening, Mum and Petra just talked and talked.
Siena and I asked if we could go on the pier and, amazingly,
Mum said yes. It was awesome. All the lights and the noise from
the rides. The hundreds of people everywhere, all so different.
Mods, rockers, punks, gays, straights. Not like Italy where
everyone sort of looks the same. All tanned and tidy with white
shirts and loafers with no socks. Here everyone looked scruffy
and there were drunk people singing karaoke at the end of the
pier. I just love Brighton.*

Several factors were behind Emily's decision to embark, at such
short notice, on a visit to England. First, after the dreadful
panic of the night of *Ferragosto*, she just felt that she needed
to get away from Tuscany for a while. The memory of running
through the square with Charlie's sleeping body in her arms
(which, in her imagination, had almost become his lifeless
corpse), searching desperately for Paris, still had the power to
turn her cold with fright. The flight in the dark, with fireworks

exploding all around her, seemed, to her, the very stuff of nightmares even if, at the end of it, she had found Paris safe in the care of Basil Fawlty. Also, the dreadful Giancarlo was hanging round more than ever and now Siena was demanding to go and stay in his holiday apartment (even the poorest Italians seemed to have these apartments, usually by the sea or in the mountains). Emily had quickly squashed that idea. She didn't trust Giancarlo in Monte Albano; she would trust him even less in a holiday apartment, miles away from her watchful eye. Better for Siena to be away from him for a bit.

Secondly, she needed to see her accountant and solicitor, both of whom were in London. Thirdly, she badly wanted to see Petra again. And fourthly, fourthly was the piece of crumpled newspaper sent by Petra with the scribbled note: 'Here is the picture of M. Still cute, eh? Izzy and Ruth are having a reunion party on 22nd. Any chance you could come?' On the morning of 16 August, Emily was sitting at her computer, with a cup of black coffee beside her, booking the flights to Gatwick.

It was wonderful to see Petra again. She looked the same, perhaps even thinner, standing like a stork dressed in bleached denim, peering over the tops of the crowds. Jake, who had grown into a serious-looking boy with Petra's long legs and blond hair, was pushing a baggage trolley. Harry, dark-haired and blue-eyed (like Ed), was standing next to Petra, both hands over his ears.

'Pete!' Emily hugged her friend. Petra felt stiff and unyielding as if she wasn't used to being hugged but she kissed Emily's cheek and said, with real affection, 'Em. It's so lovely to see you.' Emily burst into tears.

While Petra and Jake bustled about with the luggage, Emily introduced the children. 'You remember Siena and Paris, of course. And this is Charlie.' Harry took a step forward, took his hands from his ears, and kicked Charlie, very hard, in the shins.

Charlie was too shocked even to scream. 'Harry,' said Petra wearily, but without real anger, or even surprise. Instinctively, Emily clutched Charlie closer to her side. Harry stared at them impassively before covering up his ears again.

'He doesn't like the noise, you see,' explained Petra, leading them at a brisk trot towards the car park.

'I understand,' said Emily faintly.

'He hates planes,' said Jake, who was still pushing the trolley. 'He only likes Thomas.'

'Thomas?'

'The tank engine.'

'Oh.'

In the car (a dilapidated people carrier), Emily sat in the middle row with Charlie on her lap. Petra awarded Siena the front seat and Paris sat in the back with Jake. The dreadful Harry was in his child seat next to Emily. Charlie stretched out one brown leg to touch the seat in front. Harry leant forward and bit it.

This time Charlie did scream. Petra turned round. 'Harry,' she said, in the same tone as before. 'I'm sorry,' she said to Emily.

'That's all right,' said Emily stiffly. She was furious with

Siena and Paris for laughing. There were actual teeth marks on Charlie's leg.

Petra's house is in Kemp Town, just along the coast road from their old flat (now, according to Petra, renovated into 'executive apartments'). It is a tall thin house, four storeys high, narrow and steep with sloping wooden floors, like being on board a ship. Siena and Paris are delighted to be given the top floor where, from their beds, they can look straight up to the cloudy sky. The cry of the seagulls made Emily shiver with something almost like fear.

Emily and Charlie are on the floor below. They are to share a double bed and Emily is slightly ashamed of how much she looked forward to cuddling up to Charlie's warm, baby-scented body at night. Surely she had never looked forward like this to cuddling Paul at night? All she remembered were his irritating habits of stealing the duvet and turning on the overhead lights at five thirty when he had an early plane to catch. She certainly couldn't remember the sheer animal joy of having another human body beside her; those feelings were now confined to her children, memories of curling round them at night like a mother cat with her kittens. Only on nights when Paul was away, though; he always refused to let the children sleep in their bed.

Petra's boys are on the same floor as Emily, where there is also a roof garden. 'We have to keep it locked,' said Petra casually, 'because of Harry.' Petra is in the study on the floor below, next to the sitting room.

'I can't take your bed,' said Emily horrified.

'Oh, it's OK,' said Petra, 'I don't sleep much.'

Emily looked at her friend as she moved around the basement kitchen, making tea, cooking pizza, feeding the cat, gently removing sharp objects from Harry. She didn't look tired as much as worn out, almost transparent, her hair colourless, the bones showing through her skin. As she turned to lay the table, the diffused light from the low window seemed almost to shine through her, as if she were made of glass.

'Can I help?' asked Emily, sitting with Charlie on her lap (he was afraid to go anywhere near Harry).

'Yes,' said Petra. 'You can open the wine.'

After supper the girls wanted to go to the pier and Emily was too tired to stop them. 'It's OK,' said Petra comfortingly. 'It's a surprisingly safe place, Brighton. All its faults are on the surface, so to speak.'

'Don't speak to anyone strange,' called Emily as her daughters made for the door.

'This is Brighton, remember,' said Petra. 'Everyone's strange.'

Petra and Emily sat next to the open window, drinking wine and listening to the town coming alive for evening: the relentless beat of music from the pier, the shouts of people walking along the promenade, the whine of the traffic and, behind it all, the endless sound of the sea.

'I've missed the sea,' said Emily.

Petra took a slug of wine. 'I thought it was all so wonderful in Tuscany,' she said. 'All the sun and the food and the charming, rustic locals.'

Emily thought of the Villa Serena and the fig trees and the terrace. She thought of Don Angelo slicing a peach and of Giancarlo on his Vespa. She thought of the black-haired woman making porchetta sandwiches without once exchanging a word with her and of the blank faces of her neighbours when she asked them if they had seen Paris. She thought of Olimpia holding Charlie and of Paris, asleep on the stone floor.

'It's not all like that,' she said at last. 'That's what people want to read about. That's the Tuscany they want. It's not like that underneath.'

'What's it like underneath?' asked Petra.

'I don't know. I haven't been there long enough.' Suddenly an image came into her head of the women at *Ferragosto* whispering about the mysterious Raffaello: 'He is a devil.'

'There are things I don't understand,' she went on. 'Undercurrents. My Italian's not good enough to understand what's going on.'

'I would have thought your Italian would have been pretty good by now.'

'It's OK. Siena and Paris are better. Especially Paris. But, even if my Italian was perfect, I'd still be an outsider. You don't know what it's like. Even people from the village two miles away are outsiders. *Stranieri*, they say, Strangers.'

'What about the girls? Do they feel outsiders too?'

'Siena doesn't, probably because she's got an Italian boyfriend. Paris does. She says she hates it. I worry about her.

She never says anything, just scribbles away in her diary. And she's so thin.'

'Maybe she's just the sort of person who doesn't put on weight,' said Petra, reaching for her glass with a wand-like arm.

'Yes, maybe. Like you. And not like me. I must have put on a stone in the last few weeks. All that misery eating. And drinking. Life in paradise. If only they knew!'

'You should write the real story,' said Petra. 'Not all this crap about sunsets and early morning dew.'

Emily sighed. 'I can't. People would stop reading the column and it's my only source of income at the moment.'

'But Paul's wealthy enough, surely? He won't leave you destitute.'

'I don't know. That's why I want to see my accountant. You know what Paul is like. It's all show, borrowing here, borrowing there. He looks like a successful businessman but I don't know if he is really.'

Petra acknowledged that she did know what Paul was like, remembering him in the old days with his sports cars and designer suits. 'His cuffs,' she remembered, 'were always snow white'.

'With cufflinks,' added Emily.

'Yes, with cufflinks,' agreed Petra. Stooping, she picked up Harry who was asleep on the sofa. Emily had wondered why she hadn't put Harry to bed when she had taken Charlie up. Jake had gone to bed by himself, quite happily, saying he would read until lights out but Harry was allowed to play downstairs until he fell asleep, still clutching a model of Thomas the Tank Engine. Its wheels had left tiny indentations in his cheek.

When Petra came back downstairs, Emily asked her. Tactfully, she hoped.

Petra poured herself more wine before answering. 'Harry's got special needs,' she said. 'Surely you must have noticed.'

Emily, who had only thought of Harry in terms of a threat to Charlie, could only repeat, weakly, 'Special needs?'

'Autism,' said Petra shortly.

'No!'

'Yes.' Petra knelt on the floor and started to tidy away the train track. When she spoke, her voice sounded tired, as if she had had this conversation many times before. 'Apparently an obsession with Thomas the Tank Engine is almost a diagnosis of autism in itself. It's the large, blank faces, they say. Autistic children find them easy to understand. Easier than human faces anyway.'

Emily didn't know what to say, so she knelt down too and helped to unclip the track and put the engines away in their boxes.

'Make sure you put them in the right boxes,' warned Petra. 'He goes mad if they're wrong. That's another thing about Thomas. Everything has its place, everything has a name and a number. Autists like that.'

'How long have you known?' asked Emily, hastily taking Annie out of Clarabel's box.

'About six months.'

'Why didn't you tell me?'

'Well, it's not the sort of thing you say on the phone, is it? Or in an email.'

'I told you about my marriage breaking up.'

'That's different. Marriages break up all the time. Mine did. Not that it was a marriage, but still. Children are different. Everyone wants their child to be perfect. The best, the cleverest, the prettiest. I remember, with Jake, I was so proud when he learnt to read at four. Harry doesn't even know which letter his name starts with.'

'But aren't autistic children sometimes—' Emily paused, not knowing how to continue, wanting to comfort but not to patronise.

'Clever?' Petra smiled grimly. 'Good with numbers? Just don't, for God's sake, mention Rain Man.'

'I wasn't going to.'

'Good,' said Petra, in a slightly more friendly tone. 'Actually, Harry is really good with numbers. And he is quite affectionate, with me anyway. So it could be worse.'

Emily, sitting on the floor surrounded by neatly labelled boxes, said nothing.

'It's just . . . oh, Em . . . it's just the complications. When I think of the complications ahead of Harry, and ahead of me, I could weep. I really could weep.'

Emily got up and, fetching the wine bottle, refilled Petra's glass. For the first time in three weeks, she did not feel like weeping.

CHAPTER 8

Thoughts from Tuscany
By Emily Robertson

One of the joys of living in Tuscany is having friends to stay. In England, I saw my friends fairly regularly. We went out for meals or to the cinema, we had snatched cups of coffee in the middle of a crowded day, we spoke on the telephone in the evening. Occasionally, we went to each other's houses for dinner, though these events, whilst pleasant enough, would inevitably end in disappointment. Spouse would get into an endless debate about house prices, people would drink too much and fall asleep in the zabaglione and, at about eleven, the dreaded shadow of the minicab would fall over the evening.

But here, in Tuscany, I can have friends to stay. On the terrazzo we can breakfast together on slices of melone and golden cornetti. We can have lunch under the vines, cold white wine, mozzarella and sliced tomatoes. We can eat together in the evenings as the children play around us and the shadows lengthen. Suddenly, there is all the time in the world to enjoy friendship.

Emily is on the train, heading for London. She is going to see her accountant and has left the children behind in Brighton with Petra. She is slightly worried about Charlie; he has become very clingy and is still petrified of Harry. But it is absolute bliss to be on her own for a change. She stares out of the window (the train has unaccountably stopped just outside a station) and wonders when she was last able to drift off like this, her forehead pressed against the grimy glass, thinking of nothing in particular. But then, of course, all the worries come rushing back. What is she going to do in Italy without Paul? Will she have to sell the house? Will she have to move back to England?

The train starts to move but Emily's worries keep pace effortlessly, running along the track, leaping over sleepers and hurdling through the terraced houses on the outskirts of London. Is she really going to have to come back to England? Paris would be delighted but, despite her fantasies about living in Brighton, Emily feels that it would be so much like defeat, running back home with her tail between her legs. She and Paul had talked so much about making 'The Move', leaving their old life behind and starting a new adventure. How can she admit that the adventure was a dreadful failure? But can she afford to stay in Tuscany? She must make sure she listens to her accountant and not drift off like she usually does when money is mentioned.

London is a shock. The Thames shines brilliantly and there are smart new flats at Battersea wharf. The giant Ferris wheel of the London Eye, towering over the city, gives the whole place a carefree, holiday feel. Although Emily was at university in London and lived in Clapham for nearly twelve years, it has been a long time since she has been to the centre, the touristy bit. The red buses and the black cabs seem almost too picturesque to be true and when, from the top deck of her bus, she sees Big Ben and the Houses of Parliament, she has to pinch herself to make sure it is real. Surely she has strayed into the middle of a postcard? Surely snow is soon to fall from an invisible glass shaker? Surely someone is about to write 'Greetings from London' across the improbably blue sky?

Her accountant's office, behind Oxford Street, brings her back to reality. It is a dingy brown building, with black bin liners stacked up on the front steps. The air conditioning isn't working and Dermot, Emily's accountant, spends the meeting fruitlessly flapping the air with a copy of *Accountancy Today*.

Emily knows Dermot from university. He is a partner now and really too important for this kind of work but he has agreed because she is a friend. So he says, smiling sweatily but charmingly behind his desk, but Emily does not feel that she knows anything about this balding man in a crumpled beige suit. He still looks to her like a grown-up, a dad, a teacher. She cannot believe that she herself is over forty (forty-one, she adds, defensively, to herself). She cannot believe that, somewhere in London, she won't come across her youthful self, eight stone with waist-length hair, wearing jeans and a Live Aid T-shirt, hand in hand with Michael.

They talk for such a long time about university, mutual friends, their families, that it seems almost indecent to bring the subject back to finances. Eventually, Emily says, apologetically, 'About my financial position?'

Dermot shifts papers and flaps *Accountancy Today* a few times. 'Yes,' he says. 'Yes indeed.' There is a long silence during which Emily wonders if Dermot realises that she has come here on business and has not, in fact, just popped in for a chat all the way from Tuscany. She feels sweaty and sticky and longs for a glass of water.

'The house in Tuscany,' Dermot says at last. 'Is it in your name?'

'Yes,' says Emily, glad to be asked a question, especially one to which she knows the answer. 'Paul thought it was better. The London house is in his name, of course.'

'The London house is being repossessed,' says Dermot, not meeting her eyes.

'What?'

'It is my understanding,' says Dermot, speaking quickly and still avoiding eye contact, 'that your husband remortgaged the house to finance his latest business venture.' He consults his papers. 'Italian Property 4 You.'

Emily is speechless. 'I didn't know,' she says at last.

'No,' agrees Dermot. 'It seems that your husband's Italian property company has been in financial difficulty . . .' he coughs delicately, '. . . for some time.'

'I didn't know,' says Emily again.

'And the other property companies,' continues Dermot, 'they are also overstretched.'

'Overstretched?'

'The receivers have been called in.'

'My God.' Emily does not know what to say. Although she knows much of his wealth is a façade, she just can't acclimatise herself to the idea of a penniless Paul. Oddly enough, it is easier to imagine herself poor than Paul.

'What shall I do?' she asks.

Dermot is reinvigorated, as if he has been waiting for her to ask this. He even pulls out a new file, headed 'Emily Robertson' in neat type.

'My advice to you,' he says, 'is to keep the Italian house. It is in your name and so cannot be considered part of any bankruptcy proceedings. In addition, it is an appreciating asset. There may be some pressure on you to sell but, in the circumstances—'

'Paul wants me to sell,' interrupts Emily.

'My advice would be not to do so, at least not until the bankruptcy proceedings are completed. It is your security and that of the children.' He looks down, his bald head reddening. 'Am I to understand that you are getting divorced?'

'Yes.'

'Well, in the circumstances, you should hold on to the house in lieu of alimony, which I doubt will be forthcoming. Do you have any other assets?'

'Assets?' Emily thinks of the Fiat Panda, rusting gently under the fig trees. 'No, not really.'

'What about your writing?'

'My writing?'

'What happens to the income from your column?'

'Oh that,' says Emily. 'It mostly goes on food, clothes for the children, things like that.'

'So it goes straight into your own account?'

'Yes.'

'Good,' says Dermot grimly. Then, as Emily's mind starts to wander back to the house in Tuscany, now, it seems, her only possession in the world, Dermot says suddenly, 'I always read your column. For me, it's what Italy is all about.'

Siena is on the beach. They all are: Paris, Charlie, Jake, Harry and Petra. Paris is helping Harry build a sandcastle without sand (Brighton beach being comprised wholly of smooth, grey pebbles). Neither of them seem unduly concerned by this setback to their project; on Paris's face is a look of tender concentration that Siena cannot remember ever seeing there before. In addition, she is wearing an orange T-shirt, such a departure from her trademark black that, for many conflicting reasons, it actually makes Siena's eyes ache to look at her.

Jake and Charlie are standing hand in hand by the water's

edge, like an advertisement for Start-rite shoes. Petra, wearing a frayed denim skirt and a sleeveless top, is sitting nearby, watching them. Siena admires Petra's sense of style immensely (Mum would never get away with that length skirt and, anyway, would probably spoil it by wearing it with horrible kitten-heeled sandals) but she finds her rather intimidating. Only that morning, Petra had cut into Siena's monologue about how much she was missing Giancarlo with a brusque, 'For God's sake, Siena, your life's not over because you're away from your boyfriend for a few days.' Paris had laughed but Siena had been hurt. Of course, she knew her life wasn't over but she was really upset, anyone could see that. She really loved Gianni, it wasn't just some teenage crush. Petra probably didn't remember what true love was like, if she had ever known. Siena remembers Emily talking about Ed, Jake and Harry's father, and saying that he was 'terrified of commitment'. That just went to show; Petra had no idea how to hold on to a man.

Siena will hold on to Gianni, she is sure of that. She tries to imagine his dark eyes, his smooth, brown skin, his startlingly white smile, but all she can hear is his voice saying 'Siena' in the special way that he does. Until she went to Italy, she had hated her name. 'Why are me and Paris named after *places*?' she used to wail. 'It's so unfair.' She notices that they had no truck with a stupid name for Charlie. But, in Italy, being named after an Italian city didn't seem so bad. For a start, they pronounced it properly, they didn't say 'S'yena' like her friends in London, and, somehow, being named after a place in Tuscany, especially a beautiful place in Tuscany, made her feel like she belonged.

Falling in love with Gianni made her feel like she belonged as well. She remembers the first time she saw him, delivering bread on his Vespa. He had whistled and called after her but she was used to that, they all did that. 'It's because you're blonde,' everyone said, but Siena thought there was more to it than that. In Italy, for some reason, they seemed to appreciate the real Siena, to see how special she was. She had always known that Mum and Dad didn't think she was as clever as Paris and, after Charlie was born, it seemed like no one took any notice of her at all. In Italy, they took notice all right. Once, she had almost stopped the traffic in Sansepolcro, crossing the street in a tight pink top. 'Stop drawing attention to yourself,' Paris had hissed. 'I can't help it,' Siena had replied simply.

So, when Gianni had called to her that she was a *bambola*, a doll, she had simply tossed her hair and kept on walking. She had been so pleased with herself for her coolness that it was a couple of seconds before she realised that Giancarlo's Vespa was now blocking her way. He was just sitting there and grinning, dark even for an Italian, with his black brows and fathomless eyes, just grinning at her as if, she thought afterwards, he already knew everything there was to know about her.

'*Permesso*,' Siena had said primly.

Gianni had just sat there, grinning, and, despite the fact that she could easily have walked past him, she didn't. Then he put out his hand and said, in a perfect Prince Charles voice,

'Absolutely delighted to meet you.' Afterwards she found out that Giancarlo only knew a few stock English phrases which he pronounced in the tones of the BBC CD from which he had learnt them but, at the time, it seemed like a miracle, to hear perfect BBC English coming from the mouth of this dark, smiling stranger.

'How did you know I was English?' she asked, ten minutes later, when they were sitting in the piazza drinking lemon soda.

Giancarlo shrugged. 'Everyone knows. English people have moved into the Villa Serena. Two parents, three children, one *bambola*. Everyone knows.'

Siena sighs, adjusting her position on the pebbles. It had been so intoxicating to hear from Giancarlo that, in the town, she was the important one of the family. It is different here. She watches Paris and Harry sorting out stones with the utmost concentration. She knows that Petra is delighted with Paris for taking an interest in Harry. She watches Jake encouraging Charlie to jump over the waves. Siena is fond of Charlie, in a way, it is just that she and Paris disapprove of the way that Emily spoils him and, to show their disapproval, they usually conspire to ignore him. Now, she is amazed at herself for feeling jealous of Jake and of Petra, who has now joined the boys in the waves, not seeming to care about getting her clothes wet.

Siena lies on the stones (they are oddly comfortable, like one of those expensive massage chairs) and listens to the cries of delight from Jake and Charlie as the icy-cold waves splash their legs. Behind her she can hear the tinny, tragic, mesmerising music of the merry-go-round. She had been on it earlier, pretending she was doing it for Charlie but really enjoying the sensation of swooping above the crowds on her grinning horse, called 'Josie' according to the sash round its head, listening to that heartbreakingly jolly tune. She sits up. A group of boys are daring each other to jump from the pier. One does so, flailing in mid-air until he lands with a splash, sending up a spray of water that almost reaches his grinning mates who are hanging on to the rusting iron girders above. A lifeguard comes running. The boys start to climb down.

Siena turns to look back at the promenade with its parasols and shops selling jewellery made from seashells and driftwood. A man on a unicycle weaves his way through the crowds. A hen party passes by; the girls all wear bunny ears and are giggling and clutching each other as they negotiate the stones in their stiletto heels. Continental, people say, just like Italy. But it isn't; it isn't at all. Siena lies down again and dreams of being married to Giancarlo.

Petra sits on the edge of the sea and watches the boys jumping the waves. Every seventh wave is meant to be a big one but, actually, it is the small, sneaky ones that catch them unawares. The sideways swirl of water, the sudden splash of foam. The boys laugh delightedly, though Charlie looks a little nervous. Jake faces the sea boldly, a true Brighton boy, but Charlie has grown used to the calm, tideless Mediterranean. He is spoilt, thinks Petra, digging her toes into the wet stones at the water's edge, brightly coloured like little jewels. Emily can't see it but she's completely smothering him. He's a cry-baby too, anyone can see that Harry doesn't mean to keep hurting him.

She worries about Emily. Emily is so gullible, so easily taken in. Petra remembers how, in the old days, as soon as Emily met Michael, everything he said and did was perfect. From being a quiet English girl from Surrey, almost overnight Emily turned into this raving Italophile, going on about how an Italian had invented the telephone before Alexander Graham Bell had even thought of it and calling people '*simpatico*'. Petra had liked Michael, though she remembers feeling slightly chilled by his eyes. They were beautiful but oddly empty, like the eyes of a china doll. But Emily had adored him. Michael and Michael's family became the centre of her life. Petra remembers countless stories about Gina: her wonderful food, her beautiful clothes, her goodness, her kindness, her generosity. It all had the effect of making Petra want to go to Gina's snotty over-priced restaurant and spit in the food.

But then Michael and Emily split up and Petra was left to pick up the pieces. And that was exactly what it was like; Emily's life was shattered into a thousand tiny fragments and there she was, grubbing about on the floor, trying to fit them back into some sort of coherent shape. All those endless late-night conversations, during which Emily invariably managed to convince herself that it was all her fault ('I was too clingy'), all those times when Emily simply collapsed, sobbing, 'But I *love* him!' Even in the midst of their exciting new life in Brighton there had been the shadow of Michael, causing Emily to weep bitterly if another man asked her out because he never was and never could be Michael. 'Forget him!' Petra would say. 'He's gone. Forget him,' and Emily would look back at her, tears brimming in her eyes, steadfastly, infuriatingly loyal. 'I just can't,' she would say.

Then Emily met Paul and everything changed. Paul was new, he was different, he was completely sure of himself. At first Petra had deeply disapproved; Paul was a capitalist pig and he was far too old for Emily. Then she had met him and had immediately recognised the attraction. Paul was a capitalist pig but he was a charming capitalist pig, one who listened intently to your views and roared with laughter at your jokes. She still thought Emily was mad to marry him but she understood. Of course she did. They lived in a world of grotty bedsits, of weedy bearded sociology students, of grungy bedlinen and sour milk for breakfast. Paul was handsome, he was rich and he smelled better than any man Petra had ever met. Of course she understood.

Petra worried even more when, after they were married, Emily and Paul disappeared to London and Emily got pregnant almost immediately. But, by then, Petra had met Ed who was a lecturer at the university. Ed was married and they had struggled on for years through renunciations and reconciliations until, finally, Ed left his wife and moved in with Petra. This was the time when Emily had turned up on Petra's doorstep, with the girls in tow, announcing that she had left Paul. Petra remembers guiltily that her first reaction was annoyance that, having finally got Ed on his own, she was now having to share him (and her flat) with three other people. But then Paul had arrived, all charm and contrition, and Emily had disappeared again. The next thing Petra knew was that Emily and Paul were going to live in Italy.

Would she have gone back to him if I had been more welcoming? wonders Petra. She wishes now that she had sat down and talked to Emily, asked her what she really thought about her marriage, asked her whether she still loved Paul. But, at the time, she had been so relieved to be left alone with Ed, that she had barely said, 'Are you sure?' before packing Emily and Paul off into the sunset. But even if she had said something, she reasons, scuffing her way through the glittering pebbles, would Emily have listened? People never listen to advice; this is one of the first things she learnt as a teacher. And, if she had not got back with Paul, Emily would never have had Italy. Or Charlie. So perhaps it was meant after all. Petra grimaces. She doesn't believe in fate. How can she, with Harry the way he is?

Petra stands up and waves at the boys. 'Come on, Mum!' shouts Jake. Petra's heart constricts because she can see how happy Jake is to have some time without Harry, at the prospect of having just a few minutes' attention from her. She spares a quick, bitter thought for Ed, who only sees his sons a few times a year and then is apt to blame Petra for Harry's 'difficulties'. 'You're turning him into a Mummy's boy,' Ed, the politically correct sociology lecturer, had said once. Ed, whose mother still knitted him socks for Christmas and who had never once remembered Petra's name correctly. Men are an awful nuisance, she thinks; if only there wasn't more to being gay than wearing Doc Martens, she'd sign up like a shot.

'Come on, Mum!' shouts Jake again. Petra grins and steps into the sparkling sea.

Outside Dermot's offices, Emily gets out her phone and dials the number Paul gave her when she last saw him. It feels strange to have a new number for him. 0207 – somewhere in central London. Somewhere expensive, she thinks savagely. She is sure that even bankruptcy won't force Paul to give up his creature comforts. The phone rings and then clicks into an answerphone message: 'Neither Paul nor Fiona is available right now—' Thoughtfully, she presses delete.

Charlie is digging a trench with Jake. It's very important to get it right because then the sea will come in and fill it right up, up, up. That's what Jake says anyhow. There's sand here, right at the edge of the sea, but everywhere else is stony, bony, slippery pebbles. Charlie likes the way the sea makes little rivers through the wet sand. It's like he's a giant making a giant trench. If he put down a great big stone he'd squash all the little people, but he wouldn't do that, of course. He's not horrible like Harry. Harry is like the Gruffalo only worse because you could never trick him even if you were a very, very clever mouse. He never really looks at you so he'd never be tricked. Everyone knows you have to look at someone to be tricked.

Charlie digs deep into the stones. There's water at the bottom. He scoops up little shiny stones with his hands. They smell salty, like chips. He loves chips. He'll ask Mummy to buy him a great big bag of chips, except Mummy isn't here, only that Petra lady. Daddy would buy him chips. Daddy loves burgers and chips and all the lovely food that Mummy says is bad for you. Why isn't Daddy here? He'd asked Siena yesterday but she just said, 'You'll see him soon,' in the kind of voice you use for saying goodbye. Did he even say goodbye to Daddy last time? Did he give him a proper kiss and a hug? He can't remember. A tear falls into the sand and he watches it disappear.

'Good work, Charlie!' shouts Jake. Charlie starts digging again. His tears taste salty like the sea. He wishes Jake was his brother. Really really. Star light, star bright. He can't remember the rest. He carries on digging, right deep down to the bottom of the world.

Paris is not thinking of anything as she lines up the stones in order of size. Like a child she is thinking only of the job in hand. She has always liked putting things in order. In her diary she keeps careful lists of her favourite books, films and music, updating them every few months. She keeps her books and CDs in alphabetical order and is outraged when Siena borrows them without asking. In Harry, she has found the perfect companion. He, too, sorts and collects, without speaking. Sometimes, she hands a stone to him and he examines it carefully, appraisingly.

Only perfectly round specimens are allowed in his collection. Paris respects this. She hums as she sorts her stones.

Walking quickly, Emily heads along Oxford Street, threading her way through students offering her cards advertising language classes and American Scientologists wanting to assess her personality. In a dream she heads up through the little side streets with their secret green squares that remind her of university. Tourists with neon backpacks stand around on street corners and she passes a group of Hare Krishnas, wearing tattered orange robes and chanting half-heartedly. Sleepwalking, she negotiates her way through the maze of streets until she finds what she is looking for: an ornate gold and mahogany sign saying 'Vittorio's'.

On the beach, they are having lunch. Petra has packed all sorts of food: olives, roast chicken, salad in little plastic containers, but Harry will only eat Marmite sandwiches cut into triangles. Paris rather admires this, she likes Marmite too but only spread thinly and only without horrible oily butter. She lies back, enjoying the absence of a voice saying, 'Paris, you haven't eaten anything! What about a tiny piece of . . . a taste of . . . just a few mouthfuls of . . .' She hates all those words to do with eating: taste, try, chew, swallow, nibble. Nibble! That's the worst one, it sounds like a combination of nipple and Bible. Two profoundly unattractive things. Paris grins to herself and accepts an olive without noticing it.

*

Emily stands outside Vittorio's, looking at the menu with its spidery script and curling gold edges. *Linguine con vongole, costolette alla Milanese, scaloppini al marsala, bistecchine alla pizzaiola.* She lets the words roll over her like an incantation, remembering endless meals at Vittorio's and at Gina's house in Highgate: the fat, stuffed pasta, the gleaming sauces, the countless glasses of wine, different for every course. Nowhere in Italy has she had food like that. Tuscan food tends to be simple, made with fresh local ingredients. It does not have the musty, treasure-trove feeling of Gina's kitchen, where the garlic hung from the ceiling like great, beaded necklaces and Michael used to joke that his mother never needed to fear a vampire. Oh Michael, in your white coat and stethoscope, where are you now? She watches as parties of businessmen in braces settle at the outside tables, sweating and laughing as the waiters pour their wine. She knows that she will not have the courage to go in.

They can't go in the sea straight after lunch so Siena takes the children onto the pier. Jake, Paris and Charlie go on the bumper cars but Harry screams and covers his ears. Then, thank God, he finds a Thomas the Tank Engine ride and jumps on happily. Siena feeds in 50p after 50p (changing the money was almost like winning at one of the machines, the wonderful stream of silver falling into your hands) and stands watching him. His face is solemn, concentrating, as the blue engine moves to and fro, the tinny music repeating endlessly.

Why does he like it so much? Why don't Postman Pat or Bob the Builder, both standing empty nearby, have anything like the same attraction?

'I want to go on Thomas!' It is Charlie, his eyes narrowed as he considers a tantrum.

'You can go on Postman Pat's van.'

'Don't want to. I want Thomas. Why does *he* have to go on Thomas all the time?'

'Because he only likes Thomas.' Siena thrusts Charlie into the red van and feeds in another 50p. Pat's jaunty music rises up to join Thomas's.

'Siena?' says Charlie suddenly, looking out at her from the driver's seat, 'Where's Daddy?'

'He's working,' says Siena quickly. 'You know.'

'Yes but . . .' Charlie's bottom lip juts out as he attempts to make her understand, 'Where *is* he? Why isn't he with us?'

'It's complicated,' says Siena. Since that horrible day when Dad suddenly appeared in Italy and said that he and Mummy would always love them but they just weren't going to live together any more, she has had this awful feeling that she is never going to see Dad again. Of course, people get divorced all the time. She knows *that*. She's not going to get all hysterical like Paris did. It's just that she hadn't realised how weird it would feel. She's used to Dad being away but this time it feels different, as if he really has left them and isn't even in the family any more. 'You'll see him soon,' Mum says, but anyone can tell that she doesn't know when.

She turns to Charlie. What can she say to him? How can she reassure him when she doesn't know the answers herself?

'You'll see him soon,' she says, at last. 'I promise.'

But Charlie is busy hooting the horn and doesn't seem to have heard her.

Paris and Jake are on the Waltzer. Just when you think it can't spin any faster, a tattooed boy comes along and spins it some more, so fast that your head hits the cushioned back of the car and all your breath is sucked out of you.

'Faster! Faster!' shouts Paris, though in fact she wishes it would stop.

'Faster!' shouts Jake. He is hating every minute but would rather die than let Paris know.

Petra enjoys a rare few minutes of peace! She keeps imagining that she can hear Harry calling for her. His voice, low but penetrating, seems to have impressed itself on her very brainwaves. She forces herself to keep lying down. He'll be fine with Siena. She's very capable, much more so than she herself had been at sixteen. Petra thinks of herself at sixteen, dressed in black and reading *The Tin Drum*. She would never have looked after someone else's children, but then no one was likely to have asked her. Neighbours had thought her weird and they had no relatives living nearby.

It had been just her and her mum. Petra grins as she remembers how unalike they had been, her mother so stiff and correct, herself so keen to shock. Did she get it from her dad, who had died when she was six? Her mother didn't talk about him much; he had been in the army and had been killed in Northern Ireland. Petra has always assumed that, as he had been a soldier, he must have been a bastard but sometimes she thinks she can remember a soft Scottish voice reading to her. Was that her dad? What did he read? *Winnie the Pooh*, she thinks; she has a vague memory of him doing Eeyore. Remembering Eeyore's lovely gloomy voice she smiles, closing her eyes.

Emily walks away from Vittorio's, tears running down her cheeks. Get a grip, she tells herself firmly. She goes into a café and buys a roll and some water. She eats it in Fitzroy Square, watching the pigeons cluster round some tourists foolish enough to feed them. What is she crying for? Well, she's crying because her marriage is over, she is penniless and Paul is living with some tart called Fiona. Isn't that enough to be going on with? she asks herself, throwing the remains of the roll into an overflowing bin. Pigeons immediately abandon the tourists and cluster round her feet, arguing and jostling. They remind her of the children. But still, she knows her tears are not just for Paul. They are also for Michael and for Vittorio's and for Gina. They are for her lost youth.

Siena walks back from the beach, dragging Charlie by the hand. The children are hot and tired, moaning about the walk, complaining that their feet hurt. Siena's shoulders feel tight with sunburn and her feet, too, are hurting in her new, sequinned flip-flops. But there is something pleasant, something traditional, about these complaints, about the feeling of trudging home after a day in the sun. In Italy, people don't trudge. They stay inside in the heat of the day and emerge, cool and refreshed, in the evening. Siena knows that, by the evening, her shoulders will hurt and all she will want is a cool bath and a night of blissful British television.

'Come on, Charlie,' she says. 'Nearly there.'

'Carry me,' whines Charlie. 'I want Mummy.'

'I'll tell you a story,' says Siena, thinking hard. Charlie is silent, lower lip extended, waiting for her to come up with something.

'Once there was a boy called Charlie.'

'And Harry,' says Harry unexpectedly. He has been walking with Paris, and Siena didn't realise he was listening.

'And Harry,' she says. 'And Jake,' she adds for good measure. 'One day they went to the beach and they found a magic stone. They didn't know it was magic at first but, when they held it up to the light, it started to shimmer and glow. Charlie started to rub the stone and he heard a little tiny voice saying, "Throw me back into the sea and I will give you three wishes . . ."'

Her voice, slow and rhythmic, carries them up the steps from the beach, through the meandering crowds, and home.

'So I just stood there, staring at the restaurant. I read the menu as if it was a love letter. I must be going mad.' Emily takes a gulp of wine and a spoonful of special fried rice. She and Petra are in the basement kitchen, finishing a Chinese takeaway. The children are upstairs watching *Scooby Doo* (one of the few DVDs that seems to satisfy all age groups). Harry, who would normally have been howling for *Thomas the Tank Engine*, is sitting happily on Paris's lap making Scooby noises. Charlie is almost asleep, wedged between Siena and Jake on the sofa.

'You're not going mad,' says Petra, filling up her glass (but not, Emily notices, her plate). 'It's the lure of the past. It gets to us all. You want to go back to a time when you were happy.'

'And young,' says Emily gloomily, taking another gulp. She realises that she is slightly drunk. 'Sometimes I just can't bear not being young any more. Why didn't anyone tell us that when we were forty we'd still feel exactly the same as when we were eighteen?'

'We wouldn't have believed them,' says Petra. 'I thought that when I was forty I'd be sort of . . . settled. You know, resigned to staying at home, living a dull life, never falling in love again. But, deep down, I still think exciting things will happen to me.'

'Well, maybe they will,' says Emily loyally.

Petra laughs shortly. 'I'm a single mother with two children, one of them autistic. I teach in a comprehensive school. What exciting things are going to happen to me?'

'You never know,' says Emily. 'Maybe George Clooney will turn up as a supply teacher.'

Petra laughs. 'I think I'd better have a contingency plan just in case it turns out I'm not living in the plot of a crap American film.' Then, not looking at Emily, she says, 'What would you have done if he'd come out of the restaurant?'

'Who?' asks Emily, her mind still on George Clooney.

'Michael. What if he'd walked out of the restaurant and seen you standing there. What would you have done?'

Emily thinks, chasing the last crumbs of rice around her plate. 'I don't know,' she says at last. 'Laughed. Cried. Said hello. Thrown myself into his arms. I don't know. I hadn't got as far as that. I was still stuck being eighteen again. Sitting in the restaurant with Michael and having Gina bring us delicious food. God, Gina! I'd give anything to see her again.'

'I always thought she was a bit frightening. All that jewellery and dyed hair. And the way she used to fuss over Michael!'

'I loved her,' says Emily dreamily. 'She used to say that I was the only one of Michael's girlfriends she'd ever liked. She did our astral charts and said that we'd get married and have five children and live happily ever after.'

'Well, she was wrong there, wasn't she?' says Petra briskly, scraping plates. She feels that it is her duty to inject a little reality.

'Yes she was,' agrees Emily with a sigh.

'Do you ever hear from her?'

'No. She sent me Christmas cards for a few years but that stopped when I got married. I had no real claim on her, you see. It wasn't as if she had been my mother-in-law.'

'I've never had a mother-in-law,' says Petra. 'It's one advantage of never being married. What was Paul's mother like?'

'Oh, OK. Very home counties, very conventional. A bit like my mum, really, I can't think how she came to have a son like Paul.'

They are both silent, thinking of Paul. Petra thinks of the time when he made a pass at her, one evening when Emily had gone to bed and she was left alone with him, drinking brandy. She remembers his curiously guileless blue eyes and his shameless smile. 'Why not?' he had said. 'Surprise yourself.' She remembers that, for a second, she had actually been tempted. Emily thinks of the mysterious Fiona. Maybe she has money. It's a rich kind of name, a Sloane Ranger name. A velvet hairband, house-in-the-country kind of name.

'It's weird,' she says aloud. 'I don't feel jealous of Paul's new woman but I do feel jealous of Michael's wife. Still, after all these years.'

'Well,' says Petra, filling up both their glasses. 'Tomorrow you might see her. And him. For real.'

CHAPTER 9

Thoughts from Tuscany
By Emily Robertson

Parties in Italy are something different. For a start, no one would ever dream of bringing a bottle. To bring a bottle to an Italian party would imply that a) You think they are alcoholics and b) You think that they have no decent wines in their cellar, an unforgivable insult in Italy. For, whilst most Italians drink very little from a British point of view, they look on wine-making as a sacred art. For example, Prosecco, the delicious local sparkling wine, has to be bottled with the waxing moon. All around Tuscany, wine-makers consult lunar charts alongside arrays of modern scientific equipment. Even our delightful local priest, Don Angelo, bottles his wine with one eye on the moon and the other on Santo Giacomo, patron saint of wine.

Italians bring cakes to parties or maybe iced puddings. Everyone dresses up, women in flowered dresses, men in suits. As for the children, they are swathed in so many layers of satin and lace that it is a wonder they can move at all. The girls wear stiff cotton frocks, tied at the waist with huge bows; the boys wear dark shorts and knee-length white socks. Once the party starts, it divides strictly along gender lines; the men discuss football and politics, the women children and fashion. The men may have two or three small glasses of wine. Women are lucky to be offered a second glass. '*Basta, basta,*' they say primly, covering their glasses with their hands, 'One is enough.' Once, in desperation, I refilled my own glass and was known ever afterwards as the 'Englishwoman who drinks'.

'Emily!'

'Izzy!'

Emily embraces her old friend in the doorway of her terraced London house. She and Petra, having got off the bus at the wrong end of Green Lanes, have seemingly walked miles to get there. Emily's feet are aching in their unaccustomed high heels. Petra, in flat leather sandals, strode ahead like a teenager, stopping to wait for Emily at junctions, not giving her time to catch her breath.

Deciding what to wear for Izzy and Ruth's reunion party had taken hours. Not too dressy. She didn't want them, *him,* to think she was desperate. Not too casual either. She is no longer young enough to get away with jeans and no make-up. Instead, she spent hours putting on casually smudged make-up, the kind that looks as if you haven't any on. She had got up early to wash her hair under Petra's temperamental shower. She had tried to blow-dry it but Charlie woke up and demanded breakfast. When she next got to look at herself in the mirror, her hair had dried in wild curls rather than the smooth waves she had been intending. Oh well, at least it wasn't grey. Emily has vowed to dye her hair the minute the first trace of grey appears. She agrees with the Italians that, where hair is concerned, natural is not necessarily desirable. To see a group of middle-aged Italian women is to see a positive kaleidoscope of hair colours: purple, red, orange, blonde, tawny and black. But never, not once, grey.

Suddenly Emily thinks of Gina's hair, a proud synthetic red that seemed to have a life of its own, glowing in the dark of the restaurant. 'The year the Italian football team lost to North Korea,' she used to say, 'I went red with grief.'

Emily finally decided on tailored black trousers and a loose white top (it was a chilly, overcast day), but then Petra spoilt it all by swanning in wearing her faded jeans and a sleeveless T-shirt. Her arms were as toned as Giancarlo's and almost as brown. 'I still have to lift Harry up a lot,' said Petra shrugging. 'It's marvellous for the biceps.' She must be a size eight, thought Emily, watching Petra's tight, denim bum descending the stairs. She herself could still remember the humiliating relegation from size 10–12 knickers to size 12–14. Now maybe the silent horror of 14-16 awaited her. She sucked in her stomach and put on some more lipstick.

Now Izzy is embracing Petra and exclaiming at her thinness.

'You look *amazing,* Pete! Look, Ruth, doesn't Pete look amazing?' Emily teeters along in their wake, feeling like the Elephant Woman.

She met Izzy on her first day at UCL. It was at the freshers' disco, a gruesomely jolly event held in the Union Bar. All drinks were 50p and freshers were encouraged to wear badges giving their name, age and hobbies. Emily's said, 'Emily Robertson, 18, reading, swimming and painting.' She wished, more than anything in the world, that she could have thought of something more interesting. Reading! Who on earth was going to come and talk to someone who gave their hobby as reading? And painting! That wasn't even true anyhow. As a child she had had a fixation with painting by numbers (those lovely little tubs of paint, those complicated drawings neatly bisected by hundreds of numbers) but she hadn't painted a picture for years. The truth was she had had real trouble thinking of a third hobby and it looked so pathetic just to put two. She was sure everyone else had hundreds of exciting hobbies: hang-gliding, mountaineering, scuba-diving, marathon running, open-heart surgery . . .

'Hi.' Emily swivelled round and found herself face to face with a badge saying, 'Izzy Goldsmith, 18, lesbianism, cannibalism and embroidery.' Dumbly she looked up and saw a small, dark-haired girl in army surplus trousers.

'You're not gay, are you?' said the girl.

'No,' said Emily. 'Sorry,' she added.

The girl grinned. 'No need to be sorry. Even I'm not gay all the time.'

To Emily, Izzy was a creature from another world. Someone scared of nothing, who was going to guide Emily through the mysteries of university life and lead her triumphantly to her new, cooler, adult self. That evening, over a meal in an Indian restaurant, Izzy told Emily that she was bisexual, that she had spent a year on a kibbutz and that she had a tattoo on her left buttock. Emily said nothing, terrified that if Izzy found out that she had been born and brought up in Addlestone, Surrey, and that the most daring thing she had ever done was skip a violin lesson to go to the park with a boy, Izzy would evaporate in a puff of smoke, leaving Emily alone and friendless for the next three years.

Over those three years, during which Emily met Michael and no longer felt quite so adrift and unable to cope with life, Izzy tried being straight and being bisexual without seeming to enjoy either very much. Then she met Ruth, a shy, blonde law student from Edinburgh and that was it. As Petra said, it was one of those relationships that just happened to work, whatever the genders involved. And now, twenty years later, Ruth was a barrister and Izzy was a lecturer and they lived in this enviable house in Stoke Newington with Victorian fireplaces and squashy white sofas and acres of books. Emily, following Petra and Izzy through to the open-plan kitchen-cum-sitting room, feels a pang of pure envy: not only are Izzy and Ruth still together, but they have a Shaker kitchen and a stainless-steel fridge. She hasn't even got a house any more — unless you count the Villa Serena, which, at the moment, she doesn't.

Ruth, no longer shy but still blonde (highlighted?), greets her affectionately.

'Emily, it's wonderful to see you. You look great. Petra,' unconsciously, her voice drops into genuine surprise, 'you look *amazing*. How do you do it?'

'That's what I was saying,' chimes in Izzy. 'She's so *thin!*'

'Not eating helps,' says Petra drily.

'You're incredible. Now, would you like Pimms or champagne?'

Opting for Pimms (a slightly better chance of staying sober), Emily steels herself to look round the room. There is Jack, who used to be a rocker but now has thinning hair and an expensive suit. There is Bella, once a Titian-haired iconoclast, now a crop-haired mother-of-two, proudly showing photos. There is Martin, who could never find a girlfriend, holding tightly on to a smiling blonde woman as if to prove that he has finally broken his duck. There are Jenny and Tim. God, not still together? No, judging from the rueful smiles and exaggerated body language, they are having a civilised, if slightly charged, discussion about what might have been. And, oh Christ, there is Chad. Chad, who was Michael's best friend. Chad, who shared the dodgy flat in Balham. Chad, who used to call her Emmy Lou in a Texas drawl and who once kissed her on New Year's Eve. Chad, whom she last spoke to when she rang him in the night begging for Michael's number. 'I'm really sorry, Emmy. I just can't do it. Mike wants to . . . you know, draw a line.'

Clutching her Pimms like a shield, Emily negotiates the

stylish kitchen island and approaches Chad. In the old days he looked rather wild, with a Che Guevara moustache and tangled black hair. Now his black hair is drawn back into a ponytail and he looks like a riverboat gambler on his day off. Although he is bordering on too old for a ponytail, he looks good, much better than most people in the room. He is in shape too, wearing a tightish white T-shirt and jeans. Like Petra, he has had no need to dress up to compensate for lost looks. He is holding a glass of orange juice and talking seriously to a man whom Emily does not recognise.

'Chad.' Her mouth is dry.

He swings round. 'My God. Emmy Lou.'

The nickname is almost more than she can bear. To her horror she thinks she might be about to cry. Instead, she says in a clear, hard voice that she does not, at first, recognise as her own, 'Hi, Chad. Good to see you.'

Chad leans over to kiss her on the cheek. They have all been doing this. 'Hello. Great to see you again.' Kiss. Kiss. Funny, they never used to kiss in the old days at UCL, when they were real friends. Chad's lips hardly touch her cheek.

'You remember Gary.' Chad gestures at the man with him.

'Gary! Of course.' Emily is amazed. She remembers Gary as thin, camp and twenty-one. Now he is fat, camp and forty-one but, incredibly, married with two children.

'Do you have children?' she asks Chad. It seems less intrusive than asking if he's married.

'Yeah.' He grins. 'Three girls. I'm really outnumbered.'

'I've got two girls and a boy,' says Emily, though no one has asked her. At least, when talking about children, she does not feel inferior. Surely, no one has a daughter as beautiful as Siena, as clever as Paris or a son as downright adorable as Charlie?

'Izzy says you live in Tuscany,' says Gary.

'Yes. On the Tuscany–Umbria border really. In a place called the Mountains of the Moon.'

'Wow. Great name.'

'Yes, isn't it? It's a bit off the beaten track. Quite near Sansepolcro, you know, where Piero della Francesca was born.'

'I've read your column,' cuts in Chad. He doesn't say he has enjoyed it, which rather irritates Emily.

'Oh, do you really write a column?' asks Gary.

'Yes. In the *News on Sunday*.'

'I wouldn't have taken you for a *News on Sunday* reader, Chad,' giggles Gary. Can he *really* be married?

'My wife reads it,' says Chad damningly.

'Obviously a woman of good taste,' snaps Emily.

'Obviously,' smirks Chad.

'So where are you working now?' asks Emily, through gritted teeth.

'At the Maudsley. I'm a psychiatrist.'

'Oh,' says Emily faintly. She can't imagine Chad, who used to claim to have been chased by an alien at Glastonbury, as a psychiatrist. Do people really lie on couches and tell him their dreams? Her idea of psychiatry is taken mostly from reruns of

The Sopranos. She imagines that even a Mafia boss would be put off by the ponytail.

'I'd love someone to analyse me,' says Gary. 'It might cure me of my claustrophobia.'

Chad smiles rather thinly. 'I imagine a psychotherapist is what you're thinking of.'

'What's the difference?' asks Emily. She is dying to bring the question round to Michael. How can she ask what he is doing now? Perhaps, in a minute or two, she'll see him. Perhaps even now he is driving a sleek Italian car up and down Green Lanes looking for a parking space. No, he'll have children now. He'll be driving a people carrier, something bug-eyed and silver. She can't imagine Michael caring about carbon emissions.

'It's rather hard to explain,' begins Chad but then, luckily, Bella calls them over to look at some photographs. They all abandon the psychiatrist's couch with relief.

The photos are agonising. Eighties eye make-up, frilly shirts and leg-warmers. Flip-flops and shorts on a beach in Greece. Emily, in a strapless pink dress, holding on to Michael's arm. He has a cigarette in his hand and is turning to look at someone off camera but Emily is staring straight ahead, wide-eyed and guileless.

'Oh Emily, you do look sweet,' says someone.

'There's Michael,' says someone else, 'the old sod. Wonder what he's doing now.'

'I invited him,' says Izzy, 'but he didn't reply.'

Emily feels hope draining out of her body. She isn't going

to see him again. She may never see him again. The pages of the album turn. There they are in someone's room. Michael is holding a guitar and Emily appears to be singing. Chad is in the foreground, wearing what looks like a ballet tutu. God help his patients.

Emily and Petra, dressed as waitresses for some stupid rag stunt ('Petra hasn't changed at all. She's still so thin!'). Izzy cooking spaghetti. A group of medics at the Huntley Street Bar. A toga party. Emily thinks she can just recognise herself in a lilac sheet. There is an arm round her waist. Michael's? Another party. Jenny and Tim cheek to cheek. Gary wearing a blond wig. Emily in a black dress doing the wide-eyed thing again. Bella, Titian hair streaming, arm in arm with a man none of them remembers. Chad and Michael, wearing dinner jackets, asleep in Gordon Square. Emily, Petra and Izzy at London Zoo. Michael, wearing an Italy T-shirt, outside Vittorio's.

'God! Vittorio's,' says Bella. 'Did you ever go in there? The food was fantastic.'

'It was run by Michael's mother, wasn't it?' says Izzy. 'She was a bit weird. All that red hair and those mad clothes. She looked as if she might poison your pasta if she didn't like you. Lucrezia Borgia and all that.'

No one asks Emily about Gina though once she was closer to her than to her own mother. She remembers Gina's house in Highgate, gloriously chaotic, brimming over with books, children and animals, flowing with wine and good food. She remembers sitting on the terrace eating spaghetti con vongole and throwing the clam shells into the garden because Gina said they were good for the plants. She remembers the time she was ill and Gina fed her minestrone and told her stories of her life in Naples. She remembers spraining her ankle playing football in the garden with Michael and his brothers (Enrico and Mario, whatever happened to them?). Michael had picked her up and carried her into the house as if she were a child. God, how she'd longed to have a child with Michael.

She wanders through the French windows onto the patio. Petra is in the garden, sitting on a bench, talking to Ruth. Emily waves but doesn't join them; she is lost in the pages of the photo album. Etherised. Trapped behind the sticky paper. In those pages, Michael was still in love with her.

'Emily!' It's Chad. Emily can't quite believe he is looking for her and turns round to see if the garden has any other attractions. But apart from Petra and Ruth, it is deserted. It is a typical London garden, long, thin and dark with plane trees. The patio is full of expensive furniture and has one of those heaters you get outside restaurants. Chad is carrying a bottle of wine and two glasses. He sets them carefully on a wrought-iron table and fills both glasses.

'Here.' He hands one to Emily.

'Thanks.'

They look at each other for a moment. In the daylight, Chad doesn't look quite so young. There are silver threads in his ponytail and heavy lines around his mouth.

'God,' says Chad, 'those pictures.'

'Yes.'

'You and Michael. I'd forgotten.'

'Had you?'

'It was the real thing, wasn't it? You and Mike.'

Emily's defences crumble. Forgetting her dignity, forgetting her beautiful children and her house in Tuscany, she grabs hold of Chad's arm and almost wails, 'Please, Chad! Tell me how he is.'

PART 2

Autumn

CHAPTER 1

The first thing that greets Emily on her return to the Villa Serena is a huge pile of rubble blocking her driveway. The Villa Serena is situated up a hill, about two kilometres from Monte Albano, along an unmade road. She remembers when she and Paul first read the directions to the villa, several centuries ago. 'After leaving Monte Albano, take the Sansepolcro turning. After about two kilometres you will pass a shrine to Santa Maria della Montagna. Take the left-hand turning between the shrine and the umbrella pines and you will find a rough track with a sign saying "Danger Rock Falls". Follow the track up to the right and the villa is at the top of the hill.'

'Take the left-hand turning between the shrine and the umbrella pines'; it had been their catchphrase all that summer.

Now the track is blocked with a pile of what looks like earth and stones. A rock fall? Something about it looks too ordered for that. Next to the road are two neatly dug trenches, one even has a tarpaulin laid over the top. Emily brings the grey Alfa to a halt and stares helplessly. Inside the car Charlie wakes up and starts to cry.

The car has been their only stroke of luck all day. Arriving at tiny Forli airport, they discovered that there was a general strike in the area, which meant no taxis, buses or trains. Emily stood there for about ten minutes, surrounded by luggage, wondering what the hell to do. A man who could have gone on stage as the Hunchback of Notre Dame without make-up lumbered up and offered them a lift. Emily declined nervously. Charlie whined, Paris remained incommunicado behind headphones, Siena checked her messages. Scrabbling in her handbag for Olimpia's phone number (a last resort on an unprecedented scale), Emily's hand closed around a cold, solid shape. She drew it out. The Alfa Romeo logo twinkled up at her. Paul's spare car keys! She had completely forgotten the Alfa, left like a riderless charger awaiting Paul's return. Emily gave a genuine whoop of delight.

'Come on, guys! We're going home in style.'

In the luxury of the Alfa's air-conditioned interior, they all cheered up a bit. Siena, manic at the thought of seeing Giancarlo again (*why* hadn't he met them at the airport?), was in tearing spirits. Charlie yelled, 'Wheee!' as they shot out onto the autostrada. Even Paris, who had been frighteningly withdrawn since leaving England, recovered enough to shout, 'Dream on, sucker!' at any car unfortunate enough to try to overtake them.

Now, it seems, their good luck has deserted them before they have even reached their own front door.

'Why have we stopped?' asks Siena maddeningly.

Emily gestures silently at the mountain of earth.

'What is it?'

'I don't know.'

'Perhaps there's been an earthquake,' suggests Paris, sounding more cheerful than she has all day. Charlie starts to cry in earnest.

Wanting to escape them, even if only for a minute, Emily gets out of the car. After the air conditioning, the heat envelops her like a blanket. It is a heavy, airless day, the sky white, the trees totally still. Emily stares at the pile of reddish earth, finding it hard to breathe. What is it doing here? Have workmen arrived and cut off their water supply? Will it cost her millions to be reconnected? She has heard of such cases. What will she find around the corner? Will the Villa Serena have disappeared into an even bigger hole?

'I suppose we can walk,' says Siena's voice at her ear.

Emily sighs. 'I suppose so.'

Taking only a small bag containing washing stuff and essentials for Charlie, Emily musters her children for the trek up the hill. Slowly, reluctantly, they follow her, Charlie crying quietly under his breath, Paris with the exhausted patience of a martyr, Siena still vibrating with excitement (perhaps he'll be waiting for her at the house).

The climb seems endless, past silvery olive trees and row upon row of Romano's vines. Though it is past six o'clock, the sun beats down relentlessly from the milky-white sky; even the birds and insects are still. After what seems like hours, they pass the derelict well and the first fig trees and there is the villa, still standing, its terracotta walls glowing pinkly in the sun.

The children run towards the shade of the terrace and Emily stands for a minute, her bag digging into her shoulder, thinking, is this home? Am I pleased to be back?

'Why are you going back?' Petra had asked.

'It's where we live. It's my only asset,' said Emily, quoting Dermot. The day before they left she had seen her solicitor, Jane, who confirmed that Paul had filed for divorce, citing 'irreconcilable differences'. 'He won't contest custody,' said Jane kindly, 'but he thinks that mediation is useless.' Compromise, thought Emily grimly, remembering the evicted tenants, had never been one of Paul's strong points.

'So, sell the house and buy one in Brighton,' said Petra. 'It must be worth a bomb.'

'But we live in Italy now. We've made the move. The children love it.'

'Paris doesn't.'

'She does really,' snapped Emily; she was getting fed up with Petra's partiality for Paris. 'She's just play-acting.'

When she told the children that they were going back to Tuscany, Paris burst into tears. 'Oh please let me stay with Petra. I can go to school in Brighton. There's a good comprehensive in Hove. Please!'

'Certainly not,' said Emily, full of guilt and jealousy. 'Your place is with your family.'

Now Emily stands looking at her dream Tuscan home and thinks, what are we doing here?

From a long way off, she hears a faint clap of thunder. 'Come on,' she says. 'Let's get inside.'

Inside, Emily makes toast and Marmite. She stopped at the Co-op on the way but the Marmite comes from England. In its black and yellow livery it looks as British as a Beefeater and about as out of place in the wood-beamed, stone-floored Tuscan kitchen. Fortified with toast, Charlie cheers up completely and goes to find his toy cars. Siena slouches off to check her messages in private. Only Paris is left, dreamily crumbling her toast into infinitesimal particles.

'Paris,' says Emily suddenly, 'do you really hate it here?'

Paris looks up, surprised. Her face looks oddly blank, as if she has deliberately wiped it of all expression. Her wide-apart blue eyes look at Emily innocently. When she was a child, Paris, with her skinny body and fine brown hair, often looked comical beside Siena's glossy blond good looks, but now, Emily realises, she has her own beauty. White, almost translucent skin (untouched by either the Tuscan or the Brighton sun), short, dark hair, those stunning eyes, ringed with black lashes. She looks like a cross-dressing Shakespearean heroine, Viola perhaps, or Rosalind. The kind who never really looks like a boy, no matter how short their hair or how tight their breeches.

'Do you really hate it?' Emily asks again.

'Yes,' says Paris simply.

'But why?' Emily almost wails, conscious that they have had

this conversation many times before. It is old ground, indeed so old there ought to be an Etruscan burial site on it. 'It's so beautiful. You speak such good Italian. It's a real opportunity, you know.'

'An opportunity for what?' asks Paris, as if dropping the words into a cold, deep pool.

But Emily is now on full auto-rant. 'God, I would have loved it at your age,' she says. 'I was stuck in Addlestone, doing nothing. I didn't even go abroad until I was nineteen.'

There is a silence. Emily is thinking of the first time she went abroad. To Italy, of course. To Gina's holiday home in Positano. She remembers the shining blue of the sea, the houses piled on top of each other, teetering on the rocks, pink, yellow and blue. It had been like glimpsing paradise. Paris thinks of Brighton pier, of the karaoke bar and the gypsy caravan where you can get your fortune told, of the shrieking rides and the silver falls, ten-pence pieces eternally poised in a frozen avalanche.

'In that case,' said Paris, politely, at last, 'it's a shame we can't swap. I'd be happy never to go abroad again.'

Addlestone hadn't really been that bad. When Emily thought about it, which was quite often these days, the overwhelming impression was one of interconnectedness. Little roads joining onto bigger ones, neat driveways intersecting the pavements, traffic lights, mini roundabouts, zebra crossings, bridges and footpaths. There were no cul-de-sacs or one-way streets in her imagination; everything was connected to something else. It was rather a comforting thought. Emily remembers as a child playing long solitary games with a toy railway track, trying vainly to get all the pieces to join up, all the bridges to have tracks under and over them, all the crossroads to have an option of going in four directions, all the circles to be complete. She never succeeded but she remembers trying, absorbed, for hours. Addlestone gave her the safe, slightly smug, feeling of a railway track where all the points connected. Impossible to get lost. Impossible, she realises now, to go anywhere much.

The track must have belonged to one of her brothers, Alan or David, as her parents were not the sort to challenge gender stereotypes. Alan and David were ten and twelve years older than Emily and she can't remember playing with them very much. Really, they seemed to belong to another family altogether. When she arrived at secondary school, they had both already left (neither, it seemed, having made very much impression on the teachers). Dimly she remembers a motorbike in the hallway, rugby kit drying over radiators, large ungainly male bodies lurking around the house, but, try as she might, she cannot remember any real conversation she ever had with her brothers. Alan once bought her a doll in Welsh National costume (what had he been doing in Wales?) and David once took her to the funfair (she remembers being terrified on the Big Wheel) but, other than that, nothing. Alan got married at twenty and now lives in Australia. David married twice but now lives with a woman whom their parents do not like. They send cards at Christmas on which they invariably spell Siena's name wrong.

'She's not like her brothers, is she?' Emily remembers hearing this all the time. It was never clear whether it was a compliment or an insult. One thing was certain, her parents had known where they were with her brothers (indifferent at school, keen on cars and on the more violent contact sports); Emily was something different altogether. 'Why are you always reading?' her mother used to ask, fretfully. (Guiltily, Emily now hears herself asking Paris the same thing.) She can't really remember why she felt she had to read *all* the time: on the bus, in the bath, doing the washing up, walking to school, even once, embarrassingly, when she was supposed to be an outfielder at a rounders match. Dickens, Orwell, Jilly Cooper; it didn't really seem to matter what she read just that she had to do it all the time or else something awful would happen. She remembers walking those little interconnected streets, eyes on the page, terrified to look up at the world around her.

It was a teacher who first suggested that she should go to university. Her parents, who were inclined to be embarrassed about Emily's good marks for English, at first tried to dissuade her. 'But what will you *do* there?' her mother asked. 'Read, study, act in plays,' said Emily airily. She had no idea, of course. 'Act in *plays*?' her mother repeated, horrified. No one in their family had ever acted in a play unless you counted David's disastrous appearance as Joseph in his primary school Nativity play, when he stood on Mary's headscarf and made her cry.

Well, she had gone to university and she had acted in plays and she had met Michael Bartnicki in Gordon Square and she had fallen in love with him and he had left her and now her whole life was different. Emily, closing the shutters in Charlie's room while the thunder still rumbled around the valley, wondered if university had driven her away from her family or if the process had already begun, all those years ago, in Addlestone.

Certainly university hadn't helped. At least she had gone to London, not to Oxford or Cambridge, but UCL, with its solid neoclassical façade and its library and colonnades, had seemed alien enough. She remembers her dad standing in the library, looking up at the rows upon rows of leather-bound books. 'All these books!' he had breathed. 'What do they *do* with them?' 'Read them, Dad,' Emily had answered pertly, but to Doug the library could not have seemed more exotic if the contents had been written in Sanskrit and Linear B. Books were all very well in their place (he always had a Dick Francis at Christmas) but there was something excessive, something unhealthy, about all this learning.

Her parents had not understood about university but then, in a way, Emily too had always felt uncomfortable with the more Oxbridgey elements of UCL (the classics students who sat in the quad pretending they were at Balliol). No, it was Michael who finally took her away from her parents' world into another glittering existence. She vividly recalls trying to describe Gina to her mother and her mother just not understanding Gina's fateful glamour.

'She runs a restaurant, you say?'

'Well, it's not just a restaurant, it's more a sort of experience.'

'I see, dear. I suppose she does quite well out of it though?'

Absolutely hopeless.

The thunder roars again, nearer this time. Emily shuts Charlie's door, praying that he doesn't wake up. Paris appears at the top of the stairs, wearing a Snoopy nightshirt.

'Is it a storm?' she asks.

'Looks like it,' says Emily. 'Don't be scared. We're quite safe. It'll be fun listening to it.' She speaks with deliberate brightness but, in fact, she is rather apprehensive. She has never experienced a storm at the Villa Serena and she is uncomfortably aware of how isolated they are. Who would hear if they were struck by lightning? Romano's bungalow is at the bottom of the hill but he goes to bed at eight, with the chickens.

'I'm not scared,' says Paris scornfully. But she comes downstairs.

'*Dad's Army*?' suggests Emily. Paris nods. They go into the sitting room where Siena sits huddled on one of the sofas, clutching her mobile.

'Has he rung?' asks Emily. Tactlessly, she realises.

'Can't get a signal,' says Siena.

'Then why are you still holding the phone?' asks Paris. Siena says nothing, just hunches up further on the sofa. She looks wary and defensive but, when Emily sits next to her, at least she doesn't move away. Paris sits on the other side of her mother and, for a moment, Emily savours the feeling of sitting close to her daughters like this. If she doesn't move, if she doesn't spoil it, she can actually feel them both pressed against her.

The DVD clicks into play. Captain Mainwaring and the platoon have climbed a church tower and are becoming inextricably entangled in the workings of the clock.

A massive bolt of lightning illuminates the sky. On the screen Jones mounts a mechanical horse and exhorts everyone not to panic.

The thunder breaks against the house in a monstrous wave of sound. Paris shifts closer to Emily.

The thunder and lightning are now almost simultaneous.

'We're in the eye of the storm,' says Siena.

'Isn't it exciting?' says Emily unconvincingly. In Walmington-on-Sea, Mainwaring is being poked in the bottom by a mechanical lance.

A final, definitive crash of thunder and the Home Guard vanishes. The house is plunged into darkness. Siena screams.

'What is it?' whispers Paris.

'The electricity's gone,' says Emily. 'The cable must have been struck. I'll go and get some matches.'

'Mum!' Paris grabs her. 'Don't go!'

'Come with me then.' Like a three-legged race, they edge, clutching each other, towards the door. The hall, with no windows, is pitch black. Emily fumbles for the table where, she is sure, she left the matches. She can see them now, sitting in a little Chinese bowl. She reaches further. There is a crash which sounds very much like a Chinese bowl hitting an authentic stone floor.

'Shit!' says Emily.

'Where are the matches?' moans Siena.

'I've dropped them.'

Then, just as Emily is frantically running her hands over the floor, there is a loud bang on the door. All three freeze, unable to admit that the situation has suddenly, terrifyingly, got even worse.

'What's that?' whispers Paris.

The knock sounds again. As grim and ponderous as the Last Trump. Each of them wrestles with their own demon, imagining what is on the other side of the door, out there in the storm. Emily thinks of the Monkey's Paw, that unseen, terrible presence. Siena thinks of vampires and werewolves and wonders why she ever thought that Buffy was cool. For Paris it is simply all her fears coming together. It is Italy taking her revenge. It is Death itself.

'Who is it?' calls Emily, in English.

There is an indistinct shout in Italian and then a sound so spine-chilling that Emily and her daughters can only look at each other, speechless with horror. It is a cross between a moan and a howl, a sound straight out of central casting. Weirdly, its very clichéd scariness seems to put some courage into Emily. Slowly, she moves towards the door.

'Mum! Don't!'

In a trance she lifts the iron latch and pushes open the heavy door. The girls whimper in the background. Another flash of lightning tears open the sky and there, standing on the doorstep, is a tall, dark man with a body in his arms.

CHAPTER 2

Both girls scream. The lightning flashes again and illuminates the grotesque misshapen shadow. Emily feels like screaming too but somehow she manages not to. Instead she backs away, instinctively shielding her daughters. She thinks of Charlie, blamelessly asleep upstairs. If this monster murders her and the girls, will he then go upstairs for Charlie?

And then the shadow speaks. 'I'm sorry,' it says in Italian, 'but this was the only house. The dog is injured.'

And then Emily sees that the sinister bundle in the man's arms contains not a murdered corpse but a dog, its foot clumsily bandaged. She sees, too, that the man is huge and blackbearded, wearing workman's clothes, his hair plastered flat with rain. But his voice is cultured and, almost unconsciously, she finds herself standing aside to let him in.

Later Raffaello tells her that this was a typically English reaction to an animal in need. 'An Italian would have told me to take the mangy animal to the nearest dogs' home.'

'But where would you find one in the middle of the night?'

Raffaello shrugged. 'That wouldn't be their problem.'

The man steps into the hall, dripping onto the stone floor. At the same moment, Paris finds the matches and manages to strike one. Emily sees her scared white face lit up by the tiny flame; Siena is behind her, holding her sister's arm tightly (though whether for support or reassurance Emily doesn't know).

'Find a candle,' she calls.

'Torch,' says the man shortly, in English. 'Front pocket.' To her own amazement Emily finds herself approaching the strange man and fumbling in his pocket for the torch, near enough to smell his hair and skin. Sure enough, in the front pocket of his waterproof jacket there is a large, serviceable torch. Its beam, in the tomb-dark hallway, is like a searchlight. Emily directs the light towards the kitchen door.

'You'd better bring the dog in here,' she says.

The man lays the dog on the kitchen table. 'He has hurt his paw,' he says. 'I found him in one of the caves.' He speaks English fluently, with a slight American accent.

It crosses Emily's mind to ask him what he was doing in the cave but she thinks that she had better concentrate on the injured animal. In fact, she feels curiously calm, almost triumphant. She has faced her worst possible fears, the monster in the doorway, the summons in the night, and it looks as though they won't be murdered after all. Directing the torch on to the animal's dusty black paw, she undoes the bandage, which looks as if it was torn from a scrap of the stranger's shirt. The dog whimpers but does not attempt to bite. 'It doesn't look too bad,' she says confidently though she has never owned an animal in her life and, indeed, is usually rather afraid of dogs. 'I'll get a clean bandage.'

'No!' say Paris and Siena together. 'Don't go.'

The man laughs, showing startlingly white teeth. 'Don't worry. I'm not a murderer. My name is Raffaello Murello. I'm an archaeologist.'

Clear as a bell, Emily hears the words of the woman at *Ferragosto*: 'He is a devil.'

'Yes,' she says tranquilly. 'I've heard of you.'

While Raffaello stands stroking the dog, Siena finds a box of candles in one of the kitchen cupboards. Scented and wrapped with hessian bows, they had been a present from Petra. Emily lights three of them and sets them around the dog so that he resembles a sacrifice on an altar. Then, miraculously, she finds the first aid box, washes the wound and bandages it with a clean dressing. The devilish Raffaello watches her in silence.

When the bandage is tied, Raffaello lifts the dog from the table. It is a large dog, a German Shepherd, Emily thinks, but he lifts it with ease. 'You'll have to clean the table,' he says.

'I know,' snaps Emily. Italians are always telling you to clean things; they are obsessed with hygiene.

Suddenly Siena speaks. 'Mum? Shall I make a cup of tea?'

Raffaello throws back his head and laughs. 'Tea! Now I know I'm with English people.'

But that is what they do. Emily heats the water on the stove

(thank God for not having an electric kettle) and makes tea.
She also makes Marmite sandwiches for herself and the girls.
Raffaello, when faced with the Marmite, looks disconcerted for
the first time. 'To eat? My God! I'd rather starve.' Then they sit
around the kitchen table in the candlelight and eat and drink.
It feels curiously cosy with the candlelight and the dog lying
at their feet. Emily remembers times when she was a child and
couldn't sleep and her mother took her downstairs for illicit
cups of cocoa. It was unlike Emily's mother to do anything
illicit, which must be why the memory has stuck.

'So, Signor Murello,' she says. 'What were you doing in the
cave in the first place?'

Raffaello grins. Now that his hair has dried it stands up
around his face in wild curls. He doesn't look like a murderer
but he does look disturbingly like a pirate.

'I'm in charge of an excavation nearby,' he says. 'We've been
digging trenches near the caves . . .'

So you are responsible for the rubble, thinks Emily crossly.

'When the storm started,' Raffaello continues, 'I thought I
had better check on the dig, make sure the trenches hadn't collapsed. I heard a whine from the caves and went to investigate.'

'Weren't you terrified?' asks Siena.

Raffaello shrugs. 'No. Why should I be scared? It was obviously some sort of animal. So, I went into the cave and found
this fellow here. I think he's not much more than a puppy. He'd
hurt his paw and seemed terrified by the storm. I was carrying
him back to my car but it was too far. I saw your house. I'd heard

an English family lived here and I thought, perhaps they want a dog.' He grins shamelessly at Emily.

Paris's face lights up immediately. 'Oh Mum! Can we keep him?'

'Don't be silly,' says Emily. 'He'll already have an owner.'

'I don't think so,' says Raffaello. 'I think he's been living in the caves. He's probably a stray.'

'We don't want a stray dog,' says Emily. 'He's probably half wild.' They all look at the dog, who is sitting meekly on the floor, next to a bowl of water.

'Yes,' says Raffaello. 'He looks a very hound of hell, doesn't he?'

The dog wags its tail.

As the storm is still raging outside, Emily feels that she must offer Raffaello and the dog a bed for the night. The lights are still out too and the candles gutter as the wind blows through the draughty (authentic) windows.

'No need for a bed,' says Raffaello. 'I'll sleep on the sofa, with the hell-hound.'

Siena looks at him doubtfully. He seems OK but she wishes he'd stop talking about hell.

Raffaello grins at her over the pile of bedding presented to him by Emily. 'Don't worry, Miss Siena. I'll try not to murder any of you in the night.'

Emily wakes to an exceptionally beautiful morning. When she opens her shutters, the mist is still lying in the valley below, the tops of the trees poking through like prehistoric beasts from the dawn of time. The sky is washed pale blue from last night's rain and a sweet-smelling breeze wafts from the olive grove. Emily realises that it is still very early.

She wraps herself in her old Chinese dressing gown and tiptoes downstairs. For almost the first time since his birth she is up before Charlie and she doesn't want to spoil the peace. Outside the sitting-room door she pauses and then, softly, pushes it open.

Lying on the floor, on a blanket taken from Paris's bed, is the German Shepherd puppy, its paws, one neatly bandaged, twitching in sleep. Next to it, stretched out asleep on the sofa, is Raffaello. The sofa is huge but, even so, he is too long for it and he lies in a sprawled abandoned way, arms flung over his head, legs akimbo as if he has been running in his sleep, one touching the floor, the other reaching out over the end of the sofa.

Emily watches him for a moment, thinking about last night. She still can't get over how calmly she behaved. For someone who usually panics at quite ordinary domestic crises (running out of milk, say, or forgetting a dentist's appointment), she coped effortlessly with a situation straight out of the *Hammer House of Horror*. Emily has never thought of herself as a calm person. Michael had thought her sweet and naive and dreamily impractical (that is, until he found her annoying and stupid and irritatingly impractical). Paul had, at first, found her air of distraction attractive but, after a few years of marriage, he had come to find it exasperating. Why couldn't she read a map? Why was she never on time for anything? Why did she seem to treat life like a board game whose rules she had never quite bothered to learn? So where then had she found the sangfroid to welcome a strange man into her house in the middle of a thunderstorm? To put an injured dog on her kitchen table and tend to its wounds? To offer both man and dog a bed for the night and then to sleep peacefully for ten hours without dreams or nightmares?

Emily looks down at Raffaello's sleeping body and thinks that it helps that he doesn't know her and that she may never see him again. He doesn't know that she's incurably dizzy. He doesn't know of the famous occasion when she was heading for Maidenhead and ended up in Maidstone. To him she is a tough, eccentric Englishwoman. The sort who probably has a whole army of stray dogs living in her bedroom and named after the Knights of the Round Table. Emily grins; she quite likes this idea of herself. The dog wakes suddenly and wags his tail in a feeble and ingratiating way. Emily sighs. She has a feeling that she is stuck with the dog for life.

Raffaello stirs too. Then he yawns, stretches and almost falls full length onto the floor. Righting himself on one arm, he looks up at Emily through a tangle of black, curly hair.

'Good morning, Mrs Roberston. Is it time for the full English breakfast?'

Michael would have been surprised at the cool, dog-wrangling Emily, she thinks as she makes coffee and puts out bread and jam and Marmite (she draws the line at the full English). She remembers the time when Gina's dog, an Italian greyhound called Picchi, developed such a passion for her that he slept outside her room all night and, in the morning, Emily had been too scared to come out. And that had been a tiny, shivering rabbit of a dog, 'a woofter in a tartan coat' Michael called him, not a huge, hairy German Shepherd. Sighing, Emily adds cheese and ham to the breakfast table. Over the years she has tried to ration the number of times she thinks, what would Michael say if he could see this? Or, if Michael could see me now he'd be sorry he left me. She is bitterly ashamed of the fact that one of her first thoughts after Siena was born was, what would Michael say if he could see me with a baby? She even remembers having a morbid belief that the baby, so blonde and blue eyed, resembled Michael, rather than Paul.

Michael has gone, she tells herself, slapping knives down onto the table, he belongs to the past. The present is full of strange bearded men and injured animals. But still, clear as day, she sees Izzy's narrow London garden and hears herself asking Chad, 'How is he?'

'He's OK,' Chad had answered brusquely. 'He lives in South London, in Kennington. He works at King's. His wife's a sculptor. You knew he was married?'

'Yes,' said Emily. She still remembered the acute physical pain she felt, actually *literally* in her heart, when she heard that Michael had married, barely a year after they had separated. Barely a year after he had cited, as one of the reasons for wanting to part, a need for 'space', a wish to 'be on his own with all the loneliness that brings'. Jesus. And he thought *she* was pretentious.

'Mara. She's American. She trained as a doctor but now she makes these weird sculptures out of old television sets and pieces of torn-up bog roll. Can't say I get it but she seems to do quite well out of it.'

'Do they have children?' asked Emily, feeling herself wavering on the edge of the precipice again. Like a child contemplating its parents' love life, if they didn't have children she would not have to accept that they ever made love.

'A daughter. Jessica. She's seventeen.' A pause, then Chad said shortly, 'She's got CP, cerebral palsy. I think it's been a terrible strain on them all. She's a lovely girl.'

'How awful.' It *was* awful but it was not what Emily wanted to know. What she wanted to know, of course, was whether, in the midst of his new life, he ever thought about her.

Raffaello enters the kitchen with his hair wet from the shower and proceeds to interrogate Emily about her life.

'What do you do all day, stuck here in the middle of nowhere?'

'I write,' says Emily, rather defiantly, pouring herself a black coffee.

'You write? Books?'

'No. Articles. For an English newspaper.' Her novel, started when she was at university, was still upstairs in the box containing her degree certificates and Michael's love letters. It is a magic realist love story, set in turn-of-the-century Italy, and it makes Emily feel physically sick to think about it.

'What sort of articles?' persists Raffaello, chewing on bread and ham. 'How to lose weight in two weeks eating only chocolate? How to turn day into night with that little black dress?'

'No,' says Emily, with dignity, though she does wonder how Raffaello is able to satirise the genre so accurately. Surely he doesn't read English women's magazines? Maybe he has an English wife.

'I write about Italy,' says Emily at last. 'About living in Tuscany.'

'Ah,' says Raffaello, looking at her with interest. 'So you are an expert on Tuscany now?'

'Well, I do live here.'

'People have lived here for thousands of years,' says Raffaello, polishing off the last of the ham, 'and still there are secrets in these hills.'

'Of course. You're an archaeologist. Anyone after the Romans must seem a newcomer to you.'

'The Romans!' Raffaello snorts in derision. 'They are arrivistes. Charlatans. Barbarians. The Etruschi are my people.'

The Etruscans. Emily is fascinated by the way he puts this, 'The Etruschi are my people', almost as if they are his family, still present, still inhabiting the region whose name derives from theirs. The only thing she knows about the Etruscans is that they preceded the Romans. Before Raffaello can say more, the children burst in, accompanied by the dog.

'A dog!' Charlie is radiant with excitement. 'My dog!'

'He's not your dog,' snaps Paris. 'You weren't even awake when he arrived.'

'No,' agrees Siena, eyes huge, voice sepulchral. 'It was terrifying. There was a terrible storm, lightning was flashing and then this awful, awful knocking at the door . . .' She raps on the kitchen table.

Charlie gives a shriek and runs to hide behind Emily. 'Ignore them, Charlie Bear,' says Emily. 'They were scared stiff, if you want to know.'

Raffaello is sitting back in his chair, hugely enjoying the scene. The dog hobbles over to him immediately and puts his head on his lap.

'You see,' says Raffaello to Charlie, 'he is my dog.'

'Who's he?' says Charlie rudely, pointing at Raffaello. 'He looks like a pirate.'

Raffaello looks even more piratical in the daylight. He even has, Emily notes, a gold earring in one ear. Raffaello laughs heartily. 'I am Blackbeard the pirate,' he says. 'My ship is outside.'

'Is it?' Charlie runs to look.

'Don't be silly, Charlie,' says Paris. 'There isn't even any sea.'

'Ah,' says Raffaello, 'but there are places, towns, villages, that were once covered by sea. The whole of the Po valley was once under water.'

'Thousands of years ago,' objects Paris.

'Ah. Thousands of years are as nothing to me.' Raffaello

clicks his fingers impressively. Emily dimly recalls someone else saying this to her recently.

'Mr Murello is an archaeologist,' Emily explains to her children, putting Coco Pops in front of Charlie. To Raffaello, she says, 'I assume I've got you to thank for the rubble blocking my drive?'

'I apologise,' says Raffaello seriously. Then spoils it by adding, 'Nice Alfa.'

'My husband's,' says Emily repressively.

Raffaello says nothing but looks at her quizzically. His eyes are very dark brown, almost black, but full of light, like the eyes of an animal – or a bird of prey.

'Did you say you were digging near here?' asks Siena, who is patting the dog.

'Yes. I believe that there was an Etruscan settlement in this area.'

'Aren't all the Etruscan settlements down near Arezzo and Cortona?' asks Emily. She remembers going with Paul to see the tombs at Cortona.

'Well, very little has been found so far east,' concedes Raffaello, 'but I am convinced they were here. After all, the Romans were here and they usually built towns where there was already an Etruscan settlement.' He looks contemptuous of such copycat behaviour.

'Who were the Etruscans?' asks Siena. Paris snorts with derision though Emily is pretty sure that she doesn't know either.

'They were a wonderful people,' says Raffaello gravely. 'They lived here, in Tuscany, Umbria and Latium, about two thousand years ago. It was called Etruria then.'

'I've never heard of them,' says Siena candidly.

'I'm not surprised,' says Raffaello. 'Many of their cities are lost. We have very little of their writings. There are no direct translations so, even today, we don't fully understand their language.'

'What are you looking for here?' asks Paris. 'Is it a lost city?'

'One of the twelve cities of Etruria?' asks Raffaello, with a slight smile. 'I don't think so. But I think there was some sort of settlement near here. Unfortunately the Etruscans built with wood so very little will be left of it.'

'So what do you think you will find?' persists Paris.

'The one thing they did build with stone,' says Raffaello, eyes glinting. 'Their tombs.'

'What's a tomb?' asks Charlie, looking up from his cereal, dripping milk.

'A grave,' says Paris in her most terrifying voice.

Charlie looks at Emily, unsure whether or not to cry.

'More like a house,' says Emily, frowning at Paris.

Raffaello laughs. 'Your wonderful mother is quite right. Etruscan tombs are very like houses. Full of carvings, bronze figures, ordinary household objects. Quite incredible.'

'Have you found any evidence?' asks Emily, pouring more coffee.

'We have found what I think are some steps,' says Raffaello. 'It's potentially very exciting. But, before we go any further, we have to get permission from the Soprintendenza Archeologiche.' He looks rather depressed at this prospect.

Paris leans forward. 'When you find the tomb, can we see it?'

'Of course. You will be one of the first.'

'Cool,' says Paris happily and actually takes a piece of bread and begins to eat.

Emily is so pleased to see the ordinary, interested expression on Paris's face that it is a few seconds before she realises that her younger daughter is speaking to her.

'Mum,' says Paris, 'can we keep the dog?'

'Please!' says Siena, still on her knees beside the dog, caressing his ears.

'Please!' shouts Charlie, jumping up to put his arms round the dog.

Emily starts to say, 'But dogs give Charlie asthma . . .' but then she sees Charlie with his face pressed up next to the dog's furry muzzle, not wheezing or choking but in fact looking radiant with happiness.

'Please,' says Siena again.

Emily looks at their faces, identical in that instant, united by a simple, uncomplicated desire. For some reason, it brings tears to her eyes.

'Oh, all right,' she says.

CHAPTER 3

Paris's diary

*Back to school yesterday. Could have been worse, I suppose.
Having the dog makes a difference. We haven't given him
a name yet because Mum says it has to be democratic and
the others have such stupid ideas (Charlie wanted Mowgli!).
Anyway, Dog sleeps on my bed though Mum says he's not
allowed to. I can tell he likes me best. For example, he is all over
Mum when he thinks she's going to feed him but he jumps up
at me for no reason at all, just because he likes me. Of course I
am the one who takes him for most walks because Siena is too
lazy and Mum is always writing those stupid articles though
she says that they've got more difficult since Dad left. Don't
see why as they were always complete bollocks from start to
finish. Anyway, yesterday I took Dog up to the place where R is
digging. There's nothing much to see, just some pieces of string
marked out in squares but when you speak to R he makes it all
sound real somehow. He says the entrance to the tomb might*

*be decorated with carvings of the underworld, snakes and
monsters, people being tortured. I told Charlie and he went
screaming off to Mum. Typical.*

*Anyway school is not so bad. Silvia and Paola said they were
pleased to see me but that is the Italian thing, all very kissy
kissy, che carina, and it doesn't necessarily mean anything.
But Silvia isn't really like that. She wears black clothes and she
listens to Metallica. I quite like her. Siena is studying for her
Licenza Classica so I don't see much of her. She's still wrapped
round Giancarlo which makes me want to puke. I hoped they
might have split up when he didn't contact her when we got
back from England but, two days ago, he just turned up on his
stupid moped going on about having lost his phone in Forte dei
Marmi. And Siena – can you believe it? – just flung her arms
round him and it's all on again. Dear Diary, it is mortifying to
have such a stupid sister.*

*Andrea came to talk to me at school. I don't know why. He
just came up to me by the lockers and said had I enjoyed my
holiday and everything. That was nice, I think. I don't like him
or anything. But it was nice.*

Emily is at the despised Tuesday market, with the dog (now
named Totti after the footballer Francesco Totti) at her side.
Totti is a nuisance, panting loudly after the other dogs and
making sudden leaps for freedom, leaving Emily with the lead
wound round the legs of several disgruntled pensioners, but
there is no doubt that having him there makes Emily feel more

like she belongs. She knows she still looks like a tourist, with her schoolgirl Italian and her too-clean wicker basket, but a tourist would not have a delinquent German Shepherd puppy on a lead. So, as she apologises and drags Totti whimpering past the meat stall, she is pleased to be able to exchange understanding looks with other dog owners, to smile modestly when complimented on the dog's size and to roll her eyes humorously when he makes another assault on the flower seller's Pekingese.

'*È un donnaiolo.*'

'*Sì!*' She smiles brightly though it is not until she gets home and looks this word up that she realises that it means 'ladies' man'. Of course, the Italians *would* have a word for this; it is more surprising that there is an English equivalent.

'Mrs Robertson! How nice.'

She turns from the flower seller to find Don Angelo smiling at her. Though he was previously so dismissive of the market he seems quite unabashed to be discovered here, his (genuinely battered) basket containing two large aubergines and a cheese wrapped in greaseproof paper.

'Did you have a good trip to England?' he asks, in English.

'Yes. Thank you.' She has ceased to be surprised that he knows where she has been.

'Did you see your family?' He pats Totti whose head comes up to his waist.

'Well,' Emily is furious to find herself blushing, 'my parents were away. On holiday. But I saw lots of friends.'

There is a pause while she feels the unspoken censure of

parents who could go on holiday when their daughter comes to visit and the absolute impossibility of mere friends taking the places of the genuine, sacred *famiglia*. But, when the priest speaks, his voice is kind.

'And your husband?'

'Oh yes. I saw him.' On the last day of their stay in Brighton, Paul drove down to see the children. Emily had precisely ten minutes alone with him in the rock shop on Brighton pier. There, amongst the candy-striped sweets and the outsized lollipops with 'Best Mate' written on them in loopy writing, they talked about the fact that they had no money and that Paul was living with a twenty-two-year-old 'personal trainer' from Cirencester.

'She's got some money of her own.'

'Yes. I thought she would have,' said Emily, staring at a grotesque baby's dummy made of sugar.

'I'm sorry,' said Paul, awkwardly, jingling his change and not meeting her eyes.

'That's OK,' said Emily. Though of course it wasn't.

There is another pause and then Don Angelo says, briskly, 'There is a meeting tonight. At the Palazzo Comunale. About the *scavi*.'

Scavi? Frantically Emily's mind races through her sparse mental dictionary of Italian words. At first all she can think of is Pompeii and then she remembers. *Scavi*. Ruins.

'The diggings? Near our house?'

'*Sì*.' Don Angelo smiles encouragingly. 'A lot of people are unhappy. You should come. After all, the work is almost in your front garden. Have you met Mr Murello yet?'

'Yes. I have met him.'

The priest smiles again. 'Come to the meeting, Mrs Robertson. Eight o'clock. *Salve!*, He raises his hand in farewell but then stops and calls back, over his shoulder, 'A fine dog.' He points at Totti who is grinning foolishly.

'Thank you,' says Emily weakly. And she makes her way to the cheese stall, encumbered by Totti whose one aim in life seems to be to follow the priest as he wends his way through his parishioners, towards a stall selling stuffed animals made from real fur.

In Brighton, Petra too is contemplating a new term. As she dumps her tatty sports bag full of books onto the staffroom table she thinks that, as a teacher, you never grow up. You still dread the start of term, autumn means not conkers and kicking your way through the leaves but new books, a new class, a new start. She still finds herself buying new shoes for September, just like the kids do. She looks down at her feet now, shiny Doc Martens, and smiles. She has not worn heels since splitting up with Ed.

But still there is something exciting about being back again. Petra likes the staffroom, the sense of fellowship as the teachers relish the one place where they are safe from the enemy. Her friend Annie waves at her from across the room. Like the kids, she will be meeting her friends again, getting back into old routines. Because of Harry, she tends not to socialise much in the holidays. That is why it was so lovely to see Emily and her children. She misses them, especially Paris, more than she likes to admit. Petra never wanted a daughter ('I just don't *do* pink,' she used to say) but Paris is different: clever, edgy, sharp-tongued, an observer. She reminds Petra of herself and she has to actively stop herself from thinking that it is she rather than Emily (so soft and curvy, so full of diffidence and other dubious feminine virtues) who should be bringing up Paris.

Petra sighs and goes into the book cupboard to count copies of *Skellig* (like the seasons, the set books never change). When she emerges, wiping dust from her hands, she sees Annie talking to a man she doesn't recognise. Annie grins encouragingly over his shoulder (he is very tall) but, when the man turns round, Petra actually finds herself catching her breath. Oh my God, she thinks. George Clooney.

Piling Totti and her basket into the Alfa (she regards it as rather like a hostage and has no intention of going back to the Panda) Emily drives to the *scuola materna*. This term she is determined to collect Charlie herself and not rely on Olimpia. When she told Olimpia of this decision, she had been shocked by the sudden expression of hatred on the older woman's face.

'Sì, Signora Robertson,' was all that she said but that momentary flash of venom stayed with Emily for a long time. She had known of course that Olimpia loved Charlie but had not realised quite how possessive that love was. Well, now Emily was going to reclaim her son. She is going to collect her child herself, driving her Italian car with her Italian dog and her bag full of Italian groceries: aubergines, radicchio and cavolo nero. To celebrate she puts on a Puccini CD rather than the nursery rhymes. The heart-stoppingly beautiful music carries her on a wave of sound, the grey car on the winding roads like an advertisement for Italy.

The *scuola materna* is on the outskirts of the town, a low modern building with white-painted walls covered with colourful murals. A blue elephant and a pink giraffe guard an impressively secure entrance with entry phone and CCTV cameras (Italians take no risks where their *bambini* are concerned). Emily is buzzed in and finds Charlie and some of the older children playing in the shady playground. For a second, she just stands there and watches them, holding Totti tightly by the collar. Charlie, in his red dungarees and blue shirt, looks no different from the other brightly coloured Italian children who dart around the climbing frame like dragonflies. She hears him calling out in monosyllabic but perfect Italian and, for a second, her heart constricts as if she is about to cry. He looks so happy, so absorbed, so sure of himself, trotting about in his little white trainers. She doesn't want to call out and spoil it, to recall him to her claustrophobic maternal world.

But Charlie sees her and comes bounding over, though he does embrace Totti first. The other children, too, come crowding round the puppy, who is more of a draw than Emily could ever be. Charlie, bossily proprietorial, takes Totti's lead, and drags him off through the trees, all the children following, begging for a turn with the *cane lupo.* The principal, an impressively chic woman called Monica, who has been watching from the porch, comes over to talk to Emily. Emily cringes, expecting a lecture about bringing a dog into the school. She is in awe of Monica, who has those thin black-framed glasses that make her look both intellectual and fashionable, two qualities that combine to make Emily feel irrevocably inferior.

'Sorry about the dog . . .' she begins.

Monica waves her hand. 'It's OK. We're pleased to meet him. Charlie has talked about him a great deal.'

'I'm glad,' says Emily. 'His Italian's coming on then?'

'His Italian is very good,' says Monica.

'Better than mine.'

Monica shrugs. 'It's always the way.' Her own English is almost perfect.

As this moment Totti bounds back to Emily, dragging Charlie behind him. Monica sends Charlie to collect his belongings (Emily is amazed at how quickly he obeys her) but still stands beside Emily, as if she has something else to say. Emily, untangling Totti's lead from round her legs, begins to feel rather uncomfortable. Has Charlie done something wrong? Is he about to be drummed out of the *scuola materna*?

Finally, as Charlie approaches, carrying a pile of brightly coloured drawings, Monica says, 'I was talking to my friend Antonella about you.'

My God, thinks Emily, they are all talking about me. The stupid Englishwoman who can't speak Italian and whose husband has left her. Probably Don Angelo has told them all to pray for her. But then, she looks up and sees Monica's intelligent, alert face. She doesn't seem the sort of person to gossip with priests.

'Antonella teaches at the primary school,' Monica is saying. 'We belong to a book club.'

'Book club?' echoes Emily rather randomly.

'Yes. We meet and read books.' Monica grins. 'And we drink wine and we criticise men.'

'Sounds like fun.'

'Yes it is. We wondered if you would like to join us.'

Driving back through the midday heat, Puccini on the CD player (much to Charlie's disgust), Totti panting on the back seat, Emily thinks about her conversations with Monica and Don Angelo. Would she have had these encounters a year ago? No, she would have been stuck in her beautifully restored eyrie, writing about the joys of Tuscan life. As she takes the left-hand turn between the shrine and the umbrella pines, she notices that black bags have been placed under the olive trees to catch the harvest as it falls. The sunflower fields are turning brown. Although it is as hot as ever, she thinks she can feel something in the air, something sharp and invigorating, the first faint tang of autumn.

A new beginning.

And, many miles away, Michael Bartnicki is reading an email from Izzy Goldsmith. He clicks on the attached pictures and stares at them for a long time, tapping a gold pen against his teeth.

CHAPTER 4

Emily arrives at the meeting late, having had a last-minute panic about leaving Charlie with Siena and Paris.

'But he's asleep, Mum.'

'I know. But what if he wakes up?'

'Then I'll tuck him up and he'll go back to sleep again.'

'What if he doesn't?'

'Then he'll be awake when you get home. Honestly, Mum!' Siena looked at her with clear-eyed sixteen-year-old confidence. After all, what could possibly go wrong?

'And anyway,' said Paris, wandering in from the kitchen eating a Mars bar, 'we've got Totti.'

The sight of Totti snoring in his basket did not exactly fill Emily with confidence but she didn't want to irritate the girls, especially as they were being so unexpectedly helpful and upbeat. Siena had actually *offered* to babysit and even Paris had not made any of her usual comments about selling Charlie to the first gypsy family who came knocking at the door. Even so, she had dithered and fussed so long that it was seven thirty before she left the villa and nearly eight o'clock by the time she had found a parking space in the twisting medieval street.

The Palazzo Comunale is packed. It is a large, rather beautiful building in the main square of Monte Albano, used for public meetings and communal get-togethers, of which there were a surprisingly large number. The room is full of people, all happily anticipating an evening of squabbling over Etruscan remains. Emily tries, and fails, to imagine a similar meeting in England attracting more than a few fusty academics and a man who has come in to shelter from the rain.

Emily slips into a seat at the back of the hall. In the crowd she spots her nearest neighbours Romano and Anna-Luisa, farmers who are rarely seen in the town, as well as Olimpia, looking sullen, and Monica, looking intense. Next to Monica is a blonde woman. She wonders if this is Antonella. At the front, facing the audience, is a trestle table where Don Angelo is sitting, reading the *Gazetta dello Sport.* Next to Don Angelo is the mayor of Monte Albano, a mild-mannered communist called Umberto Biagotti. Next to Biagotti is a woman whom Emily does not recognise, dressed in a dark suit and wearing the same sort of frightening glasses as Monica. She asks her neighbour who this woman is and is told that she is the Soprintendenza Archeologiche, a professor at Bologna University, who is responsible for all archaeological sites in the area.

Suddenly there is a stir by the main doors and people are looking round and whispering. Emily twists her head and sees Raffaello steaming into the room. His arms are full of papers and he is frowning in concentration. He is dressed more smartly than when Emily last saw him, in a blue suit and open-necked shirt, but his hair is still wild and he still has the air of someone who doesn't really belong indoors. The door bangs after him and a cold wind blows through the hall. Emily's neighbour shivers and tugs her fur jacket over her shoulders.

With Raffaello's arrival the meeting is ready to start. Mayor Biagotti speaks first but Emily's Italian is not good enough to follow everything that he says and, besides, he has a strong regional accent. As far as she can make out, he is introducing Raffaello as a world-famous archaeologist and an expert on the Etruscans. He says the findings in the mountains are of great importance, both culturally and commercially. As he says the last word, his lip curls; he is, after all, a communist. He stresses that any excavation must be done 'sympathetically' and he calls upon Don Angelo to represent the views of the community. He sits down to sparse applause.

Emily expects Don Angelo to resent being introduced by a Godless communist but he shakes Biagotti's hand with real warmth, calling him 'Umbertino'. Then he turns to his audience, sighs and spreads out his hands. *Che peccato*, he begins, what a shame. What a shame that it is such a contentious subject that brings us together this evening, dear friends. What a shame that it is controversy that brings such a dear son of Monte Albano back to his home town. (Emily starts at this. She had no idea that Raffaello was actually a native of the town). What a shame that such an eminent archaeologist should busy himself with such a petty, such an unimportant site, when there are clearly great things he could be doing (the further away the better, he seems to imply). What a shame that he wishes to disturb the rest of souls who, though they may come from pagan times, are our compatriots, fellow Tuscans, our brothers.

It is a tour de force. He is humble, he is moving, he is strangely compelling. He looks at Raffaello like a sorrowing father, he twinkles at the audience like a roguish neighbour gossiping over the fence, he addresses Biagotti with simple dignity, he smiles at the Soprintendenza with creaking charm. Even though Emily only understands one word in ten, she understands this: Don Angelo does not want the excavations to continue and he will call on all his powers, heavenly and earthly, to prevent it.

The Soprintendenza stands up next. Emily had expected her to support the dig but she seems to be set against it. The ruins should be left as they are. If they are excavated, exposed to the wind and rain and (far worse) the curious eyes of the world, they will be destroyed. Archaeology is a finite resource. Only in the future will we have the necessary skills to excavate without harming the artefacts. All we can do is register the site for future generations of archaeologists. She sits down with a wintry smile. Emily, looking at Raffaello, sees him bury his head in his hands.

Now it is Raffaello's turn to speak. Emily sees him take a deep breath and square his shoulders as he faces the audience.

To her surprise she finds herself leaning forward in her seat, her hands tightly clasped together. Why on earth is she on his side? He's the one who wants to dig up her land, turn her house into a building site and probably unearth a huge, spooky graveyard just where she wants to plant her new peach trees. Really she should be on the side of the snooty Soprintendenza who just wants to leave well alone. But, despite this, she finds herself willing Raffaello to put up a good show.

He does his best. He has slides, he has artefacts, he has his own piratical charm. He stresses the importance of the site, the status it will bring to Monte Albano. It is rare, he says, to find Etruscan remains so far to the east, so near the Alpe della Luna. He hints at the commercial possibilities of tourists flocking to the town (Biagotti shifts uncomfortably in his seat). He dwells on the skills and brilliance of the Etruscans and reminds the audience that they are their descendants. He reminds them of the tombs at Cortona, the immense curved ceilings, the clay horses, the bronze figurines. We know so little about these people, let us find out some more, he begs. Let us shine a light on the past. To know and understand the past is, after all, the best way to understand the future.

Raffaello sits down, running a hand through his already wild hair. Biagotti stands up again. Wearily, he invites the audience to question the speakers. Emily is not really surprised to see Monica standing up, cool and self-possessed. 'I'd like to ask our priest,' she says, 'why he is so against adding to the sum of human knowledge.'

Don Angelo smiles widely. 'Ah,' he says, spreading out his hands. 'Human knowledge.' Emily waits expectantly but that is apparently the only answer that Monica is going to receive. The priest smiles beatifically, Monica sits down, angry but, Emily feels, not really surprised. An elderly woman stands up and rants about the evils of tourists. Don Angelo nods enthusiastically, Raffaello smiles thinly. Another woman asks if the Etruscan graves are cursed. Very possibly, says Don Angelo smoothly. Raffaello snorts. Then, to Emily's surprise, Olimpia stands up. Large and calm in her flowered dress, she addresses Raffaello without apparent emotion.

'Dottor Murello,' she says, 'we are surprised to see you back in a place which must hold such tragic memories for you.' A tremor runs through the hall. Emily sees Romano whispering to Anna-Luisa and the glint of Monica's glasses as she looks up sharply. 'Doesn't Dottor Murello think,' asks Olimpia sweetly, 'that the dead should be *left in peace*?' She says these last words so vehemently that Emily is quite shocked. She looks at Raffaello and is surprised to see that he, too, is shaken. He runs his hand through his hair again, starts to speak and then stops. He looks at Don Angelo, almost pleadingly.

The priest makes a small gesture to Olimpia (halfway between commiseration and censure) and then says quietly, 'I am sure Signor Murello is aware of the many memories that reside in this place. I am sure we can rely on his sense of what is right.'

'Thank you,' says Raffaello meaningfully.

Biagotti stands up and declares the meeting over.

Emily is left with a feeling of anticlimax. What has been decided? Will the excavations continue or not? Will Raffaello ever remove his pile of rubble from her drive? Why was Don Angelo so vehemently opposed to the excavations and why did he come to Raffaello's aid like that? And what the hell was Olimpia so upset about? Emily longs to ask someone but knows that her Italian is not up to such niceties. So she smiles and waves at Romano and Anna-Luisa and turns to make her way out of the hall. Don Angelo is moving amongst the audience, laughing and gesticulating, but Raffaello is still sitting on the dais, gathering his papers together. His hands are quite steady but Emily can see a muscle pounding in his cheek. Does she dare go over and speak to him? What would she say anyhow? She is still dithering when she hears somebody calling her name.

'Emily!' It is Monica, glasses gleaming, expensive tote bag over her arm. 'I'd like you to meet Antonella Di Luca.' She gestures towards the blond woman.

'*Piacere*.'

'*Piacere*.'

'I believe my son is a friend of your daughter,' says Antonella, smiling.

'Siena?' Emily knows that every red-blooded male in the town is a friend of Siena's. She wonders what it can be like to be so popular. She has examined her feelings conscientiously and knows that she is not jealous, as she believes mothers sometimes are. Rather, she fears for Siena. Beauty, she knows, has its price.

'No. Paris.'

'Oh.' She looks at Antonella with interest. Paris often tells her that she has no friends in the town and certainly no male friends. Italian boys, she says, are pathetic.

'So,' cuts in Monica, 'what did you think of tonight's entertainment?'

'I'm afraid I didn't understand it all.'

Monica laughs shortly. 'No, it takes a lifetime in a small Tuscan town to understand it all.'

'Why is Don Angelo so against the excavations?'

Monica shrugs. 'Superstition. Small-minded Catholic superstition. What more do you need to know?'

'And Olimpia. My . . . er . . . my *collaboratrice domestica* . . . she seemed to have some real grudge against Raffaello . . . Signor Murello.'

It is Antonella who answers, her voice gentle. 'Well, a lot of people in the town do not like Signor Murello.'

'Why?'

'They think he murdered his wife,' says Monica.

CHAPTER 5

'He's here,' says Petra.

'Who's where?' asks Emily, confused. It is early in the morning and she has been woken by Petra's voice, sounding very loud and English in the hazy Italian morning. Emily is sitting up in bed, hair wild, and Totti is lying on her feet, wagging his tail ecstatically. Outside, she can hear Anna-Luisa's cockerel crowing.

'George Clooney's here. In my school.'

'*What*?'

'Well, not him exactly, of course.' Emily can hear Petra taking a drag of her cigarette. 'But he's the new ICT teacher and he's just *gorgeous*. Not like somebody in real life at all.'

Emily is trying to see the time on her watch but it has fallen onto the floor. 'Petra. What time is it in England?'

'Oh,' says Petra vaguely, 'six-ish. I had to ring before the boys are up. Harry hates it when I'm on the telephone.'

Emily turns her watch over with her foot. Five to seven. She sinks back on her pillows, resignedly. Totti jumps up and looks hopefully at the door, whining gently. 'Shh, Totti,' says Emily.

'Who are you talking to?'

'The dog.'

'You've got a dog?'

'Yes,' says Emily, rather proudly. 'A German Shepherd.'

'What? Is this the woman who once crossed the road to avoid a poodle?'

'It was a big poodle,' says Emily defensively. 'Anyway, Totti's very sweet, not scary at all.'

'*What's* his name?'

'Totti. After an Italian footballer.'

'Jesus.' There is a silence and then Petra says, rather wistfully, 'Anyway, I just wanted to tell you about George.'

'It's great! I can't believe it.' Emily tries to inject some enthusiasm into her voice. Hearing it, Totti starts to caper wildly. 'And he isn't married?'

'No. Not even divorced.'

'Gay?'

'Apparently not. He's just split up with his girlfriend.'

'How do you know all this?'

'We went out for a drink last night after work.'

'Pete! You've been on a date!'

'Well, not really. I mean, there were other people there at the beginning.'

'But not at the end?'

'No,' admits Petra. 'At the end it was just the two of us.'

'And?'

'And nothing. We just talked and then I had to go back to collect the boys from the childminder.'

'Are you going to see him again?'

'Yes. Every morning in the staffroom.'

'You know what I mean.'

There is another silence and an intake of smoke. Even a thousand miles away, Emily can feel her throat constricting in sympathy. 'I don't know,' says Petra at last. 'It's difficult. I mean, he said things like – we were talking about Woody Allen and he said he'd like to see his new film and I said so would I and he said, well, why don't we go?'

'Sounds like he was asking you out.'

'But then we started talking about something else. He didn't exactly get his diary out and say, let's make a date.'

'Looks like you're going to have to ring him up and make a date.'

'I don't know, Em,' says Petra. 'It's just all such a hassle. I don't know if I can be bothered.'

'For George? Of course you can.'

Petra laughs. 'Actually, his name's Darren.'

'Oh dear.'

'I know.'

'Even so, it's still worth it. I mean, a good-looking single man of forty-odd—'

'Thirty-nine actually.'

'Even better. A younger man.'

Petra laughs again. 'I'll think about it,' she says. 'Anyway, how are you? Any news?'

'I'm OK,' says Emily slowly. She tells Petra about the storm and Raffaello's appearance with the dog in his arms. She doesn't tell her about the meeting on Tuesday night. *They think he murdered his wife.*

'God! It sounds like something out of *Wuthering Heights*. What is he like, this archaeologist?'

'All right. Not my type. Black curly hair and a beard.'

'A beard? Gross. Still, he could always shave it off.'

'Maybe but he's still not for me.'

'How are the kids? How's Paris?'

'Paris is OK. She's actually been a bit happier since we got the dog. She adores him. Siena is still with the ghastly boyfriend. Charlie is a darling. His asthma seems to have gone completely and he doesn't seem to be allergic to nearly so many things.'

'Well, give them my love. Look, I'd better go. I can hear Harry moving about upstairs. Bye, Em.'

'Bye.'

It is only afterwards, when Emily has gone downstairs and let Totti out for his first wild gallop through the fig trees, that she realises that she didn't ask Petra how Harry was. Or Jake.

Siena is woken by the sound of Totti barking amongst the fig trees. Stupid dog, she thinks, lying back and watching the bars of early morning sun shining through her shutters. Totti was turning out to be almost as embarrassing as Paris. What had Paris called Giancarlo last time she saw him? Yes, a *libertine*. What a ridiculous word. Actually, she'd had to look it up because she didn't understand it at first. She has to hand it to Paris, she knows a lot of words. And, luckily, Gianni hadn't understood it at all. But, *libertine?* 'A morally dissolute person', that's what her dictionary had said. She'd had to look up 'dissolute' too.

Siena lies in bed, feeling very conscious of her body beneath her sheet and single blanket. Last night was the first time she'd needed a blanket in months. Summer must be nearly over. She shivers, though in fact she is hot now, with the sun falling across her bed. She feels the shiver running the length of her body, right down to her silver-painted toes. She is aware of everything: the warmth of the sun, the cool sheet, the bees buzzing somewhere in the eaves, Totti barking in the garden. Is this awareness, this uncomfortable, prickly consciousness of her body, a sign that she is ready for sex? Gianni would say so, *has* said so, would doubtless say so again tonight and the next night. 'If you loved me, you would sleep with me,' he says, his bottom lip stuck out slightly, his dark eyes accusing. But she does love him, she nearly died when they came back to Italy and she thought she'd lost him. She'd never believed the story about the lost mobile. How stupid did he think she was? But she understood this: she'd been given another chance.

If she sleeps with him, surely that means they will be together forever. Not that people always marry their first lovers, she knows that. Even Mum told her this really embarrassing story about her first boyfriend, some medical student called Michael. Although she didn't actually say so in so many words, Siena knew she was meant to understand that Mum had slept with this Michael. 'I thought he was the one,' Mum had said, with this really sad little smile. Yes, but look how much Mum knows about men. She lost this Michael and now she's lost Dad. And Siena knows, though Paris doesn't, that Dad has found a new woman. She rang Dad once and this woman answered the phone. Quite nice, posh voice, sounded youngish.

Anyway, she'd asked Mum and Mum had said that, yes, Daddy had got a girlfriend but don't tell the others as they wouldn't understand. Siena was happy with that (Paris really didn't understand *anything*) but she did feel a bit sorry for Mum. Poor thing, she's far too old to find another man now. Anyhow, she's got Totti and everyone knows that dogs are good company.

So Mum was no use. Sometimes, Siena even wished she could talk to Petra because Petra seemed more modern than Mum somehow. She understood the way the world was, not just because she wore more fashionable clothes but because she seemed to live a more modern life, being a teacher and a single mother and all that. Mum seemed to be stuck in some awful time warp, floating about in this old house, shopping at the market, trying to garden, writing those soppy articles.

A couple of days ago Emily had tried to talk to her about Giancarlo. 'I understand,' she had said, 'that you like Giancarlo very much and he is very good looking—'

'You told Paris that he looked like a lizard in chinos.'

Emily had the grace to blush. 'Paris quoted that right out of context. The point is, I know *you* like him and I worry that he might pressure you to do something you're not ready for.'

'Like what, Mum?' Siena wasn't going to make it easy for her.

'Like, you know, sex and things.'

'Sex *and things?* What do you mean, *and things?*'

'Oh, you know,' said Emily irritably. 'I worry that he'll pressure you to sleep with him and that you'll regret it.'

'What if I sleep with him and don't regret it?' Siena had asked.

But now she has to admit that she is worried about the whole *irrevocableness* of it. If she sleeps with him that will be it, she'll have no bargaining power left, and what if he still leaves her? God, if only you could lose your virginity by a text message, she'd do it like a shot. Send Gianni a text saying 'Fuck me' and then it would be all over. But, then, would he ever call her again?

In the shower, feeling the hot, hard water on her body, she thinks, yes, she will definitely do it. It seems stupid to agonise over it. She'll be seventeen soon, for God's sake. And part of her wants to sleep with him very much. The trouble is, that's all she really wants to do, sleep. She wants to lie against his beautiful brown chest and feel him breathe. She wants him to cuddle her all night and wake her up by kissing her neck. If only he'd be satisfied with that. But he wants to have sex and, now, every time he kisses her, she feels that she is letting him down. She is being stupid and childish and, God forbid,

English. 'English girls are very cruel,' he said to her last night. She understood the implications of that, all right. Sooner or later he'd find a girl who wasn't so cruel and wasn't so English. Someone who'd have sex without turning an immaculately groomed hair. Someone else.

Going slowly downstairs, she thinks, if he loved me he wouldn't pressurise me. But then her thoughts skitter away from that like a moth trapped behind glass. She knew when he didn't contact her for those two days, that the power in the relationship has changed. She knows it every time he laughs and jokes with Angela from the café. She knows it every time he says that Paris is getting quite pretty. She knows it every time he doesn't answer her texts, every time he loses his phone, every time he wants to meet her in the piazza instead of collecting her from the house. She knows he doesn't love her and oddly, scarily, this doesn't seem to stop her from loving him. It only makes her more determined to hold on to him. Whatever it takes.

They eat breakfast sitting on the terrace. The leaves on the ivy are turning yellow but the sun is still hot as it breaks through the awning of vine leaves. The grapes are ready to pick now and Siena plucks one and eats it with her Weetabix.

'We should make wine really' says Emily vaguely.

'I hate wine,' says Paris, predictably, feeding Totti with crusts.

'Don't feed him,' says Emily. 'He's getting far too fat.'

'He was hungry,' says Paris, in the special baby voice that she puts on solely for Totti's benefit. 'Weren't you sweetie-kins?'

'Why does Paris talk to Totti like that?' asks Charlie, who has certainly never heard that honeyed voice directed to *him*.

'Because she's mad, that's why,' says Siena briskly, leaning back in her chair and letting the sun warm her wet hair.

'You can talk,' says Paris. 'It wasn't me who missed a Johnny Depp film, *in English*, just so she could listen to Giancarlo's crummy band rehearse.'

'They're not crummy,' retorts Siena. 'They've nearly got a recording deal.'

'Yeah, and I'm nearly the Pope.'

'Girls,' says Emily warningly though she is only half listening. She is reading this week's article and thinking how boring it sounds. Can anyone really be interested in the recipe for torta della nonna? Anyone apart from Nonna, that is.

'Mum. Raffaello,' says Paris.

'What?'

'Raffaello. There, coming up the hill.'

Emily stands up and sees Raffaello approaching through the olive trees. He is pushing aside the silvery branches like an explorer fighting his way through the jungle. He is wearing a baseball cap and looks hot and rather cross.

'Hello,' says Emily. 'Would you like some coffee?'

'Just water please,' says Raffaello as he reaches the terrace. He pulls off his cap and his hair springs up wildly. He has scratches on both arms and his T-shirt is ripped. He sinks down on the stone bench and Totti immediately comes over and puts his head on his lap.

'Good dog,' says Raffaello, grinning at Paris. 'You know your true master.'

'He's our dog now,' says Paris. 'He's got a collar.'

'And has he got a name?'

'Totti. After Francesco Totti.'

'Totti! That amateur. What's wrong with Alessandro del Piero?'

'His name doesn't sound like a dog's name, that's what.'

'Good point,' says Raffaello.

Emily puts a glass of water in front of him and asks, 'What are you doing here so early?'

Raffaello takes a gulp of water. 'I think I've found something,' he says. 'Up by the caves.' He drains the water and holds out his glass for a refill.

'What is it?' asks Paris excitedly 'Is it a tomb?'

'I don't think so,' says Raffaello. 'But I have found some bodies.'

CHAPTER 6

Emily feels slightly nervous as she drives into Monte Albano for the book club evening. What if Monica really has only asked her there to quiz her about Paul and her failed marriage? What is the Italian word for 'unfaithful bastard'? What if they are all impossibly beautiful Italian women, with perfect nails, wearing designer clothes? Emily's hands, clenched on the steering wheel, are still slightly muddy from picking olives earlier. And she is wearing jeans (size 14 jeans, she adds despairingly to herself). She is sure no one else will ever even have heard of size 14.

Monica's apartment is on the top floor of a palazzo in the very centre of Monte Albano. By the time Emily reaches the top of the twisting staircase she is quite out of breath. 'Some flowers for you,' she manages to pant, thrusting some wilting roses in Monica's face (she knows enough not to bring lilies; these are considered bad luck in Italy).

'*Grazie*,' says Monica. 'How kind.' She ushers Emily into a long sitting room which seems to be full of flowers and antiques. At the end of the room, the doors are open onto a tiny balcony overlooking the piazza. The evening light casts long shadows over a piano, a carved wooden sofa and a table laid with impressive-looking food and numerous small tables overflowing with silver-framed photos. 'My *nipoti . . .*' says Monica, seeing Emily looking. 'How do you say it? Nephews.'

Emily, who has never imagined Monica having anything as homely sounding as nephews, makes admiring noises. Antonella, who is sitting on the sofa surrounded by velvet cushions, says, 'Monica, she is the perfect auntie. I wish Andrea had an auntie like her.'

'He has me as well,' says Monica, coming in with a tray of glistening crostini.

'That's true. Lucky him.'

Monica introduces Emily to the fourth woman in the room, who is called Lucia. Emily is relieved to see that, although extremely pretty, Lucia is not a terrifying designer-clad virago. She is even wearing jeans, though they look a depressingly small size. Lucia is an architect, working on the restorations at the church of St Francis in Assisi.

'What a waste of money!' snorts Monica, who clearly has a very personal animus towards the church. 'You should be building hospitals and schools for children.'

'Oh, well, it's our heritage,' says Lucia mildly. 'All those beautiful frescos.'

'Frescos! Italy has too many frescos. You can't move without coming across another stupid picture of the holy family.' Emily is reminded of Don Angelo's dismissal of the fresco of the Annunciation, though she does not dare make this comparison to Monica.

'It is a problem though,' concedes Lucia. 'Every time we dig the foundations for a new building, we find another lot of Roman remains. It slows everything down.'

And bodies, thinks Emily, thinking of Raffaello's grisly discovery. For a second, she has a nightmarish vision of Italy as a country built upon human remains, with Etruscans, Romans, Renaissance noblemen and English expatriates all building their own vainglorious structures, higher and higher, upon the bones of the dead. Aloud she asks, 'What happens when you find the remains? Do you have to stop building?'

'Only if the find is really significant,' says Lucia, taking a delicate bite of her breadstick. 'Usually, we just note the findings, take a photograph and then build on top.' Emily is reminded of the meeting at the *comune* and the Soprintendenza's argument: leave well alone.

'So our multi-storey car parks all have Roman amphitheatres underneath,' says Antonella.

'Best place for them,' says Monica.

'It's a question of layers,' says Lucia. 'If the layers are all in place, future archaeologists can work it out. Technology will have improved so much, they may not even have to dig.'

The book they are reading, a rather syrupy tome entitled *Va' dove ti porta il cuore*, does not occupy them for very long. From Emily's point of view the best thing about the book is that it is short and relatively easy to read. They have a brief conversation about the themes, marriage, infidelity and the importance of the family, before settling down to a more absorbing discussion about men, work and the importance of sex. Emily does not always find the talk easy to follow (her Italian reading is better than her conversation) but she is able to nod vigorously when Monica says she would rather be on her own than with the wrong man and to sigh sympathetically when Antonella says that she has not heard from Andrea's father since she announced her pregnancy, sixteen years ago.

To her relief, no one asks her about Paul.

Monica is talking about her ex-boyfriend, a painter who claimed to need to be free for his art but is now married with four children. Emily thinks of Michael and the lurch in her heart when she learnt that he was married.

'I still think about my old . . . *amico speciale*,' she says, 'and I haven't heard from him for twenty years.'

'Twenty years!' says Monica. 'He must have been special.'

'He was,' says Emily, taking a gulp of wine. 'He was my first . . . you know.'

The women all nod understandingly. It turns out that Lucia is married but her husband is away working in Rome ('there are no jobs around here') so the four of them are united in their solitary state.

'It's hard to meet someone new,' says Monica, 'especially when you live in a tinpot town like this. Especially when you work with children. Week after week, the only men I see are that mad priest and the man who delivers my pizza on a Friday.'

'Oh, Gennaro. He's quite cute,' says Antonella.

'I know,' says Emily. 'The only man I have seen recently is Raffaello and he only wants to talk about dead bodies.'

Since she is a little tired and a little drunk, she doesn't at first realise the impact of this statement. She takes another slug of wine (she *must* stop drinking, she has to drive home) and looks up to find the other three staring at her.

'Raffaello Murello?' asks Monica. 'The archaeologist?'

'Yes.'

'When do you see him?'

'Well, he's digging near my house,' says Emily rather defensively.

'I didn't think the dig was approved,' says Lucia. This is true and Raffaello has admitted as much. His excuse for carrying on is that if he waited for official approval, the human race might well die out before he can begin his excavations.

'Do you like him?' asks Monica curiously.

Emily thinks for a minute before answering. She thinks of Raffaello appearing on her doorstep, huge and sinister, outlined against the storm. She thinks of him sitting in her kitchen, drinking her coffee and teasing Paris about the dog. She thinks of him at the meeting, isolated on the dais, and the oddly vulnerable look in his eyes as Olimpia attacked him.

'Yes,' she says at last. 'I do like him.'

'He's quite sexy, I have to admit,' says Antonella. 'But all that business about Chiara, it makes me a little afraid of him.'

'Who is Chiara?' asks Emily though she thinks she can guess.

'His wife,' says Monica after a short pause. 'She was from Monte Albano, you know. In fact, she was the niece of your cleaner, Olimpia. Well, they were childhood sweethearts and they got married but Raffaello was away a lot, digging here and there, you know. Well, Chiara got sick and she wouldn't leave the house and, in the end, well—'

'She died,' says Antonella. 'She starved to death.'

'*What?*' says Emily. Antonella's words sound too gruesome, too gothic for this setting. For the antiques and the flowers on the balcony and the plates of dainty finger food. People don't starve to death in this day and age. Not in Italy anyway.

'They didn't find her,' says Monica, 'for weeks. Not until Raffaello got back from wherever he'd been digging.'

'So he found her?'

'Yes.'

'How awful for him.'

'Yes,' says Monica, thoughtfully peeling a peach. Then she says, 'But a lot of people blamed him, you see. She'd been so sick and he hadn't got help for her. Some people said—'

'Well, Olimpia said,' corrects Antonella.

'Yes, Olimpia's hardly been his greatest fan over the years. Well, she said that he kept her locked up.'

'What?' says Emily again.

'Olimpia was very fond of Chiara. Well, she was a lovely girl.

I remember her from school. Anyway, she says, and a lot of people believe it, that Raffaello drove her mad, then kept her locked up and left her to die.'

'Why would he do that?' asks Emily.

Monica shrugs. 'I don't know. Perhaps he had another woman. Most of them do.'

'Archaeologists?'

'Men.'

Emily thinks of Paul and his flight into the arms of an independently wealthy fitness trainer from Cirencester. 'It's amazing that he came back,' she says in English. 'Raffaello, I mean.'

'Oh, he came back for the Etruscans,' says Monica. 'He's obsessed with finding those remains.'

'But at the meeting,' says Emily, 'you were on his side.'

'Well, yes, I'm always on the side of science against religion,' says Monica, rather proudly. 'I think the last thing this town needs is another old heap of stones but if that old nutcase Don Angelo is against it, then I'm for it.'

'But you know,' says Antonella in her gentle voice, 'Don Angelo has always believed Raffaello's story. He doesn't think he killed Chiara.'

Emily remembers Don Angelo coming to Raffaello's aid at the meeting and Raffaello's look of silent gratitude.

'But people seem to believe Olimpia,' she says, thinking of the faces of the townsfolk as Olimpia stood up to address Raffaello. She thinks of the woman at *Ferragosto*: 'He is a devil.'

'Well, she has a lot of influence, you know. Her son's the local doctor and her father was the chief of the partisans in the war. A lot of people respect her family.'

'The war was a long time ago.'

Monica laughs hollowly. 'Not for Italians, believe me.'

Siena and Paris are playing cards. For the second time in two weeks, Emily has left them in charge of Charlie and they are quite enjoying the sensation. Siena has reasons of her own for submitting to such tame entertainment on a Saturday night but, for some reason, neither of them really minds being alone in the house any more. The presence of Totti, snoring in front of the television, helps but, though neither of them discuss it, they both feel that if they could survive the night of the storm, they can survive anything.

They have switched on *Dad's Army*, more from reflex than anything else, but, since they both know it by heart, they have turned down the sound and are playing double rummy at the huge dining table at the far end of the room. A tiny, barred window looks out over the dark valley and the light from the (modern, very expensive) chandelier casts a conspiratorial glow on the table. Paris lays down her cards with a professional swagger.

'I'm out.'

'Paris! How can you be?'

'I'm a better player than you,' says Paris simply. 'Shall we play again?'

'All right,' says Siena, though she has now lost three games in a row. She starts to shuffle the cards, noticing that Charlie has coloured the ace of hearts green. That ought to help her recognise it, she thinks. She'd make a rotten card shark.

'Why do you think she doesn't ask Olimpia to babysit any more?' she asks Paris, dealing briskly.

Paris shrugs. 'She doesn't like Olimpia much, does she? And maybe she thinks we're grown-up enough to look after Dear Little Charlie.'

Siena grins. '*Dear* Little Charlie.' This is the start of one of their favourite routines.

'He's *so* sweet.'

'*Such* an angel.'

'No trouble at all.'

'My baby!'

'He's so perfect. OK, so he still wears a nappy at three and he throws a tantrum if you don't let him have his own way but he really is *absolutely perfect*.' This last is Paris, who always has to go over the top.

'But actually,' says Siena, squinting at her cards, 'I think he has got a bit better.'

'Like how?'

'Well, he didn't have a tantrum when we wouldn't let him stay up tonight. And he's quite sweet with Totti.'

'I'll take your word for it,' says Paris, laying her cards on the table with a flourish. 'I'm out.'

*

Charlie is lying in his bed but he's not asleep. He can hear the girls downstairs playing one of their stupid card games. They never want to do interesting things with the cards, like make little houses and hide toy soldiers underneath them. They just want to say silly made-up words that they think are so clever, like 'trumps' and 'tricks' and 'heartsclubsdiamondsspades'. Mummy says teach Charlie but Paris says he's too stupid to learn. He's not stupid though. He knows all sorts of things. He knows that Totti likes him best really, he knows that Mummy cries at night sometimes, he knows that Paris hides Mars bars in the old oven and he knows that there is a man in the house, right at this minute, watching them.

It is after midnight when Emily leaves Monica's apartment. She can't think how it has got to be so late. Still, at least it has given her the chance to sober up a bit. She has had three espressos and her head is buzzing. She embraces Monica in the hallway, which is crowded with more antiques, including a curly hat-stand that reminds Emily of Vittorio's.

'It's been a lovely evening. Thank you.'

Monica smiles, slightly sardonically. 'Don't mention it.'

As she drives home through the inky-black night, Emily feels happier than she has felt for a long time. She has finally found some Italian women friends. Of course, they can never replace Petra and her English friends (and she can only understand one word in seven that they say) but it is still a start. She realises how much she has missed having friends to talk to. Emails are all very well but she has missed the cosy pleasure of sitting around with friends and just chatting. *Chiacchierata,* that is the Italian word for chat. It's wonderfully onomatopoeic and apt, too, as the Italians spend more time chatting than any other people she knows. Standing on street corners, sitting outside cafés, holding up traffic at the lights, leaning out of windows, yelling from balcony to balcony. *Chiacchierata, chiacchierata, chiacchierata.*

But, for all that she enjoyed it, the chat had some dark moments. She is troubled by the story of Raffaello and Chiara. It has all the more disturbing elements of a fairy tale. The beautiful princess locked up in the tower, spinning gold out of silences. The evil king, the robber baron, riding off into the hills and abandoning her. Does she believe that Raffaello is capable of this? She doesn't know, she only knows that she badly wants to keep Raffaello in the light of day: dog rescuer, bringer of much-needed relief to her family, the only man in the world who thinks she is organised. She badly wants him to stay on the side of the angels.

As she turns into the unmade road she sees the pile of rubble, now moved to the side of the road, ghostly under its tarpaulin, and wonders exactly what Raffaello is doing up there in the hills. The excavation seems quite organised, with teams of fresh-faced students from Bologna University coming every day with their spades and trowels and portable radios. Who is paying them? she wonders. Or do they do it purely 'to add to the sum of human knowledge'?

The Villa Serena is in darkness, the crickets *chiacchierating* like anything. She stops for a minute to breathe in the scent of basil, lemon balm and thyme from the garden. She realises now that she is resigned to letting the herbs grow where they like and will never have her perfect herb garden. As she approaches the back door, she can hear Totti barking madly. Stupid dog. He must know it's only her. Why's he carrying on like this? 'Shh, Totti,' she hisses, opening the door which is unlocked as usual. Totti greets her ecstatically, jumping up and licking her face, but then he immediately heads back through the house to the front door and starts barking again.

'Totti!' Emily chases after him. 'Be quiet! You'll wake the kids.' Totti stops barking but he keeps looking at the door, whining, his head on one side. 'What is it?' Emily asks him. The front door is bolted (ridiculous, she knows, when the back door is left open) and the hall is in darkness, the dark-wood furniture looming unpleasantly. She remembers the night of the thunderstorm and her frantic search for matches. Quickly, she switches on the overhead light. Everything looks better now and the furniture retreats to its usual places but Totti is still looking at the door and whining. Exasperated, Emily lifts the heavy iron latch and opens the front door. Totti shoots out into the darkness barking but there is nothing in sight except the driveway with her car parked on it and the cypress trees, black against black.

'See, Totti,' says Emily, going out to call the dog. 'There's nothing there.' It is only as she turns to go back into the house that she sees the skull on her doorstep.

CHAPTER 7

That night Emily dreams of Michael. Nothing surprising in that; after they split up she had dreamt about him every night for almost a year. Awful, heartbreaking dreams where they had got back together and Emily would wake, cocooned in happiness (it was all a mistake!) and feel reality creep back in with the first cold light of dawn.

This time, though, she wakes feeling oddly frightened. The room seems cold, empty, the morning sun casting harsh bars of light across the white walls. A fly, one of the last flies of summer, buzzes helplessly in the rafters. Everything is as it should be. So why does she feel so nervous, as if she is waiting for something to happen?

The church bells, ringing across the valley, make her jump. Of course, it is Sunday. Slowly the events of last night come back to her. The book group, the pleasure of the talking and laughing with other women, the drive back home, the house, peaceful in the moonlight, Totti barking at the door, the skull on the doorstep.

She had not known what to do with the skull. She had not wanted to bring it into the house and she did not want the children to find it in the morning. Eventually, she had picked it up and carried it to the terrace where there was a barbeque covered with a tarpaulin. The barbeque, expensive, black and gleaming, had been one of Paul's purchases but Emily never used it. There was an outside pizza oven that was much easier to use and didn't require endless cleaning and oiling. So, Emily picked up the skull (it was surprisingly light), put it on the barbeque under the tarpaulin and went back into the house, Totti trotting happily beside her.

Who could have put it there? It hadn't been there when she left for the book group because she would have seen it when she got into the car. That left the truly terrifying thought that someone must have come to the house in the dark, while the children were alone inside, and left the skull on the doorstep. Why? Was it a warning and, if so, what for? Suddenly she thinks of Raffaello. He thinks he has found some bodies. Does this, in fact, mean skeletons? Was the skull from this recent, grisly find or was it Etruscan? She has no idea how you tell if bones are old or not. The skull had certainly looked clean and white, gleaming in the darkness. Should she tell Raffaello? Clear as a church bell she hears Monica's voice in her head: 'Raffaello drove her mad, then kept her locked up and left her to die.' How much does she trust Raffaello?

Shivering, Emily gets up and has a hot shower. While she is in the shower Charlie barges in and demands to come in with her. Holding his slippery, wet body under the water, she thinks, who hates her enough to try to frighten her, and her children, out of their wits? Olimpia? She certainly dislikes Emily but Emily doesn't think she would want to scare her beloved Charlie. And why a skull? Does it have some sinister meaning that she is unaware of? Paul had been a great fan of the *Godfather* films and she remembers a character in one of the films being sent a dead fish as a message. It meant apparently that some mobster was 'sleeping with the fishes'. Was the skull a message that she was about to die? Dust to dust, ashes to ashes?

Nonsense, she tells herself, drying Charlie briskly; she is becoming carried away by lurid Mafia fantasies. This is Tuscany, after all, not Sicily. The skull was probably meant as a joke, because of the archaeological work on her land. Not a very funny joke, she thinks grimly, walking downstairs with Charlie, but a joke all the same.

She gives Charlie his breakfast and, when he is happily playing with his cars, she goes quickly out to the terrace. The girls are still asleep and Totti is chasing rabbits in the olive grove. It is a beautiful morning, calm and golden, still misty in the valley and fresh with the first faint chill of autumn. The bells ring out joyfully as Emily approaches the sinister green tarpaulin. Perhaps it won't be there. Perhaps it was all a dream. Gingerly, she lifts the corner of the tarpaulin.

'Mrs Robertson!'

Emily screams and drops the tarpaulin. Raffaello stands grinning under the vine leaves, Totti at his side.

'What is this?' he asks. 'Guilty conscience?'

'You just scared me, that's all,' says Emily, trying to get her breath back.

'I thought we had all agreed that I wasn't an axe murderer.'

Emily laughs loudly. 'Don't be ridiculous. I was just surprised to see you here this early.'

Raffaello looks at his watch. 'It's not that early. I've been digging since eight.'

'It's Sunday' says Emily. 'Day of rest and all that.'

'Rest is overrated, in my opinion,' says Raffaello. 'Now are you going to tell me what's under that tarpaulin?'

Shrugging, Emily pulls back the tarpaulin to reveal the skull, grinning evilly in the morning sun.

'*Dio mio*,' breathes Raffaello. 'Where did you get that?'

'It was left on my doorstep last night.'

'My God.' He comes closer, looks at the skull for a long minute before picking it up and turning it over in his hands. He looks like a hairy, Italian Hamlet.

'Is it Etruscan?' asks Emily.

Raffaello laughs. 'Etruscan! God, no! It's modern. A hundred years old at the most.'

Emily marvels again at Raffaello's definition of modern. 'Is it from the . . . you know . . . the other bodies? The ones that you found.'

Raffaello shakes his head.

'How do you know? Have you checked?'

In answer, Raffaello holds the skull out to her. Stamped on its base is a tiny number, 192.

'What's that?' asks Emily, shivering, thinking of concentration camp victims with numbers tattooed on their arms.

'I think it means that this is an exhibit. From a medical school or a museum. They number the pieces of the skeleton, you see.'

'But how did it get here?' Emily almost wails.

'I don't know,' says Raffaello, 'but I have an idea.'

It is late afternoon. Emily sits on the terrace, facing away from the tarpaulin, and tries to write her 'Thoughts from Tuscany'. 'Sunday mornings at the Villa Serena . . .' she types, and stops to take a swig of water. God, she feels dehydrated. It must be the espressos last night on top of all that wine. Below the terrace she can hear Charlie playing with his stuffed animals. He is making the tiger eat Mowgli, which Emily finds rather worrying. Siena is out with Giancarlo and Paris has taken Totti for a walk.

'Sunday mornings at the Villa Serena,' she types, 'the bells ring across the valley . . .' And crack my head open because I've got a hangover, she adds wryly to herself. What the hell can she say about Sundays in Italy? The bells ring all day and the Co-op is shut so you run out of bread and your children sulk because they can't eat Marmite sandwiches? No, not nearly lyrical enough. Has she mentioned the sunset recently? It must be about time for a good sunset.

'Mum!' Charlie suddenly appears beside her, all bare brown legs and tousled hair. Emily reaches out to hug him but he neatly evades her.

'Mum! I'm bored!'

'Why don't you play another game with your animals?'

'They're all eaten. By the tiger.'

'Oh dear.'

'No, they like being eaten.'

Emily sighs and shuts her laptop. 'Shall we go for a walk?' she says. 'Go and feed the hens?' Anna-Luisa has hens which run free in her garden, sometimes roosting in the olive trees like ungainly songbirds. She also has a herd of the white cows for which the Mountains of the Moon are famous. Emily always hopes that Charlie will not ask what happens to their sweet white calves.

'All right,' Charlie says grudgingly.

Emily drinks some more water and gathers up some crusts for the hens. Charlie puts on his policeman's helmet and says that he is a spaceman. Together, they walk down the steep, stony track that leads to Romano and Anna-Luisa's farm.

'Mum,' says Charlie chattily as they head down the hill, scattering the loose stones beneath their feet. 'Do you believe in the tooth fairy?'

Emily looks at him. Charlie recently lost a tooth and she had left a euro and a note from the fairies under his pillow. Has Paris been telling him that the tooth fairy doesn't exist? She really is too nasty sometimes.

'Of course I believe in her,' she says sharply.

'How does she get into our house?'

'By magic, of course.'

'Does she look at me when I'm asleep?'

Emily stops. 'What do you mean?' she asks.

Charlie's face is bland. 'Nothing. Next time, can I have two euros?'

Emily thinks of beauty and death, of the skull beneath the skin. Do the locals resent her because she lives in this beautiful house and they live in tiny apartments in Monte Albano? But she knows that, to most Italians, a modern apartment is worth a hundred crumbling villas. Italians are great ones for communal living (even the ancient Romans lived in three-storey apartment buildings) and for modern bathrooms. She can't imagine that anyone would envy her anyway, abandoned by her husband, blatantly struggling to bring up her children. Was the skull maybe another type of warning? *Et in Arcadia ego.* Even here, there is death.

As they reach the gate to the farm, Emily hears voices coming from the other side of the lavender hedge.

'You have to be careful,' says one voice. 'Give him a little bit of food at a time.'

'I give him my food,' says the other voice. 'I'm too fat as it is.' It is Paris. Paris and Raffaello.

There is a pause and then Raffaello says, in a voice Emily has never heard him use before, 'Paris. That is dangerous talk. You have to feed yourself and you have to feed your dog. Understand?'

Paris mumbles something in reply and then Totti barks and Charlie rushes through the gate, yelling, 'My doggie! My doggie!'

Paris and Raffaello are standing beside a neatly dug trench which is running the length of the lavender hedge. Raffaello is holding a diamond-shaped trowel and Paris is holding a small stone. Totti has a bone in his mouth, which must have been why they were discussing his eating habits.

'Are you sure that isn't an Etruscan bone?' asks Emily brightly.

Raffaello and Paris both raise their eyes heavenwards. 'It's the shin bone of a cow,' says Raffaello. 'It won't hurt him.'

'Mum,' says Paris, 'Raffaello says we have to feed Totti little and often.'

'As opposed to continuously,' says Emily. 'He's probably right.'

'I usually am,' says Raffaello. Emily ignores him.

'Are you going to throw that stone for Totti?' she asks Paris.

'It's not a stone,' Paris says pityingly. 'It's an arrowhead.'

Raffaello nods. 'Probably Neolithic. You can find examples of worked stone all over these hills.'

Charlie is trying to get the bone away from Totti. 'Mu-um,' he whines, 'I want to go to the farm.'

Emily gives him the bag of crusts. 'Go with Paris,' she says.

Suddenly Paris drops her world-weary air. 'Come on!' she shouts to Charlie. 'I'll race you.'

As Paris, Charlie and Totti race down the slope, the dog barking, the children's hair flying, Raffaello smiles at Emily. 'Have you found any more skulls?' he asks.

'No,' says Emily. 'Aren't you going to tell me who you think left it there?'

'Not until I'm sure,' says Raffaello. 'But don't worry, I don't think you're in any danger.'

'Easy for you to say,' says Emily sulkily, running her foot along the edge of the trench.

Raffaello laughs. 'I'll protect you, Mrs Robertson.'

There is a short silence, then Emily says, in a rush, 'Have you found out any more about your skeletons. The modern ones?'

'No,' says Raffaello, picking up the arrowhead, which Paris has dropped in her haste. 'I don't want to do any more excavation on that site until I find out more about the bodies. I want them examined by an expert, I don't want the layers disturbed. For that I really need a forensic archaeologist I'm going to see one tomorrow, in Badia Tedalda.'

Emily has never heard the phrase 'forensic archaeologist' before. It seems to her to combine two equally unpleasant disciplines – cutting up bodies and digging up the past.

Raffaello is looking past her, down into the valley. They can hear the children's voices, punctuated by Romano's Tuscan growl.

'You can come with me, if you like,' Raffaello says suddenly.

'To Badia Tedalda?'

'Yes. It's a nice trip.' He grins at her. 'Up into the Mountains of the Moon.'

'What about the children?'

'We can be there and back before Charlie is out of school.'

Emily does not know what to say. A trip into the mountains seems to take their relationship into another dimension, away from the safety of the Villa Serena and jokes about the dog. Instead of answering, she asks a question that has been on her mind a lot recently. 'You know,' she says, 'I've never asked. Why are they called the Mountains of the Moon?'

'Well,' says Raffaello slowly, 'the most usual explanation is that the white stone in the mountains gleams in the moonlight and looks like the surface of the moon. There is another story though.' He pauses.

'What?'

'Hundreds of years ago, a countess used to meet her lover up in the mountains. They met by moonlight. Then, one night, he didn't come. She leapt to her death.'

'She committed suicide?'

'Yes.'

They are both silent. Emily is thinking uncomfortably of the locked doors and the princess dying in her tower. To break the tension, she says, 'Thank you for what you said to Paris.'

'What?'

'About eating. I worry about her. She's so thin.'

'You are right to be worried,' says Raffaello bluntly. 'She's far too thin.'

Far from being offended, Emily is acutely relieved. She is so used to people like Petra saying that Paris is fine, she's just naturally thin, and feeling embarrassed, as if she is compensating for her own increased weight by going on about Paris, that it is incredibly comforting to hear someone say that, yes, she is right to be worried.

Raffaello continues, looking away from Emily, his face in shadow. 'And her self-image is bad. She lacks confidence so she exercises the only power she has, by refusing to eat.'

Emily gapes at him. This is the second time that he has shocked her by sounding like a woman's magazine.

'What do you know about it?' she asks. It comes out more rudely than she intended.

Raffaello shrugs and turns to look at her. 'My wife died of anorexia,' he says. 'Now what about that trip into the mountains?'

Emily stares at him. She can hear Paris and Charlie coming back up the hill, arguing gently. In the distance, the bells start ringing again. 'Yes,' she says. 'I'd like to come.'

CHAPTER 8

Thoughts from Tuscany
By Emily Robertson

Sunday mornings at the Villa Serena, the bells ring across the valley and reverberate in my head because *I've got a hangover*. I was out late last night with a newly discovered species: Italian women who are neither mammas nor madonnas. Professional women, two teachers and an architect. Single women (either through choice or circumstance) who love their jobs and their families but who would also like to meet a man one day. Friends, I suppose you'd call them.

As I stayed up late, chatting and drinking with these friends, I thought about my life and the choices I have made. I wanted to come to Italy; it was my dream, no one else's. I thought that here, in this beautiful place, I would have the perfect life. That my family would be happy and united. That my husband and I would rediscover our marriage.

Instead, my middle child, in the midst of the culinary splendour that is Italy, is battling with anorexia. She weighs barely six stone and you can see the skull beneath her skin. She has a fine, pale down on her arms that is her body's last, desperate attempt to keep her warm. She won't see a doctor but she does consent to eat something, however small, whenever the dog eats. The dog eats rather a lot.

My elder daughter is in love with a rotter. The word might be quintessentially English but the genus is universal. He has knowing eyes and a sly grin and I know that he wants to sleep with her. Will she hold out against him? Knowing eyes and a sly grin are attractive when you are sixteen. Will she see through him? Of course not. I didn't. Did you?

My youngest child is spoilt rotten. He is only three but can have tantrums in two languages. He cries for our cleaner, the monstrous Olimpia, but I won't let her babysit because she hates me.

And me? I sit on the terrace and try to write my column. I am forty-one and two stone overweight. My husband has left me for a younger woman and I have no money. My only assets are this house, a grey Alfa Romeo and a sudden belief in my own ability to pull up out of this mess. And my friends.

CHAPTER 9

Autumn becomes more advanced the higher they climb into the mountains. As Raffaello's beaten-up Jeep negotiates the helter-skelter road to Badia Tedalda, Emily notices that the leaves on the trees are turning yellower with each death-defying twist of the tarmac. Finally, they reach an avenue of trees, completely yellow, as if they have travelled in time as well as space.

For a time, Emily amuses herself by looking at the three road signs that flash past regularly every few kilometres. First there is the sign rather like a pair of huge, pneumatic breasts, which indicates hills. Then there is the festive, Christmassy snowflake which must, she assumes, be warning of heavy snows in winter. And finally there is a charming picture of a deer, which appears to be leaping joyously across their path. Breasts, snowflake, deer; eventually they merge in her mind into one monstrous snow-covered, silicone-breasted deer. Emily closes her eyes. Her ears have popped and she thinks they must be very high up.

'Are we nearly there?' she asks, sounding like a parody of her own children.

Raffaello shoots a glance at her. 'Another ten minutes. This road is very slow.' As he has been driving like Michael Schumacher on uppers, she assumes that this is a figure of speech only.

The mountains are densely wooded, with the occasional gleam of white stone. Here and there she sees ploughed fields, the earth rich and brown, or white cows grazing on a vertiginous hillside. Far below she can see the lake, a tributary of the Tiber, that stretches between Sansepolcro and Pieve San Stefano.

'It's very wild,' she says to Raffaello. 'I can almost imagine bandits hiding in the woods.'

Raffaello laughs. 'This is bandit country, all right.' Then he says, 'In the war these hills were called the *Linea Gotica,* the last line of defence between the partisans and the Nazis. They say there was a partisan hiding behind every tree.'

The *Linea Gotica,* the Gothic line. The name strikes Emily with an odd mixture of fear and fascination. 'Was there a lot of fighting up here?' she asks.

'Yes,' says Raffaello, speeding up to overtake on a bend. 'Partisans against Nazis, the Bersaglieri against the partisans, sometimes partisans against partisans.'

Emily has shut her eyes to avoid looking at the road. When she opens them again they are approaching a town perched on the very top of the hill. The breasts, snowflake and deer fly past them.

'Who were the Bersaglieri?'

'Crack Italian troops. They stayed staunchly pro-fascist. Others didn't. My grandfather was a communist, he'd fought in Spain. You can imagine how popular this made my family.'

Emily has completely forgotten that Raffaello was born in Monte Albano. His American accent, his archaeological jargon, his air of slightly amused abstraction, all combined to make him appear an outsider. Someone who appeared out of nowhere. In a flash of lightning.

'What happened to your family?' asks Emily.

'Well, my great-grandparents owned a trattoria—'

'*What*?'

Raffaello looks at her, surprised. 'A restaurant. What's so odd about that? Anyway, at first the Germans used to come and eat in the restaurant every night. They were very friendly, despite knowing that the owners had a communist son. They always left big tips. You see, the Germans had . . . *monete di guerra* . . . war money, that could only be spent in Italy. So they were big tippers. But then those Germans left and the SS arrived. Then everything changed.'

'What happened?'

'A lot of people just left town, went to hide in the hills.' He waves his hand towards the woods that rise, dark and impenetrable, on either side of the road.

'Where did they hide?'

'Well, some people had hunting lodges, or just shelters for the animals. Others lived in caves.'

'Really?'

Raffaello laughs. 'Yes, really. These were desperate times. You could be shot for harbouring a partisan. You could be shot for anything really. One morning, the SS rounded up all the young men, including my grandfather's two younger brothers, and were going to shoot them in the town square. But then orders came from above and they let them go. That was always the way. One day, the Germans would be sharing food and drink with the townspeople, the next minute they would be shooting them.'

'What happened to your grandfather's brothers?'

'One of them became a member of the Cichero Division, the best partisan group in the hills. He was killed in the Genoa uprising. The other kept his head down and became rich.'

'I've never heard of the Genoa uprising.'

Raffaello laughs. 'That's not surprising. History is written by the victors and the English are adept at airbrushing out any examples of Italian heroism.'

Emily tries to think of something to refute this but, when she thinks about the Italians in the war, the only images that come to mind are that of sad-eyed prisoners-of-war on the Isle of Man or of Mussolini, swinging upside down beside his mistress. The only thing she can remember about the Italian army is the old joke about tanks with five reverse gears. She doesn't think she should share this with Raffaello.

'What about your grandfather?' she asks.

'He was killed in Spain. My father never knew him.'

'Are your parents still alive?'

'No. My father died about five years ago, my mother last year. What about your parents?'

'Oh, they're still alive. They live in England, in a small town called Addlestone.'

'You're lucky.'

'What? Oh, yes, I suppose I am.' Emily had never thought of it like this. In her world, parents are still alive, going to bingo or on Saga holidays, perhaps having a timeshare in Spain. It seems a million miles away from the desperate partisans fighting in the hills, fascist from versus communists or the Spanish Civil War. Her father's father fought in the war, she thinks he was in the D-Day landings, but that seems to belong to history books rather than real life. She dimly remembers a picture of her grandfather and some other soldiers standing beside a captured German tank and a story about him getting a piece of shrapnel in his knee ('It travelled all the way to his stomach,' her grandmother used to say, 'and got trapped in his small intestine.').

They have reached the town and Raffaello parks the Jeep at an angle in the main square. There are a few shops and a café with tables outside. The three elderly men sitting silently at the tables look at them with suspicion. In the doorway of a house opposite a woman is plucking a chicken.

'Shall we have a coffee?' asks Emily.

'A coffee,' Raffaello mimics her. 'Only English people say "a coffee". "Let's have a cappuccino."' He says this last in a high-pitched, affected English accent. Emily finds it rather offensive.

They march past the café (the men all turn to look at

them, as if hypnotised) towards a modern building with a sign saying 'Information'. Inside is a small tourist office with framed maps and photographs on the walls and a stuffed wolf in the hallway.

Raffaello has a quick, unintelligible discussion with the girl at the desk and she goes out of the room.

Raffaello turns to Emily. 'She's gone to get Stine. She's in the library.'

'Stine?'

'My friend. The forensic archaeologist.'

Stine turns out to be a stunning, six-foot Danish blonde. Emily who is expecting a bearded, middle-aged man, is momentarily shocked into silence.

'Pleased to meet you,' says Stine, in English, holding out her hand. 'You're the lady with the skeletons.'

It is not quite how Emily likes to think of herself but she manages to smile and say hello. 'They're not, strictly speaking, my skeletons,' she says.

'But I thought they were on your land,' says Stine.

Emily turns to Raffaello who looks away. She had not realised that the hillside with the caves and the skeletons was officially on her land. She wonders if that is why Raffaello has brought her along today.

'It's on the borders of your land,' says Raffaello hurriedly. Then, turning to Stine, 'I think they're modern,' he says.

This is the first Emily has heard of this.

'How do you know?' Stine asks.

Raffaello looks at her. 'I didn't excavate but there was a jawbone. I think I saw a filling.'

'But that must be very modern,' says Emily, thinking of her skull, number 192, which Raffaello has taken away with him. No wonder Raffaello had been so quick to say that it didn't belong with his skeletons. 'Shouldn't you have called the police?'

Raffaello dismisses the police with a shrug. 'I wanted Stine to look first. I don't want the site contaminated.'

Emily realises that he is thinking about his Etruscans. In his mind they take precedence over the recently deceased. But then Raffaello says, 'Another thing, I think they have been buried.'

Stine draws in her breath sharply but Emily doesn't understand the significance of this. 'What do you mean?' she asks.

'I think they have been buried deliberately,' says Raffaello. 'It's not a grave, there's no sign of ritual burial, but I don't think they died naturally. They have been arranged in the ground and earth has been piled on top of them. And the vegetation is different.'

'What does that mean?' asks Emily.

It is Stine who answers. 'A grave is a disturbance,' she says in her perfect, sing-song English. 'Some people call it a footprint of disturbance. If you dig a grave, you break up the layers of topsoil, clay, et cetera. And when you fill in the grave, the layers become mixed. And vegetation grows differently. Nettles grow higher, for example.'

'That's why I need Stine,' says Raffaello. 'This is her speciality.'

'You mean the people in the graves might have been murdered?' Emily says.

'Exactly,' says Raffaello, grinning. For a second he looks exactly like the wolf in the hallway.

Paris is sitting in class, reading. As the lesson is English and she has no need to learn English, she is allowed to read quietly. She is meant to be reading a Primo Levi book but instead she is rereading *Wuthering Heights*. She loves the cold, desolate Englishness of it. She sees herself as Heathcliff though, rather than Catherine, as she always identifies with the male characters in stories. For years, she had a secret identity as Renny, the hero of the Jalna books. Before that it was William Brown.

Paris sits lower in her chair so only her head is visible over her desk. She is uncomfortable and there is an odd, nagging pain in her stomach. It's a bit like one of those pains that are almost pleasurable, like period pains sometimes. Though it has been six months since Paris has had a period. She hasn't told her mother this though she rather despises Emily for not noticing. If she told Emily she might even put on that dreadful worried face and ask if she might be pregnant. Paris's spine recoils at the thought. She can't imagine ever, ever having sex. It's all right for men, for people like Heathcliff and Renny, they can do sex in a hearty, rollicking sort of way, an outdoor activity, a bit like bareback riding or white-water rafting. For women, though, sex seems more of an indoor event; a ghastly, moist, embarrassing experience, fraught with connotations of losing something. She remembers reading some graffiti on the loo door of her school in London. 'Virginity is like a balloon, one prick and it's gone for ever.' Presumably the pricks, too, lose their virginity. But, for a man, the loss doesn't seem to come into it. It's more a question of conquest and achievement, notches on the bedpost and all that stuff. Paris is never going to be a notch on anyone's bedpost.

Has Siena slept with Giancarlo? She hopes not. Not that she cares for her sister's virginity, more that she wants to deny Giancarlo any sort of triumph. She's seen that look on Giancarlo's face when he's with Siena, a sort of 'Look at me, I'm so clever, I've got a blonde, English girlfriend' look. If he persuades his blonde, English girlfriend to sleep with him, he will become even more unbearable. 'You're getting quite pretty,' he said to her the other day. Wanker. 'Wish I could say the same for you,' she had replied.

She shifts again in her chair. She wishes she was at home, lying flat on her stomach. Except that, when she gets home, she'll have to take Totti out for a walk. Mum will be too tired as she will have been on this mysterious journey with Raffaello, 'up into the mountains'. She talked about it as if it was a polar expedition though the mountains are really no more than large hills (though they do have snow on in winter, she has to admit that). Paris doesn't really mind taking Totti for walks. He's so keen, jumping up at her the minute she gets in, grabbing his lead as if it was a trophy, and he's excellent company, better than any human she knows. The bad thing is she'll have to feed him before they go out and she's promised Mum that she'll eat something too, otherwise Mum will go on and on about eating disorders and doctors and other things that it really makes her too cross and wound up to think about. It's just all so embarrassing. *Painfully* embarrassing. She can feel the horrible, sicky pain of it churning round in her stomach. She *hates* talking about it. Still, she has promised and she will do it. Paris prides herself on keeping her promises. Maybe just a piece of melon or something.

Paris tries to concentrate on Catherine dying. She's a bit of a drip really. Girls in books are always dying of stupid things like chills or coughs (they call it consumption but it's still really just a nasty cough). Not the men though; they never die of things like that. She sighs and tucks her legs under her to try to make herself more comfortable. She has identified the odd pain in her stomach; it is hunger.

Siena sits at the café in the piazza and knows that Giancarlo won't come. She has texted him and his phone is switched off. They had arranged to meet at one o'clock and now it is nearly half past. Siena has her afternoons free, theoretically to work, but usually she meets Giancarlo, who is meant to be studying at the technical school in Sansepolcro. He is training to be a master baker.

Siena sips the last of her lemon soda and wonders about ordering another, but she is embarrassed about asking Angela, the curvy waitress, who is, amongst other things, a friend of

Giancarlo's. Angela comes over now, swinging her hips with mechanical provocation.

'*Finito?*' she asks.

'*Sì,*' says Siena. '*Grazie.*' Then she gets up, switches off her mobile and walks slowly out into the bright sunlight.

Charlie is painting a picture. He is trying to paint Totti but all he can really do are the ears. 'That's lovely!' says Monica-with-the-glasses. 'Are they mountains?' Mountains, fountains, mountains of the moon. Mummy is going up a mountain with Raffaello-with-the-beard. He likes Raffaello-with-the-beard. He can walk on his hands and he can whistle with two fingers in his mouth. He likes him better than the other man; the one that just watches. Maybe they'll buy him a present. Daddy always brought presents. Those huge tubes of Smarties with a plastic toy at the top. He'd like a Smartie right now. The orange ones are the best. Monica-with-the-glasses always gives them fruit for a snack. Charlie hates fruit. It makes him feel sick. So sick that only lemonade can cure it. Proper lemonade not that stuff Mummy makes with awful bits of lemon floating in it. Proper lemonade from a shop.

Charlie starts another picture. He's drawing Totti again. He can't see the point of drawing lots of different things. Maybe there'll be a sweet shop on the mountain.

Stine takes Raffaello and Emily to see the finds she is investigating at Badia Tedalda. They climb a steep hill to the church, a plain, Romanesque building clinging to the side of the mountain. The view is spectacular, though Emily is so out of breath she hardly notices it. The church is called San Michele Arcangelo.

Stine unlocks the door and Emily finds herself inside a curious mixture of a church and fortress. The walls are thick and the windows small but there are ceramic frescos around the walls just like the ones in the Palazzo Comunale at Monte Albano. Emily is startled to see Raffaello crossing himself with the holy water. She has never thought of him as a Catholic somehow.

'This church was built on the site of a Roman temple,' says Raffaello as they walk briskly up the aisle towards a door beside the altar.

'The frescos are beautiful.'

'School of della Robbia,' says Raffaello dismissively.

The doorway leads to a small room full of priests' vestments and cleaning gear. There, incongruous amongst the mops, is a large piece of stone archway, beautifully decorated with carvings of leaves.

'*Che bello*,' breathes Raffaello. 'Roman?'

'Yes,' says Stine. 'I think so. It was found when they were building a new house for some foreigners.'

Raffaello grins at Emily. 'These foreigners with their houses and swimming pools are very useful sometimes.'

'The leaves are lovely,' says Emily ignoring him.

'They are oak leaves,' say Raffaello. 'It's a symbol of this area.'

Emily has always thought of the oak as a particularly English tree, but, when she looks closely, she sees that there are acorns interspersed among the leaves. She realises that the Mountains of the Moon are, in fact, covered in oak trees.

As they leave the church, Stine invites them to stay for lunch but Emily says she has to get back for Charlie. Raffaello looks put out, which isn't fair of him as Emily made it clear that she has to collect Charlie from nursery school. She is feeling twitchy now; she has always had a horror of being late for her children.

'*Va bene*,' says Raffaello. 'Stine, will you come down and look at our skeletons?'

'If that is all right with Emily,' says Stine.

Emily, who has been feeling slightly surprised to hear them described as 'our skeletons', says yes, of course.

Stine agrees to come in two weeks' time, when she has finished at Badia Tedalda. They shake hands outside the café, where the same old men still sit, immobile over their espresso cups.

Raffaello says very little on the journey back to Monte Albano. Emily leans forward, worried about the time.

'Don't worry,' says Raffaello, glancing at her. 'You worry too much.'

'I can't help it. Charlie goes mad if I'm late.'

'Charlie is spoilt.'

'He's not!' says Emily furiously. Then, hitting below the belt, 'You wouldn't understand. You haven't got any children.'

'On the contrary,' says Raffaello smoothly, 'I have a daughter in America.'

'But I thought your wife was—'

Raffaello laughs. 'Oh, I'm not married to her mother. But we were together for a long time and the result is Gabriella.'

'Gabriella,' says Emily at last. 'That's a pretty name.'

'She's a pretty girl. She takes after her mother, thank God.'

Emily looks at Raffaello's wild hair and curved, Roman nose and thinks that he is right. His features would be unfortunate on a girl. They look all right on a man though.

'You must miss her,' she says. 'How old is she?'

'Seven,' says Raffaello. 'Yes, I do miss her. I'm hoping to see her next month.'

'Are you going to America?'

'Yes. I worked there for many years, you see. I was a lecturer at Penn State University.'

That explains the American accent. 'Will you stay there for a long time?' Emily asks.

'That depends.'

'On what?'

Raffaello laughs but doesn't answer. They are silent for the rest of the drive down the mountain.

CHAPTER 10

For some reason, Emily finds it hard to settle that evening. Totti doesn't help either, prowling round the house, hackles up, jumping at every shadow. 'You're meant to make me feel safe,' says Emily, dragging Totti out of the sitting room where he has been growling at the table for the last ten minutes, 'not acting as if there's a murderer behind every piece of furniture.' She thinks of Raffaello: 'They say there was a partisan hiding behind every tree.' Has her house suddenly become the front line in some undeclared war? 'Nonsense,' she says to herself, leading Totti into the safety of the kitchen. 'The skull was a one-off. Someone having a joke. It won't happen again.' Totti stiffens and starts growling at the fridge.

'Calm down, Totti,' says Emily, offering him some food. Greed fights with fear in the dog's eyes for a few seconds before greed wins. He settles down to eat, his muscular tail banging against the wall. Emily starts at the noise. God, she is jumpy this evening. She goes to the back door and looks out. An owl calls from the olive grove but, otherwise, all is silence. Emily bangs the door shut and, as an afterthought, locks it.

Charlie is in bed. Siena is in her room with her headphones on, incommunicado. Paris is, rather encouragingly, out with some friends from school ('Are they good friends, darling?' 'Not really.' 'Would you like to invite them home one day?' 'No thanks.'). Emily is meant to be getting on with her next 'Thoughts from Tuscany' but the drive up through the mountains, the meeting with Stine, the starkly beautiful church with its miraculous view and, most of all, the rather disturbing talk with Raffaello on the way back, keeps swirling around inside her head. 'These hills were called the *Linea Gotica* . . . They say there was a partisan hiding behind every tree . . . A grave is a footprint of distur-bance . . . On the contrary I have a daughter in America . . .'

Suddenly the Tuscan hills (described so lovingly in many 'Thoughts') seem to be teeming with desperate partisans, with skulls, bones, skeletons, long-dead Etruscans, long-buried enmi-ties, half-remembered loyalties. And Raffaello himself, is he her guide in this whole bewildering landscape, her protector, or is he part of the mystery, the man who abandoned his wife, who has a child halfway round the world and who cares more for the dead than for the living? Emily sighs and switches on her laptop. She wishes life was as simple as a newspaper column. Nervously, she wonders what Giles, her editor, thought of her last attempt.

After circling maddeningly for a few minutes, Totti eventu-ally settles down in front of the stove and Emily clicks on to

'ThoughtsfromTuscany60'. As she does so, the Facebook icon winks at her. 'What harm can it do?' she thinks. 'Just one last look at his name on Facebook. Just one quick google.'

She is about to type in 'Michael Bartnicki' under 'Search' when she sees a small flag at the bottom of the screen: '1 unread mail message'. She clicks on her in-tray, wondering who could be emailing her. Petra with the latest on George? Her brother Alan from Australia?

The address in the inbox reads: chad.buchanan. Chad! Emily can't remember giving him her email address. Remembers, in fact, that he left the party without even asking for her phone number. She opens the message. It is brief.

> Emily,
> I'm in Bologna for a conference next month. Do you want to meet up?
> Chad.

She hesitates for a long moment, her finger hovering over the delete key.

Paris is almost enjoying herself. She is at Silvia's house and they are listening to The Darkness. 'They come from near me in England,' she says. The Darkness come from East Anglia but she doesn't expect the others will know that. 'Cool,' say Silvia and Paola respectfully. The curtains are drawn and all three girls are wearing black. The only light comes from three candles placed carefully in front of a Metallica poster. Burning joss sticks give the room a musty, dreamy atmosphere that reminds Paris of Brighton.

These, very mild, signs of rebellion – wearing black, burning joss sticks, listening to music played by foreign transvestites – are viewed by Silvia's parents with extreme alarm. On the one hand, they approve of Paris, she is English which they think is classy, her mother is a writer and her sister is extremely pretty. On the other hand, they think she must be a bad influence as, before she came to the school, Silvia was a perfect Italian girl in pleated skirts and loafers. They have even gone as far as to ask Don Angelo for advice. 'How nice that Silvia has a new friend,' said Don Angelo, misunderstanding completely. 'It is wonderful to learn new things from our friends.'

'Do you miss England?' Paola asks. She is painting her finger-nails black and the smell of the nail varnish mingles toxically with the joss sticks.

'Yes,' says Paris, which is what she always says. 'England's so cool. You can wear what you like, do what you like. Nobody talks about football. Most of the men are gay anyway.'

'Cool,' says Silvia but then adds, hesitantly, 'The boys, though, the ones that aren't gay, they aren't very handsome, are they?'

'No,' admits Paris. 'They're pug ugly.'

'Italian boys are stupid,' says Paola, finishing her nails with a flourish. 'But some are very handsome.'

'Yes,' says Paris, leaning over for the black varnish. 'Some are handsome. Is there anything to eat?' She is suddenly very hungry.

CHAPTER 11

Emily does not intend to sleep with Chad in Bologna. Her only plan is to have a bit of a break from the children and to interrogate Chad for news of Michael. She has decided to spend the night in Bologna though not, of course, with Chad. She has taken a room in a small hotel near the station. In the event, she never sees it.

Monica has agreed to come and stay the night and look after the children as Emily thinks a whole night is too much responsibility for Siena and Paris. Charlie adores Monica so is beside himself with excitement. Unfortunately Monica has to go to a conference in the morning so Emily has been forced to ask Olimpia to take over. Still, she won't be late back, especially as this is the day when Stine is due to come to look at the skeletons. The children are beside themselves with excitement at the thought of more grisly finds. Emily tells Raffaello that she is going away for a night 'to see a friend'. Raffaello smiles sardonically. She feels sure he knows it is a man.

Emily likes Bologna. It is a terracotta city, the buildings all in various shades of yellow, orange and pink. It is a city of colonnades, endless lines of covered walkways, filled with young people, lounging, laughing and talking. Above all it is a young city, full of students, far more multicultural than most Italian towns and far grungier too. Instead of the ever-present ironed jeans and white shirts, Emily sees leather jackets, piercings, dreadlocks. Paris would love it, she thinks.

She goes straight to Chad's hotel as she was late leaving home. Just before she left she had a call from Giles, her editor at the paper. His voice, sometimes so posh as to be practically unintelligible, was almost plebeian with irritation.

'Emily what the fuck is this last column all about?'

'I thought I'd try a bit of honesty for a change.'

'Well, don't. Our readers like homemade pasta and Chianti by moonlight. They don't want to hear about your daughter's anorexia, for Christ's sake.'

'But it's true,' said Emily sulkily.

A deep breath down the phone line. In the background Emily could hear two other phones ringing. 'Well, I'm sorry to hear that,' said Giles at last. 'Anything I can do to help and all that. But, in the meantime, write me a column about porcini mushrooms and the olive harvest. There's a good girl.'

Chad's hotel is a very smart one, near the Piazza Maggiore. Emily instantly feels scruffy as she waits in the chrome and marble foyer for Chad to descend. She is wearing a long, red skirt and a white T-shirt. It looked all right in the age-spotted (authentic) mirror in her bedroom, but here it feels too peasanty, not tailored enough. The woman behind the reception desk is wearing a perfectly cut olive linen suit. Emily wishes they could swap clothes, like Siena and her girlfriends used to do.

'Emily!' Chad comes down the stairs wearing a dark, pin-striped suit and a pink shirt. Emily feels even worse about her clothes.

They kiss, awkwardly, on the cheek. In fact, for a second, Emily is so overcome with embarrassment that she wants to run away, straight out of the gilded doors of the hotel, and never see Chad again. It feels all *wrong* somehow, being with Chad in a foreign city, wearing make-up and high heels for him, having the receptionist describe her, with a hint of archness, as 'your visitor'.

'Chad . . .' She begins. She doesn't know what she is going to say. 'I've just remembered I've left the oven on'? 'I've remembered that I never really liked you after all, you were just the friend of someone I was in love with'? 'Let's forget all about it, I'll go home and we won't contact each other for the next twenty years'? But Chad seizes her elbow in a masterful kind of way and steers her out through the swing doors. He looks up and down the street in a businesslike manner. 'I've booked a table at a restaurant,' he says. 'It was recommended by someone at the conference.'

Emily is surprised to find herself thinking that the restaurant is over-priced and pretentious. Maybe she is turning into a real Italian at last. There are no menus, just some swirly writing on a blackboard. The wine list, though, is as thick as a Bible and comes with tassels like a prayer book. Chad orders something red and expensive.

'Is this on expenses?' asks Emily faintly.

'Sure,' says Chad. 'The drug companies will pay.'

Over black risotto with truffles he tells her about his work ('mostly private these days'), his wife ('she's a wonderful horse-woman') and his daughters ('they all play two instruments and do ballet, bloody nightmare'). Emily eats and says very little. She starts to tell him about the bodies on the hillside but he pulls a face and says, 'Bit grisly, isn't it?' She would have thought doctors would be used to bodies.

Over the veal (him) and sea bass (her), he tells her about his house in Wiltshire, his boat in Chichester and his ski chalet in the French Alps. Emily eats and says nothing. He tells her that he likes Italy but the inefficiency drives him mad. He tells her that he thinks aromatherapy, past-life regression and Catholicism are all cons. He tells her that he once had a cabinet minister as a patient.

Finally over tiramisu (him) and sorbet (her), she asks him if he has heard from Michael recently. He looks up, his gambler's face dark in the candlelight.

'He's got problems,' he says. 'Forget about him.'

He pays the bill, pockets the receipt and steers her out of the restaurant. Outside, the streets are thronging with young people, someone is playing a guitar outside the gelateria opposite, three girls walk past, arm in arm, to a chorus of wolf whistles. Chad is marching Emily through the milling, loitering crowds and she is just wondering if she should get a taxi back to her hotel as she has had quite a lot to drink (she had brought the new Marian Keyes novel and maybe she'll be able to watch CNN news), when Chad suddenly steers her into a dark alleyway and kisses her violently.

Emily is amazed, horrified and turned on, all at once. There is no denying that the new, passionate Chad, pushing her against a barred shop window so that she feels the iron grille against her back, is an improvement on the model who sat over his risotto and talked about his boat. All the same, he is married and she isn't in love with him and it all still feels just *wrong*.

'Chad . . .' She manages to push him away.

'What?' He looks at her, panting slightly.

'What are you doing?'

He grins. 'What does it look like?'

'Did you invite me here just so that we could go to bed together?'

He shrugs. 'What's wrong with that? I've always fancied you.' Emily knows she shouldn't be but she is slightly swayed by the compliment. It seems such a long time since anyone has fancied her and Chad is very good looking. Also, the 'always' reminds her of her favourite place, the past.

'You mean you fancied me when I was going out with Michael?'

'Sure,' says Chad. 'He used to tease me about it.' And he starts to kiss her again.

Eventually, he pulls her away from the iron bars and they

walk, arm in arm, back to the hotel. Emily is in a trance, she doesn't particularly want to go to bed with him, but how can she resist? Isn't this how such evenings end? And it is nice, very nice, to feel his arm round her and occasionally to feel his lips brush her hair. It would take more willpower than she has got to break away now, back to safety and the Marian Keyes novel.

Back in his hotel room, Chad is on top of her like a madman. For some reason, Emily expects him to be a sophisticated, resourceful lover. Michael had been the master of the long drawn-out foreplay (so long, she has to admit, that sometimes she just used to long for him to get on with it) and she imagines that all doctors are similarly attuned to the human body. But Chad, she remembers, finds bodies a bit grisly. Anyway, he puts on a condom and is on top of her and inside her without more than the most perfunctory nibblings and lickings. Afterwards he actually, she can't quite believe it for a second, asks, 'How was it for you?'

'Oh, earth-shattering,' she says, sarcastically, but he doesn't get it. He just looks smug, rolls over and goes to sleep.

As she lies beside him, listening to the traffic outside and the sounds of the youth of Bologna at play, Emily thinks, I've slept with Michael's best friend, and wonders why she doesn't feel worse about it. She doesn't feel unfaithful to Paul. He, after all, is happy in the arms of his young, rich fitness instructor. She doesn't feel unfaithful to Michael. He left her years ago. In fact she feels quite triumphant about Michael. 'See?' she says to him in her head. 'I'm not so obsessed with you. I'm just as happy sleeping with your best friend. What do you think about that then?' She suppresses the feeling that Michael wouldn't care if he did know (what sort of problems did Chad mean, anyhow?). No, the person she feels bad about is Petra. Petra would be horrified to learn that she slept with Chad. She must never tell her. With that thought in mind, she sleeps.

In the morning, it all feels different. Emily feels cool, in control, a woman of the world. She banters happily with Chad as they get dressed and rejects his offer of breakfast. 'I'll get something on the way back.'

Chad is surprised into being slightly sheepish. 'Hey, Emmy Lou,' he says, in the hotel lobby. 'When will I see you again?'

Emily reaches up to kiss him on the cheek. 'I'll text you,' she says. Though, come to think of it, she doesn't even know his mobile number.

She drives back along the motorway in unreasonably high spirits. She stops at a service station and has a coffee and a *cornetto* (which, in Italy is not an ice cream but a kind of crois-sant). She buys chocolates for Monica and Olimpia, magazines for Siena and Paris and a toy car for Charlie. She also buys an L plate for the car. Siena will be seventeen in November; she will teach her to drive.

She reaches Monte Albano at eleven and is driving past the pile of rubble at twenty past. She parks in a screech of dust and saunters into the house. It is deserted. No children, no Olimpia, no Totti running round in excited circles. For a minute, she almost panics, then she sees a note in Siena's writing, stuck to the fridge with an Action Man magnet. 'Gone to the caves to see the skellys. Sx'

Pausing only to put the presents on the table and drink some water, Emily sets out for the caves. It is a long walk and the day is sultry. The sky is overcast and the air is still. She thinks there might be another storm on its way.

She sees Raffaello first. He is wearing a red shirt and is sitting on a rock, leaning forward, frowning, concentrating. Siena and Paris are standing behind him, Paris holding Totti by the collar. Olimpia and Charlie are standing slightly apart. Emily notes with irritation that Olimpia is carrying Charlie.

All five are looking towards the trench at the foot of one of the caves. In the trench stands Stine, cool in a blue shirt and jeans, wearing surgical gloves, shaking some soil through a sieve. The soil already taken from the trench has been put into plastic bags and there is a groundsheet on which Stine is placing other items. Emily cannot quite see what they are but they look like stones. Occasionally Stine stops and takes a photograph, calmly clicking and focusing as if she is taking holiday pictures.

There is a strange sense of anticipation and almost of foreboding in the air. The dark sky gives off an odd light, like a stage set, casting long shadows across the rocks and the coarse grass and the stunted oak trees. Nobody speaks. That is the strangest thing. Emily's cheerful greeting to her children dies on her lips and, though she raises her hand to say hello, she too stands silently beside Olimpia, watching Stine as she sieves and digs and clicks with the camera. She doesn't know how long this has gone on when, suddenly, there is a subtle shift in the atmosphere. Stine bends down to examine something. She brushes away soil and then leans closer to take a photograph. Raffaello, from his vantage point, leans forward too, but he says nothing. Then, slowly, painstakingly, Stine lifts something white out of the trench and places it on the waiting groundsheet.

Still nobody speaks. Stine lifts out more bones and some pieces of material. Raffaello lets out a stifled exclamation but sinks back into silence. Still more bones are lifted free and placed on the groundsheet. And then Stine bends closer to the earth, brushes away more soil and slowly, carefully, unearths something, two things, that shine brightly in the doom-laden light. She turns to face her audience, palm outstretched, to show what is in her hand.

Emily is only conscious of Charlie falling to the ground and crying as Olimpia puts her hands to her face and screams and screams.

PART 3

Winter

CHAPTER 1

'. . . the bodies discovered in the grounds of the Villa Serena are confirmed as being those of Carlo Belotti and Pino Albertini. Belotti, the leader of the local partisan brigade, disappeared in 1944 and was thought to have been killed by German SS troops stationed in the area. Albertini was his deputy.

In November 1944 the German General, Wolfgang Ramm, ordered a crackdown on partisan activities in the area after a parachute drop of radios and weapons was intercepted. Belotti and Albertini disappeared at this time and were believed to have been executed.

Belotti's body was identified by his daughter Olimpia Gazzi. Signora Gazzi said that she recognised a gold ring always worn by her father, which was found by his body. The autopsy report showed that both men were killed by gunshot wounds to the head. The evidence of forensic archaeologist Stine Nielson confirmed that the bodies had been deliberately buried in the hillside, with heavy stones placed on top of the graves.

The bodies were unearthed as part of archaeological excavations carried out by—'

Monica pauses and puts down the paper, which she has been translating for Emily.

'That must have been some moment,' she says.

'It was awful,' says Emily. She remembers Olimpia falling to her knees and screaming for her father. '*Mio babbo*,' she cried. 'My daddy.' It struck Emily as unbearably sad that this elderly woman in her sensible floral housecoat should be calling for her daddy, just like a little girl. She can't have been much more than a little girl when he disappeared, she realises.

'Did she recognise the ring at once?'

'Yes, as soon as she saw it she just started screaming. There was a cross too but she didn't seem concerned about that. She just kept screaming that it was her father's ring.'

'What did you do?'

'Well, I tried to comfort her but she just shook me off. She clung to Charlie and cried into his hair so, of course, he cried too. Even the girls were scared. It was Stine who saved the day really. She went up to Olimpia and said, "Now you can bury him." That really seemed to calm her down. But then we had to move the bones somehow, so I phoned Romano and asked if he could bring his tractor.'

'You phoned Romano?'

'Yes. Why not? He's our nearest neighbour, you know.'

'Romano is the son of the man who was mayor here during the war. A dedicated fascist.'

'No! Really?'

'Yes. You can always tell because, at one time, all fascists called their children Romano and Romana. So, if you see an Italian of a certain age called Romano, you know. You got extra money if you called your children after any of Mussolini's children so there are a lot of Romanos, Vittorios and Eddas around.'

'But Romano was really respectful towards the bodies. He crossed himself and everything.'

Monica snorts. 'That's just superstitious reflex. They all do it round here, cross themselves, pray to the Virgin and then just carry on as usual.'

They are sitting in the piazza drinking coffee. Charlie sits opposite, solemnly finishing an ice cream. It is late October but still warm enough to sit outside. Monica's apartment is visible across the square, an aerial oasis of flowers.

'I suppose you had to call the police,' says Monica.

'Yes, of course, though Raffaello didn't want to. He was worried about his precious excavations, but Stine insisted.'

Monica smiles. 'He's got a very anti-authoritarian streak, Raffaello.'

'So have all Italians,' retorts Emily.

Monica smiles, rather smugly. 'True. So what did the police say?'

'Oh, they asked lots of questions. Raffaello kept quiet about the fact that he'd known the bodies were there for weeks. He made out they'd just discovered them. He seemed to know one of the policemen, kept calling him Tino.'

'Agostino Pieri. They were at school together.'

'God, Monica, you know everybody.'

235

Monica sighs. 'It's the worst thing about still living in the same town where you grew up. Well, one of the worst things anyway.'

'Anyway, the police took the bodies away. Olimpia had calmed down a bit by then so I said I'd drive her home, but she said she wanted to go to the church.'

'Typical! I hope you told her not to be so ridiculous.'

'Of course I didn't. I drove her to the church. Don Angelo was there so I left them together.'

'I'm sure the old nutter was beside himself with excitement.'

'Actually, he seemed very shaken. I realised what an old man he is.'

'Oh, he'll go on forever, these religious nutcases always do.'

'Well, he's burying the bodies next week. Full funeral Mass. I'm sure you'll be there.'

Monica shakes her head. 'I'd rather be buried myself. Don't tell me you're going?'

Emily looks uncomfortable. 'Well, I thought I ought to.'

'Emily!' Monica explodes.

Charlie slurps up the last of his ice cream and looks at his mother to see if she has noticed. No, she is too busy chatting. Chat, chat, chat. Chat, cat, fat, bat. English words are funny when you make them rhyme. Italian words rhyme all the time. *Bello bimbo.* That's what people say to him. Paris laughs but she's just stinky. Siena's boyfriend's just come in. Charlie doesn't like him although he did once give him some chewing gum, which he's not allowed. He's got it safe somewhere. He can't remember where. Siena's boyfriend is talking to that lovely girl who gives him special straws. She says Charlie's her special boyfriend. Not him. He's just smelly. Smelly, welly, jelly.

'Isn't that Siena's boyfriend?' asks Monica.

'No,' says Emily. 'They've split up. She says she doesn't want to talk about it.'

When Emily gets back to the house, it is in silence. Siena is out and Paris seems to have taken Totti for a walk. After the warmth of the morning, the air is cooler and there is a cold wind (known locally as the *tramontana*) blowing. Emily cooks lunch for Charlie and for herself and puts on the central heating. It is actually against the law in Italy to turn on the central heating before the first of November, but everyone ignores this. Emily hears the boiler spring into noisy life and thinks that she will put on a DVD and snuggle down with Charlie on the sofa. A special treat. She might even get ten minutes' sleep.

In the sitting room, she sees something bright glinting on the mantelpiece. Thinking it might be money (she is always short of euros for the supermarket trolley) she goes over to find that it is a cross, the very cross that was found on Carlo Belotti's body. The policemen must have left it there. She remembers them asking Olimpia if she wanted it and her saying no, she only wanted to keep the ring.

For a few minutes, Emily stands with the cross in her hand. It is small and looks as if it was once attached to something else, a rosary perhaps. It is obviously not valuable, the metal has rusted and the enamel covering has partly chipped away. Even so, Emily wonders why Olimpia, who held her father's ring as if it were the relic of a saint, was so uninterested in the cross. Surely these sorts of things are important to Catholics? And Olimpia is very Catholic indeed; Emily has seen her going to Mass in full armour of headscarf, missal and giant rosary. Why didn't she value this evidence of her father's faith?

Emily looks again at the cross. It fits neatly into her hand and is rather attractive in design. It has curved corners, a little like a Coptic cross, but is otherwise unadorned. (She remembers a story from England about two girls comparing crucifixes and wondering why 'the one with the little man on' was more expensive.) There is no little man suffering and dying on this cross. Even so, Emily feels that it deserves some respect. She puts it on a high shelf, out of reach of Charlie and Totti, next to a picture of the girls, taken at Hampton Court.

Emily and Charlie are halfway through *The Jungle Book* when the door slams and Totti bursts into the sitting room and jumps onto the sofa.

'Down!' orders Emily, trying to sound stern.

Totti just grins goofily at her. Charlie puts his arms round him. 'He *likes* it on the sofa, Mum.'

'He's got a perfectly good basket over there.'

'He likes it here.' Totti and Charlie settle down together to watch the DVD. After a few minutes Paris wanders in.

'Hi, darling,' says Emily. 'Have you fed Totti?'

Paris eyes her narrowly. 'Yes,' she says.

Emily makes a desperate attempt at lightness. 'And did you have something yourself?'

'Yes,' says Paris. 'I had some bread.'

'What about some cold pizza? There's some in the fridge.'

'I had some bread,' repeats Paris evenly.

Emily decides to let it go. Paris has been eating a lot better in the last few weeks. She even dares to hope that she might be putting on some weight.

'Did you have a nice walk?' she asks.

'Yes,' says Paris, lying down on the floor to watch the video. 'I saw Raffaello.'

'You did? What was he doing?'

'He was looking at the site. He said he wanted to do some more digging before the rains came but he's going away next week.'

'Next week?' Emily doesn't know quite why she feels so shocked. She knew that Raffaello was going to America, she just didn't know it was so soon. She also feels obscurely offended that he hasn't told her about his plans, has just left her to find out second-hand from Paris.

'Yes. After the funeral. You know, the funeral of our famous skeletons.'

Both Siena and Paris have adopted an attitude of half ironical proprietorship towards the skeletons found on their land. They call them Luigi and Mario, after two characters on television.

'I found out their real names today,' says Emily and tells Paris about the newspaper article.

Paris is impressed. 'Cool. So they were real freedom fighters.'

'Yes, I suppose they were.'

'I'd have done something like that if I was alive then.'

Emily sighs. 'I'm sure I would have been far too scared. We just can't imagine what it was like, having your town taken over like that.'

'Londoners lived through the Blitz,' Paris points out. She 'did' the Second World War while she was still at school in England.

'That must have been awful as well. It just seems worse to think of having the enemy actually living in your town, not knowing who is a friend or who's going to betray you. Not knowing whether to collaborate or whether to fight.'

'I would fight.'

'I expect you would.' Emily fears that she herself is a natural collaborator.

'Fighting's naughty,' says Charlie in a virtuous voice, without taking his eyes from the screen.

'Yes, you're right, Charlie,' says Emily. 'It's just that it's sometimes a bit more complicated than that.'

Siena is in church. She doesn't know quite how this has happened. She only knows that she didn't want to go home after school and she especially didn't want to go to the piazza where she'd probably find Giancarlo drooling over Angela. She'd thought she might just go for a walk but it suddenly got very cold and Siena has never been much of a girl for exercise, not like Paris. She wanted somewhere quiet and somewhere warm and then, somehow, she found herself walking up the shallow steps that lead from the piazza to the church.

The church smells of candles and flowers. A red light glows on the altar, which Siena thinks must mean something significant but she doesn't know what. It is dark and empty apart from one old man kneeling by the altar rails. Siena slips into a pew. She doesn't kneel; she would find this too embarrassing, even though she is on her own. She just sits there, huddled in her red jacket, thinking about Giancarlo and about the frightening emptiness inside her where her feelings for him used to be.

This is almost the worst thing. When Giancarlo stood her up at the café, she walked out into the piazza and suddenly, just like that, she didn't love him any more. The square, with its cobbles and timbered shops and posters for the Festa dei Porcini, was still the same but she, Siena, was totally different. She felt a moment's panic and wished, more than anything, that she could go back into the café and still be in love with Giancarlo. Even if he continued to stand her up and treat her badly, if she still loved him she would know who she was. But it just couldn't be done. Siena had stood there, with Vespas and Fiats swerving round her, and realised that this was it. Love had died.

Giancarlo had come to see her the next day and said he was sorry and that he still loved her. But Siena was quite calm. 'I'm sorry,' she had said, 'I don't love you any more.' Giancarlo had even cried but Siena remained dry-eyed and oddly detached.

She had looked at Giancarlo, with his trendy jeans hanging off his skinny frame and had wondered how she could ever, ever, have contemplated sleeping with him. Really, it was all she could do to look at him without shuddering. And eventually Giancarlo had got the message.

Paris had been delighted. 'Well done,' she said, with rare warmth. 'I didn't know you had it in you.' But Siena couldn't feel triumphant. It still felt like a failure to her, not to be in love any more. After all, that was what life was about, wasn't it? Being in love? She was sixteen and she knew she was pretty. She should be in love. She should be riding about the countryside on someone's motorbike, the wind in her hair and delicious anticipation in her heart. But now she just feels numb. Numb and cold and rather old. Suppose she never falls in love again? Suppose Giancarlo was her one chance and she has blown it? She will die an old maid and Paris and Charlie's children will patronise her and she will never get to wear a wedding dress.

Siena stands up. She is stiff from sitting so long but she feels that her visit to the church deserves some formal gesture. A sort of symbol. Catholics are good at symbols, she thinks, looking round at the Stations of the Cross (gloomy depictions of suffering in shiny oil paint), at the statues, at the fading fresco on the wall of the high altar, at the holy water, at the banks of candles. That's it. She will light a candle.

Slowly, hesitantly, Siena approaches the side altar, where there is a friendly plaster statue of Mary, all blue and white with surprising blond hair. In fact, she looks a bit like Siena herself.

Siena lights a candle (it is just like one of those tea lights that Emily plonks all over the house) and places it on one of the spikes provided. There are four or five candles already burning. Who has lit them? she wonders.

Siena looks up at Mary and addresses her silently. 'Dear Mary, help me fall in love again one day. Thank you.' Mary smiles blandly down at her. In one hand she holds a rosary, and one bare foot, Siena notices, is planted firmly on a snake. 'Amen,' she adds. She wonders why Mary is stamping on wild-life. It doesn't seem very environmentally friendly somehow.

As she turns to go, she passes the man at the altar rails. It is only when she is outside in the gathering dusk that she realises who it was. It was Don Angelo.

And he was crying.

That night Emily receives two rather surprising phone calls. The first is from Petra, telling her that she has a date that night with George/Darren. Emily is surprised. In their last few conversations Petra has given the impression that she has given up on George/Darren because of the sheer logistical difficulties involved in 'the dating thing'. She can't find a babysitter who can cope with Harry, she can't park in the middle of town and can't afford a taxi and she can't be bothered to shave her legs. But, here she is, announcing that they are going to go to a play at the Theatre Royal and for a meal afterwards. 'He arranged it all,' she says, rather defensively. 'I couldn't say no.' Emily says of course she must go, have a good time, don't do anything I wouldn't, etc. She puts the phone down feeling slightly, just slightly, jealous. She still hasn't told Petra about the evening with Chad.

The second phone call is from her mother. This is even more unusual. Emily always phones her mother on a Sunday morning, she knows her mother likes routine and she times her phone call to coincide with the end of the *Archers* omnibus. But here is her mother ringing on a Tuesday, just two days after they last spoke. Something must be wrong.

'Is anything wrong?' These are Emily's first words.

'No,' says her mother, rather huffily. 'I'm allowed to ring my own daughter, aren't I?'

'Of course. It's lovely to hear you. Is anything wrong?'

Of course something is wrong. Emily's parents had been going to spend Christmas with David and his partner, Kelly. But Kelly has (of course) messed up the arrangements and has also invited her parents from Newcastle.

'Can't you all go?' asks Emily tactlessly.

'Well, there's hardly room, is there, in that tiny little house?' Emily's mother lays the blame for David's lack of material success squarely on Kelly, despite the fact that David was equally badly off when he was with his first wife, Sue (a local girl), and his second, Linda (Sue's best friend). It is true to say he has become worse off still since he left Linda for Kelly but Emily finds it hard to see why this is entirely Kelly's fault. She rather likes Kelly who is a beautician and is always promising to 'tidy up' Emily's eyebrows.

'It's her,' says Emily's mother. 'She doesn't want us.'

'I'm sure that's not true.'

'Of course it's true. She'd rather have her parents with their karaoke machine and their funny-coloured cocktails. And they're bringing that sister of hers. Did you know she was pregnant?'

'Kelly?'

'No, her sister. Leanne I think she's called.'

'I thought Leanne was still at school.'

'She is. That's the sort of family they are.'

'Have you talked to David?' asks Emily, but without much hope. In her experience her mother doesn't talk much to either of her sons. Despite this, she gets on better with them than she does with Emily.

'There's no point talking to him. He's always on her side.'

'Well, she is his wife.'

'She's not his wife,' hisses Emily's mother.

'His common-law wife then.'

A sniff. 'That says it all.'

'Mum! Kelly's all right. She loves David and she's great with the kids.'

Her mother is silent. A buzzing, expensive silence. Then she says, 'I can't expect you to understand. Living in your great big house in Italy.'

And Emily says, as, perhaps, she was always expected to, 'Why don't you come to us for Christmas?'

CHAPTER 2

The church is full for the funeral of Carlo Belotti and Pino Albertini. It is also All Saints' Day, a feast day which has hitherto passed Emily by (in England, the previous day, Halloween, always seemed the important one) but one that is clearly of great significance in Italy. All the statues have been cleaned and the church's one relic (one of St Anthony's fingernails) has been brought out, resplendent in a gold case. Banks of flowers fill the church with a sickly, heady scent and the candles fairly blaze on the altar. Even Don Angelo is wearing magnificent purple robes more suitable, in Emily's eyes, for an emperor than for a parish priest.

Emily slips into one of the back pews. The front rows seem to be completely taken up with Olimpia's family. There is Olimpia herself, all in black from head to toe, complete with a black veil, flanked by her husband, her two sons and their families. Emily knows that Olimpia is the youngest of seven children and the only girl, so she assumes that some of the elderly men in the front rows must be her brothers, though surely not all of them are still alive. There are plenty of young people too: children looking over-excited in their Sunday best, babies whose sudden cries are quickly silenced, sullen-looking teens with long hair and leather jackets.

Pino Albertini has no family left alive, apart from a distant cousin who sits nervously with his wife, surrounded by the Belotti clan. Monica has told Emily that Olimpia's family have paid for everything, a hero's funeral for their dead father.

The coffins, both covered by Italian flags, are brought into the church by black-suited undertaker's men. There is absolute silence, broken only by the pacing footsteps on the stone floor. The silence surprises Emily; she had expected music, hymns, general religious uplift. Instead the silence, the stillness of the congregation, the black gloves of the coffin bearers, all strike her as deeply sinister. She finds herself, probably the person in the room least connected to the tragedy, wanting to cry out loud, anything to break the awful tension. Looking down, she is surprised to see her hands clenched on the back of the pew in front.

Don Angelo speaks at last. He sprays holy water from a silver container and invites Olimpia and Albertini's cousin to come forward and place Bibles and crucifixes on the coffins. Olimpia does so with proper theatrical relish; the cousin just looks embarrassed. Then the funeral starts.

Emily is rather relieved to find that the service is just like the usual Catholic Mass, though with a few extra flourishes. The choir sings in Latin, quite beautifully, and one of the sullen youths gets up and does a long reading (from St Paul, she thinks). Then Don Angelo moves over to the pulpit for the sermon.

Emily has to admire his style. For a full minute he just stands there, his purple robes glowing in the light of the candles. Then he raises one hand and says, 'Dear people . . .' Emily is reminded of his performance when he urged the townspeople not to allow Raffaello's excavations. 'Dear people,' says Don Angelo, 'this is a sad day for us all. This is a day that must reopen the wounds of the past. Must call to mind a time which some of us remember and all of us have heard about. A time when neighbour was set against neighbour and great fear and turmoil was in all our hearts. But it is also a happy day. It is a day when we welcome our dear departed brothers back into our community. It is a day when we remember them with great respect and affection, it is a day when we can pray for their souls and commend them to our Lord, Jesus Christ. It is a day when we can bury our beloved brothers in the consecrated soil of our churchyard and it gives us a place where we can remember them and continue to pray for them and commend their souls to God. For their families who, I know, have been praying for their loved ones every day of these past sixty years, it offers a final resting place. A place where they can lay down their heavy burden of grief.'

There is a harsh sob from the front pew and Emily is sure it is Olimpia. She has her head down and her shoulders are heaving. Her husband pats her, rather hesitantly, on the back.

Don Angelo continues. His voice is so slow and measured that, for once, Emily can understand every word. 'Dear people. These were two extraordinary men. At a time when member-ship of a partisan brigade was punishable by death, these men led and organised armed resistance to the enemy. These were men without fear, without . . .' He pauses for a second and looks towards Olimpia's family, '. . . without the usual human doubts.' He pauses again and looks down, seeming to falter for the first time. He passes a hand over his brow. The church is absolutely still, waiting. The dust motes dance in the air and Emily watches her neighbour pass her rosary beads from finger to finger. Click, click, click.

Then Don Angelo raises his head. 'I knew both these men,' he says. 'Not well. I was only a boy but I knew these men by reputation, I knew their families, I knew the risks they took. And I honour them.'

At these words there is a slight stir in the church. Emily looks round and catches sight of Romano and Anna-Luisa, sit-ting a few rows to her left. Why would Romano, the son of a fascist, come to the funeral of a partisan leader? Emily does not know, but Romano's face, calm and respectful, shows no sign of unease. He looks just as he did when he crossed himself before removing the bodies from Emily's land. Superstition, Monica would say. But it seems to Emily that there is some-thing stronger than superstition at work in the church this day. Something, perhaps, equally dark and unknowable, but something that binds this community together, some shared memory, some shared belief, perhaps even a shared fear. It is there in the candles and in the relics of the saints. It is there in Don Angelo's face as he addresses the community in his purple robes, it was there in the sullen youth's voice as he read from St Paul, it is there in Romano's clasped hands as he prays for his father's enemy, it was there, Emily realises, in Raffaello's words when he told her about the partisans hiding in the hills.

Don Angelo continues, speaking in a stronger voice now, so that his words carry right to the back of the church. 'I honour them,' he says, 'not just for their courage, which was indisputable, but also for their certainty. They did not suffer the doubts and fears that assailed many of us at that time. They had their certainty and so they kept their integrity, even to the end. And we pray, dear people, we pray to our Lord Jesus Christ, who also lived in an occupied land, we pray to Him that we may never suffer such times again. We pray that we may never again have to bury our brothers, our comrades, in such circumstances. We pray not to be put to the test. We pray that the angels will take their souls to heaven where they will sit at the right hand of the Father. And we pray that we will join them when our time comes, when all hurts will be healed and the world is at peace.' He says something else, but so softly that Emily doesn't, at first, catch it. Then, as if rewinding a tape, her brain picks up the words and replays them to her, first in Italian, then in English. 'We pray,' Don Angelo had said, 'that we may forget.'

Don Angelo bows his head and Emily does not know if he has finished or not. But then he raises his arms and says, '*Credo . . .*'

As one, the congregation stands and chants after him, '*Credo in un solo Dio* . . .' Emily stumbles to her feet. She can never get used to the way that Catholics do things in unison. The chanting seems to go on for ever, the woman next to her sways back and forth, her eyes shut. Twisting round, Emily sees Antonella standing next to her son Andrea. Antonella grins, which makes Emily feel a lot better.

More chanting, more singing, more prayers. The air is thick with incense and Emily is starting to get a headache. 'There are only two smells in the afterlife,' she remembers a priest at Oxford saying to her, 'brimstone and incense.' She wonders whether brimstone might actually be preferable. Then, at some unseen signal, the congregation rises and starts to shuffle forward for Communion. To do so, they have to pass right by the two coffins, which stand in the centre aisle. Emily watches as Romano and Anna-Luisa go past. As they reach the Italian flags, Romano places one hand on Carlo Belotti's coffin and his lips move silently. Anna-Luisa watches impassively.

Emily notices that Antonella is almost the only other person who does not go to Communion. Is she excommunicated because she is an unmarried mother? Surely that can't be possible in this day and age? Emily remembers the first time she went to church with Michael. He had crossed himself as they passed the altar and she had thought how remote that made him seem, how Italian, how somehow *glamorous*. To think that this man, her boyfriend, belonged to this shadowy, secretive religion. To think that he shared some mysterious Catholic

DNA with Graham Greene and Evelyn Waugh and the Gawain poet. She remembers feeling deeply impressed and also deeply inferior. Her own parents went to church only for weddings and funerals, they had never had anything as romantic as doubts. Sin, sacrament, doubt, salvation – she has a feeling it is still all beyond her.

Doubt. Don Angelo had talked a lot about doubt. Odd, perhaps, for a funeral Mass. He honoured the dead men for their certainty, he said. Certainty of what? Certainty of a life after death? But Don Angelo, as a priest, must share that. Certainty that fighting the Germans was right? But surely everyone had felt that? Everyone except the fascists, that is. She watches as Romano passes the pews containing Olimpia's family. He stops and embraces Olimpia fondly. Anna-Luisa does the same. Emily's head is starting to swim.

One more hymn and the coffins are passing out of the church. People bow their heads as they pass and Emily is amazed to hear some clapping (Antonella explains afterwards that clapping is a sign of respect at Italian funerals). Emily edges out with the rest of the congregation. She tries to stop to find Antonella but the crowd sweeps her on, out of the church and towards the graveyard.

Outside, a strong wind is blowing and Don Angelo's purple robes are blown out behind him like a banner. The tall, hand-held cross rocks violently to and fro. Don Angelo's words, as he stands by the open graves, are lost on the wind. But, at the back of the crowd, Emily hears a sigh, like another gust of wind, pass through the crowd as Olimpia and her brothers throw soil onto their father's coffin. The Italian flags have been removed and one of Don Angelo's attendants (Emily is not sure of their proper title) folds them and passes them reverently to the families. Then it is over and the people start to walk away, suddenly laughing and joking and lighting cigarettes. The spell is broken.

As the crowd thins, Emily is surprised to see Raffaello standing there amongst the graves, unusually smart in a long, black coat. Emily walks towards him, avoiding looking at the two new graves, where the undertaker's men are already at work.

'I didn't see you in the church,' she says.

Raffaello shrugs. 'I didn't go in. I . . . I don't like funerals very much.'

It is on the tip of Emily's tongue to say that no one likes funerals very much but then she remembers. His wife. Raffaello must have buried his wife when she was still in her twenties. No wonder he doesn't like funerals.

'I waited outside,' says Raffaello after a pause. 'I wanted to pay my respects. After all, I was married into the Belotti family.'

Of course, Raffaello's wife Chiara had been Olimpia's niece. Carlo Belotti would have been her great-uncle.

'It's all very strange,' Emily says at last.

'What is?'

'The whole thing. The funeral. These men died sixty years ago but it all seems so . . . *raw*, so painful.'

253

'Sixty years.' Raffaello shrugs. 'It's nothing.'

'To an archaeologist.'

'Not just to an archaeologist.' He stops and points back towards the graveyard, where Olimpia and her brothers still stand beside their father's grave. 'To these people. There are still plenty of people alive who remember the war. They remember who was on whose side, who betrayed who. And when they die, their families will remember.'

'Don Angelo said we should pray to forget.'

'He is a wise man.'

They have reached the steps that lead down to the road. Emily sees Antonella and Andrea talking to Giancarlo's parents. Antonella raises her hand to call Emily over.

'Antonella di Luca,' says Raffaello. 'She is a lovely woman.'

'Yes, she is.' Emily hesitates, not quite sure what to say next. At last she says, 'Paris says that you are going to America.'

'Yes. In a few days' time.'

'When will you be coming back?' As soon as she has said the words, Emily curses herself. How *could* she have asked him that?

But Raffaello just smiles. 'I'll be home by Christmas,' he says.

As she watches Raffaello lope off down the road, his black coat flying out behind him, Emily thinks about what he has said. *Home,* he said. 'I'll be home by Christmas.' Where is home for Raffaello? Monte Albano, where half the people think he is the devil himself? Or in the hills with his Etruscan graves? Emily shakes her head to free herself of the image and walks slowly over to join Antonella.

CHAPTER 3

Three days later it is Siena's seventeenth birthday. Siena has been behaving so oddly recently that Emily does not know quite how to suggest they celebrate it. Last year Siena had a party at the house and Giancarlo broke Emily's precious Venetian mirror (Emily hopes he gets the full seven years' bad luck) but when Emily asks if she wants some friends round she says no. Does she want to go for a trip somewhere, to Florence or Pisa perhaps? No, thank you. Eventually Siena says that what she would really like is to go out for a meal: 'With your friends?' asks Emily. 'No,' says Siena. 'With you and Paris.'

Emily is amazed. For a second, she fears she is going to cry. Siena, who usually treats her like the village idiot's less intelligent sister, actually wants to spend time with her. Siena, who is normally at the centre of a circle of laughing, confident friends, actually prefers to go out with her mother and her sister (though not, it is true, her brother). Then, almost immediately, she starts to worry. Does this mean that Siena has fallen out with all her Italian friends? Does the break-up with Giancarlo mean that she will now be ostracised in Monte Albano? With a superhuman effort, she manages not to say all this to Siena.

'That would be lovely, darling,' she says. 'Where do you want to go?'

Siena shrugs. 'I don't care,' she says, in the usual dismissive voice she uses for Emily. Emily is quite relieved to hear it again.

Monte Albano has three restaurants. The first is a large pizzeria, where all the young go. There are tables outside and a large, wood oven inside. You can buy a pitcher of wine for three euros and the pizzas are the size of tea trays. It is a lively, friendly place and Emily and the kids have been there many times. But for Siena's birthday she feels, that they need somewhere special. Besides, Giancarlo will probably be at the pizzeria.

The second restaurant is tucked away down a dark alleyway just off the main piazza. It is mentioned in several guide books and the duck with figs is supposed to be out of this world. But there are only six tables and Emily always feels that she is on show when she eats there. The chef's wife brings plate after plate of beautiful food and you have to ooh and aah and say how wonderful it all is. The food is undeniably wonderful but the whole experience is rather exhausting. The first time that Emily and Paul went there, Emily had a morbid feeling that they were not going to get out alive. Stuffed to bloating with food, she began to dread the tap, tap of the chef's wife's high heels heralding the arrival of yet another dish. Eating stopped being a pleasure and became torture. Emily was reminded of Hansel and Gretel being fattened up by the witch. Come to think of it, there was something rather barley-sugary about the dining room with its strawberry-coloured walls and curly candy-striped chairs. When, eventually, they were allowed to leave, the chef's wife pressed a bag of homemade biscuits into their hands, presumably in case they got hungry on the way home. There was a lipstick kiss on the napkin.

The third restaurant, La Foresta, is popular with the families in Monte Albano. It is an old-fashioned place, all dark wood and gilt frames inside, with a few tables outside on a wooden platform. It is not mentioned in any guide books but Emily has heard that the food is good, so she decides to go there on Siena's birthday. She doesn't think she will need to book on a Thursday night. The restaurant is also in the piazza, opposite the pizzeria, so they will be able to have a little *passeggiata* first. She hopes Paris won't make too much fuss about the food.

It rains all morning on Siena's birthday. The November rains, Olimpia tells Emily, with gloomy relish. Olimpia still comes twice a week to clean, though her relationship with Emily has changed since the bodies were found. It is not that she likes Emily any more (in fact Emily has caught her looking at her with something very like hatred), more that she now dislikes her as an equal rather than as a stupid foreigner. She now always speaks to Emily in Italian which, while it sometimes leads to misunderstandings, seems a gesture towards acceptance. And, though she still disapproves of Emily's kettle and her propensity to pile dirty towels on the bidet, the words '*tipicamente Inglese*' are heard less often.

Siena opens her presents when she gets home from school. She said she would rather do it this way and Emily is pleased to see that she is carrying several small packages and cards from friends at school. She had also been pleased to see, a few days earlier, a package arrive addressed to Siena in Paul's writing. And she hadn't even had to remind him. Maybe the fitness instructor is a good influence after all.

Paul's present is a cheque and a bag (small and chic, more evidence of the new woman's taste). Emily gives her new jeans and a bracelet, Paris some bubble bath ('It hasn't been tested on animals'). Siena pronounces herself pleased with her gifts, puts on her jeans and the bracelet and stuffs her mobile into the bag. So far, all is going well.

Even the rain has stopped as they drive into Monte Albano. Charlie was quite happy to be left with Monica and even Totti only howled for a few minutes (or for as long as it took Monica to open a tin of dog food). Emily parks by the town walls and the three of them walk through the darkening streets to the piazza. Emily loves winter evenings in Italy, the lighted shops are like little jewels and the cobbled streets shine with the day's rain. Italian shops seem more restrained about Christmas too. Though it is November, the shop windows still show harvest wreaths, stacks of walnuts and chestnuts and baskets of tiny clementines. Even in December, Emily knows, their decorations will only consist of displays of panettoni in colourful boxes and, of course, the ubiquitous crib.

In the piazza, fairy lights glimmer in the trees and a band is playing. Siena goes as far as squeezing Emily's arm. 'Isn't it lovely, Mum?'

'Lovely,' agrees Emily, squeezing back.

Even Paris admits that the music is nice. 'Better than the stuff Giancarlo plays anyway.'

'Signora Robertson and her two lovely daughters!'

Emily swings round. There, sitting outside one of the cafés, is Raffaello, hair wild, earring glinting. He is with a group of men, one of whom Emily recognises as Tino, the policeman who came to investigate the discovery of the bodies.

'Hello,' says Emily, rather nervously.

'To what does Monte Albano owe this honour?' Raffaello looks rather pleased with himself, Emily thinks. The other men are laughing, obviously admiring his cheek at chatting up the *Inglese*.

'It's Siena's birthday.'

'Ah, happy birthday, Miss Siena.'

'Thanks,' says Siena, looking coy.

'Sweet sixteen?'

'Seventeen!' She isn't about to let him get away with this.

'Sorry, seventeen. Even sweeter. Are you going for a meal?'

'Yes, we're going to La Foresta.'

Tino laughs and says something in Italian. But Raffaello just nods gravely. 'Good choice.'

'We'd better be going,' says Emily.

'*Buon appetito.*'

'Thank you.'

As Emily moves away she thinks she can hear them laughing again. Really, Italians can be very annoying sometimes.

At the opposite end of the piazza, the pizzeria is full. Emily thinks she can see Giancarlo at one of the tables, part of a roaring, gesticulating crowd. She doesn't know if Siena has spotted him. Although it has started to rain again, the square is filling up with people and Vespas, even an illegal car or two. The *passeggiata* is at its height. Emily is rather relieved to be able to dive into the welcoming gloom of La Foresta.

But then, disaster strikes. The restaurant is full. Apparently there is a convention of *cacciatori* (hunters) and the tables are crowded with bearded men discussing guns and ammunition. The waiter is sympathetic but spreads out his hands helplessly. 'A thousand apologies, signora, but what can I do?' Emily stands irresolute in the doorway. Paris has started to mutter under her breath and Siena seems sunk in despair. How can they go outside again and face the laughing crowds with Giancarlo holding court at the pizzeria? And it is raining. Oh, why didn't she book a table?

'What shall we do, Mum?' asks Paris.

'We'll have to go home,' says Siena. 'Great birthday this is turning out to be.'

'I'm sorry—' Emily begins for what feels like the millionth time in her life.

But then a voice behind them says, 'Can I help?'

It is Raffaello, filling the doorway as he shakes rainwater out of his hair. Emily starts to explain about the *cacciatori* and the pizzeria and the lack of a booking but then she sees that Raffaello is not looking at her but at the waiter.

'Signor Raffaello!' says the waiter in apparent delight. 'Why didn't you tell us you were coming?'

'I'm not coming in,' says Raffaello. 'But have you a table for my friends?'

'*Sì, sì*,' says the waiter without turning a hair. 'If you wait just one minute, I will find a table.'

And he bustles away to procure a table, seemingly out of thin air. Emily turns, open-mouthed, to Raffaello.

'How on earth did you manage that?'

Raffaello smiles. 'You remember I told you that my family had a restaurant?'

'This is it?'

'Yes. La Foresta has been in the Murello family for generations.'

Emily remembers the story about the Germans dining at the restaurant and leaving big tips. She looks around at the crowded tables, imagining them filled with Nazi uniforms, imagining Raffaello's great-grandmother, out in the kitchen, cooking for her life.

'So your family still run the restaurant?'

'Yes. Remember I told you that one of my great-uncles kept his head down and became rich?'

'Yes.'

'Well, he inherited the restaurant.'

'Is he still alive?'

'Very much so. Zio Virgilio. He's in his late seventies now but as sharp as ever. His grandson Renato's supposed to be in charge but Zio Virgilio still calls all the shots. That's Renato over there.' He points to a young, dark-haired man who is chatting to some of the hunters. The dark-haired man raises his hand in greeting but doesn't come over. He is shorter than Raffaello and somehow less substantial.

The waiter comes hurrying back. 'I have prepared a beautiful table,' he says proudly, pointing at a small table which has miraculously appeared next to the window. More waiters are rushing around with cutlery and glasses.

'Thank you so much,' says Emily. 'Well, thank *you!*' She turns to Raffaello. 'Won't you join us?'

'No, this is a family meal. But I will join you for coffee, if I may.' He leans over and whispers something to the waiter, then, raising his hand in farewell, backs out of the door.

It is a wonderful meal. Somehow, the near-disaster at the start serves to make everything else seem more exciting. They love the restaurant with its stuffed deer's heads on the walls and its framed pictures of the Mountains of the Moon. They even love the hunters, who keep bursting into raucous song and shooting appreciative glances at Siena. They love the food, which is simple and good, traditional Tuscan dishes like *ribollita* and *tortellone in brodo*. Emily and Siena eat heartily and even Paris consents to eat almost all of a plate of risotto.

By the time they reach the *dolci*, Emily is completely full but Siena persuades her to share some profiteroles ('Go on, Mum, it is my birthday'). The waiter, all smiles now, whisks away and Emily is just turning to Paris to ask her if she is sure about not having a piece of chocolate cake when all the lights go out. Siena screams and Paris says, in a world-weary tone, 'What's happening *now*?'

'Happy birthday to you, happy birthday to you, happy birthday, dear Siena, happy birthday to you.' The waiter's accented English is joined by the lusty singing of the *cacciatori* as he makes his way through the tables carrying a cake glowing with seventeen candles.

Laughter, applause, (delighted) embarrassment from Siena. She blows out the candles and the whole restaurant cheers. The hunters start singing again.

'But however did he know?' wonders Emily.

'A little bird told him,' says a voice behind her. It is, of course, Raffaello.

'Did *you* tell him it was my birthday?' asks Siena, who is bright pink.

Rafffaello laughs but does not answer. As he sits at their table, glasses of sparkling wine appear, as if by magic.

'I hate wine,' says Paris. But she says it quietly, almost dreamily.

'I'll have yours then,' says Siena, who is thoroughly overexcited by now.

'You're like a magician,' Emily says to Raffaello. She is rather over-excited herself.

'Why? Because I can make tables appear?'

'Tables and birthday cake and sparkling wine.'

'And dogs,' adds Paris, 'and skeletons.'

'And dogs and skeletons,' agrees Raffaello. 'I am indeed a necromancer.'

Not a necromancer, Emily thinks later, more a shape-changer. With Raffaello's arrival, somehow their lives have assumed a different shape. They are now a family with a dog, a family with friends. They are at the centre of a discovery and a mystery that still seems to reverberate in the town. Emily is a woman who can sleep with a man she does not love and not feel ashamed. Siena is a woman (a woman now, surely, at seventeen?) who can dump her boyfriend and go out to dinner without a backward glance. Paris is a girl who can, almost, eat a proper meal in a restaurant. Not all this is due to Raffaello, of course, but his arrival seems to have made things possible. He has opened doors, not only to this restaurant, but to the past. He has made Emily see Tuscany not just as the perfect middle-class holiday haven, but as a place of secrets, of long-buried bones and of doorways in the hills. He has made her see death, betrayal and murder and, somehow, instead of terrifying her, this has given her strength.

During that meal at the restaurant, with the familiar waiters, the complimentary drinks and the sense of being at home in a public place, Emily wonders why she is not reminded more of Michael. When Michael took her to Vittorio's, it was a rite of passage, the key to a hidden world. But, dazzled as she was by Michael and by Gina, she still never really felt that she belonged there. Michael could sit and backchat with the waiters, but she was still worrying about her tutorial. Michael could sprawl in the sun at Gina's house in Positano but Emily was still too embarrassed to sunbathe topless. But Raffaello is another outsider. True, he is an outsider who was born and bred in the town, who can drink with the local policeman and whose family own the restaurant. But he is an outsider all the same, the man who married the local beauty and left her to die, the man with an American accent and an American child. Raffaello offered Emily La Foresta as if it was a present from one foreigner to another. The result was to make Emily feel not inferior, but powerful.

Eventually Renato himself comes over to their table and Raffaello introduces Emily and the girls.

'You're from England?' says Renato, in fluent English. 'I spent a few years on the south coast in England.'

'I used to live in Brighton,' offers Emily.

'Brighton! I know it well.' He is charming and hospitable (calling for coffees and *digestivi*, asking Paris if she'd like another Coke) but Emily gets the feeling that he dislikes Raffaello and, more surprisingly perhaps, that he fears him.

Afterwards, Raffaello walks them to their car. They stand talking in the shadow of the ancient walls with the rain falling like a friendly chorus around them.

'Thanks for everything,' says Emily.

'It was nothing. I'm glad you enjoyed the evening.'

'It was lovely. Siena had a wonderful birthday.'

'I'm pleased.'

A pause and then Emily says, in a rush, 'Perhaps you could come and have supper with us one evening.'

Raffaello gives a strange little bow. 'Sadly I am leaving for America tomorrow.'

'Tomorrow?'

'Yes. November the fifth. Firework night in England.' And he smiles his pirate's smile, raises his hand and disappears into the night.

Paris's diary

Siena's birthday. An OK evening. S was quite nice about my present (so she should be, it cost 10 euros!) and at least we didn't have to put up with ghastly Giancarlo slobbering all over her. I still can't believe that S had the sense to chuck him. She says she doesn't miss him but she doesn't want to talk about it. I didn't see if he sent her a card. Andrea did though.

We went out for a meal. I hate restaurants (all those awful people chewing away, dribbling and making disgusting noises) but this one wasn't too bad. For a start it was so dark that you couldn't see people eating and then there were all these hunters making such a racket you couldn't hear anything either. I ate some rice and Mum didn't nag me too much. At first, they said the restaurant was full and I thought Mum was going to make it into some big tragedy but then R came and sorted it all out. It turns out his cousin owns the restaurant or something. The cousin came over afterwards and was all slimy. R was quite funny, winding him up about his restaurant being old fashioned and suggesting he put in a karaoke machine and serve burgers. I could tell the cousin was really pissed off.

When we got back to the car, Mum and R talked for ages in the rain. So stupid. Mum doesn't talk to him when she gets the chance and then stands there in the freezing cold, yakking and yakking. Siena and I kept yelling at her to hurry up and get in the car but she didn't.

On the way home Mum told us that Grandma and Grandad are coming for Christmas. Bloody hell.

CHAPTER 4

Emily's parents arrive at Forli airport on 23 December. Emily is there to meet them, glumly aware the plane is late, so, for her mother, the holiday will already be a disaster. A disaster bravely borne, but a disaster all the same. Emily has Charlie with her (surely the sight of Charlie would cheer *anyone* up?) and the girls are at home with instructions to prepare a welcome supper. As Siena was last seen plugged into her iPhone, straightening her hair, and Paris was putting the finishing touches to Totti's Christmas stocking, she is not too confident about the meal. But at least the house looks wonderful. There are wreathes of ivy on every door, a giant Christmas tree in the sitting room and scented candles on every available surface. Pine branches hang from the ceilings and she has made a real Tuscan Christmas cake. Surely even her parents will be impressed.

When her parents finally emerge from the Arrivals gate, pushing their neat wheeled suitcases, Emily takes it all back. Of course they won't be impressed. How could she ever have thought they would be? Her mother's first words are, 'Fifty-five minutes late and not even a complimentary cup of tea.' Her father's: 'We've brought our own tea bags. They're in the hand luggage.'

'It's lovely to see you,' says Emily, kissing them. 'Look, here's Charlie. Hasn't he grown?'

Her parents survey him pessimistically. 'He's not as tall as Ashley,' says her mother at last. Ashley is Alan's youngest child. Her parents visited Alan and Debbie in Australia last year.

'No,' snaps Emily. 'Well, Debbie is practically a giant, isn't she? Come on. Let's go and find the car.'

Emily's mother, Virginia (Ginny), is the sort of woman for whom the word 'feminine' was invented. She is small and dainty and is fond of telling people that she buys her clothes from the 'petite' range. Emily is small too but, next to her mother, she immediately feels untidy, an uncouth peasant wench with wild hair and food stains on her blouse. Ginny Robertson's clothes are always immaculate. When travelling she wraps her jumpers in tissue paper and has special bags for her shoes. She has her hair tinted ash blonde and always, always wears heels. She teeters along now, being brave about her case, which got scratched on the luggage carousel, and wishing that Emily wouldn't wear jeans all the time.

Emily strides along, feeling butch and unattractive beside her mother. She pulls the absurd little case behind her and Ginny whimpers slightly. Charlie skips to catch up; he hasn't spoken a word to either grandparent.

When they reach the Alfa, Emily's father, Doug, delivers a

masterclass on the correct way of folding the cases into the boot.

'Do you like the car, Dad?' asks Emily.

'An Alfa,' says Doug dubiously. 'I've heard they're very unreliable.'

'Actually,' says Emily, 'it's the best car we've ever had. It was Car of the Year.' This is the sort of information she is always offering her father.

Doug Robertson was originally from Glasgow. He met Ginny whilst at a training course in Guildford (they were both working for a supermarket, he as a management trainee, she on the pharmacy counter). Swiftly she persuaded him to seek a transfer to Surrey, take out a mortgage on a small terraced house and marry her. Of course, he probably didn't need much persuading; Ginny was a pretty girl at eighteen, her famous femininity in full flower. And Doug was all too happy to leave Glasgow for the soft south. Today, his only concessions to Scottishness are a mild liking for whisky and a gentle burr on his 'Rs'.

When she was a child, Emily loved spending time with her father. She was his little princess, his longed-for daughter after two sons and, though she couldn't articulate it at the time, she probably felt, even then, that she was a disappointment to her mother. 'I wanted a daughter,' Ginny used to say, 'so I could do her hair in a French plait.' But Emily had wild, curly hair that wouldn't stay in a smooth plait and she soon learnt to run and hide whenever she saw her mother approaching with brush, comb and pink ribbons. Ginny took her to ballet lessons but Emily preferred reading. Ginny bought her a Barbie doll's house but Emily preferred playing with her brothers' battered railway track. Ginny made Emily beautiful dresses with smocking and embroidery, but Emily preferred jeans. Even then.

When she was young, Emily took Doug's silences for companionship. He would occasionally call her 'hinny' (another relic of Scottishness) and make her little men out of pipe-cleaners. But, as she got older, Emily started to want someone to talk to and here Doug was as little use as her mother. 'Our Emily could talk for England,' he used to say, but Emily knew that, although quite affectionate, this was not a compliment. It was then, she supposes, that she started to remember bits of information to tell him, guessing that he preferred fact to fiction. But, in the telling, the information somehow lost its power to please and Doug never seemed very interested in the number of countries in Africa or the moons of Saturn. Gradually, Emily, too, started to relapse into silence, retreating almost entirely into a world of books. When, occasionally, she tried to share her growing excitement about books with her parents, she could never quite seem to make them understand. She remembers once trying to explain the plot of *To Kill A Mockingbird* to Ginny. 'And then Boo Radley, he was sort of like a mockingbird too, you see, and if they brought him out into the light it would be like killing him . . .' 'Boo Radley?' said Ginny, pausing with feather duster on the stairs. 'What sort of a name is that?'

Doug and Ginny are silent as Emily negotiates the roads

around the airport and finally emerges onto the motorway. Her father sits tensely in the front seat, hands clenched on his knees and, in her mirror, she can see her mother sitting in the back with her eyes shut.

'Are you OK, Mum?'

'These roads! How can you bear it?'

'Bear what?'

'All those cars driving on the wrong side of the road.'

'Well, it's the right side for them, you see. You get used to it after a while,' says Emily, pulling out to overtake a juggernaught. 'The Italians are actually brilliant drivers. There are fewer crashes here than anywhere else in Europe.'

There is a disbelieving silence. Then Doug says, 'It could be that they just don't report the crashes . . .'

'Yes,' says Emily, eagerly seizing on the chance to share a fact. 'Apparently sixty per cent of minor incidents go unreported.'

'There you are then,' says Doug with satisfaction. In the back Ginny winces as a Ferrari overtakes on the inside.

It is dusk when they reach the Villa Serena. Emily's parents have visited the house before, two years ago, when the renovation work was first completed. It was summer and Ginny moaned constantly about the heat and the mosquitoes. Doug fell asleep in the sun and burnt his face so badly that he had to go to casualty. Emily is looking forward to them seeing the house in the kindly cold.

They bump up the unmade road ('This road, Emily! Can't you tell the council?'), pass Raffaello's rubble and finally approach the house, mellow in the soft, brown evening. Emily takes out the suitcases and then goes to lift Charlie out. He has fallen asleep in his car seat.

'Would you like to carry him, Mum?'

'He'll be too heavy for me with my back.'

I thought he was so small compared to Ashley, thinks Emily crossly as she hoists Charlie onto one shoulder and lifts her mother's suitcase with the other hand.

'Be careful with that case, Emily. It's got my medication in it.' Ginny is diabetic and is constantly referring to her medication. Since her children have left home, she has taken a part-time job as a doctor's receptionist and considers herself practically medically qualified. She never has a cold, always a 'strep throat' and invariably refers to sickness as 'D and V'.

Siena and Paris come out of the house to meet them and Ginny brightens visibly. Siena is her favourite grandchild. She is blond and pretty and has even been known to do her hair in a French plait.

'Siena! You've grown your hair. It looks lovely.'

'Hello, Grandma.'

'Hello, Paris. Goodness me, you look thin.'

'Thanks, Granny,' says Paris, effectively silencing Ginny who did not mean it as a compliment. She also detests being called Granny.

As they enter the house, they are met by a glorious smell of pine needles and lasagne. Unfortunately, they are also met by Totti, whose presence has not yet been explained to Emily's parents. He leaps happily at Ginny, tongue flapping, giant paws on her shoulders.

'Get it off me!' shrieks Ginny.

'Down, Totti,' says Emily, grabbing his collar and yanking.

'Oh my back, my nerves . . .' Ginny collapses onto the wooden bench in the hallway.

'Whose is that creature?' asks Doug faintly.

'He's ours,' says Paris. 'He's called Totti.'

'You never said you had a dog,' says Ginny reproachfully. 'You know I'm allergic.'

'I didn't know you were actually allergic,' says Emily, pushing Totti into the kitchen. 'I just thought you didn't like dogs.'

'No, I'm allergic,' says Ginny firmly. She is fiercely proud of her allergies, which become more numerous by the day. 'I'm asthmatic too, you know.'

'Well, the air here is excellent for asthma,' says Emily, helping her mother to her feet. 'Charlie hasn't wheezed once since coming to Italy and you remember what he used to be like in London.'

Supper is a moderate success. Siena and Paris have put the lasagne in the oven though they haven't made a salad or heated up the bread. Ginny eats very little, blaming, variously, her allergies, her nervous exhaustion and her traumatic experience at the paws of Totti. Doug, though, cheers up after several glasses of Chianti and says that the house is looking lovely, that Emily is a talented woman and that Paul must be mad.

'He's OK,' says Emily, helping herself to more lasagne. 'He's got a new girlfriend now.'

Ginny moans gently. She liked Paul; he was her idea of the perfect son-in-law: good looking, charming and rich. She feels that Emily must have done something dreadful to drive him away. Paris looks up with interest. This is the first she has heard of the girlfriend.

'What about you, Siena?' asks Doug. 'Still breaking the hearts of all the Italian boys?'

'No. I had a boyfriend but we split up.'

'Plenty more fish in the sea,' says Doug complacently. 'How about you, Paris?'

'Actually,' says Paris, 'I'm a lesbian.'

Paris's diary

A mixed-up sort of day. The morning was lovely. We decorated the tree and I'm making a stocking for Totti with all his favourite things in it. Bonios and a rubber ball and some of Mum's old tights. Then Mum went to collect G and G and Siena and I played cards and watched the Dad's Army Christmas Special. Then the Gs arrived and it was all, 'Oh, Siena, you're perfect. Oh, Paris, you're a skinny dyke.' I got my own back though. Over dinner, I told them I was a lesbian. It was brilliant! I thought Granny was going to have a fit. Mum yelled, 'Of course she's not,' which sounded rather homophobic if you ask me. Grandad didn't seem to understand at all. They probably don't have lesbians in Glasgow.

I'm pretty sure that I'm not a lesbian. It's more the opposite. I don't like women very much. They're always going on about pathetic things like clothes and hair and who said what to who. And, after they get to about sixteen, they refuse to do anything fun like running or horse-riding or swimming. 'Oh I can't. It's that time of the month.' 'Oh I can't. My leg will fall off.' 'Oh I can't. I'm allergic to chlorine/grass/horses/enjoyment.'

Petra is the only woman I know who's different. She goes running every morning and she swims in the sea too. 'Isn't it awfully cold?' asked Mum. Honestly! I'm ashamed of her sometimes.

Anyway, Mum let slip one interesting thing at dinner. Dad's got a girlfriend! I'd sort of guessed this from some things Siena's said but I really want to know more. Who is she? Will I meet her when we go to stay with Dad in the New Year? I must grab Mum tomorrow and make her tell me everything.

I'm not sure how I feel about Dad having a girlfriend. On the one hand, I can see that he needs someone to look after him. He's so rubbish at looking after himself. On the other hand, why couldn't he stay here and let Mum look after him? She's good at all that stuff. I suspect the answer's got to do with sex and money and all those things I'm supposed to be too young to understand. I understand all right. I think it's sad and pathetic and utterly selfish. But I understand.

CHAPTER 5

Christmas Eve starts well. They wake up to a frosty morning and there is snow on the Mountains of the Moon.

'Snow!' breathes Charlie in ecstasy leaning out of the window in Emily's bedroom.

'It's not snow, it's frost,' says Paris crushingly from the doorway.

'It's as good as snow, isn't it, Charlie Bear?' says Emily, hugging him. His cheek feels smooth and cold.

'My feet are freezing,' says Paris, looking down at her bare feet on the stone floors. 'Can I put the heating on?'

'Put some socks on first,' says Emily, struggling into her jumper. 'Anyway, the heating's already on. We'll have a wood fire later. Nice and Christmassy.'

Paris snorts in her most Scrooge-like way but, when she comes back, she is wearing red socks with little Santas on them. 'Christmas socks,' she says.

'I want some!' wails Charlie. 'I want some Santa socks.'

Emily looks down at Paris's festive socks and suddenly finds that she wants to cry. This time last year Paris would not have worn Father Christmas socks, however cold she was. She would not have made a Christmas stocking for Totti either, or helped with the tree. This time last year, she was huddled in her black clothes complaining about the lack of proper Christmas cards in Italy. But then, this time last year Paul was with them and they were a proper family. It is all very confusing.

Ginny and Doug emerge for breakfast complaining about the cold.

'I didn't know it could get this cold in Italy,' says Ginny fretfully, wrapping a pink pashmina round her shoulders.

'It's these houses,' says Emily, from the stove where she is frying bacon (she knows that a proper English breakfast will be required). 'They've got thick walls and stone floors, you see.'

'You need some fitted carpets,' says Doug. 'I could help you fit them if you like.'

'There's not even a word for fitted carpet in Italy,' says Emily. She remembers learning this at evening classes in Clapham. 'Just *tappeto*, which means rug.'

Siena wanders in with her hair wet, making Ginny worry aloud about chills.

'It's OK, Grandma,' says Siena. 'I haven't had one cold since we've been in Italy.' Emily tries not to look triumphant.

Emily serves eggs, bacon and fried bread to her parents, a boiled egg to Charlie and a bacon sandwich to Siena. She watches Paris silently helping herself to bread and Marmite.

'Have some bacon and eggs, Paris,' says Ginny. 'Goodness knows you could do with fattening up.'

Paris puts down her bread and Marmite and stalks out of the room. Emily is furious.

'Mum! Look what you've done!'

'What have I said?' enquires Ginny plaintively, turning to Doug for support. 'Could someone tell me what I've said?'

'Nothing,' says Emily, crashing plates into the dishwasher. 'Nothing, nothing.' She has a feeling it's going to be a long day.

After breakfast they go into Monte Albano to look at the shops. Emily is rather surprised to find that both Siena and Paris elect to go with them, squashed into the back of the Alfa with Charlie on Siena's knee ('Is that legal here?'). Totti has been left behind because of Ginny's allergies and his howls follow them all the way down the unmade road.

Monte Albano is packed. It seems that everyone has left it until the last minute to do their Christmas food shopping. Stalls line the piazza selling chestnuts, olives, *panettoni* and a bloody abundance of meat: turkey, duck, goose and a thousand cuts of beef. Despite the crowds, the atmosphere is cheerful. From one shop comes a tinkly traditional tune, '*Viva, viva Natale arriva*', but there is none of the taped Christmas music, the Mud/Slade/Wombles horror compilations, that Emily remembers from her Christmas shopping days in England. People stop every few yards to exchange Christmas greetings, '*Auguri! Auguri! Buon Natale!*' Everyone is dressed in their best clothes and the narrow medieval streets are a seething mass of fur as the women parade their minks, sables and foxes (just as no Italian woman has grey hair, no Italian woman of a certain age would be seen in winter without her fur coat).

Ginny is fascinated by the Nativity scenes in every shop window. The bread shop has a Madonna made from a loaf and a baby in a basket of plaited bread. The clothes shop has three artfully draped kings and a Virgin Mary in shocking pink. One of the butchers (rather tactlessly) has a mass of furry animals worshipping at a stable made from lollypop sticks.

'Look at that, Emily!' Ginny points to the craft shop where a Mary made entirely from shells gazes at a knitted baby Jesus. 'Whoever made that was good with their hands.'

'I like it,' says Doug. 'Not like in England, with noisy great toys in every window.'

'Italian children get most of their presents in January, on the Epiphany, or on Saint Lucy's day,' says Emily. 'Christmas is much more of a religious day here.'

'We're getting ours tomorrow, aren't we?' asks Paris anxiously.

Charlie's mouth goes square. 'Want presents!'

'Yes, yes,' says Emily hurriedly. 'You'll get yours tomorrow.' Trust her children to show her up.

After two circuits of the piazza, they go into the café for coffee and hot chocolate. The windows are steamed up and there is a lovely, cosy feeling inside.

'Why is everyone standing up?' asks Ginny. 'There are lots of tables free.'

'Coffee costs more here if you sit down to drink it,' says Emily. 'Most Italians drink their coffee standing up.' As she says this, she can hear Raffaello's voice: 'Only English people say "a coffee".' Where *is* Raffaello? Didn't he say that he'd be home by Christmas?

They sit down and Angela, resplendent in scarlet cashmere, brings them their drinks. Siena greets her with composure, complimenting her on her jumper. Ginny complains that the coffee is cold, but half-heartedly. She is in a remarkably good mood.

'Emily!' Looking up through the fur coats, Emily sees Antonella coming towards them. She is wearing a beautiful suede jacket and her cheeks are flushed with the cold. She looks extremely pretty.

'Antonella!' They kiss on both cheeks and Emily introduces her parents. She can see her mother looking approvingly at both Antonella's jacket and her high-heeled boots.

'Won't you join us?' says Emily.

'Just for a second. Thank you.' Doug, ponderously polite, brings over a chair and Antonella thanks him charmingly. Doug goes bright pink.

'I wanted to meet with you,' says Antonella, switching to English in deference to Ginny and Doug. 'I have a little . . . *regalo* . . . for you.' She produces a small, beautifully wrapped box.

'Oh, really . . . you shouldn't . . .' stammers Emily, embarrassed because she hasn't thought to get a present for Antonella.

'Please! It is nothing. And Andrea . . . my son . . . he ask me to give this to Paris.' And she passes another, less well-wrapped, box to Paris. Paris goes Ferrari red.

'Paris!' Ginny is always quick to pick up on embarrassment. 'Have you got an admirer?'

Paris ducks her head and mutters furiously, 'No! Of course not!'

'It's from a school friend,' says Siena, coming to the rescue. 'It's sort of like a tradition here.'

'Oh,' says Ginny, but she sounds unconvinced.

Antonella turns to Emily 'I have a card from Raffaello today,' she says.

'Oh?' says Emily but she feels her mouth go unaccountably dry.

'Yes. He stays in America for Christmas but he will be back in the New Year. He send you his regards.'

'Oh,' says Emily again. But all through the ensuing conversation, at Antonella's good-humoured attempts to ask about English Christmas traditions, at her parents' evident admiration of this attractive Italian woman, at Paris's continuing embarrassment, at Charlie's squirming boredom, all she can hear is Raffaello's voice, 'Antonella di Luca. She's a lovely woman.' So lovely, evidently, that she deserved a card where Emily did not. So lovely that she has brought Emily a present and even her son is apparently lovely enough to make Paris blush for twenty minutes. So lovely that, all through the rest of the day, Emily is assailed by tiny but violent darts of pure jealousy.

*

Petra is making mince pies. Although both the boys hate mince pies, she feels that it is the right thing to do at Christmas and, besides, her mother is coming in the afternoon. Petra does not really get on with her mother, a strong-minded Yorkshirewoman who used to be a headteacher and whose professional verdict on Harry is that he is 'spoilt', but again, it seems the right thing to do at Christmas. And, really, Christmas Day with just her and the boys is too depressing. The boys don't like turkey either so last year they had tuna pasta and ice cream. Jake and Harry ate every scrap with evident enjoyment but Petra, clearing the table afterwards, felt that it was all just *wrong*: she should be covering a turkey carcass in cling film and complaining that they would be eating cold turkey for a week, she should be sweeping up crinkly paper and discarded jokes from the crackers (they can't have crackers either because they terrify Harry), she should be really *doing Christmas* like every other mother in the world. So, this year, she and her mother are going to have a turkey crown from M&S and she is damn well going to make mince pies.

The telephone rings and Petra reaches for it with a floury hand. She has a vague feeling that it will be Ed, ringing to wish the boys Happy Christmas. She hopes it will be Ed, for their sakes, but she dreads the inevitable battle about getting Harry to the telephone. He hates the phone but Ed can never understand this and invariably accuses Petra of turning his son against him. At least Jake can be relied upon to chat. He loves his dad. God knows why, thinks Petra sourly.

'Hello?'

'Hello, Petra. It's Darren.'

Darren. George Clooney. Petra pushes back her hair, covering it with flour and leaving tiny bits of pastry dangling from her fringe. This is the last thing she expected. After their theatre outing, she has hardly spoken to Darren in the end-of-term rush. He didn't even give her a card. The only presents exchanged at school are in the 'Secret Santa' (buy a present for five pounds and put it in the lucky dip; Petra got a pair of fishnet tights) so she didn't expect a present from him. She doesn't expect anything really. Their evening out had been great. They had sat high up in the circle, looking down at the gilt and crimson of the stalls; the play was amusing (Alan Ayckbourn) and well acted; afterwards they had a lovely meal in an Italian restaurant and they clinked glasses and Darren had said how much he was enjoying the evening. And then – nothing. Beyond helping her on and off with her coat, he hadn't even touched her. Was he gay or did he think she was? She should have worn heels, just this once. They had walked back to her house and he had reached out his arm, almost, but not quite, touching her. 'Good night,' he had said. 'Thank you.' And that had been it.

'Darren! Hello.'

'Happy Christmas and all that.'

'Same to you.' With a sinking heart, Petra saw that Harry had wandered into the kitchen. If there was one thing he hated more than the phone, it was seeing her on the phone.

'I was wondering, would you like to come to a party tonight?'

'A party?' If he had said a human sacrifice with ritual dancing afterwards, Petra couldn't have been more surprised.

'Yes. Alan in the science department is having a Christmas party. Do you fancy it?'

Petra almost laughs. Alan in the science department has a full-face beard and collects Star Wars memorabilia. She can't think of anything she'd fancy less. Harry starts tugging at her sleeve. 'Mum!' he hisses.

'I can't really,' she says. 'My mother's coming to stay.'

'What about a drink then? Just a quick one?'

'I'm sorry, I don't think I can.'

'Mum!' yells Harry, eyes dilating with fury.

'What about a walk along the beach. Ten o'clock. I'll bring some champagne.'

'Mummeee!'

'OK,' says Petra at last. 'That sounds lovely.'

And she puts down the phone, very carefully, as if it might break.

Emily and Paris are in one of the outhouses putting together a bike for Charlie. This is one of the times when Emily misses Paul the most. He was good at all the traditional male things: putting up the Christmas lights, mending fuses, fixing punctures, sleeping with women half his age. But Emily has to admit that Paris is a pretty good substitute. Emily has long ago been relegated to the role of assistant: holding the spanner, steadying the bike, murmuring tactful words of encouragement.

'He's spoilt, Charlie is,' says Paris, indistinctly, through a mouthful of screws. 'I never had a bike at three.'

'Darling! You did!'

'Siena's cast-off. That's different.'

'We got you your own bike later,' says Emily defensively. 'That red one with the stabilisers.'

'Yes,' says Paris, reminiscently. 'I loved that bike.'

'Do you remember you insisted on taking it to bed with you?'

'I even knitted it a scarf in winter.'

'You called it Malcolm.'

'Yes. I don't know why.'

They are silent for a minute. Emily thinks of the house in Clapham, all creaky boards and awkward corners, of the stained glass in the front door and the view over the rooftops at the back. A real family house, she used to say (mostly when defending the mess that crept over all surfaces and piled up, like silt, in the basement). By the time Charlie came, they had given away all Siena and Paris's toys. Their afterthought baby. 'Was it a mistake?' friends asked breathlessly, but it wasn't, not at all. After Paul had come galloping down to Brighton for her, declaring his undying love, promising her anything, *anything* if only she would come back to him, she had said that she wanted to move to Italy. She had to move away from Clapham, where the Other Woman lived only two streets away. She wanted a new challenge, she wanted a fresh start and she was still, after all these years, in love with Italy. So she and Paul had come to Tuscany, they had taken the trip up the unmade road and they had seen the Villa Serena. And, that night, in a hotel in Siena, Charlie had been conceived.

Emily shivers as she holds the bicycle wheel. It is very cold in the outhouse, which was once a dairy (it still has a tiled floor and high, slatted windows). Once, she and Paul had planned to convert the outhouses into self-contained apartments so they could rent them out and make their fortunes. But the money had run out before they had even finished the main house, and the self-contained apartments, like the swimming pool, remain unfinished, a testament to their naivety.

'Mum?' Paris's accusing voice breaks into her thoughts. 'Why didn't you tell me that Dad had a girlfriend?'

'I'm sorry,' says Emily. 'I meant to.'

'What's she like?'

'I haven't met her. She's called Fiona. She's a fitness consultant.'

'Cool.'

'I thought you might think it was cool,' says Emily wryly.

Paris is irritated by her mother's humble expression. 'For God's sake!' she explodes. 'I only said it was cool, not that she was going to be my new best friend or anything. I just meant that it might be nice to have someone else about the place who likes sport, that's all.'

'I know. I'm sorry.'

'Will she be there when we go over in the New Year?'

Paul has asked if the children can come to England for a week in January. Emily does not see how she can refuse to let the girls go, he is their father after all, but she really doesn't want to send Charlie. How can she put her darling baby into the care of a twenty-something Sloane in a designer tracksuit? 'He'll be in *my* care,' said Paul. 'Are you saying you don't trust me to look after my own son?' Well, yes, she was, but she knows better than to say these things aloud. And then there is the cost. Despite (because of?) being declared bankrupt, Paul still seems mysteriously to have money. But who is going to pay for the air fares, not to mention the running costs of the three children for the week? She can imagine Paul letting them live on McDonald's and fizzy drinks. Charlie is sure to have a bilious attack.

'I don't know,' she says to Paris. 'Would you mind if she was?'

Paris shrugs. 'Not really. I can't really imagine Dad on his own, can you?'

'No,' says Emily, 'I can't. Is the bike finished? Shall we leave it here and I'll come and wrap it up after Charlie's gone to sleep?'

Emily is surprised when Ginny offers to come with her to midnight Mass, and she is even more surprised when, a few minutes later, Siena offers to accompany them. Doug says he will stay at home and look after the children but, as he is snoring in his chair by ten o'clock, Emily resigns herself to relying on the dubious guard dog skills of Totti who, having eaten two Christmas decorations and five mince pies, is sitting smugly in front of the fire.

Emily packs Charlie's stocking (she will have to do the girls' later), puts another log on the fire and chases Paris up to bed. Then she, Ginny and Siena venture out over the icy roads into

Monte Albano. The sky is clear and full of stars. The white cows in Romano's field look like ghosts in the moonlight, surrounded by clouds of white breath.

'Do you think they kneel down at midnight?' asks Siena, leaning forward from the back seat. 'Like in the poem?'

'I don't know,' says Emily. 'Let's look when we come back.'

'They look dangerous to me,' says Ginny, pulling her coat round her. 'Are you sure they're not bulls?'

'They have buffalo in Italy Grandma,' says Siena. Ginny screams.

Paris's diary

Christmas Eve. I'm sitting up in bed trying to feel like a kid again. It's really frosty outside so everything kind of looks like a Christmas card. Before she went to midnight Mass, Siena and I got the bell from Totti's old collar (the one he won't wear because of the noise) and rang it outside Charlie's window so he would think it was Santa's reindeer. It was funny but standing out there in the cold it sort of felt like it was Santa's reindeer. I mean, I know we were making the noise ourselves, I know it wasn't sleigh bells ringing, but it felt magical somehow because it was Christmas Eve and everything. I looked at Siena and I know she felt the same but then she said something stupid about Andrea and I went back to despising her again.

I don't know why Andrea gave me a present. Does he like me? Do I like him? He's not good looking really but he has got a nice face. He's got blond hair which is a relief after everyone round here being so dark. And he's got really nice blue eyes. He looks at you like he's really listening to you. Siena says he's really clever which might not mean anything because, to Siena, anyone who can spell 'Wednesday' is clever. But somehow I think he is clever because sometimes he says things which are funny but nobody gets them. He doesn't mind, he just says them for the hell of it. I can understand that, I do it myself sometimes. It's like saying 'I know something you don't know' but to yourself, not out loud. But he doesn't make people feel stupid, like when Francesca didn't know what a gynaecologist was. He could have made her feel really thick (specially considering what kind of doctor it is) but he didn't. I like that.

I wonder what's in the present?

Charlie lies totally still in his bed. He heard them, he really heard them. Paris will never believe him but he heard them. A sort of magical jingling sound. It was sleigh bells, anyone could tell that. Right outside his window. Perhaps Santa is here now, parking the reindeers under the trees, tramping up the path with his sack full of presents. Will he come right into Charlie's room like the other man once did? He'd put his fingers to his lips to tell Charlie not to make a sound. It's funny, he'd looked quite friendly when he did that, like Monica-with-the-glasses when she tells them to be quiet at nursery. So Charlie hadn't made a sound. He'd shut his eyes and when he opened them the man wasn't here. That's why he'd thought he was magic, like the tooth fairy. Or like Santa.

Charlie really doesn't want Santa to come into his room. For a moment he thinks he'd even rather not have any presents, even though he wants a bike more than anything. Maybe Santa will wait until everyone's asleep and come creeping upstairs like a burglar. He wishes he hadn't thought of the word 'burglar'. It's a scary word, like 'ghost' or 'murderer'. Once he heard Olimpia say Raffaello-with-a-beard was a murderer. He doesn't know what it means but it has a horrible, hard, scary sound.

He can hear Paris moving about in her room and somehow that makes him feel safe. Even a murderer would be scared of Paris.

The church is boiling. The heat is on full blast and everyone is wilting in their fur coats. Emily sees Olimpia at the front of the church, resplendent in something that looks like mink. Siena is immediately pulled into a scrum of young people, all dressed in their best clothes. She looks back apologetically over her shoulder at Emily who waves an understanding hand. She is delighted to see that Siena is still popular, despite finishing with Giancarlo (who is also here, looking sheepish as he holds Angela's hand).

Remembering how well the shop window Nativities had gone down that morning, Emily takes Ginny to see the *presepio*, the crib. Here, the emphasis is on realism. A mountain cave, made from local stone, houses an almost life-size Holy Family.

It is artfully lit, casting long shadows, and the ox and ass peer suspiciously from the sidelines.

'Why are they in a cave?' asks Ginny.

'Well, maybe it was a cave,' says Emily. 'Up in the hills here, some farmers still use caves as shelter for their animals.' She is uncomfortably reminded of the cave on her own land, the cave that, for so many years, sheltered the bodies of Carlo Belotti and Pino Albertini.

Emily enjoys the Mass. The church is dark and the only light comes from the candles which cast dramatic shadows over Don Angelo's face as he preaches a brief sermon about being kind to asylum seekers and turns his assistants into sinister presences as they move to and fro in darkness behind the altar. The music is lovely, though there is none of the jolly communal singing that she remembers from English services. She knows that carols are not part of the Italian Christmas tradition but she feels that the silence of the congregation goes deeper than that. A priest (the incense and brimstone one) once told her that English Catholics are quiet in church because once they used to have to hold their Masses in secret. But this does not explain the silence in Italian churches where, as far as she knows, Catholics have never been persecuted. Privately, she interprets it as rather hostile. 'Go on then,' Italian congregations seem to be saying, 'Entertain us, uplift us, but don't expect us to help.' So the choir sings expertly and the congregation fidgets in its furs. Emily misses bawling out, 'Born, to raise the sons of earth, born to give them second birth,' but, even so, she appreciates the high-flown Latin duet between priest and choir. It is far easier to think spiritual thoughts when you don't understand what's being said.

After Mass there is coffee and wine in the cellar below the church. Emily remembers her shock when she first saw this underground room, which is essentially a fully equipped taberna, complete with bar. The heat here is even more stifling and Ginny fans herself with the order of service whilst Emily battles her way through the fur coats to get them a cup of coffee. When she returns, Romano, her next-door neighbour, is deep in conversation with a slightly hypnotised-looking Ginny. 'Just chatting to your dear mother,' says Romano genially when Emily appears. She has already discovered that having her parents to stay is a sure-fire route to local approval. 'We hope you will come over for drinks on Boxing Day,' continues Romano. 'We even have some English beer.'

'We'd love to,' says Emily politely. She does not really fancy an evening of stilted conversation drinking warm beer but she knows the invitation is a great honour. She has never been in Romano's house before.

Siena, flanked by two girls in full party warpaint, now appears at her side.

'Mum! Can I go to Francesca's house? She's having a party.'

'How will you get home?' asks Emily, ignoring Ginny's look of horror.

'I'll take her home,' says one of the girls. 'I've got a car.'

'Well, no later than two, OK?'

'Thanks, Mum. Happy Christmas!'

The light touch of Siena's lips and, more than that, her look of uncomplicated happiness, warms Emily throughout the cold ride home listening to Ginny's outrage at her lax parenting.

'Letting her come home at two in the morning! That girl driving her is sure to be drunk.'

'People don't drink much at Italian parties,' says Emily, swerving to avoid a fox. 'You'd be surprised.'

'I would be!' returns Ginny with what she obviously thinks is brilliant repartee. 'I certainly would be.'

It is pitch black when they reach the Villa Serena. Looking up, Emily sees a tiny sliver of a new moon, like the faintest ghost of a smile. 'Mum!' She grabs Ginny's arm. 'The new moon! Make a wish.' Suddenly she realises that, for the last twenty years, she has always automatically made the same wish: on moons, wishbones, mince pies, throwing coins in fountains, hearing the first cuckoo of spring. She has always wished that she will see Michael again. Now, she decides, it is time to change.

Fixing the moon with a determined glare, she wishes, 'Make me happy.'

And, on Brighton beach, Petra and Darren lie in each other's arms while fireworks explode into the night sky.

CHAPTER 6

On Boxing Day afternoon Emily feels even less like trekking out over the frozen, dark fields to have a drink with Romano and Anna-Luisa. The fire is lit in the sitting room and the children are curled up on the sofa watching their new DVDs. Emily wants nothing more than to sit with them, eating chocolates and watching the complete *Blackadder Collection*. But she knows that she must honour the invitation (hospitality is a sacred thing in Italy) and also, for some unknown reason, Ginny and Doug are actually keen to come with her.

So far, she thinks cautiously as she changes into her boots, Christmas has been a success. Everybody liked their presents (even Ginny's home-crocheted cardigan for Siena turned out to be the height of retro chic) and the children hurried away after breakfast to play with, listen to and wear them. Emily and her parents had had a civilised glass of Prosecco and Ginny and Emily prepared lunch, with less friction than you might expect. Emily gave in to her mother on every culinary decision and Ginny unbent so far as to say that Emily had turned out to be 'a nice little cook'. Even a phone call from David and Kelly had not dented Ginny's good humour; in fact she was delighted to hear that Kelly hadn't even started peeling potatoes by midday and that Leanne's new PlayStation wouldn't work on their TV ('What a shame, dear. We've got a spare black and white if you'd like it?').

After lunch, Emily and Paris had taken Totti for a walk through the olive trees. It was already dark and Emily lit their way with a torch (Raffaello's torch, she realised with a jolt, the very torch that she had taken from his pocket the night that he had appeared with Totti in his arms).

'Just like Clapham,' Paris said, shivering in her new black skirt.

'What do you mean?'

'Well, it was always just you and me going for walks then. I used to wish we had a dog to make them more interesting.'

Emily waited for some comment about the superiority of London parks over Tuscan olive groves but, amazingly, none came. Emily stumbled over some loose stones and Paris grabbed hold of her. 'Steady on, Mum. It's nice that we've got one now, isn't it?'

'One what?' asked Emily stupidly. Her ankle felt as if it had been twisted right round.

'A dog, of course.' And Paris let go of her to greet a returning Totti with a rapturous hug. Still, it had definitely been a good moment.

Now Paris, Siena and Charlie hardly look up from the screen when Emily says goodbye.

'I won't be long. Call me on my mobile if you need me.'

'Yeah, OK,' says Siena vaguely, eyes fixed on Baldrick wearing a giant turnip.

Outside it is very dark and Emily shines Raffaello's torch carefully in front of Ginny as her mother is, of course, wearing high heels. Ginny squeaks and holds on to Doug's arm as they negotiate the stony path through the olive trees.

'You want to tarmac this, Emily,' she says more than once.

'Mmm,' says Emily, not listening. She is thinking about Blackadder and about Christmas and about Paris eating a whole leg of turkey and about Raffaello's face when he said he was going to America. 'I'll be home by Christmas.' She has the horrible feeling that she will never see him again.

At the end of the olive grove is a small, white gate leading to Romano's land. His house is comparatively new, built of white stone with a low, sloping roof. Once the Villa Serena had been the farmhouse, surrounded by stables and dairy and barns, but now Romano runs the farm from this modest bungalow. He rents most of Emily's land, for which he pays very little, but he does provide Emily with bottles of her own olive oil, cloudy and green like a witch's potion, and with wine grown from her vineyards. This seems the perfect arrangement to Emily. It used to drive Paul mad though.

They knock on the door and it is opened almost immediately by Anna-Luisa, magnificent in an embroidered housecoat.

Romano, hovering by her elbow, is in shirtsleeves and braces. They greet Emily's parents as if they are royalty and usher them to the best chairs in the sitting room. Emily looks around with interest. Never, she thinks, has she been anywhere that is less like a farmhouse. When renovating the Villa Serena, she took care to preserve the wood stove, the farming implements, the rush baskets, the hooks for hanging and preserving meat. She exposed bricks and left the uneven floors and low ceilings. Here, the keynote is modernity and comfort. Velvet sofas, black ash furniture, a giant flat-screen TV, chandeliers, endless glass-fronted cabinets containing photographs and ornaments. Row upon row of ornaments, most of them religious: Madonnas, ivory crosses, framed prayers, wooden Nativity scenes, holy water from Lourdes, holy soil from Jerusalem, sacred wood from the coffin of Santa Francesca of Rome (encased in lace and framed in gold).

Anna-Luisa promises 'proper English tea' and emerges with a tray so laden with tea-making paraphernalia that it is almost impossible to locate the actual tea: bone-china cups and saucers, sugar tongs, tea strainer in its own case, ornate teapot, Apostle spoons, three types of coloured sugar. Ginny is enchanted. Emily can feel her comparing it to her own chipped mugs and one bent teaspoon (the kids keep throwing them away inside yoghurt pots). Anna-Luisa also offers cake, *biscotti* and special Christmas *amoretti*. Ginny purrs with pleasure and relays compliments for Emily to translate.

'What lovely cups. Tell her, Emily. Lovely cups! I love these almond biscuits, don't I, Emily? Emily, tell her how much I like these biscuits.' Emily complies, smiling so widely that she can hardly fit her cake into her mouth. Anna-Luisa beams, eating nothing, but filling up their plates with deadly regularity.

In the background, Romano is asking Doug about British politics. Emily's heart sinks. Doug could talk forever on the iniquities of the prime minister; she just hopes she won't be asked to translate. What is 'self-satisfied bastard' in Italian, anyway?

'You prefer, what is her name, Margaret Thatcher?' asks Romano, dunking a biscuit into his tea.

'Oh aye,' says Doug, blissfully unaware of his shipbuilder father spinning rapidly in his grave. 'She was a strong woman.'

'Strong. *Sì*,' agrees Romano.

'What England needs,' continues Doug, who finds that this always goes down well at the Rotary Club, 'is a dictator.'

He could not have foretold the effect this remark would have. Romano slams down his teacup and leaps to his feet. He crosses the room to grasp Doug by the hand.

'*Sì*, my friend, *sì*. A dictator. You are wise, very wise. When was Italy strongest? When was Italy most feared? When was Italy most prosperous? When we had Il Duce, of course. When Mussolini was in power.'

'Mussolini,' repeats Doug faintly.

'*Sì, sì*. He drained the marshes. He built the roads. He defeated the Mafia. He won us back our empire. People feared us. Rome lived again.'

Doug looks at Emily in confusion. What has he said? Everyone knows that Mussolini was a clown, not even accorded the same fearful respect as real monsters like Hitler and Stalin. And didn't the Italians kill Mussolini anyway? How come this chap is singing his praises like this, bringing over a photo of the fat fascist himself, sitting on a horse?

'A wonderful rider. *Sì, sì. A* great fencer. A skilled linguist. Yes, a wonderful man. And do you know who else thought so?'

'N-no,' stammers Doug.

'Your Churchill! Winston Churchill himself. He admired Mussolini very much. In fact . . .' Romano lowers his voice impressively, 'he say to his wife, "Mussolini is one of the most wonderful men of our time." Churchill wanted a friend on the Axis' side in case the Axis powers win the war. Oh yes, this is all the truth, my friend.'

Doug looks stunned. 'Churchill? Really?'

'Oh yes, my friend.'

Emily attempts to come to her father's rescue. 'You must have some great stories about Monte Albano during the war,' she says to Romano.

'Ha,' says Romano. He pauses with the picture in his hand, then kisses it reverently and puts it back on a shelf. He seems to have become depressed suddenly. The ebullience with which he remembered Mussolini has disappeared.

'Surely you are too young to remember,' compliments Ginny.

Romano grins a gap-toothed smile. 'No, I remember. I was a child. But I remember. My father was mayor. He was loyal to Il Duce. Yes, to the end. But, the others! One day they are shouting "Duce! Duce!" the next they are spitting on his grave.'

'There was a lot of partisan activity in this area, wasn't there?'

Romano comes back to life with a roar. 'The partisans! Pa! I spit on them! Italy changes sides and suddenly every man, woman and child is a partisan. Not my father. No. He says, "I am Mussolini's man until the day I die." The Americans locked him up. Everyone else says, "No, no, I'm with the partisans. God bless America." Pa!'

'Did you know Carlo Belotti?' asks Emily, suddenly really wanting to know, oblivious both of Ginny's blank stare and Doug's discomfort.

'Sì,' says Romano. 'Yes, I know him. A brave man, I admit. I know the family well. Olimpia, she is my friend. Yes, Carlo Belotti was a brave man but, in the end, he was in the pay of the Americans. An occupying power. So, to me, he is a traitor. God rest his soul,' he adds piously.

Anna-Luisa, who has been listening to all this with a calm, inscrutable expression on her face, rises to her feet and offers drinks. A glass of Prosecco? Grappa? English beer? Emily and her mother accept a glass of Prosecco (though Emily knows it will make the walk home even harder work) and Doug has a beer. Romano, drinking grappa, relapses to his former amiable silence. Anna-Luisa brings out photographs of her children and grandchildren. There is a son called Benito (ha!) who helps run the farm but he lives in Monte Albano and is away visiting his in-laws, and there is a daughter called Italia who lives in Rome. There are numerous grandchildren in a succession of baptisms and first Communions.

After half an hour of this, Emily makes a move to leave. It is late and she wants to get back to Charlie. She is also sleepy from the wine and the hot room and wants to leave before Romano can get back onto the subject of Il Duce. Her parents get to their feet slowly, Ginny still exclaiming over the photographs and the cakes. Anna-Luisa smiles graciously. Emily can tell that her mother has made an excellent impression.

In the crowded hallway they stand exchanging awkward pleasantries in mangled Italian. There are more religious objects here: water stoops, plaster saints and a huge oil painting of the Pope. Anna-Luisa points out a tiny wooden Madonna that comes from Medjugorje, the town in Croatia where assorted children saw regular visions of Mary ('every day, at twenty past six'). Ginny and Doug obediently turn to the statue but Emily is looking at something else. Round the base of the statue hangs a rosary. A ceramic rosary with a cross that has curved Coptic corners.

'Lovely rosary' she says.

Romano is pleased. 'Ah,' he says. 'When I was a boy every schoolchild was given one of these. Do you know who gave them?'

Emily thinks she can guess.

'Il Duce! Mussolini gave a rosary to every schoolchild. He put the cross back into the classroom. Every classroom had a crucifix and every child had a rosary. Like this one.'

On the way home, Ginny and Doug talk endlessly about Romano and Anna-Luisa. They are fascinated, and a little stunned, by their introduction to Italian life. 'To think she made all those cakes!'

'He was a proper fascist, all right. Did you see him kissing that photo?' But Emily is silent. She is thinking that, if the rosary was given to all schoolchildren, then the cross found on Carlo Belotti's body cannot have belonged to Belotti himself. It must have belonged to someone much younger. Someone who was at school during the war. Someone who was at school with Romano.

CHAPTER 7

Buona fine, buon principio.

Happy end, happy beginning. Emily hears this phrase every-where in the days leading up to New Year's Eve and it never fails to give her a little jolt of surprise and recognition. Her life feels suddenly to be full of beginnings and endings and her emotions, too, seem to veer between extremes of happiness and sadness. Quite often she feels both at once, teetering on a kind of schizophrenic see-saw.

Two days ago, her parents went back to England. Emily hugged them at the airport feeling, again, torn between sad-ness at seeing them go and utter relief at getting rid of them. It hadn't been so bad, really. At least this time Ginny and Doug seemed actually to enjoy Italy. Ginny, in particular, loved the shops and the quaint hill towns. She made firm friends with Anna-Luisa, they spent a morning making gnocchi together and Ginny went home with a bag packed full of homemade pasta, cakes and salami. Doug avoided Romano, not wishing to be dragged into another all-fascists-together conversation, but he did take several walks with Paris and talked to her about football. He also, to his own great satisfaction, mended Emily's shower and nailed back the banging shutter that was driving them all mad in the night. He even softened towards Totti, having play fights with him and calling him a 'great soft doggie', his Scottish 'r's coming out with a flourish.

Even so, it was an undeniable relief to be saying goodbye. Emily was beginning to dread her mother's 'little chats' about Paris's thinness, Totti's dirtiness (Ginny's attitude to Totti did not change: she continued to circle around him as if he were the Hound of the Baskervilles) and the likelihood of Emily getting back with Paul. 'But I don't *want* to get back with him,' Emily had wailed at last. Ginny's mouth disappeared in disapproval. 'Well, I'm sorry. I brought you up to think that marriage was for life.' Emily did not remember David getting half this much grief when he left Sue for Linda (or Linda for Kelly).

The children, too, were relieved to see the back of their grandparents. All in all, they had behaved very well. Of course, it was easy for Siena. She will always be Ginny's favourite and only has to smile and look pretty to retain her position. But Paris was really very patient with the constant comments about her weight and her sulkiness and her mysterious 'admirer'. Here again, Totti helped. Whenever Ginny got too much, Paris could just grab the dog and go out for a walk. Going out for a walk by yourself is a temper tantrum; with a dog it is just another good deed. Charlie, too, was constantly being asked, 'What's the magic word?' and compared unfavourably to

Ashley. He didn't care though. He was too busy riding his bike (the stabilisers have already come off) and playing with a giant talking Barney, a deeply irritating present from Paul.

Paul is the only fly in the ointment. Emily has had to agree that the children go to visit him for a week, later in January. Paul is paying for everything apparently; she hasn't asked where the money is coming from. She is dreading it. Paul has promised to come to Forli to collect the children but, even so, saying goodbye to them (even for a week) will be a hundred times worse than saying goodbye to her parents. No mixed feelings there.

When she got back after seeing her parents off, Emily found another ending lying in wait for her. She found a message to ring Giles at the paper ('Some posh git rang, can you ring him back?' was Paris's actual wording). She did so to receive the unwelcome, if not entirely unexpected, news that the paper was dropping her column.

'But why?' she asked. Don't get emotional, she told herself sternly.

'To be honest, darling. It's gone off.'

'Gone off?'

'Yes, you know. It seems to have lost its magic a bit.'

Emily did know. She had been trying very hard to continue to be lyrical about porcini mushrooms and sunsets over the olive grove, but reality kept insisting on creeping in.

'For example,' Giles continued, 'when you wrote about your divorce.'

'Well, I couldn't pretend it wasn't happening, could I? Keep writing about Spouse like he was this cute little helpless character when all the time he was off with his new girlfriend.'

'Don't see why not. Lots of columnists do it.'

'Well, I couldn't.'

'Anyway, darling, I think the whole Tuscany thing is just the teeniest bit over now. It's all Slovakia these days. No hard feelings and all that.'

No hard feelings. She supposed not. It had been increasingly difficult to write the column now that her rose-coloured spectacles were well and truly off. She kept finding herself wanting to write about the bodies on the hillside, about Monica's desperate search for a man and the problems of anorexic women in the land of plenty. It was hard to keep writing the same old Sunday supplement stuff when she really wanted to write about life in Italy as it really was; so much richer, deeper and darker than she had ever imagined when she first started writing the 'Thoughts from Tuscany' column two years ago.

It is the money that is the real problem. The column was Emily's only real source of income. Giles, salving his conscience, offered her some reviewing and a special about 'Life in Tuscany, two years on' but that was it. She has ten thousand pounds in the bank, enough for about six months if she is careful (there is no mortgage on the Villa Serena though the utility bills are huge). Her second New Year's resolution (after losing weight) must be to get a new job. And quickly.

Emily stands at her mirror, getting ready for the New Year's

Eve party at Antonella's. It seems a long time since she has actually looked at herself, besides horrified glimpses of herself in shop windows, hair wild, skirt the wrong length. Now she peers at her reflection with almost scientific interest. Her hair is still dark; she supposes that, at forty-one, she should be grateful for this, but it is shaggy and badly in need of a cut. Also, her springy, dark hair only serves as an unwelcome contrast with her white, anxious-looking face. How has she got so pale? She was really quite brown in the summer (Emily is old fashioned about suntans, seeing them as highly desirable). But now she looks like a ghost. Her eyes look very dark but, sadly, so too do the circles under them. Where have they come from? She always used to pride herself on her fresh-faced, healthy look, not needing much makeup, only some mascara and lipstick. Now, she feels in need of the whole of Elizabeth Arden, and about a vat of Oil of Olay. Her skin looks dry and chalky with new lines appearing round her mouth and in the corners of her eyes. My God, she thinks, peering closer, I have finally turned into my mother.

But, stepping back, she has an even worse shock. How the hell has she got so fat? She has been dimly aware for some time that she needs to diet but, as she hasn't got any scales, she has been able to close her eyes to the awful reality. There are genuine rolls of fat around her stomach. Actual rolls! And her arms have flesh swinging from them. Her boobs, always her best thing, are still perky enough but now, rather than nicely curvaceous, they seem huge. Monstrous. In need of the sort of bra that contains underwiring of molten steel. She poses, Playboy style, in front of the mirror. A grotesque middle-aged woman leers back at her.

'Mummee!' calls Charlie from downstairs. Emily hastens to get dressed. She doesn't want to put Charlie off women for life, after all. How on earth could she have slept with Chad? More to the point, how could Chad have slept with her? (Rather to her surprise, Emily has had several emails from Chad since their encounter in Bologna. He even sent her a Christmas card hoping to see her soon. She didn't send one back.) Oh well, maybe she should just give up on men for ever, resign herself to getting fatter and fatter, until she will have to be lifted out of the Villa Serena using the old farmyard hoist. Emily goes over to the mirror and starts, carefully, to apply her make-up. She is not ready for that just yet.

As she paints over the dark circles under her eyes, she thinks about Antonella's party. She is wearing the earrings (tiny amber orbs) given to her by Antonella as a Christmas present. She feels guilty that her gratitude is tinged by something which she does not quite want to recognise as jealousy. What could be more natural than that Raffaello should be attracted to Antonella, a beautiful single woman from his own home town? Let's face it, he is not going to fancy an overweight Englishwoman with three unruly children. He was obviously only being friendly because he wanted to get his hands on her Etruscan remains. Come up and see my etchings and all that. In Raffaello's case, he really is only interested in the etchings. But, says a stubborn voice in her head, what about finding a table at the restaurant on Siena's birthday? What about encouraging Paris to eat? Come on, says another voice (which sounds faintly like Petra's), he was just being friendly, that's all. Those are the sorts of things a friend would do. After all, he's never shown the slightest sign of being attracted to you, has he? No, says Emily sadly to herself, rubbing rouge onto her cheekbones, he hasn't. It's been so long since anyone has been attracted to her that she is not sure she would recognise it anyway. She doesn't count Chad.

On Boxing Day she received a surprising, and faintly unsettling, call from Petra.

'Guess what?' Petra's breathless voice was incongruous amongst the sad remnants of Christmas Day (bags full of wrapping paper, wilting tinsel, plates of leftover food). 'I did it!'

'Did what?'

'Slept with Darren. You know, George Clooney.'

'You didn't?'

'I did.' Petra sounded triumphant. 'On Brighton beach. We went for a walk on Christmas Eve night, had some champagne, got talking, he kissed me and that was it.'

'What do you mean, that was it?'

'Oh, you know.' Petra laughed. 'It was fantastic. You know the sort of sex you had when you were a teenager? Wild and a bit dangerous. It was like that. It was amazing.'

Emily tried to sound enthusiastic but actually she had been rather shaken. She had not had wild, dangerous sex as a teenager. Michael was the first man she had slept with and, by then, she was nineteen, almost not a teenager at all. And sex with Michael had been wonderful, of course, but it hadn't been wild. She had been too inexperienced and somehow she had never quite had the courage to interrupt Michael's virtuoso performance with requests of her own. Paul, well, sex with Paul had been wild to start with. She remembers being amazed at how *abandoned* you could feel, in bed with someone you didn't really love. Later on, when she had come to love him, sex became less exciting. By the time they had children, it had really become a sort of indoor tennis, fun and good for you but not really earth-shattering. She cannot imagine, even in her promiscuous post-Michael days, having sex on Brighton beach.

Emily sighs and starts to get dressed. She feels too depressed to put on anything too dressy so she settles for her favourite black trousers and a ruffled shirt. At least the trousers are slimming and the shirt shows her cleavage, the only place where spare flesh is acceptable. She sprays on perfume and looks at herself in the mirror once more. All right as long as no one gets too close. Fat chance, she thinks gloomily, going downstairs to round up Paris and Charlie. Siena is out with friends but Paris and Charlie are coming with her to the party. There'll be lots of young people, Antonella says. She has to admit that Paris has been quite good about it; she has hardly complained at all.

Paris, too, is looking in the mirror. She does this so rarely that she hasn't even got a mirror in her bedroom. She has had to go into Siena's bedroom (a ghastly mess of fluffy cushions and stupid pictures of Siena's friends pulling faces in photo booths). Now she stares at herself in Siena's dressing-table mirror (dressing table, how sad is that?). Short brown hair, pale skin, blue eyes. Is she pretty? Mum says so but then she would, wouldn't she? She thinks Charlie is gorgeous and he looks like a troll. She knows Siena is pretty but Siena is easy. Siena looks just like girls in magazines: blonde hair, brown skin, hips and boobs and all that stuff. She, in contrast, is all straight lines: flat chest, skinny legs, no in-and-out bits. Once, when she looked in the mirror, she saw a fat person. Although, deep down, she knew she wasn't fat, that was what she saw. Now, she supposes, she is over that (whatever *that* was, she refuses to give it a name). Now all she sees is a thin girl with short hair. The question is, what will *he* see?

'See you tonight,' Andrea said when she saw him in the marketplace that morning. He was with his friends and he didn't come over or anything. Just smiled and waved and said that. Paris could feel herself blushing, as if her whole skin was burning. She'd had to pretend to be looking at these really gross jeans, the kind with stupid flowers embroidered on them. When she'd looked up from the jeans, he'd gone.

It's not like a *date* or anything but she is going to see him, spend some time with him. She still doesn't know how she feels about him. His Christmas present to her, a book on training German Shepherd dogs, was reassuringly unromantic, but the fact that he gave it to her at all still has the power to make her go hot and cold at odd times of the day. It must mean that he *thinks* about her. It must mean that he remembers her telling him about Totti and how hard he was to train. She tries to imagine him going into a shop and choosing the book and writing her name on the card ('To Paris with love from Andrea'). Love. What does it all mean? For a second, she almost considers talking to Emily but then she stops herself. Poor old Mum, she must be way past all that love stuff by now. It's not as if she ever knew much about it anyway.

Antonella lives in a modern apartment, just outside the town walls. From the outside it looks fairly grim, all wrought-iron grilles and stained plaster, but inside it is large and comfortable with polished wood floors and white-painted bookshelves. Antonella, stunning in a black velvet dress, greets them affectionately and establishes Charlie in front of a DVD and sends Paris off to play computer games with Andrea. Emily is surprised to see Paris looking back at her with rather a pleading look. She thought that Paris liked Andrea. He always seems such a polite, well-mannered boy. Perhaps Paris thinks he's dull. Anyway, there is nothing she can do to save her. Andrea ushers her through the door of what can only be his bedroom. If it was Siena, she would have been quite worried.

The party is in full swing. Jazz is playing on the stereo (Emily hates jazz; she hates not knowing when it will end) and the rooms are all full of people. Emily spots Monica in the kitchen, deep in conversation with a grey-haired man in a startling pink shirt, and Lucia on the sofa, holding hands with a dark man who must, she supposes, be her husband. Antonella gets Emily a drink and introduces her to people. 'This is Emily. She's British. She's a writer.' Emily smiles and smiles but she finds it hard to follow the conversation and, once people have established that she is not J. K. Rowling, they do not seem very interested in talking to her. Emily smiles and drinks her wine too quickly. She sees people looking over her head for someone more interesting to talk to but she hangs on grimly. 'Have you lived in Monte Albano long?' she asks the smooth, blonde woman next to her, smiling some more.

'All my life,' says the woman coolly. 'And you?'

'Just two years. My husband and I bought a house—'

'Ah, Alberto!' The blonde woman spots someone coming into the room. 'Do excuse me.' And Emily is left alone, still smiling.

'Are you OK, Emily?' It is Antonella, circling the room with wine bottles.

'Yes, fine. Thank you. And thank you for the earrings. They're lovely.' She shakes her head to display them.

'I'm glad you like them. Did you have a nice Christmas?'

'Yes. Well, yes and no.'

'Yes and no?'

Emily takes another slurp of wine. 'It was lovely having my parents. Well, some of the time. But I've just lost my job.'

'Oh no.' Antonella looks genuinely concerned. 'I'm so sorry.'

'Well, it's OK. I was finding it harder and harder to write the column anyway. But I do need to find another one.'

'Why don't you teach English at my school?' says Antonella. 'We're looking for someone. It wouldn't pay much but it would be something.'

'But I don't know anything about teaching.'

'You don't need to. They're only little. Just sing them English songs or something.'

'I'll definitely think about it,' says Emily. Her mind has gone blank and the only English song she can think of is 'God Save the Queen'. The Sex Pistols' version.

An elderly woman comes over to claim Antonella's attention and Emily drifts off to find Monica. She is still in the kitchen talking to the pink-shirted man.

'Emily! Have you met Emilio? He works at the university.'

'Everyone seems to work at the university.'

'No,' says Emilio gravely. 'Only about half of them.'

Emily laughs loudly, delighted to have got a joke in Italian. She likes Emilio, who is the sort of suave, slightly camp figure that she associates more with Brighton than Tuscany. He launches into a description of his tutorials, teaching lounging sports-obsessed youths about Dante. Like many Italians, he assumes that she is completely familiar with Dante's works.

'I'm afraid I haven't really read the *Commedia*,' says Emily apologetically.

'But I thought you studied literature,' says Monica.

'I did, but it was really just English writers.' Emily feels English universities sinking lower in their estimations. It is certainly true that whilst any educated Italian is familiar with

Shakespeare, Emily is willing to bet that most of her contemporaries at UCL know nothing about Dante or, if they do, can only quote the first line, the one about being halfway through the journey of one's life.

Charlie wanders in, bored with the film, and Emily is suddenly much more popular as the Italians crowd round him commenting on his blond good looks. She wonders how Paris is but doesn't like to invade the teenage sanctum. She must be all right surely, or she would have come to moan at Emily. As the clock nears midnight, more people crowd into the kitchen, forcing Emily, Monica and Emilio out into the hall.

'In England,' says Emily, 'we say that a tall, dark stranger should cross the threshold at midnight, carrying a lump of coal.'

'Coal?' says Emilio. 'Why coal?'

'I don't know. Maybe it's something to do with keeping warm through the winter.'

'I've heard it's very cold in England,' says Emilio sympathetically.

Antonella switches on the television so they can see the countdown in Rome. 'Ten, nine, eight, seven, six . . .'

Emily finds herself by the front door, Charlie on her hip, trying not to spill her champagne. Emilio is talking to her about the myth of the Green Man and she tries to look suitably intelligent.

'Five, four, three . . .'

Suddenly, there is a loud knocking at the door. Emily, startled, reaches over to open it.

'Two, one . . .'

As New Year explodes in an excited babble of voices and laughter, Emily pulls open the door to reveal a tall, dark man, but not a stranger.

'Raffaello,' she says.

Buona fine, buon principio.

CHAPTER 8

'Mummy! Don't go!'

It is awful. It is worse than she ever expected. It is as if her heart is being ripped out of her body. She is breathing hard, bent almost double, she feels as if she is about to die.

It had all started quite well. The children had been excited as they packed the suitcases in the car. Paul had met them at the airport, grinning as the children ran towards him, scooping Charlie up in his arms. It will be all right, Emily told herself, they've missed Paul, they need some time with him. She will enjoy being by herself, she can get on with odd jobs around the house, really get down to doing some writing (her piece on Tuscany Two Years On is overdue).

Paul looked well. Thinner, wearing a zip-up top and jeans. He looked vaguely sporty, something she attributed to Fiona's influence. He did not look like a man who had just gone bankrupt.

'Emily,' he said.

'Hello, Paul.'

'You look well.' She knows that she doesn't but she supposed he was trying to be nice.

'So do you.'

Emily handed him a list of instructions about Charlie, his bedtimes, his asthma stuff, his favourite books and DVDs, his need to have the talking Barney with him at all times. Paul put it in his pocket without reading it.

'You will read it, won't you?'

'Yes,' said Paul, sighing. The distillation of a hundred such conversations over the course of their marriage.

They waited in a café before the flight was called and Emily managed not to comment as Paul bought Coke for the kids. It's just important that they're happy, she told herself. Charlie sat on Paul's lap, playing with Barney and singing tunelessly. The girls were plugged into their music but they looked reasonably happy. Paris even volunteered that she would miss Totti and Emily (in that order; her list of instructions on Totti's care is even longer than Emily's list about Charlie).

The trouble starts at the departure gate. As soon as Charlie realises that Emily is not coming with them, he pulls back. 'Mummy!' he shrieks.

'Darling.' Emily squats down to his height. 'I'm not coming this time. You're going to have a lovely holiday just with Daddy. I'll see you very soon.'

'No!' shouts Charlie, clinging on to Emily's leg with strong, desperate arms.

'Come on, Charlie.' Paul prises him away with difficulty.

'We'll have fun. We'll go to the zoo. You remember the zoo. We'll go to the funfair. You can have candyfloss.'

'Want Mummy!' yells Charlie, twisting round in Paul's arms.

'You'll see Mummy very soon. We'll phone her when we get to England. How about that?'

'No! No! No phoning. Want Mummy!'

Eyes streaming, Emily kisses her daughters and presses her lips to Charlie's flushed cheek. 'I'll see you soon, precious. Mummy loves you.'

'No! No!'

'Look after them,' she says wretchedly to Paul.

'Of course I will,' says Paul impatiently, still struggling to hold Charlie. 'Look, this is only making it worse, we'd better go.' And he strides away, holding a still-screaming Charlie, with both girls trotting after him.

Emily waits until they are out of sight and then she makes her way to a bench, sits down and weeps bitterly. She knows it is ridiculous (they are only away for a little over a week) but she cannot help herself. She folds herself up on the bench and cries and cries.

'Mrs Robertson! Emily!'

It is a few minutes before she realises that someone is calling her name. Then, slowly looking up, she sees scuffed workboots, faded jeans, a red jumper, a dark pirate's face. Raffaello.

'What's the matter?' Raffaello squats down to her level, rather as she had done earlier with Charlie.

'The children. Gone. Charlie,' she sobs.

'Have they gone to stay with your husband?'

'Yes.' She sniffs horribly.

'Well, then, they can't be gone for long. A week?'

'Ten days,' sniffs Emily.

'Well then.' He reaches out a hand and pulls her to her feet. She rubs a hand over her eyes, thinking how awful she must look, tear-stained and blotchy. Raffaello passes her a handkerchief, a proper one, crisp linen, with his initials on it.

'Come on,' he says, not unkindly. 'Wipe your eyes.'

She does so and can't stop herself blowing her nose as well although she knows it looks disgusting. Raffaello takes her arm and begins to guide her out of the airport, past the milling tourists and the gum-chewing, machine-gun toting policemen.

'Have you got your car?' asks Raffaello as they reach the exit to the car park.

'Yes.'

'Then, go home, drive carefully and have some rest. I'll come round later and take you out to dinner.'

Emily nods, hardly taking this in. Then something strikes her and she asks, 'What are you doing here anyway?'

'I'm here to collect some geophysics machinery,' says Raffaello. He smiles at her, not his usual slightly mocking smile but something rather harder to fathom. 'I'll see you later. I'll be round about eight.' Then he turns and disappears into the crowd.

*

When Emily saw Raffaello standing on Antonella's doorstep on New Year's Eve, the first thing she thought was that there was something different about him. The second thing she thought was that she should kiss him, at this moment, with the alibi of the clock striking in the background. But then Antonella called from inside and the opportunity was lost. Raffaello was drawn into the party, just pausing to grin at Emily as he passed her by, close enough for her to touch his coat, wet with the night's rain. As he passed, she realised what was different: he had shaved off his beard.

'What happened to your beard?' she asked later, as they sat on the sofa beside a sleeping Charlie. Paris was still nowhere to be seen.

'I shaved it off,' he said. 'Gabriella didn't like it. She said it was too scratchy.'

'How is she?'

'Wonderful. Talks all the time. Has an imaginary dog called Peter. Thinks that Italy must be near China because noodles look so much like pasta.'

'It's a logical idea. Didn't Marco Polo bring pasta back from China anyway?'

'Rubbish! Pasta is Italian. Anything else is heresy.'

'I thought you believed in historical fact.'

'Not where pasta is concerned.'

At that moment Monica and Emilio came over and the talk turned to America. After a little while, Paris appeared, looking tired, and Emily reluctantly decided that she ought to go home.

Raffaello had carried Charlie out to the car saying that he would see her soon. That had been ten days ago.

Now Emily drives home, feeling light-headed after crying so much. It is raining and the road to Monte Albano is full of tunnels, treacherous little openings in the mountainside, dimly lit and full of dangerous corners. Emily knows she needs all her wits about her but she keeps drifting off into thoughts of the children (will Charlie have stopped crying? Will Paul remember to give him sweets to suck during landing and takeoff?) and, more disturbingly, of Raffaello. In what sense is he taking her 'out' to dinner? Does he just feel sorry for her? How *could* she have blown her nose on his handkerchief like that?

It is still raining when she reaches the villa. She can hear Totti barking madly from inside and is glad of his presence as she walks through the unusually silent house. The clock ticks loudly and she can hear her footsteps echoing across the stone tiles. Charlie's abandoned bicycle in the hall makes her cry for a few minutes but mostly she feels too wound up for tears. She is itchy, unsettled, disturbed, as if all her nerve endings are exposed. When Totti brushes up against her it is like an electric shock, when she drinks a glass of water she imagines that she can feel it dripping through her body, as if she is dissected, cross-sectioned, on display. She wanders around, tidying things, putting away the breakfast dishes. Siena has left a Jilly Cooper book open on the kitchen table. Paris's black boots lie in the hallway. Emily puts these things away, giving the boots a surreptitious hug, mud and all. Totti watches, tail wagging.

She can't face lunch but forces herself to eat an apple, chewing each mouthful without tasting it. She flings the core out of the window. Perhaps an orchard will grow there in a hundred years' time. She hears Don Angelo's voice: 'A hundred years? That is nothing.' The house is silent apart from Totti's frantic scrabbling at the front door. She will have to take him out for a walk. Paris's list (1. Walk Totti *every day*) rebukes her from the fridge door. Her laptop lies open on the table. She should really get on with the article. Instead, she sits down and idly flicks on to Google. Out of habit she types in 'michael b—' and then stops. She closes the laptop. Outside the rain is thundering on the low roof. She hopes the guttering lasts the winter, she cannot cope with another expense. She has taken the job teaching English at the primary school but it pays very little. She could sit down now and plan her first lesson. Instead she gets up with a sudden burst of energy. She will tidy upstairs and then she will have a bath.

In her luxurious bathroom, all natural stone and marble (it was the bathroom that finally bankrupted them), she lies in the scented water and thinks about Raffaello. She hasn't thought so much about a man since she stalked Russell Edwards, a boy in her school chemistry class, and followed him home every night for a week. With Michael, it just happened, their sudden explosive romance. She hadn't had time to become obsessed with him beforehand. He had just appeared, in the twilight of Gordon Square, and taken over her life. With Paul, he had become obsessed with *her* and had pursued her with single-minded certainty. It had really been very restful. But now she seems to have all this time to wonder: does he like me, do I like him, is he in love with Antonella, is he in love with Gabriella's mother, is he still in love with his first wife, the tragic Chiara? It makes her very uneasy, all this wondering, but she has to admit it adds interest to life. She turns on the hot water tap with her toe.

The telephone rings and she goes to answer it, pink and dripping. It is Paul. They have landed safely and the children are fine. Yes (impatiently), even Charlie. He is quite happy and is playing with his Happy Meal toy. Are they in McDonald's then? Yes (defensively). Can she speak to the girls? Siena comes on the line. Yes, the flight was OK. It is nice to be back in England, it's cold but sunny (she is delighted to hear that it is raining in Italy). Dad has taken them to McDonald's and then they are going shopping. What for? Oh, you know, stuff. Does she want to speak to Paris? Paris is quick and businesslike. How is Totti? Has she taken him for a walk yet? England is OK, she supposes, a bit dirty after Italy. And she hates the chips in McDonald's, they smell of sick. Bye, Mum. Love you too.

As Emily puts the phone down she has the strangest feeling. As if there is someone there in the room with her, watching her. The feeling is so strong that even when she turns round slowly and sees that her bedroom is completely empty, apart from Totti looking at her hopefully, the sensation does not go away. The back of her neck prickles and she suddenly feels far too exposed, wrapped in a towel, hair dripping. She clicks on the radio which bursts into a saccharine Europop monstrosity. Perfect, no one could feel scared whilst listening to '*Bim bim bim, bom bom bom, ti voglio bene, he he he.*' She dresses hurriedly, pointless to wear anything revealing on a night like this and, anyway, she feels as if she wants to be very covered indeed. Black trousers, grey cashmere jumper, black boots. Right. Ready for anything. She stomps downstairs, Totti following.

She lets Totti out but is relieved when he doesn't go far. 'I'll take you for a proper walk tomorrow,' she promises. He wags his tail hard and knocks a lamp off a small table. It is half past seven, time for a glass of wine. She thinks she feels quite calm and in control and is surprised to see her hand shaking as she pours the wine. Get a grip, she tells herself. She'll do some work on the article and then Raffaello will come in to find her sitting poised at her typewriter, the model of a calm, self-possessed woman.

In fact, when Raffaello appears, half an hour later, letting himself in through the open door, he finds her clearing up Totti's sick. The dog, obviously bored without Paris, has been gorging himself on a box of liqueur chocolates, left over from Christmas. The sick smells disgustingly of crème de menthe.

'Ah, Mrs Robertson,' says Raffaello, observing her from the doorway. 'You shouldn't have gone to all this trouble.'

'Shut up and pass me the bucket,' says Emily through gritted teeth.

Ten minutes later she is on her way out to Raffaello's Jeep. The rain is falling in solid sheets and a muddy beige waterfall is cascading down the slope.

'Very unusual,' says Raffaello, opening the car door for her. 'This much rain so early in the year. Must be because it's so mild.'

'Mild?' shivers Emily, climbing awkwardly into the Jeep. 'It's freezing.'

'It's normally much colder than this in January,' says Raffaello, shutting her door and sprinting round to the driver's side. Despite the rain, he has no hat or hood and his black hair is soaking, flattened to his head. Without his curls he looks different, more dangerous somehow.

Emily never had any doubt that Raffaello would take her to La Foresta. Like Michael, he seems to believe that his family's restaurant is his own private kitchen. In fact, he acts as if he has cooked the food himself, ordering her complicated items that do not appear on the menu but which, apparently, the chef will be delighted to prepare for her. 'We do a famous ribollita,' he says. 'You must have that.' He then describes in detail how it is made, though Emily doubts that he can actually cook at all.

'I love this sort of food,' she says.

'It's the *cucina povera*,' he says with a grin. 'Poor people's food, bread and pasta with a little olive oil and garlic. Nothing exotic, nothing fancy. Not like French food.'

Emily nods, thinking of Vittorio's with its elaborate gourmet menu. Once she had thought that Vittorio's was the very essence of Italy but now that she actually lives in the country, she finds that it is something very different. And Michael? Perhaps, she thinks with a sudden jolt of recognition, perhaps he wasn't the real thing either. And if he wasn't, she is free at last. Slightly dizzy, she takes a gulp of wine. It tastes of woods and berries and winter.

'Lovely wine,' she says. 'What is it?'

Raffaello shrugs. 'I don't know. Something local.' He grins wickedly. 'You don't want to get like all those English tourists going on about wine all the time.' He puts on a terrible English accent and mimics, 'Oh, look, a lovely Montepulciano 1982. Let's take it home and bore everybody senseless talking about it.'

Emily laughs. 'It's a big part of people's experience of Tuscany,' she says, 'the food and the wine. I read somewhere that because tourists don't speak much (because they usually don't understand the language), the other senses are heightened: taste and touch and sight.'

'Must be why they're called sightseers,' says Raffaello. 'Seeing is everything.'

'And they take photos to prove that they've seen it,' says Emily, feeling smugly removed from that sort of tourist, sitting in an Italian restaurant with the owner's nephew, drinking delicious wine that does not appear on the wine list.

'So you are not a tourist then?' says Raffaello teasingly.

'No,' says Emily, offended. 'I live here.'

'I was born here,' says Raffaello, leaning back as their steaming plates of ribollita are put in front of them, 'but I don't feel at home here. I'm still Raffaello Americano. I'm still the mad archaeologist.'

'But you're *their* mad archaeologist,' suggests Emily, trying not to eat too greedily. The ribollita, a sort of soup made with chunks of bread, is unbelievably good.

'Maybe,' says Raffaello. 'But I'm still the evil man who killed his wife.'

Now it is out in the open, Emily feels rather relieved. The dead wife, beautiful and doomed like someone in a fairy story, no longer lies between them.

'They can't really think that surely?'

'No? On the anniversary of her death, every year, someone sends me a picture of her. Underneath it says, "Chiara Belotti, murdered by R. Murello 1992".'

'No!' says Emily shocked. 'Who would do a thing like that?'

Raffaello shrugs but Emily thinks he has a shrewd idea. She has a suspicion herself, come to think of it. Raffaello sighs, takes a gulp of wine and then says, 'I didn't know she was anorexic, at first. Sounds stupid now, but I didn't. She was very thin, of course, but so are lots of girls. And she seemed to eat well. When I took her out, she always seemed to like her food.'

'Did you bring her here?' asks Emily, knowing the answer.

Raffaello nods, his eyes dark and fathomless. 'She loved it here. Everyone loved her too. They used to make her a special pudding, a raspberry torta. How was I to know that she was making herself sick as soon as she got home?'

'What about after you got married? Didn't you guess then?'

'Not at first. But then I started to guess. Her gums bled, her breath smelled odd. I started to read all the books, all the

329

magazine articles, trying to find out about it. But I couldn't talk to her.'

'Why not?'

'She just wouldn't talk about it. I know it sounds ridiculous but she just blanked it out completely. Just refused to admit it was happening. She was a living skeleton, for God's sake, but she insisted there was nothing wrong. I didn't know what to do. If her mother had been alive, perhaps she could have done something but she died a few months before our wedding. Looking back, maybe that was the start of it. Chiara was very close to her mother.'

'Did you persuade her to see a doctor?'

'Eventually. In the end I tricked her. She was desperate to have a baby. My God! She was barely five stone, she had stopped menstruating months before but she couldn't understand why she hadn't got pregnant yet. So I told her I had made an appointment with a fertility expert. Of course, he was actually a specialist in eating disorders. He took one look at her and admitted her to his clinic.'

'That must have been hard.'

Raffaello gives a harsh laugh. 'She was furious. She said I had betrayed her, that she hated me. She refused to see me for days. But she got better. That was the main thing. Slowly, she got better. When she came back home she was still dreadfully thin but she was eating again. I really thought that everything would be all right.'

'Then what happened?'

'I went away,' says Raffaello, frowning into his glass. 'I was offered a dig in Australia, using new techniques, and I went. I knew how weak she was but I still went.' He looks angrily at Emily as if it was somehow her fault. 'Our apartment was on the fifth floor. One day she walked up all the stairs, came in, laid down on our bed and her heart just gave way. All her organs were damaged, you see. I found her when I came home a week later.'

'How awful.'

'Awful, yes. Her family have never forgiven me.'

'But Raffaello,' says Emily, voicing something that has been in her head a long time, 'couldn't her family have looked out for her while you were away? If you ask me, it's as much their fault as anyone's.'

Raffaello laughs bitterly. 'Her family didn't visit. They didn't like me so they didn't visit the apartment. She could go to them but they wouldn't come to her.'

'Well then, I think it was their fault,' says Emily stoutly.

Raffaello laughs, and puts his hand on hers. 'You're a sweet girl, Emily, you know that?'

Emily laughs too, embarrassed. She looks down at their hands, lying on the red linen tablecloth, his so large, with black hairs on the back, hers white and feeble-looking, the nails bitten.

The waiter comes with their second course and Raffaello says suddenly, 'Do you miss your husband? Do you miss Mr Robertson?'

'He wasn't Mr Robertson. He was Paul Hanson. Still is, of course.'

Raffaello smiles. 'Hanson is as Hanson does.'

'Exactly.' Emily drains her wine, Raffaello immediately refills her glass. Don't get drunk, she tells herself. 'Yes,' she says after a pause. 'I do miss him sometimes. I miss having someone about the house, I miss having someone to discuss the children with. But . . . I don't know. I miss us, together. I keep thinking back to the days when we were happy, when we were first married, when the children were young. But I don't miss him, not really. By the time we separated, we didn't really have much of a marriage. I mean, we lived together, when he wasn't working, but we never really talked. Just practical stuff about the kids and the house. We were like two mechanics, servicing some monster machine, not like two people in love.' This is the first time she has admitted this to anyone.

'What about the children? Do they miss him?'

'I think the girls do. Charlie is too young really. Paul doted on him in theory because he's a boy but, in practice, he didn't have much to do with him. But Siena misses him, I think. Paris too. She says he needs someone to look after him and she's probably right.'

'She probably is. She's a highly intelligent girl.'

'Yes, she is.'

Raffaello is about to say something else when there is a general hubbub in the restaurant behind them. Raffaello turns round and Emily sees an elderly man, beautifully dressed in a light grey suit, making his way through the tables. It is like a royal progress: diners reach out to greet him, to touch him. He raises his hand in benediction, offers a word here, an embrace there. The waiters hover around him like acolytes, anticipating his commands. He walks slowly, leaning on a gold-topped stick.

Raffaello turns to smile at Emily. 'Now you will meet Zio Virgilio,' he says.

The elderly man is making his way towards them. He shows no surprise at Raffaello's presence. Raffaello rises to his feet. 'Zio!' He embraces the old man, kissing him on both cheeks. 'Allow me to present Emily Robertson.' Emily rises too and Virgilio extends a hand. It feels like a leaf, brittle with age.

'Won't you join us?' says Raffaello. For a second time, Emily sees a waiter conjure a chair, as if by magic. Virgilio sits down, handing his stick to another hovering waiter. 'Champagne,' he says. 'Bring champagne.'

'Sì, Signore Virgilio.' The waiters melt away. Virgilio turns to Emily. He has an extraordinary face, like a portrait by El Greco, thin and aesthetic-looking with dark, dangerous eyes. Raffaello's eyes.

'So. You are the lady from the Villa Serena?' He speaks in English, strongly accented but fluent.

'Yes.'

'I've heard a lot about you.'

'Good things, I hope,' says Emily nervously.

'Of course,' Virglio makes her an odd little bow. 'I hear that you are very beautiful and that you have two lovely daughters and one delightful small son. I hear that my great-nephew torments you by digging up your land and filling your house with skeletons.'

The waiter brings the champagne and presents it to Virgilio with a flourish. He gestures impatiently for it to be poured.

Raffaello laughs. He seems very relaxed in his great-uncle's rather intimidating presence. 'Yes, it is true that I have been a great torment to Mrs Robertson.'

'No,' mumbles Emily. 'You've been very kind.'

'Kind?' Vigilio looks quizzically at Raffaello. 'You say he's been kind?'

'Very kind.'

'He must have changed,' says Virgilio simply. He holds his glass up to the light. '*Salute!*'

'*Salute!*' they chorus. It feels as if they have strayed into a film; the candles on the table cast dramatic shadows on to Virgilio's face and gleam on the cut-glass of the champagne flutes. It only needs the music from *The Godfather*, thinks Emily.

Virgilio turns to Raffaello. 'What news of the skeletons?'

'Well, you know we buried them with great honour.' Raffaello smiles with an irony that is drily acknowledged by the older man.

'Yes. I didn't attend the funeral myself but Giovanni and Renato were there. They say it was quite a spectacle. Angelo did us all proud.'

'So I hear,' says Raffaello gravely.

'Did you know Carlo Belotti?' asks Emily.

Virgilio smiles widely but does not answer for some minutes. When he does, it is in a softer voice than he has used so far. 'Yes. I knew him. We all knew him. He was a brave man, though he put all our lives at risk.'

Emily thinks that, while everyone has called Carlo Belotti brave, everyone, Romano, Virgilio, even Don Angelo, has added a qualifying clause.

'Were your lives at risk for hiding the partisans?' she asks.

Virgilio nods, his face dark in the shadows. 'Yes. General Ramm, the Nazi general, he was a terrible man. They say that, in Lucca, in retaliation for a partisan uprising, he ordered a baby to be thrown into the oven in the town square. Ordered him burned alive while his family watched.'

'God!' says Emily, horrified.

'Yes,' says Virgilio with a mocking smile. 'You think it was easy for us, sandwiched between the Nazis and the partisans and the Americans? When the partisans cleared Monte Battaglia for the Americans, Ramm ordered that the entire village be destroyed. Even I know what it was like to be marched to the town square with my brother to face a firing squad. "Say your prayers," they told us. I remember I asked Our Blessed Lady to look after my mother. I was proud of that later, that my last thoughts were for my mother.'

'But you were spared?'

'As you see,' Virgilio gestures to himself and somehow to the whole restaurant, to the whole glittering room with its deer's antlers and its photographs of the mountains in the snow. This too, he seems to say, survived the Nazis, even if it had to feed them first.

'Why?'

'Who knows? Ramm had orders from above, they say. We will never know. We were saved, my brother Severino and myself. He was killed a year later, in the Genoa uprising.'

'Your other brother, Raffaello's grandfather, was killed in Spain, wasn't he?'

'Yes.' Virgilio reaches out an affectionate hand towards Raffaello. 'Yes, poor Amadeo. It was his fault, of course. We were the brothers of "The Communist". That is why Ramm hated us so much. Even now some people in the town call this the red restaurant, *il ristorante rosso*. All Amadeo's fault. God rest his soul.'

'The Nazis ate here, didn't they?' says Emily, thinking that the red restaurant probably hasn't changed much in the last sixty years.

'Yes. Not the SS but the first Germans who were stationed here. They were gentlemen, my mother always said. There was one she was very fond of, he gave us the warning that the SS were coming, told us to hide our valuables and head for the hills. Yes, my mother liked those first Germans. Except for the potatoes. She always said they ate too many potatoes. They ate them the way Italians eat bread.'

'Speaking of which,' says Raffaello, 'your ribollita is better than ever.' And the conversation turns, gracefully, to food. But Emily, following Virgilio's gesture as he points towards the kitchens, praising the excellence of his chef, suddenly notices something that had previously escaped her attention. Sitting on a shelf, between a photo of the Monte Albano football team and a row of dusty Chianti bottles, is a human skull.

They drive home through the apocalyptic rain. Neither speaks and the only sound is the relentless beat of the windscreen wipers. Emily is glad they are in the Jeep as its tyres spin wildly on their way up the unmade road. A lake has formed below her terrace and the gutters are bent under the weight of the water.

Raffaello turns off the engine, yet still neither of them moves. For a moment, the headlights illuminate the terracotta villa, hazy in the rain, but then Raffaello flicks a switch and they are plunged into darkness.

'Thank you for a lovely evening,' babbles Emily suddenly. 'The food was wonderful and it was fascinating to meet your uncle—'

'Shh.' Raffaello leans towards her. 'The time for talking is over.'

Emily opens her mouth to disagree, to say goodbye, to be cool and poised and all the rest of it. Instead, she finds herself reaching for him and kissing him wildly, desperately, as the rain thunders against the roof.

CHAPTER 9

Emily wakes to find that the rain has stopped. The winter sun is streaming in through the open shutters and Totti is lying snoring on the bed. There is no sign of Raffaello. A note on her pillow, written on a page torn from a diary, reads: 'Dear Mrs Robertson, Have gone to see what the rain has done to my excavations. Back soon. R.' Emily smiles, the thought that Raffaello can still call her Mrs Robertson (after the car, after the hallway, after the stairs, after the bedroom) strikes her as irresistibly funny.

She opens a window and breathes in the bright, cold air. There is a drenched smell to everything, a smell of grass and earth and wet leaves. I am alive, she thinks, delightedly, foolishly. Yesterday's mood of frenzied expectation has given way to a heavy, dazed contentment. Who would have thought, says Emily to herself, shutting the window and going into the bathroom, that this was what I was waiting for? To go to bed with Raffaello. To go to bed (and the stairs and the hallway, etc.) with Raffaello and for it to be so straightforwardly fantastic. No guilt (she checks herself carefully for the signs), no embarrassment, no agonising. Afterwards she had fallen into the deepest sleep she had had for years, a drowned sleep that blotted out past, present and future, that obliterated (God forgive her) her children, her ex-husband, the fitness trainer from Cirencester, the dead wife, the skeletons in the cave, the look on Virgilio's face when he told her about the war.

Emily showers briskly, dresses and goes downstairs, Totti sticking anxiously to her heels (his meal was inexplicably forgotten last night and he wants to be sure that it doesn't happen again). She puts on coffee and starts grilling bacon. Today, she thinks happily, today is the day for the full English.

She feeds Totti (at last!) and puts out the breakfast plates. She must play it cool, she tells herself, she mustn't frighten him off by getting clingy as soon as they have slept together. But, even as she thinks these thoughts, squeezing oranges so joyously that the pips ricochet across the table, she doesn't really believe them. This time, she thinks, I won't screw things up. This time everything is going to be just perfect.

Finally, at nearly ten o'clock, she hears footsteps running (running!) up the terrace steps. The kitchen door flies open, banging back against the wall. Raffaello stands in the doorway, his face alight with happiness, with a joy (she has to admit) that surpasses anything she saw last night.

'I've found them!' he shouts. 'I've found my Etruscans!'

PART 4

Spring

CHAPTER 1

It was the rain, they said. The rain that thundered down all night and washed away stones and mud and laid bare the bones of the mountain. When Raffaello left Emily's bed that January morning to go and check the excavations, he found that half the hillside had been swept away into a muddy waterfall that was still rushing down the slope several hours after the rain itself had stopped. What was left were the white rocks of the Mountains of the Moon and a gaping black hole in the hill that made Raffaello's heart leap in his chest.

Falling on to his knees, Raffaello began to scrape away mud and stones with his hands. The rain had done a neater job than any archaeologist could and several large grey rocks were exposed. Below these, almost a metre high, was an opening; unmistakably a doorway of some kind. Forgetting Emily, forgetting everything, Raffaello scraped and dug for almost an hour, widening and deepening the hole, exposing more stones, regularly spaced, like giant building blocks. Then, very carefully (he didn't want to get buried in a mud slide, after all),

Raffaello lowered his head and upper body into the opening he had created.

Afterwards he thought of Howard Carter's words when he first saw the tomb of Tutankhamen. 'What do you see?' 'Wonderful things.' Raffaello looked into the darkness under the hill and he knew that his life's work was fulfilled. He knew that nothing would ever be the same again.

Running into Emily's kitchen, half laughing, half crying, he shouted, 'I've found them! I've found my Etruscans!' He grabbed Emily by the hand and half dragged her out of the house, up the muddy hill, Totti capering madly at their heels ('A walk! At last!'). At the top of the hill, Raffaello pointed grandly to newly exposed stones, white in the thin sunshine.

'My God,' said Emily slowly. 'A mudslide.'

'That's not all,' said Raffaello. 'Look. Look inside. Here, have my torch.'

Reluctantly, because she was wearing her best jeans, Emily knelt and looked into the narrow opening between the stones. To her utter amazement, she found herself looking into a room, a square stone underground room, complete with benches and chairs cut into the wall. The wavering light of the torch picked out pillars, carvings, intricate frescos.

'What is it?' she breathed at last.

'It's an Etruscan tomb,' said Raffaello, almost dancing on the spot.

'But it's like a little house. There are seats and things.'

'Those are seats waiting for dead ancestors,' says Raffaello.

'I think there's an altar too, for sacrifices. There may be more tombs, perhaps a whole cemetery. I've got to get help.'

And with that he turned and ran back down the hill, leaving Emily kneeling on the muddy ground.

Now it is evening and Raffaello and his volunteers have been digging all day. They are a diverse crew: students from the university, Stine from Badia Tedalda, Tino the policeman, and even a small crowd of onlookers including Umberto the mayor and Romano's son Benito. Raffaello has infected them all with his own manic enthusiasm as he shouts orders, marks out grids and lays out the finds on plastic sheeting. Now he is setting up arc lights, helped by Tino's brother, an electrician. Evidently the dig is going to continue well into the night.

Emily, too, has been digging for most of the day. Her back aches, her feet are freezing and she is covered in mud but she doesn't mind. The Etruscans have been found and on her land! Actually, the tombs are just outside the border of Emily's land, but she doesn't know this yet. At the moment she thinks of them, like Luigi and Mario earlier, as her relatives. And it is incredibly exciting, watching the ground give way beneath their feet, revealing almost unimaginable treasures.

By mid-morning, they had uncovered the door of a second tomb. Raffaello was convinced there were many more. 'It's like a whole street of the dead,' he cried and Emily felt a slight shiver run along her spine. Did she really want to live next door to a street of the dead? By afternoon, they had dug down to a sunken road that seemed to lead right into the heart of the hill. By evening, they have excavated a third, smaller, tomb. 'Belonging to a less important family,' says Raffaello.

'They were very snobbish,' says Emily. Her back is beginning to ache badly and she feels less well disposed towards the tomb-builders.

'They were organised,' says Raffaello. 'Everything is regular, controlled. This tells us a lot about how they lived.'

'Emily!' cries a voice in the crowd. It is Monica.

'Monica!' Emily is pleased to be able to escape from her trench. It is hard work. She had always imagined archaeology to be a cautious, painstaking business, brushing away gently at the soil or carefully digging with tiny trowels. But all day the volunteers have been working with huge shovels, removing wheelbarrow after wheelbarrow of soil. Tino the policeman is stripped to the waist like a navvy, hauling wheelbarrows up a makeshift ramp. Raffaello, his shirt torn and streaked with dirt, is literally burrowing into the hillside, sending out a spray of mud and stones behind him.

'Come on,' says Emily to Monica. 'I'll make some coffee and we can bring it back up to the site.'

'My God,' says Monica. 'The site. It really has become "the site".'

In the kitchen, Totti greets them hysterically. He is not allowed near the site and has, in his opinion, spent an unreasonable amount of time shut up in the house. Emily makes coffee and Monica starts to make salami panini. Emily realises that, for tonight at least, she is stuck with feeding the volunteers.

'My God, how Raffaello's enjoying this,' says Monica, absent-mindedly eating a piece of salami.

'Well, this is what he was waiting for, isn't it?' says Emily. 'He thought there was a major Etruscan site here and he was right.'

'It was luck really though, wasn't it?' says Monica. 'If it hadn't rained, he would never have found them.'

'I'm sure he would have eventually,' says Emily, prompted by some strange loyalty. 'I think it's just that they are so far away from the original wall. Apparently the tombs were usually on the north and east of the town. This is on the west.'

'You seem to know a lot about it,' says Monica curiously. 'Has Signore Murello been boring you rigid with archaeological tales?'

Emily turns her head so Monica won't see how much she is blushing. 'No,' she says. 'It's just that I've been here all day. You can't help picking some stuff up.'

'How long's all this going to go on anyway? You can't go on making coffee and panini for twenty.'

'I don't know. It depends if they get the backing. That woman from the university is coming up here soon. If it becomes an official dig they can make their own supper.'

Emily sighs as she fills a Thermos flask. She is thinking of last night, of the rain lashing the windows and the surprising tenderness in Raffaello's eyes as he looked at her. 'Why, Mrs Robertson,' he had said, only half ironically. 'You're beautiful.'

'You look tired,' says Monica. 'You should go to bed. Leave them to it.'

'I will later,' says Emily. 'I just want one last look at the site.'

In the darkness, the tombs look less cosy and more threatening. The white stones loom out of the darkness and the volunteers are silhouetted in grotesque shapes against the arc lights. Emily starts to think of the Etruscans less as relatives and more as spectres, haunting her house and casting their long shadows over her family.

Raffaello is standing slightly apart, examining some of the finds, which are laid out on a groundsheet. When he sees Emily, he calls out for her to come over.

'Look,' he says, pointing to some ornate, rusty pieces of metal, looped together in fantastic circles.

'What is it? A necklace?'

'I think it's a horse's bit. It was found in one of the tombs. Probably signifies that the dead man was rich and owned lots of horses.'

Emily thinks of those other relics of the dead, the ring and the cross found in Carlo Belotti's grave. It would be handy if these, too, could be so easily explained away. She is lost in thought for a moment, looking down at the greenish coils of metal. Then Raffaello looks quickly over his shoulder and leans forward to kiss Emily, hard, on the mouth.

She is so surprised she can hardly speak. Then she says, in an attempt at lightness, 'What was that for?'

'We have unfinished business, Mrs Robertson,' he says. And, with that, she has to be content.

That night, when she finally goes to bed, she can still see the lights on the hill and the little black figures going to and fro in front of them.

Paris's diary

Well, we're back and everything is different. The house is full of people, archaeologists, students, assorted weirdos, and Raffaello is striding around as if he owns the place. I couldn't believe it when Mum told me that he'd finally found his Etruscans. When we were away! What a cheek! He even admitted as much. 'I'm sorry, Paris,' he said. 'I meant to wait for you but even I can't control the weather.' Even I! Who does he think he is? King Canute?

Mum is different too. I mean, she was really pleased to see us and everything, said she had really missed us and it wasn't the same without us but she didn't seem quite as worked up as I'd thought she'd be. I'd imagined her really going to pieces without us (I'd felt quite bad about it, to be honest) but she seemed to have lost weight, cut her hair and got some new clothes. Siena and I noticed immediately that she was wearing new jeans, boot-cut ones, much nicer than her old ones. And she was wearing perfume. She used to only wear perfume when she was going out for the evening with Dad.

It was great to see Dad. Really. I mean it. He took us to lots
of cool places and he bought me a new leather jacket. But, I
don't know, he's got a different life now, him and Fiona. She's
all right as well, Fiona. I mean she speaks with this really
affected voice and everything ('Oh realleah!'), Siena and I were
cracked up when we first heard her speak, but she's OK. She
was really good with Charlie, kept taking him to the zoo and to
watch Disney films and stuff. She just left Siena and me alone,
which was what we wanted I suppose. At first, we just wanted
to watch TV all day. My God, English TV is so brilliant! And
Dad (of course) has all these other channels so we watched hours
of MTV. We just sat there in front of the TV all day, eating
Pringles. It was fab. But then, I don't know, I got a bit bored. I
kept thinking about home and Mum and Totti. I wanted to be
out walking with Totti. Fiona took me to her super-cool health
club but it wasn't the same. I hate places like that, all designer
Lycra and mirrors. I just wanted to be walking with Totti, up on
the hills.

One thing happened that was good but a bit weird all the
same. My periods started again. It gave me a bit of a shock. I
was changing after swimming at the club and I saw this blood
on my costume, really bright. I mean, I knew what it was (even
before I first came on Mum had talked and talked to me about
it so it wasn't exactly a surprise) but I had sort of forgotten
how bright it was, how much like real blood, as if you were
actually wounded. Anyway, I borrowed some money off Fiona
and got some tampons from a machine. It felt quite good,

actually, saying to Fiona I'd got the curse, what a pain it was etc. etc. It made me feel just like everyone else. Not that I want to be like everyone else, of course. But just occasionally it isn't too bad.

Anyway, England was good. I'm glad Dad is happy with Fiona. They are revoltingly kissy and cuddly – she calls him Paulie! Yuk! But, after a bit, I just wanted to get home. I kept thinking about school and my friends here. All right, I admit it, I was thinking about Andrea.

When he kissed me, on New Year's Eve, I was so surprised. And I was kind of scared, to be honest. I mean, I kissed him back and everything but afterwards I didn't know how to behave, whether to hold his hand or talk to him in a different way or just to pretend it hadn't happened. Halfway through, he said, 'This is all right, isn't it?' and I said, 'Of course,' but I wasn't sure what he meant. It was all right for him to kiss me, in fact it was brilliant. I had been worried that I wouldn't know how to kiss but there was nothing to it! I'd worried that my nose would get in the way but it was as if we didn't have any noses at all! And I wasn't sure what to do with my tongue (keep it still or wiggle it around in some really gross way) but, in the end, it didn't seem to matter. I just did what felt right and Andrea seemed to think it was OK. Of course, he is an Older Man (16). That probably made a difference.

Andrea texted me in England and we are meeting up tomorrow, in the café after school. But now I'm stuck all over again. Are we going out? I don't know. Pathetic, I know, but

I've never been out with anyone before. Not like Siena who'd had tons of boyfriends at my age. But I've never really liked any boy before. I know it sounds stupid but I knew I liked Andrea when I saw him eat a piece of pizza at Ferragosto. Usually I hate the way people eat. Dad slurps his soup, Siena eats with her mouth open, Mum sort of picks at food in a really irritating way and Charlie, well, Charlie is just disgusting. But Andrea just ate his pizza, neatly and cleanly, without fuss. It was sort of how an animal eats. Not that I mean he slobbers and drools like darling Totti but he just ate it, you know, without making a big deal of it. Without making a meal of it, ho, ho. It was food and he ate it. I liked that.

Anyway, am I going out with him? In a way, I want to but in another way I'm scared. I don't know how to be a girlfriend (Siena was probably born knowing) and I don't want to do it all wrong. Perhaps it's better just being his friend. I mean, I know how to do that. But, then again, I do want to kiss him again. Maybe we can be friends with added kissing. I wouldn't mind that.

CHAPTER 2

Tuscany, Two Years On
A Travel Section special by Emily Robertson

Two years ago, my husband and I fell in love with a square terracotta house in the east of Tuscany. The region is known as the Mountains of the Moon. It's a strange place, less manicured somehow than the west of Tuscany, the rolling hills around Siena, the picturesque rooftops of San Gimignano. The mountains are inhospitable, snow-crowned and densely wooded, a last line of defence before the sea and the barbarian hordes of Rimini. During the war it was here that the Germans had their defensive line, the *Linea Gotica*, the Gothic line. In these dark woods and rocky mountain passes the Italian partisans fought desperately to free their country from the German invaders. Doubtless many Italians feel the same about the red-faced, camera-clicking tourists who fill their streets each summer, complaining loudly about the heat and the lack of proper English tea.

So we fell in love with a house and this love has lasted,
through extensive renovation, through loneliness and alien-
ation, through traumas both personal and professional;
though our love for each other ultimately has not.

The house, called the Villa Serena, was not, at first, much
to look at. Set on the top of a hill, against four ink-dark
cypress trees, it had a rather intimidating aspect, more like
a fortress than a family home. It was an old farmhouse,
four-square and solid, complete with outhouses, stables and
barns, but for more than ten years it had stood empty,
the farmer now living in a modern bungalow at the end
of the drive. The Villa Serena had been allowed to decay:
bats roosted in its high ceilings, plaster was falling from
the walls and part of the roof had fallen in, allowing a
glimpse of the almost shockingly blue Tuscan sky. But, as
we stood there, that bright spring day, amidst the rubble
and the bat droppings, we both felt, unmistakably, the first
stirrings of love.

Buying it was a nightmare. The land was sold separately
from the house and it turned out, at first, that we did
not have the right of way to our own driveway. It was a
listed building and, initially, the local council refused permission for our renovations. But our architect (a charming
Florentine called Massimo) persevered and, eventually,
the Villa Serena was ours. Then began the longer nightmare of the renovations: the plumber who worked only on
Wednesdays, the carpenter who worked not at all, the tiler

who was such an artist that he burst into tears if criticised, the plasterer who hated the British, and British women in particular. But, eventually, our dream home began to take shape. Dark rooms were lightened, luxurious bathrooms emerged out of linen closets, subtle lighting picked out the low beams and intricate herringbone brickwork typical of the region.

It was at about this time when, proud possessor of a Tuscan dream home, I began to realise that I knew nothing about the area in which we had made our home. Oh, I'd read all the books. In fact I probably knew more about Tuscan regional customs than most Tuscans, but I just didn't belong. My children belonged, they went to local schools and soon began to speak fluent Italian. One of them passionately hated Italy, but she still belonged. It was me, with my phrasebook Italian and my authentic Tuscan recipes for bean soup, who was an outsider.

Then two things happened. First, my husband left me. In retrospect, I should have seen it coming. He had been coming home less and less, sometimes not even unpacking his suitcase. When at home, he was like a stranger. He had mysterious texts and emails which were instantly erased. He forgot my birthday but seemed to remember the words of every corny love song ever written. He sang them in the bath or when alone on the terrace. When I appeared, he shut up. Worst of all, he seemed to have forgotten his love affair with Italy and moaned about the late opening hours of the banks and the lax parking habits of the inhabitants. If I did not belong in Italy, he belonged even less. He did not understand the simplest sentence in Italian and insisted on pronouncing the 'g' in *tagliatelle*. Obviously the marriage was doomed.

The second thing was that I made some friends: two highly intelligent women, both teachers; a mad archaeologist; and, strangest of all for a lifelong agnostic, the local priest. The teachers introduced me to other women and I learned that, for an educated woman in Italy, living an independent life is a constant struggle against family, traditions and the church. I also learned that many of them manage it. The archaeologist was digging for Etruscan remains on the very borders of my land. From him I learned that the Etruscans were a highly organised people, living in well-planned towns, who worshipped the traditional family, practised divination and believed in conscription. So far they sound like old-style Tories, but my archaeologist friend tells me that they were not all bad. They also believed in the education of women, for one thing.

And the priest? Well, strangely enough, from the priest I learned that it is dangerous to dwell too much on the past.

So, here I am in Tuscany, two years on. I have a job teaching English at a primary school. The children I teach are like children anywhere – lively, affectionate, demanding and often completely baffling. My own children now seem totally integrated into Tuscan society – the girls have both had Italian boyfriends (one charming, one a complete rotter), while my four-year-old son now speaks with a Tuscan accent and has a Juventus football shirt. We have a dog. We go to friends' houses, they come to ours. At the carnival that takes place before Lent we are all dressing up as angels (though my son refuses to wear wings). We are, if not members of the family, at least welcome guests.

Emily finishes spell-checking and clicks on 'send'. From the start, she thought of her columns about Tuscany as messages, letters in bottles, sent out to people she could no longer reach in any other way. She thought of old school friends, acquaintances from university, people she had worked with on newspapers, picking up the paper with a pleased smile and saying, 'Emily Robertson! That must be the Emily Robertson I used to know. Isn't she doing well?' In reality she soon found out that almost no one she met ever read the columns, or admitted to having read them. And, she came to admit, they were more likely to grind their teeth over her unremitting smugness than smile in a fond way and wish her well. But still she couldn't help thinking that, somewhere, somewhere, there was someone who read her columns and knew they were a private message meant for them alone. She was thinking of Michael, of course.

Now she imagines Michael reading her article, learning that she is divorced and rushing to her side. For so many years, this fantasy had sustained her: Michael declaring undying love, admitting that his marriage had been a terrible mistake, vowing never to let her go again. Now, tentatively, she turns this fantasy over in her mind. Does it still have the power to make her weak with longing? She is aware that she has neglected to mention that, in addition to teaching her about the Etruscans, her archaeologist has also made mad, passionate love to her. She hasn't mentioned that she thinks about him most of the time and that just his voice on the phone can make her itch with desire. So why does she still want Michael to think that his life is meaningless without her? Why can't she just be happy that he is successful and fulfilled in his own life? Why does he still *matter*?

Because Michael was more than a boyfriend, she supposes. He was her youth. The years they were together, from when she was nineteen to when she was twenty-two, were the years when she changed from Emily-who-is-nothing-like-her-brothers to a woman with her own personality and opinions. All her tastes – in music (deeply sad, according to Siena), food, wine, books, everything – they were all formed during those years. Which is why, even now, she has a secret weakness for Soft Cell and sweet German wine. And Italy. It was during those years that she fell in love with Italy through falling in love with Michael. And with Gina, of course.

Gina encouraged her to believe that she would marry Michael and have five children. Even now she believes that Gina wanted it to happen. When Michael broke up with her, she remembers Gina ringing up, furious. 'I want you to be together,' she said. 'You will be together, I promise you.' Emily remembers how much hope she had pinned on those words, believing in Gina's promise. But weeks passed and she began to understand that they were just words. In this instance, at least, Michael was not going to obey his mother. He had cut Emily out of his life. She would never see him again.

It is that, too, she realises. Michael vanished so completely, disappearing into the secret world of the hospital, it was as if he had never been. She moved to Brighton, met Paul, got married. But, even when they moved back to London, she never once bumped into Michael in the street, saw him getting on a tube, read about him in the paper, spotted his picture in the alumni magazine. Only the restaurant was still there. Vittorio's. Unchanging with its Gothic printed menu and its gilt and velvet interior. She never went in but she went as far as the doors many times, she read the menu until she could recite it in her sleep (*Prosciutto Melone, Risotto Milanese, Saltimbocca alla Romana*) and, somehow, she always thought that one day she would push open those heavy glass doors and there he would be. Waiting for her.

And so, with every episode of 'Thoughts from Tuscany', she had been writing him a letter. Telling him about her life, telling him that she was happy, successful, living in a beautiful place. And now that the truth is no longer so enviable, she finds that she still wants him to know.

'Mum!' Paris wanders into the room. She is wearing jeans, a rugby top and a pair of angel's wings. She looks sulky, stroppy and very pretty. 'Mum! This costume's ridiculous!'

'Well, you're not meant to wear it with jeans.'

'I'm not wearing that awful white dress thing. I look demented in it.'

'We've all got to wear them on the float. We're meant to be a heavenly chorus.'

'Heavenly chorus,' snorts Paris, kneeling down to cuddle Totti. 'If you ask me, Monica's gone completely mad.'

Monica is organising the school's float for this year's carnival and her theme is angels. For such a diehard atheist it seems a strange choice but Monica argues that the costumes are easy and the children will look sweet with their golden wings and haloes. Some adults, Emily and family included, have been press-ganged in to help.

The spring carnival is a huge event in Italy. Meant to be a final blow-out before the deprivations of Lent (the Italian word *carnevale*, as Emily noted in a previous 'Thoughts from Tuscany', actually means 'to put away meat'), they have metamorphosed into week-long extravaganzas with floats, fire-eaters, acrobats, masks and costumes. The carnival in Cento, a small town north of Bologna, is actually twinned with the famous Rio carnival and, every year, the winning float is shipped off to Brazil. In Viareggio, the carnival stretches over four weeks.

The carnival in Monte Albano is more modest but it still seems to have taken weeks of organisation. There is to be a parade at twilight, with floats and jugglers and mime artists. The famous porchetta grill is once again to be set up in the main piazza and there will be free cheese and wine. The whole thing culminates in a spectacular firework display at midnight on Shrove Tuesday. Emily is excited because the carnival will coincide with Petra's visit. Petra is snatching a rare three-day holiday without the children (their father, Ed, is taking them to Disneyland Paris – 'More fool him,' says Petra). Emily is longing to see her friend and, she has to admit, to tell her about Raffaello. At last she has some wild sex of her own to boast about.

Paris slouches out of the room, wings glinting. Emily closes her laptop, puts on her coat and decides to take Totti for a walk up to the site. She will have to keep him on the lead but even so, she reasons, it will be good for him to get out. It's not as if she is only going up there to see Raffaello; it's not like that at all.

When she gets to the site, she knows that something strange is going on. Raffaello is standing by the main trench, legs apart, arms folded. Even from a hundred yards away, Emily can see the tension and hostility in his stance. Facing him, incongruous in a well-cut suit and polished shoes, is his cousin, Renato.

Getting closer, dragged by a panting Totti, Emily hears Raffaello say, 'You wouldn't dare!'

'You don't think so?' Renato gives a high, unpleasant laugh. 'You don't think your friend at the university would be interested to hear about how you found two corpses on the site and didn't even bother to tell the police.'

'I did tell the police,' says Raffaello, between gritted teeth.

'Oh, your mate Tino. Very convenient.'

'Get out!' Raffaello takes a step towards him. Covered in

mud, fists clenched, he looks like a madman. Emily is not surprised to see Renato step back quickly.

'I'll be back,' he says. Turning and seeing Emily, he adds nastily, 'Good afternoon, Mrs Robertson,' before heading back down the hill at a brisk trot.

'What was all that about?' asks Emily.

'Nothing,' says Raffaello who is breathing hard.

'Raffaello, I heard him. He was threatening you.'

'Oh, it's just my cousin making trouble.' Raffaello takes a deep breath and makes an attempt at a grin. 'He is threatening to tell the Soprintendenza about the bodies.'

'But she must know about them already. It was in the papers.'

'Yes, but not that I knew about them for two weeks before telling the police.'

'How does Renato know?'

Raffaello shrugs. 'I don't know. *Una bustarella*.' Emily has been in Italy long enough to recognise this word. A little envelope. A bribe.

'Tino?'

'No, Tino would never inform on me. But there are plenty of others who would.'

They turn and start walking back towards the Portakabin where Raffaello is storing the finds. Emily is surprised to see Siena coming out of the cabin, accompanied by a young man in a camouflage jacket (almost all the volunteers wear camouflage; it's like having an army about the place). Siena waves in a 'don't come any nearer' way, so Emily doesn't wave back.

'But Raffaello,' says Emily at last, 'I don't understand. Why does Renato want to stop the dig?'

Raffaello sighs. 'He wants me out of Monte Albano.'

'But why?'

'He knows I'm Zio Virgilio's favourite. He's afraid he's going to leave the restaurant to me.'

'But Renato's his grandson. He runs the place.'

'I know. I think Zio Virgilio's got every intention of leaving La Foresta to him but, being a wily old fox, he likes to keep him on his toes. He's probably been telling him what a comfort it is to have me around. That sort of thing.'

'What will happen if he does tell the Soprintendenza?'

'I don't know. If she turns against me, it would take the discovery of the lost city of Atlantis to get her to approve the dig.'

'Raffaello,' says Emily suddenly, 'do you think it was Renato who left the skull on my doorstep?'

Raffaello looks at her curiously. 'Why do you say that?'

'Because I saw a skull at La Foresta, on one of the shelves.'

Raffaello laughs. 'That skull used to belong to a friend of Virgilio's who was an artist. He used to paint all these weird pictures, the skull with flowers coming out of it, stuff like that. It's not Renato's.'

'Maybe there's another skull.'

'One's enough, wouldn't you say?'

'I don't know,' says Emily doubtfully. 'I still think it could have been him. He could have been trying to frighten me so I stop the dig. It is on my land, after all.'

'He wouldn't come after you,' says Raffaello. 'It's me he has a quarrel with. He'll try some dirty trick now, you wait, just to try to mess things up for me.'

'What will you do?' asks Emily.

Raffaello grins, teeth very white in his mud-spattered face. 'I won't give up without a fight. You can be sure of that.'

CHAPTER 3

The first thing both Emily and Petra think is that the other looks remarkably well. Emily has lost a stone and her hair has been cut and highlighted (Italian style). Petra has actually put on some weight and her hair is longer than Emily has ever seen it, just skimming the tops of her shoulders.

'It's lovely to see you,' says Emily, hugging Petra who, as usual, holds back slightly.

'You too. You look great.'

'So do you.'

They smile at each other, sensing there is more to be said. But at first they concentrate on the kids (Jake is playing for the school football team, Harry is seeing a speech therapist) and on the amazing fact of being alone together in Italy. Instead of driving straight home, Emily takes Petra to Arezzo and they have lunch at a tiny restaurant in the oldest part of the town, where the houses crowd together around the fan-shaped piazza.

'They have jousting here in the summer,' says Emily. 'It's part of the Palio.'

'I thought the Palio was in Siena,' says Petra, twirling pasta round her fork.

'Every Tuscan town has a *Palio*,' says Emily. 'Even Monte Albano. Everyone dresses up in medieval clothes. It's amazing.'

'Tell me about this carnival,' says Petra. 'Are we really having to dress up?'

'Not if you don't want to. It's just that we, the children and I, have promised to be on the float and we're all dressing up as angels.'

'Jesus. You're not getting religious on me, are you?'

'No,' says Emily, scooping up her sauce with a piece of bread. 'Though I have got quite friendly with the local priest.'

'Jesus,' says Petra again but she says it without heat. She seems remarkably relaxed, the usual tense blend of humour and despair absent from her voice.

'So,' says Emily, when they are drinking their coffee. 'Tell me about Darren.'

Petra laughs, sighs and then laughs again. 'What's to tell? We go out, we go back to his place to make love then I go home and pretend that nothing's happened. At school we try not to speak to each other. It's like having an affair except that neither of us is married.'

'Do you like him?'

'Like him? Of course, I *like* him. I fancy the pants off him. But, if you're asking if I *love* him, I don't know. I honestly don't know.'

'Have the kids met him?'

Petra laughs but without humour this time. 'Christ, no. I want to keep him interested a bit longer.'

'Does he . . .' begins Emily and then stops. She had been going to ask 'Does he know about Harry' but then realised that this sounded as if she sees Harry as some kind of obstacle, which seems tactless to say the least.

But Petra answers a different question. 'Oh yes, he wants to meet them all right. He keeps going on about it. It's just, I don't know, I'm a different person when I'm at home with the kids. I'm a mum. I don't know if I want him to see that side of me. He knows me as a teacher, as a *person*. I want to keep it that way.'

'Aren't you a person when you're with the kids?' asks Emily, though she knows exactly what Petra means.

'No,' says Petra immediately. 'I'm a thing. A chair for sitting on, a hanky to wipe noses, a tape recorder to read stories, a machine to produce lunch. I don't want Darren to see the nose-wiping, bad-tempered, sandwich-making me. He actually thinks I'm quite cool.'

'You are cool. *And* you're a cool mum.'

'Gee thanks, honey,' drawls Petra, draining her coffee. 'Now tell me about you. Why are you all lit up like a Christmas tree?'

Emily blushes. 'Actually . . . I've had a bit of a fling.' She giggles nervously at the inappropriateness of the word. A fling. It sounds like some weird country dance. Take your partners for the Tuscan Fling.

'A fling?' echoes Petra. 'Who with?'

'Raffaello. The archaeologist I told you about.'

'I thought he had a beard.'

'He shaved it off. Anyway, he's been digging near our house and we got friendly, he's brilliant with the kids and he gave us a dog, remember I told you about him?'

'Yeah, he's a Great Dane or something.'

'An Alsatian. Well, when the kids were in England with Paul, Raffaello took me out to dinner and, well, that was that.'

'You went to bed with him?'

'Yes.' Emily thinks how inadequately this phrase describes their hungry, desperate love-making with the rain pounding against the windows. 'Yes I did. It was incredible.'

'Bloody hell, Em,' says Petra. 'You're a dark horse. So are you an item then, you and this what's-his-name?'

'Raffaello. I don't know. I mean we went to bed together and it was brilliant but since then he's been totally obsessed with this dig. He's found an Etruscan tomb, you see.'

'So he'd rather dig up dead bodies than sleep with you?'

'Well, if you put it like that . . .' Emily thinks of the dead bodies, first the two skeletons and then the mysterious Etruscans (though there are no bodies in the tombs; the Etruscans apparently cremated their dead). Does Raffaello love them more than he loves her? Does Raffaello love her at all? She remembers his face when he said that he wasn't going to give up without a fight. Is she just part of the fight to realise his ambition?

'I don't know,' she says aloud. 'I don't know what's happening. But something is.'

Petra smiles. A rather uncomfortably knowing smile. 'So when am I going to meet this Raffaello then?'

'Not at the carnival,' says Emily. 'Angels aren't quite his thing.'

In fact, Raffaello is at the carnival. Emily doesn't spot him at first, she is so preoccupied with the float and its chorus of hyperactive angels, trying to keep hold of Charlie and stop Paris sloping off to see Andrea. The night is a chaotic tumult of loud music, men in medieval dress carrying banners, monstrous masks and flashing lights. When the procession is over, Paris and Siena disappear and Emily takes Charlie to buy a porchetta sandwich. She meets Petra by the stall, drinking mulled wine from a plastic glass.

'Look,' she says. 'Is that your archaeologist over there?'

Emily looks. 'Yes,' she says. 'How did you know?'

'Because he's covered in mud.'

Raffaello is indeed covered in mud. He is wearing heavy boots and a reflective jacket, the kind dustmen wear in England, and must have come straight from the site. He is watching the tail end of the procession with the familiar half-ironical grin on his face.

'Raffaello!' Emily raises her hand.

'Mrs Robertson.' He strides over to meet them, scattering a small crowd of children dressed as jungle animals.

'I'd like you to meet my friend Petra.'

'Delighted to meet you,' says Raffaello gravely.

'You speak good English,' says Petra.

'Unfortunately I learned it in America. Emily tells me that I have a terrible accent.'

Emily is so surprised to be called 'Emily' instead of 'Mrs Robertson' that she actually jumps.

'She's an awful snob,' agrees Petra.

'I'm not a snob,' protests Emily hotly. 'It's you who won't let your children watch *EastEnders*.'

At that point, Emily's own child regains her attention by dragging her sharply towards the porchetta grill. By the time they return, Petra and Raffaello are deep in conversation. Emily catches a few words, 'extraordinary finds' (Raffaello), 'wonderful food' (Petra). She is glad that Petra is getting on with Raffaello (otherwise, knowing Petra, she wouldn't spend this long chatting to him) but she is beginning to feel rather marginal. She is also bitterly cold. It is a freezing February night and she is only wearing a white sheet over jeans and a jumper. Her hands are blue with cold around her porchetta sandwich.

'Here,' she says to Petra. 'I bought one for you. They're delicious.'

'Where's mine?' asks Raffaello.

'I didn't get you one,' says Emily.

Raffaello laughs. 'What a cruel woman you are, Mrs Robertson.' Then he takes off his coat. 'Here,' he says. 'You look frozen.' And he wraps the heavy jacket around Emily's shoulders. She is so taken aback that she can't speak. 'I'll go and get us a drink,' he says and he disappears through the brightly coloured crowd.

'You lucky cow, Emily,' says Petra slowly.

Later, they wander up to the piazza to watch medieval jesters juggle with fire. Raffaello, with Charlie on his shoulders, is chatting to Tino the policeman. Petra is talking to Monica. They have taken to each other immediately; funny how it has only just occurred to Emily how alike they are. She wonders why she is more drawn to the acerbic Monica and Petra than to the sweet-natured Antonella. Across the square she can see Paris and Andrea, he has his arm around her and even at this distance Emily can see that she looks happy. Earlier Antonella had asked Emily if she minded Paris going out with a boy two years older. 'Mind?' Emily wanted to say. 'I'm overjoyed.' But she had just smiled and said of course she didn't mind, Andrea was such a nice boy. She doesn't think Andrea is totally responsible for the change in Paris (for that she also credits Totti and the Etruscans) but he sure as hell has helped.

As she watches the jugglers (it is very clever but rather boring after a while; you couldn't do it yourself but why would you want to?), she hears someone calling her name. It is Don Angelo, wearing a Russian hat that makes him look like a spy. He is surrounded, as usual, by admiring elderly women, Olimpia amongst them. Emily walks over to them.

'Are you enjoying the carnival?' asks Don Angelo.

'Very much,' says Emily politely.

'It's not as good as last year,' says one of the women.

'I didn't come last year,' says Emily. Where had she been last year? Entertaining Paul's clients, she thinks, or writing a column about the joys of living in a Tuscan community.

'How are the excavations going?' asks Don Angelo. Despite his earlier objections, the priest now seems fairly resigned about the dig, even coming up to see it one day (sprinkling holy water over the sunken road and praying loudly for the dead, to the amusement of the volunteers).

'Fine, I think,' says Emily.

'Is it approved yet?' asks Olimpia insinuatingly.

'Nearly,' says Emily defiantly. 'You can ask Raffaello. He's over there. With Charlie.'

'Poor child,' mutters Olimpia.

Looking over, Emily sees that Raffaello is now talking to Renato. She is too far away to see their expressions but she thinks that Renato looks faintly conciliatory, his hand gestures performing wide apologetic arcs. Characteristically he is smartly, even formally, dressed, wearing a long black coat and a dashing red scarf. Next to him Raffaello looks every inch a labourer.

Don Angelo cuts into her thoughts with a polite cough. 'With your permission, I would like to come to the house one day next week,' he says. 'Olimpia here would like me to say some prayers. She is concerned about her father's spirit.'

'I have felt him,' says Olimpia suddenly. 'I have felt him around the place. His spirit is not at rest.'

'Nonsense,' says Emily sharply. She does not like to think of Carlo Belotti's spirit wandering uninvited around her house.

'Nonsense, is it?' says Olimpia sullenly. 'Well, listen to this, Signora Robertson. One day, when I was sweeping the hall, I distinctly heard someone whistling "*La Donna è mobile*". What do you make of that?'

Emily makes very little of it but Don Angelo says, in a gentle voice, 'Ah, how Carlo loved that tune. Many, many times have I heard him sing it or whistle it.'

Olimpia clasps his hand, deeply moved, but Emily finds herself wondering how, if Don Angelo barely knew Carlo Belotti, as he claimed, he comes to have such an intimate knowledge of his musical tastes.

Before they even get to the fireworks, Charlie is asleep in Raffaello's arms and Emily is frozen with cold, despite the dustman's jacket. She has lost sight of Paris, and Siena is at the centre of a wildly excited group of young people milling around outside the pizzeria. Petra and Monica are still deep in conversation. They are now on to how men are afraid of strong women and look set to keep going all night.

Raffaello puts a hand on Emily's arm. 'Do you want to go home?' he asks.

'I'd love to,' sighs Emily. 'But what about Petra and the girls?'

'Petra could drive them home in your car. I'll take you and Charlie in my Jeep.'

But Petra, surprisingly, is nervous of driving a left-hand-drive car. 'It's so dark,' she says. 'I'd never find the turning.'

'Don't worry,' says Monica. 'I'll take them home. You go with Raffaello.' She looks hard at Emily as she says this.

'Oh, thank you, Monica. It's just that Charlie is exhausted.'

'No problem. You can leave your car here and collect it in the morning.'

'Yes,' says Emily gratefully. 'Is that OK with you, Pete?'

'Fine,' says Petra. She looks cold but still full of energy, eyes sparking under her woolly cap. 'I wouldn't want to miss the fireworks.'

'Siena'll probably go home with Francesca anyway.' Francesca is now Siena's best friend. They spend hours every day texting and phoning and, amazingly, still have plenty to say to each other when they meet up. Having a best friend, says Siena, is much better than having a boyfriend.

Paris is located, standing by the porchetta grill with Andrea, watching a jazz band. Emily does not remind her that, at *Ferragosto*, Paris said that the smell of porchetta made her feel sick. She does not want to remember *Ferragosto* when, in so many ways, she thought she had lost Paris.

'Is that OK, darling?' she asks when she has outlined the plan.

'Yeah, fine,' says Paris vaguely. 'I'm not nearly ready to go yet.'

'I'll look after her, Mrs Robertson,' says Andrea seriously.

Paris gives him a punch, playful but hard. 'I can look after myself,' she says.

Walking up the hill with Raffaello, Emily thinks again of the night of *Ferragosto*. She remembers running through the crowds with Charlie a dead weight in her arms, frantic about Paris. She remembers how terrifying the fireworks sounded, like gunshot, blitzkrieg. She remembers her relief at finding Paris safe at home, asleep in front of a mad Torquay hotel owner. Now, Raffaello carries Charlie, his loping pace hardly affected by the child's weight. She is not sure exactly what is in Raffaello's mind or why he was so keen to leave the carnival early. All she knows is that the dark night, the shouting crowds, the sound of the fireworks just starting in the piazza no longer seem hostile but friendly, positively soothing.

'What were you talking to Renato about?' she asks, skipping to catch up with Raffaello.

'Oh, he was asking what we had found. Pretending to be interested. He's hoping we don't make a really big discovery. Then I'd never be out of his hair.'

'Haven't you already made a really big discovery?'

'Yes,' admits Raffaello. 'But people have found tombs before. I'd love to find something totally new. Something that changes the world.'

'The lost city of Atlantis?' teases Emily.

Raffaello laughs. 'Something like that.'

Looking at Raffaello, his face rapt in the moonlight, Emily feels a jolt of the same protective feeling she has for the children. She loves the way Raffaello is so passionate about his Etruscans, those mysterious people who have been dead nearly two thousand years. But privately she thinks he is asking too much. How can any discovery be so earth-shattering? How can a bit of old stone change the world?

They have reached the Jeep. Emily takes Charlie from Raffaello and, as she does so, a piece of pink paper flutters out of her hand.

'Oh dear,' she says. 'Now I'll never win the raffle.'

Raffaello grins, illuminated in the headlights of a passing car. 'You've won me,' he says. 'I'm the first prize.'

That night their love-making is different. There is none of the feverish intensity of the first time. They hold each other, they take their time and they enjoy themselves. Once or twice Emily feels herself about to say, 'I love—' but she stops herself just in time. I love this, she tells herself firmly. Nothing more.

Raffaello leaves before the girls return but for a long time afterwards Emily lies absolutely still, smiling in the darkness.

CHAPTER 4

The letter that Emily has been expecting for twenty years arrives a week after Ash Wednesday. The day starts like any other. She collects the post, as usual, from the box where it is delivered, American style, at the end of the unmade road. She throws the letters onto the front seat, says, 'All right, Charlie Bear?' to Charlie in the back and continues the drive to the *scuola materna*. They play the nursery rhymes CD and from time to time Emily looks down at the letters scattered over the Alfa's classy leather seat. The top one is a bill, below that is a postcard from Petra showing the Brighton Pavilion; she can't see the rest. She drives on happily, stopping for a ginger cat that walks slowly and contemptuously across the road, taking the corners very carefully because the road is still frosty.

'I don't like these songs any more,' says Charlie.

She drops Charlie off at the *scuola materna*, noticing happily how he is immediately absorbed into the laughing, shouting mass of children. She waves at Monica who is trying to get the laughing, shouting mass to sit quietly in a circle, and goes back to her car. She doesn't open the letters because she only has ten minutes to get to the *scuola elementare*, the primary school where she is teaching English.

The primary school is an old stone building in the very centre of Monte Albano. She parks the car in the tiny car park and gets her bag out of the boot. As an afterthought she shoves the letters into the bag. Maybe she will get a chance to read them at break.

Her first class is a group of six-year-olds. They sing 'One, two, three, four, five, once I caught a fish alive' because it is supposed to teach them their numbers. A little girl called Sharon (after Sharon Stone, a very popular name in Italy at the moment) insists on holding her hand throughout. A boy called Kevin (after Kevin Costner) whizzes around the circle pretending to be a car. Emily ignores him as long as she can and then gets him to sit down next to her. He looks up at her with melting brown eyes. 'I like you, Signora Robertson,' he says, unanswerably.

They sit in their circle and the children pretend to be animals, introducing themselves in English. 'I am cat. I eat mouses.' Emily loves the children but she finds them exhausting. She can't understand how people like Antonella can do this sort of thing all day. By the time she finishes at midday she is almost too tired to speak.

At break time she forgets her letters because the head, a charming nun called Sister Caterina, wants her to help translate an Easter song into English. Emily struggles, partly because she can't think of an English word for '*novena*'. She often feels a bit uneasy with the more Catholic side of school life, though Sister Caterina assures her that her lack of faith is not a problem. 'We want you to feel at home in our school family.' And she does really. She loves the repartee amongst the staff, idealistic and cynical at the same time. She loves assembly when the children sing with such innocent relish, the words filling up their mouths like cake. She loves being part of it all, Signora Robertson, with her bag full of English fairy tales and folk songs.

After the service, she has a class of ten year olds who are writing a story in English. It is a joint effort and is called 'Robin Hood plays for Manchester United'. She rather enjoys the mix of old and new cultural icons (David Beckham appears as Robin Hood's long-lost twin brother). After this class, she has finished for the day and rushes out to her car. She has to collect Charlie at twelve thirty and she doesn't want to get caught up in the Friday tourist traffic.

She is lucky. The roads are clear and she reaches the *scuola materna* with ten minutes to spare. Only then does she remember the letters. She gets her bag out of the boot and scrabbles for them under the mess of pens, receipts and finger puppets. She ignores the bills and smiles at Petra's postcard ('Home safely. Had Darren and chips for tea. Love to the kids and to sexy R.'). Then her heart skips a beat. The last letter has been sent on from the newspaper's head office. It is an expensive cream envelope, addressed in bold black ink. She turns it over and reads the return address: 'Mrs Gina Bartnicki'. Hands trembling, she opens the envelope. A letter and an advertising flyer fall out onto her lap.

My dear Emily,

I hope you won't mind my writing after all this time but I have thought of you so often over the years. As you will see, I am opening a new restaurant in Bologna and I would be so happy if you could come to the opening night. I have been wanting to return to Italy for some time and, after my dear Nick died last year, I have decided to take the plunge.

I do hope all is well with you. I used to read your column every week and was so glad to know that life had treated you so well.

With love, as ever,
Gina

PS. Do come to the opening. Michael will be there. He is now living in Italy and I know he would like to see you again.

Emily looks at the flyer. Glossily printed in black and gold, it tells her that a new restaurant called Vittorio's will be opening in Bologna in March. The opening night will be on Easter Saturday. On the back is a photograph of Gina holding out a tray of bruschette. She has hardly changed at all: red hair, gold earrings, wide, challenging smile. How nervous Emily had felt the first time she met her. How ridiculously grateful she had felt when Gina had accepted her. How miraculous it had seemed that Gina, so dazzling and glamorous, actually approved of her as a possible wife for Michael.

Michael. After all these years, she is actually going to see him again. See, she had been right all along. One day she would open the door of Vittorio's and there he would be. All right, this is a different Vittorio's but the result is the same. She is going to see Michael again. 'He is now living in Italy and I know he would like to see you again.' That devastating PS. Michael. In Italy. All this time she had thought he was so far away and he was right here, in Italy. Had Chad known all the time and, if so, why hadn't he mentioned it, that time in Bologna? She sees Michael moving slowly towards her, like one of the arrows at the beginning of *Dad's Army*, advancing inexorably across Europe. She shivers. What is the matter with her? This ought to be the happiest day of her life.

'Mum!' Emily looks up with a jump. A furious Charlie is standing at the car window, Monica is behind him.

'Darling!' Emily leaps out of the car. 'I'm so sorry!'

'Charlie was worried when you didn't come to the gate,' says Monica. 'But I saw your car so I knew you were here.'

'I'm sorry,' Emily says again. 'I was reading a letter.'

'You were in another world,' says Monica. 'Not bad news, I hope?'

'No,' says Emily. 'Not bad news.'

*

Not far from the Brighton Pavilion (geographically at least), Petra is in the supermarket. Harry is with her, crammed protestingly into the child seat of her trolley. Normally she avoids shopping with Harry because the lights, the crowds and bewildering array of goods distress him. But today she has no choice, it is Jake's birthday tomorrow and she has to buy a few last-minute things for his party. She has half an hour before she has to collect Jake from his after-school club and the stress of this is making her nervous and communicating itself to Harry.

She tries to take a deep breath and force herself to calm down. 'Now,' she says to Harry in a falsely bright voice. 'What next? Sweets for the party bags. What shall we get?' The speech therapist has told her to ask open questions.

'Cheese,' says Harry in his loudest voice. 'Cheese! Thomas!' So much for the open questions.

'In a minute,' says Petra, slightly less brightly, whizzing her trolley around a corner and nearly knocking over a stack of Easter eggs.

'Cheese! Thomas!'

'OK, OK.' She backtracks, grabs a packet of CheesStrings and gives one to Harry. She used to despise mothers who did this (couldn't they even wait until they were out of the store?) but now she doesn't think twice; anything to keep Harry quiet.

Harry is mercifully silent, chewing, as she throws packets of brightly-coloured E numbers into the trolley. Sweets, squash, paper towels, balloons, Football Crazy tablecloth. Harry starts to make an ominous keening sound.

'Nearly there,' she pants, hurtling into the drinks aisle. She'll have to get some booze to keep the mothers happy. Red wine? White wine? Turps?

Harry's noise becomes louder, she sees people looking their way and mutters, 'Shh,' more for their sake than because she thinks it will do any good.

The tannoy bursts into life. 'Will all queue busters go to the checkout.' Harry screams. Harry's scream is the most piercing noise in the world, produced only at moments of severe stress, and Petra knows that once started he will not stop.

'Shh, shh,' she begs.

Harry continues to scream. More horrified glances come their way. 'He's a big boy to carry on like that,' someone says disapprovingly.

'He may be big,' Petra wants to shout, 'but he's also autistic. Leave us alone!'

Pushing her trolley with its screaming occupant, she runs down the aisle, past another Easter egg display and comes slap into Darren.

For a moment they just stare at each other. Darren, looking at his most George Clooney-ish, is carrying a basket containing bachelor shopping: red wine, steak, French fries. He is wearing a tracksuit and has obviously just come from the gym, his hair is still wet from the shower and he has a sports bag over his shoulder. In that instant, the contrast between their lives makes Petra feel physically sick.

'Petra,' says Darren at last.

'Hi, Darren,' says Petra. 'Meet Harry.'

Emily drives home in a daze. She is going to see Michael again. Should she write to Gina to say that she will be coming? Oh my God, what will she wear? Thank heavens she has lost some weight. Is there enough time to have botox done?

'Mummy,' says Charlie from the back seat. 'I learned a new song today, shall I sing it?'

'Yes please.'

As Charlie sings tunelessly, Emily thinks about Michael. Will he have changed? Would he still be arrogant, generous, impatient, gloriously certain? Would he still be beautiful? She knows she isn't beautiful any more, not that she ever was, but Michael must surely be as handsome as ever. She couldn't bear it if he had got fat or was losing his hair.

In the back, Charlie sings about a cuckoo and spring coming back.

Spring returns, she thinks, but not my friend. Where was that from? But he was returning, wasn't he? Miracles do happen. Winter has gone, the snow has vanished and the green shoots begin to show. She is going to see Michael again.

When they reach the house, Raffaello is outside. He is holding an axe in his hand and, for a moment, looks like someone out of a fairy tale, the woodsman who saves Little Red Riding Hood perhaps.

'I thought I would chop you some wood,' he says, pointing

to a tree trunk that had fallen in the January floods. It has now been transformed into neat, fire-sized logs.

'Thank you,' says Emily flatly. 'That's very kind.'

'I've learned a new song,' yells Charlie as Raffaello lifts him out of the car. 'Can I have the axe?'

'Not on your life, Carlito. You can help me carry some wood though.'

'Thanks very much for chopping the wood,' says Emily again, following them into the house. 'You didn't have to.'

'No problem,' says Raffaello in the exaggerated American accent that usually makes her laugh.

'It's very kind,' she repeats. Raffaello looks at her curiously. 'Are you OK?'

'Yes, fine. Would you like some coffee?'

'No thank you. I've got to get back to the site. We are doing some soil analysis today. Oh, by the way, I have an invitation for you.'

'An invitation?' repeats Emily stupidly.

'Yes, to Zio Virgilio's eightieth birthday party. Easter Saturday at La Foresta. Will you come?'

'I'm sorry, Raffaello,' says Emily slowly. 'I don't think I can.'

CHAPTER 5

Freezing February gives way to rainy March, but it is not the joyful returning spring of Charlie's cuckoo song. The dig is waterlogged and filthy; the volunteers tramp across Emily's terrace and destroy her lemon balm. Emily has a cold and Charlie has been coughing for four nights. But, worst of all, Raffaello is away. He has gone to Rome for a conference.

When she said she couldn't go to Zio Virgilio's party, he had asked why. Come on, he said, it'll be fun. I can't, she said, I'm going to a restaurant opening in Bologna. A restaurant opening? Who did she know who ran a restaurant? The mother of a friend of hers from university. My God, not that stupid medical student boyfriend she had told him about. Yes, as it happened, only he was now a world-famous brain surgeon. Perhaps they'll be serving offal then, Raffaello had growled, before stamping off, back to the site.

And that had been the last time she had spoken to him. She had seen him in the distance, digging or shouting orders. Once she had seen him playing football with Charlie and his friend

Edoardo. But when she had raised her hand to wave, he had ignored her. She wanted to go and apologise, but what for? She was entitled to go out without him, surely, even if it was to see an ex-boyfriend? After all, Raffaello had gone swanning off to America at Christmas and she hadn't been jealous, had she? Well, only a bit and she'd never told him.

She tries to fix her mind on the glorious prospect of seeing Michael again but she finds it hard to recapture the elation of the moment when she first saw Gina's name on the back of the letter. She becomes increasingly irritable and forgetful. Totti often goes a whole day without a walk and twice she forgets to collect Paris from Andrea's house (not that Paris seems very worried about this).

It is with resignation then that she drives up to the house one morning after dropping Charlie at the *scuola materna* to find Olimpia and Don Angelo waiting on the doorstep. Oh God, she had forgotten that it was the day of the Great Exorcism. She hopes she has biscuits or something to offer them. She is sure Don Angelo won't want to cast out demons on an empty stomach.

'I'm so sorry,' she says, jumping out of the car. 'Have you been waiting long?'

'*Non fa niente*,' says Don Angelo, waving a regal hand. He is looking rather frail in the spring sunshine, his black coat hanging loosely on his shoulders. There is no sign of his Vespa; he must have come with Olimpia in her three-wheel van.

Olimpia looks as if she could have a lot more to say on the

subject but she, too, smiles graciously as Emily ushers them into the house. Totti greets them noisily, hopefully offering them a ball to throw for him.

'A beautiful dog,' says Don Angelo, patting him.

'He is very dirty,' says Olimpia disapprovingly. 'He should really be kept outside.'

Emily makes coffee and hastily arranges some broken shortbreads on a plate. When she goes back into the sitting room, she finds Olimpia looking accusingly at the wood-chopping axe.

'Very dangerous with the little one around,' she says.

'Oh yes,' says Emily. 'I was just about to put it away. Raffaello's been chopping wood for us, you see.'

Olimpia looks more disapproving than ever but Don Angelo says, 'Ah, dear Raffaello. How pleased he must be to have found his Etruscan remains.'

'But you were against the dig,' says Emily.

Don Angelo dismisses the past with an airy hand. 'That was then. I was worried . . . but now all seems well. The dead are being treated with dignity.' He sighs and pats Olimpia's hand. 'And now, Olimpia, we must address the more recent dead. Your father's spirit. You have felt his presence, you say?'

Olimpia shudders. This is her big moment. 'Many, many times,' she says impressively. 'Sometimes, in this very room, I have felt him very close, almost at my elbow. I have heard breathing though the room is quite empty. Other times I have seen something out of the corner of my eye, his red shirt (he was a great admirer of Garibaldi, you remember, Don Angelo), his black hair, that cap he used to wear. And the music! "*La donna è mobile*" coming out of the empty air. I think he is trying to tell me something, Padre. I think he is not at rest as he should be.'

Emily is amazed how disturbed Don Angelo looks at this load of superstitious nonsense. She supposes priests have to take the supernatural seriously but she would have expected Don Angelo to retain at least a shred of healthy scepticism. Instead he looks positively ghost-like himself, his face chalk-white. He raises a hand that is shaking slightly. 'I will say the prayers of exorcism,' he says. 'We must pray together for his soul.'

'Oh no,' protests Emily. 'You don't want me here surely? I'm not a . . . well, I don't really . . .'

'Of course we want you here, Signora Robertson,' says Don Angelo. 'This is your house.'

'Perhaps they don't have ghosts in England,' suggests Olimpia waspishly.

This stings Emily's sense of national pride. 'Of course we have ghosts,' she says heatedly. 'What about Anne Boleyn? Her ghost walks at Hever Castle. And at the Tower of London.' Her eye suddenly falls on a photograph placed on a high shelf. 'What about Hampton Court?' she says triumphantly. 'That has *tons* of ghosts.' She reaches out for the picture of Siena and Paris at Hampton Court, taken years ago, when Paris was just five. As she does so, she dislodges something which falls to the floor. It is the cross. The cross that was found by Carlo Belotti's dead body.

Don Angelo picks it up. 'Here,' he says to Olimpia. 'You will want to keep this. It must be precious to you.'

What happens next happens so fast, so unexpectedly, that it is several days before Emily can quite put the sequence together. When she does so, though, she knows it will be imprinted on her memory for ever.

Olimpia stares at Don Angelo. He looks back at her, first with benign concern and then with slowly mounting horror.

'*Assassino*,' she screams suddenly. 'Murderer!'

'No,' says the priest, backing away, his hands out in supplication. 'No . . . I swear to you—'

'*Assassino!*' screams Olimpia again. And she lunges for the wood axe.

'No!' shouts Emily. Too late.

Olimpia advances on Don Angelo. 'No . . .' he says, but in an oddly despairing voice. 'No . . .' She raises the axe. Don Angelo falls heavily to the floor.

'Don Angelo!' Emily rushes over to him. He is lying on his side, one arm stretched out awkwardly, his face like putty. It is some seconds before Emily realises that the axe has not actually touched him.

'Heart attack,' comes Olimpia's detached voice from the centre of the room.

'For God's sake!' shouts Emily. 'Call an ambulance!'

But Olimpia just stands there, axe in hand, like Lizzie Borden's grandmother. Emily grabs her mobile (thank God it is in her pocket) and calls the emergency services.

'Ambulance. Villa Serena. Quickly!'

She takes so long stumbling over the directions that she fears Don Angelo will die before she has finished. But, when she puts her mobile down, he is still breathing; awful, hoarse, rattling breaths. Olimpia is nowhere to be seen.

'Emily . . .' says Don Angelo.

'I'm here,' says Emily. 'Don't worry. It'll be all right. Don't try to talk.'

Don Angelo smiles at that. A wistful, painful smile that stretches over his blue lips.

'I must . . .' he says, 'must . . . tell someone. I killed them, you see. I killed Carlo and Pino. No . . .' he says, seeing that Emily is about to speak, 'let me finish. Oh, I didn't pull the trigger but I killed them. I was the lookout boy. I was fifteen. I used to . . . run errands, take messages for the brigade, that sort of thing. I knew . . . all their secrets . . .'

His breathing is shallow, his eyelids fluttering with pain. Emily tries to tell him again to rest, not to worry, but he waves her away with a feeble hand.

'I am dying,' he says. 'I know it. I am at the gates of my Father's kingdom. I must tell someone or I cannot enter . . . '

It suddenly strikes Emily that she is hearing a priest's confession.

'I knew where they were hiding,' he says. 'Only me. I knew they were in the caves. My father used to keep sheep in these hills. I knew every inch of the land. Ramm, the Nazi general, he called all the townspeople together and he told us . . . either give up the partisans or you will all die. I knew he would do it.

I knew what he did to that baby in Lucca. I knew Ramm would kill us all without a second thought. He was a monster.'

Don Angelo is silent for a minute. Emily can hear the rain starting to fall outside and Totti crashing about in the kitchen. She wills the ambulance to arrive.

'So I told him,' says Don Angelo, in a slightly stronger voice. 'I went to him the next morning and I told him where they were hiding. He made me take him there. He said, "Call them." He knew there would be a password, you see. So I called them. "Dante is dead", that was our password. They came out of hiding and he shot them, just like that, point blank. But just before he died . . . Carlo looked at me. He knew.' There is another silence. The wind blows in the pine trees. From the site come the faint sounds of laughter, the radio playing. Voices from another world.

'I buried them,' says Don Angelo, his voice fainter now. 'I couldn't leave them there, everyone would know what had happened. I buried them and I put my rosary in the grave. I had been given it at school, we were all given them. I put my rosary in the grave and it was then I decided . . .' He lapses into silence again and Emily bends closer.

'What did you decide?' she asks. She knows now that he must finish his story. She also knows that there is not much time left.

'To be a priest . . .' Don Angelo whispers, at last. 'To make amends for what I did.'

'And you have,' says Emily urgently. 'You've lived a good life.' She is not sure if he has heard her.

'It was hard,' he says with a slight smile. 'It was hard to give everything up. I had a girlfriend . . . Olimpia.'

'What about her?'

'She was my girlfriend. Carlo's daughter. A double betrayal. That is why I did not want Raffaello to dig here. I knew what he would find.'

'But you buried Carlo,' says Emily gently. 'He is at peace.'

Don Angelo sighs. 'I did what I thought was right,' he says at last. 'I wanted to save the town. But I betrayed them. It was a terrible sin.'

'Listen,' says Emily, bending very close so he can hear her. 'You did save the town. You didn't kill them, Ramm did. You did what you thought was right. You were only a child.'

Don Angelo is silent for a long time, his eyes closed. When he does speak, it is in such a faint voice that Emily can hardly hear him.

'I'm sorry' he says.

Emily knows what she must say. Leaning down so that her lips are close by his ear, she says, 'You are forgiven.'

A faint, very faint, smile flickers across the priest's face. By the time the ambulance arrives, he is dead.

CHAPTER 6

They bury Don Angelo on Good Friday and the symbolism is almost more than Emily can bear. The church, its statues shrouded in purple for the Easter vigil, seems bowed down under the weight of so much grief. Added to this, it rains all day, the sky full of grey tears, falling endlessly. *Dies irae, dies illae*, day of mourning, day of weeping.

In the terrible weeks after Don Angelo's death, Emily finds herself telling her story many times: to Tino the policeman, to the coroner, to Antonella, to countless weeping women in the marketplace. The details never vary, the sudden heart attack, the peaceful death, the ambulance that comes just too late. '*Che peccato*,' say the women, 'God rest his soul, he was a good man, a holy man.'

Only to Monica does Emily tell the truth. The night before Don Angelo's funeral they sit up drinking wine and Emily tells her friend the whole story about the moment when Don Angelo's knowledge that the cross belonged in Carlo Belotti's grave marked him out as his murderer. 'Because Olimpia didn't recognise the cross when she first saw it. She'd never seen it amongst her father's things. The only person who would recognise it would be the person who put it in the grave. All those years ago.'

Monica is surprisingly sympathetic. 'Poor man,' she says. 'What a burden. To go through life thinking that, at fifteen, you murdered two men, one of them your girlfriend's father.'

'But he thought that if he didn't betray them, the whole town would be killed.'

'He was probably right. Have you heard of Sant'Anna di Stazzema? It's a little village not far from here. The Nazis killed over five hundred people there, men, women and children, for harbouring partisans. They found the bodies in stables and barns where they'd been herded together. The youngest was just a baby, twenty-one days old.'

'That might have happened in Monte Albano.'

'Yes, and none of us would be here today.'

They are silent for a few minutes. The kitchen is quiet. All the children are in bed. Totti lies slumbering noisily in front of the fire. Emily fills up their glasses. 'I thought there was something odd,' she says at last, 'at Carlo Belotti's funeral. I thought there was some secret but I didn't know what. I keep thinking about something Don Angelo said. He said, "We pray that we are not put to the test." How can anyone know how they would behave in those circumstances? Paris says she would fight but I'm not so sure that I would. Maybe the so-called collaborators were only doing their best.'

'Maybe,' says Monica. 'I know Virgilio feels guilty because he hid in the hills and didn't fight like his brothers, but he kept Raffaello's family going. He helped a lot of people, including my grandmother. My grandfather was a prisoner in North Africa. Virgilio used to give the family food. Probably saved their lives.'

'But he still felt guilty.'

'Yes. It's a Catholic speciality, guilt.' But she says it sadly and without rancour.

'Don Angelo felt guilty all his life,' says Emily. 'I hope he's found peace now.' She is thinking of those last whispered words: *I'm sorry. You are forgiven.*

'I hope so too,' says Monica sombrely. 'He wasn't a bad sort really. He always stood up for Raffaello when Olimpia used to bad-mouth him.'

'Olimpia! She tried to kill him. I'll never forget the look on her face when she went for him with that axe. She was like a madwoman.'

'Have you seen her since?'

'Not to speak to. I saw her in the town once and she didn't even acknowledge me.'

'She must be wondering what you've said about her.'

'What would be the point of telling anyone? She didn't kill him.'

'She may have given him the heart attack though.'

'Maybe. We'll never know.' Emily thinks for a moment about Don Angelo, not just his last tortured minutes on earth but about his face at the funeral as he prayed for the two men he had betrayed, about the way he had first appeared in her garden, an unlikely angel in dirty plimsolls.

'You know,' she says, 'I think he knew. I think he knew he hadn't got long to live.'

'He did have a weak heart,' says Monica. 'He'd already had one minor heart attack.'

'How on earth do you know?'

'Fabio,' Monica laughs shortly. Fabio is Monica's new boy-friend, a heart surgeon from Padua.

Emily laughs too, thinking of Monica and Fabio, of herself and Michael. She hopes that Monica's medical romance will turn out better than hers did. 'Can you believe Olimpia was Don Angelo's girlfriend?' she says. 'That must be another reason why she was so furious with him.'

'I've heard Romano was in love with her as well. She must have been quite a girl.'

Emily thinks of Olimpia with her shapeless body and her dyed black hair. It is hard to think of her as a young girl, full of confidence in her beauty.

'Romano has been very kind,' she says. 'He and Anna-Luisa looked after the children while I went to the hospital with . . . with Don Angelo.'

'Romano's not a bad chap for a raving fascist.'

'He's still in love with my dad. He sent him a book about Mussolini.'

Monica laughs, draining her wine. 'There's a lot of it still

about, fascists, communists, memories of the past. It's a wonder
that we can go on living with it, but we do.'

The funeral is led by Don Angelo's younger brother who is a priest
in Naples. What sort of a mother, thinks Emily, brings up two
sons to be priests? Looking at Charlie squirming next to her, she
thinks that her own family seems to have escaped the religious
gene. Siena and Paris are also with her, Siena guiltily enjoying the
drama, Paris sulky, only brightening up when she sees Andrea.

The church is packed, standing room only. It seems the
whole town is there to say farewell to their parish priest. Zio
Virgilio, elegant in deep black, next to his son Giovanni and
his grandson, Renato. Romano and Anna-Luisa with their son,
Benito, and his family. All the teachers at the school, Sister
Caterina in tears. Angela from the café, Giancarlo, Antonella,
Tino the policeman, Umberto the mayor (who bursts into tears
in the middle of his eulogy). Even Monica is there, paying her
last respects to the 'old nutter'. Everyone is there except the one
person who Emily looks for, over and over again, long after it
has become obvious that he isn't going to come. And, despite
everything, Emily is not surprised to see Olimpia, majestic in
her lace veil, making her way to the front of the church. Emily
exchanges glances with Monica who smiles back, rather grimly.

Besides the brother from Naples, there are at least ten other
priests on the altar. The candles are lit and the faded fresco of
the Annunciation looks down at them. By the time the children from the primary school have sung a song about all being

members of God's family, everyone is in tears. The readings pass in a miasma of emotion. Then the congregation shuffles up to Communion and it is over, the coffin led out of the church by its triumphant guard of priests.

Outside, it is still raining and the raised umbrellas look like the banners of an army. The graveyard, on a slope behind the church, is muddy and treacherous. Slogging along in the wet, Emily is rather disconcerted to find herself next to Olimpia, who nods coldly. Under a black umbrella held by an altar server, Don Angelo's brother is saying the final prayers, his voice shaking. Two children (Don Angelo's great-nieces, Emily learns later) throw red roses into the grave. Other family members follow suit, an elderly woman who might have been his sister, younger people, awkward in formal clothes. A priest can have no really close family, no sons or daughters, no grandchildren. Only this muttering crowd, this surrogate family, the community whose lives Don Angelo saved at such terrible cost, so long ago.

Then, before the undertaker's men can start filling in the waterlogged soil, Emily feels a sudden disturbance beside her. Olimpia is making her way through the mourners, they are parting to let her pass, she is standing on the very edge of the newly dug grave. Emily cranes forward to see. She sees Olimpia stretch her hand over the grave and let something fall. Something that falls with a gentle clunk on the coffin lid.

'What is it?' people are saying. 'What is it?' But Emily knows. She knows that it is the cross from a rosary given to every Italian child by Mussolini.

CHAPTER 7

Paris's diary

The priest's funeral today. Completely weird. Lots of people crying, everyone saying what a saint he was. Even Monica was there and she is always going on about how she hates priests, how organised religion oppresses women etc. etc. etc. I didn't know Don Angelo all that well but he seemed OK to me. He once gave me and Siena money to buy ourselves ice creams when we were in the piazza and it was boiling hot. Giancarlo was there too but he (Don Angelo) said he could buy his own. That was quite funny, I must admit.

Andrea said Don Angelo was really good to his mother when she was first a single mother because people in Italy, even today, think that it's really shocking to have a baby without being married. I told Andrea that, in London, I was the only person in my class with parents who weren't divorced and he couldn't believe it. It's funny, I used to be quite embarrassed that my parents were still together but, when they separated, I hated it.

I'm OK about it now but I'm a lot older and I've seen a lot more of Life.

Mum was all emotional at the funeral because Don Angelo actually died here, at this house. Siena and I think it's a bit freaky. Apparently he was chatting with Mum and Olimpia and he just fell down dead with a heart attack. Mum called an ambulance but it was too late. I can't decide whether I wish I'd been there or not. I've never seen a dead body and perhaps I ought to. Andrea says he's in no hurry to see one but, when he's a doctor, he'll actually have to cut dead bodies up. Gross. I can't imagine Andrea doing it. Even the smell of Totti's dog food makes him feel sick.

Anyway, Siena and I said, just joking, that maybe now Don Angelo's ghost would haunt us and Mum went mad. Not cross but really, actually mad. She laughed in a sort of crazy, gulpy way and said, 'Oh no, not another one.' I've no idea what she meant but perhaps the whole thing has unhinged her. She's been really odd lately, even for her. She keeps mooning around, looking out of windows, and she sits in front of her laptop for hours and doesn't write a thing. The other day I caught her crying over a torch! And she wears this ridiculous fluorescent jacket all the time. She looks like a demented lollipop lady (another thing they don't have in Italy).

All through the funeral Mum kept twisting round as if she was looking for someone. God knows who. Don Angelo's ghost perhaps? And afterwards she wouldn't stop for a drink with everyone else. No, she had to come dashing back here, going on

about Totti being all alone. How come she's Totti's best mate
all of a sudden? No, she's definitely gone mad. Perhaps it's the
change of life. I read all about it in Cosmopolitan so I speak
from medical knowledge.

Emily is taking Totti for a walk. After all the rain, it is a beautiful evening, the sky washed a clear, azure blue, the cypress
trees dark against the setting sun. She lets Totti off the lead
because he has been shut up all day and he goes bounding
up the hill towards the dig. Emily sighs and follows him. The
ground is a swamp after all the rain, her boots make disgusting
squelchy noises as she plods after her dog. She hopes he's not
digging up priceless artefacts but she just can't be bothered to
call him back.

The site is deserted because it's nearly Easter. The volunteers are either at home or raising a glass to Don Angelo in
the church's underground bar. Where is Raffaello? Wining and
dining the Soprintendenza in some smart Roman restaurant?
Laughing with his fellow archaeologists over some hilarious
joke from the Rosetta Stone? She had thought he would come
home for Don Angelo's funeral; in fact that thought had been
the only thing that had sustained her during the dreadful hours
after the priest's death. After Don Angelo had been pronounced
dead and his relatives contacted, Emily had got a taxi home
from the hospital. But then, on impulse, she had found herself
directing the driver into the centre of Monte Albano and asking
him to stop outside La Foresta.

It was early evening and waiters were setting out the tables. She expected to find Renato there but was amazed to find Zio Virgilio sitting alone at a corner table with the newspaper and a glass of grappa.

'Mrs Robertson!' He stood up, arthritic but gallant.

'Signor . . .' She didn't know what to call him.

'Please,' he waved an airy hand, 'call me Zio Virgilio.'

Emily hesitated. It seemed such a presumption somehow, but eventually she managed it. 'Zio Virgilio, do you know how to contact Raffaello?'

He looked at her intently. 'Yes, I have his cellular number somewhere but, sit down, Mrs Robertson, you look very pale.'

Emily sat down. She hardly noticed when one of the invisible waiters placed a second glass of grappa in front of her.

'What's the matter?' Zio Virgilio asked gently.

'Don Angelo . . . Don Angelo's dead.'

She remembers how Zio Virgilio did not look surprised or even shocked. He simply put his hand on top of hers. 'So,' he said at last.

Emily was surprised to find tears running down her face. 'He's dead,' she repeated. 'I thought Raffaello ought to know.'

She will never forget how Zio Virgilio looked, his face dark in the shadows, as he said, more to himself than to her, 'Poor Angelo. Pray God that he can lay down his burden at last.' Zio Virgilio knew, she realised, he knew all along.

In the end, she hadn't told Raffaello. He would get to know soon enough, from Zio Virgilio, and what would be the point?

He obviously didn't want to see her. And he hadn't come home, not even for the funeral, though Monica said that he had sent flowers. He doesn't like funerals, she tells herself, but the thought remains that he had an excuse to come back and he didn't. Perhaps she'll never see him again.

Totti has left the main site and is digging happily near the caves where the bodies were discovered. Emily can see his feathered tail wagging as he burrows deeper into the soft soil.

'Totti!' she yells. Oh God, he'll probably dig someone else up and the whole awful business will start all over again. Just how many secrets lie buried in these hills?

'Totti!'

He looks up cheerfully and keeps digging. Paris's training is obviously having no effect at all. Panting, Emily catches up with the dog and pulls him back by his collar. There, exposed by the rain, and the Alsatian's frantically scrabbling paws, is a square stone slab.

She has found the lost city of Atlantis.

CHAPTER 8

Easter Saturday evening and Emily is preparing to go to Bologna. Paris is out with Andrea and Siena is staying the night with Francesca. Emily is going to drive Charlie to Monica's house and then go to the opening of Vittorio's. Beyond that, she hasn't thought. Will she see Michael? Will she fall weeping into his arms, as she has so often imagined? Will he be there with his wife on his arm, all cool and American? Would she care? She doesn't know. She is moving as if underwater. The events of the last few weeks have left her in a sort of daze. Raffaello is gone, Don Angelo is dead and, outside, still buried in the mud, is probably the greatest Etruscan find ever made. All that she can do, she feels, is move very slowly through her preparations for the evening and let the thinking take care of itself.

On the table in front of Emily are her smartest handbag, the invitation to the opening and the old newspaper cutting about Michael. He looks up at her from the grainy paper, clear-eyed and confident as ever. 'Dr Michael Bartnicki, consultant in neurology at King's College, London—' Is she really going to see him again?

Emily sighs and goes outside to call Charlie. She left him on the terrace, playing with his cars. He is insisting on taking a whole truckload to Monica's. She'd better start getting him ready. He travels with more luggage than the Sun King himself.

'Charlie!' she calls.

Totti, who is also coming to Monica's, barks from somewhere amongst the olive trees. Otherwise everything is silent. The trees shiver in a sudden breeze and then are still again. Sighing, Emily climbs the steps to the terrace. The toy cars are there, frozen in disastrous motorway pile-ups, but Charlie is nowhere to be seen.

'Charlie!'

She runs round to the front of the house, trampling through Paul's abandoned vegetable patch, the place where she first saw Don Angelo. Her car is there, parked at an untidy angle on the gravel, but there is no sign of Charlie.

'Charlie!' Emily's voice is now hoarse with suppressed hysteria. She runs back in through the house, her footsteps echoing on the stone floors. Through the sitting room, monstrous clock ticking, across the hall and into the kitchen.

Charlie is sitting at the kitchen table, looking at the newspaper cutting.

'Charlie! Thank God! Where did you get to?' She hugs him fiercely, breathing in his lovely outdoor scent of grass and wood smoke.

Charlie disengages himself briskly. 'Mum,' he says, pointing at the picture in the newspaper. 'There's that man who's always watching me.'

Paris and Andrea are in the graveyard. They hadn't really meant to come here. It's just that there's not really anywhere else for them to go. They have been in the café for an hour nursing two lemon sodas but Angela has started looking at them oddly and they don't have the money for any more.

'I'm going to get a job this summer,' says Andrea, striding between the graves. 'Then we can go to places. The cinema, restaurants, a trip to Florence maybe.'

'You've got to study too, remember,' says Paris. She's not going to let Andrea forget his dream of being a doctor, even if he does. Her own ambition is currently to be an archaeologist though she thinks she'll specialise in the Egyptians. They seem to have done a bit more building than the Etruscans.

Andrea grins. 'You sound like my mother.'

'Thanks a lot.'

'It's a compliment,' protests Andrea.

'Look, I love my mum too. I just don't want to sound like her.'

'You don't,' says Andrea, sitting down on an ivy-covered tombstone. 'Your Italian's much better.'

'I know. Poor Mum, three years in Italy and she still can't roll her *r*'s.'

Paris sits next to Andrea on the tombstone. It is starting to get dark and the gravestones cast crazy, elongated shadows across the grass. A bird flies up, out of the darkening trees and, somewhere far-off, a dog barks. Paris is glad of Andrea's solid presence next to her.

Next to the church, in the space reserved for priests (a kind of ecclesiastical club class) is the newly dug grave of Don Angelo. There is no headstone yet but the grass around the grave is covered with flowers: elaborate wreaths, cheap bouquets in crackling plastic, single flowers, plastic sunflowers, even a football shirt or two (Don Angelo was a passionate Juventus supporter). By contrast, slightly further up the hill, the graves of Carlo Belotti and Pino Albertini seem lonely and forgotten. But someone has remembered them. Peering round, Paris sees a gleam of red, white and green. She gets up to have a better look.

Lying up against the new, white tombstone (*Carlo Belotti, patrioto, 1902–1944*) is a large wreath of red and white roses interspersed with green foliage. The colours of the Italian flag.

Paris bends down. 'There's something written on it.' She reads: '*Meglio vivere un giorno da leone che cento anni da pecora.*' She translates slowly into English. 'Better to live one day as a lion than a hundred years as a sheep. What does that mean?'

Andrea comes and stands beside her. 'It was a famous saying of Mussolini's. It means, I suppose, it is better to die young, having achieved something, like these two did, rather than grow old peacefully.'

Paris shivers. 'I don't like that,' she says vehemently. 'I want to live a hundred years as a lion.'

Andrea puts his arm round her. 'You will, Paris,' he says. 'You will.'

'What do you mean?' whispers Emily. 'The man who's always watching you?'

Charlie's mouth goes square with the frustration of not being understood. 'That man,' he jabs a finger at Dr Michael Bartnicki, consultant neurologist. 'That man. He watches me.'

'He *watches* you? How? Where?'

'Here!' yells Charlie. 'In this house. He watches me.'

Emily feels her whole body go cold, as if she has stepped into an underground tomb.

'Why,' she says, almost to herself. 'Why would he be watching you?'

'I don't know,' says Charlie brightly. 'Why don't you ask him?'

Emily swings round and there, standing in her kitchen, looking as calm and sure of his welcome as he had that evening in Gordon Square, is Michael.

Emily screams and grabs hold of Charlie.

'Don't be afraid, Emily,' says Michael kindly. 'It's me.'

'What are you doing here?' whispers Emily, still clutching Charlie so tightly that he whimpers.

'I came to see you,' says Michael simply. He looks the same. Slightly older maybe, his blond hair thinning slightly, lines at the corners of his eyes, a suggestion of grey around the temples. But he is still staggeringly handsome and assured. Standing in her kitchen, dressed formally in a dinner jacket and bow tie, he looks as if he has come from another world.

'I thought you might like a lift to the restaurant opening,' he says. 'You are going, aren't you?'

Emily glances at the table where the invitation glints dully beside her smart handbag.

'Yes ... I was,' she says slowly.

'Great. We can go together.'

'Michael,' says Emily, hearing a strange, almost pleading, note in her voice. 'What do you mean, we can go together? I haven't seen you for twenty years. You can't just waltz in here and take me out for the evening.'

'No,' says Michael, smiling. 'But I've seen you.'

'What?'

'I've been here before, loads of times. I've seen Paris and Siena playing cards, I've seen Charlie playing with his cars. I've seen that mad old cleaner woman. I used to whistle bits of opera just to make her jump. I've seen that oaf of a boyfriend of yours, lumbering about the place with his shovels and pickaxes. I've even seen your parents. Dear Ginny. She always liked me.'

Emily starts to back away. 'You've been spying on me.'

Michael laughs. 'It's not spying! You still love me, I know it. You look me up on Google every night. I log into your computer and it's always there, under "history". You know we belong together.'

'But you're married,' says Emily, still moving away, dragging Charlie with her. He is silent for once, eyes huge, moving his head to and fro like a spectator at a tennis match.

Michael shrugs. 'It didn't work out. It's been a very difficult time for me. I've been a bit depressed, to tell you the truth. So, when I saw those pictures of you at Izzy's house, it was like a bolt of lightning. You hadn't changed at all. I just knew I had to come and see you. Dear little Emily. The only woman who's ever loved me. Apart from my mum, of course.'

'Why didn't you just ring me up?' asks Emily, edging towards the back door.

'I don't know,' says Michael. 'I just wanted to see how you were doing. I know all about you. Even when I was in England, I always read your columns. I knew you wrote them for me.'

The columns! With shame, Emily remembers how she had, in truth, written them for Michael. Look what a good time I'm having, she had wanted to tell him, look how wonderful my life is without you.

'You seemed to be having such a perfect time,' says Michael, as if reading her thoughts. 'I used to be sad, thinking that you didn't miss me at all. But then it all changed. You got rid of that ridiculous Spouse character and I knew you needed me. And it's not too late, darling. I've come back.' He takes a step towards her.

'It is too late,' snaps Emily. 'My boyfriend's due back in a minute.'

'No he's not,' says Michael calmly. 'He's left you. I saw him driving off one day with a face like thunder. He's gone to Rome. That's what they say in town anyway. I had a very interesting chat with the young man who runs that ridiculous excuse for a restaurant. What's it called? La Foresta. He says that lover boy has left you. He says he was only ever interested in the Etruscans anyway. Poor little Emily, you were totally taken in by him.'

Despite herself, Emily finds herself believing him. Raffaello never loved her, he was only ever interested in the Etruscans. He is never coming back. She wonders if she has ever felt more alone in her life.

'Anyway,' says Michael briskly, 'what do you care? You don't love him anyway.'

'I do,' says Emily sadly. 'I do.'

'Nonsense. You love me. We'll be one happy family. You, me, Siena, Paris, Charlie and my daughter Jessica. You'll like Jessica. My mum can move in with us too. She always liked you.'

'Your mother . . .' Emily remembers Gina's letter with the delicate, enticing PS: 'Michael will be there . . . I know he would like to see you again.' Did Gina know what her beloved son was planning? Was her letter meant to lure Emily into Michael's trap? 'Does your mother know what you've been doing?'

'What do you mean?' asks Michael, looking genuinely puzzled. He moves forward to pick up the invitation that is lying on the table. Emily backs further away, pulling Charlie with her. If only they can reach the back door . . .

'Does she know that you've been breaking into my house and spying on me?'

'Spying on you?' repeats Michael in an outraged tone. 'I

412

haven't been spying on you. I've been looking after you, just checking that you're all right, my darling.'

Guiltily Emily thinks of those evenings spent staring at Michael's name on Facebook or googling him desperately, trying to find a recent photo, wanting somehow to be part of his new life. She thinks how carefully she conserved the newspaper cutting sent by Petra and how greedily she grabbed any scrap of information let fall by Chad. Is she really so different? Then she thinks, well, I didn't break into his house and I'm not trying to frighten him and his family to death. There are limits, after all.

'I wanted to see you,' Michael is saying in a dreamy kind of voice. 'I kept thinking about how it used to be when we first met. We were happy, weren't we? Going round London, hand in hand, listening to terrible music and thinking we would stay young for ever.'

Emily thinks back and finds, for the first time, that the past has deserted her. She can't, for the life of her, remember anything about being young and in love with Michael. All she can think about is the present: herself and Charlie trapped in the kitchen with the new, mad-sounding Michael, Raffaello miles away, nobody within yelling distance.

'I should have married you,' Michael is saying. 'My mother always said I should but I wasn't ready to settle down. I wanted to be free.' He laughs bitterly. 'Free! I was never free for a second with Mara. My mother was right about her. She never loved me. She never even loved Jessica. She was always forgetting her appointments, her medication. Without me, she would have died a hundred times over. And now she wants custody, if you please!'

Silently wishing Mara luck in her battle for custody, Emily edges closer to the back door. Thank God it is never locked. She reaches out one hand and grabs the handle. It is locked.

'I locked it,' says Michael informatively. 'It's dangerous, the way you never lock the doors. That'll have to change when I move in. I did for the dog too. He's an awful nuisance, isn't he?'

'What did you do to him?' Emily thinks of Totti's earlier barking from the olive groves. That must have been when Michael got him. Poor Totti, her stupid, lovable, useless guard dog. What has happened to him?

Michael laughs. 'Never you mind. I don't like dogs. I never liked my mother's stupid woofter in a tartan coat, if you remember. Now, we'd better get going. The opening starts in an hour and it's a long drive to Bologna.'

Emily wills her voice to stay calm. Surely someone will come and rescue her? But who? Paris is at Antonella's, Siena is with Francesca. Romano, her nearest neighbour, is as deaf as a post and is probably asleep in front of Fascist TV.

'Michael,' she says, 'I'm not coming with you.'

'Of course you are,' says Michael. 'You need a man to take charge round here.'

'Michael.' Emily tries to make her voice sound firm and authoritative. Tries to make it, in fact, like she remembers Gina's voice sounding. 'Please leave my house at once.'

In answer, Michael makes a sudden grab at her. Emily screams and tries to run past him, half dragging, half carrying Charlie. Michael bars her way, still smiling, his blue eyes wide and innocent.

'Michael! For God's sake! Let me go!'

Smiling sweetly, Michael lifts his arm to let her pass. Emily ducks past him and is out into the hall. The front door is only a few yards ahead of her. She runs blindly and falls headlong over the small table that had once held a Chinese bowl and some matches. Charlie screams as she lands on him. Emily scrambles to her feet and reaches for her son. But Michael has got there first.

'I'll take Charlie,' he says firmly. 'We're old friends, aren't we, Charlie? I used to pop in and see him at night. He never told anyone, though. He was a good boy. He kept our secret. Charlie wants me to move in, don't you, Charlie? He needs a father. Come on, Charlie boy, let's get you in the car.'

'Mummy!' yells Charlie. 'Help me!'

Michael strides towards the door, holding Charlie by the back of the neck. Emily screams and flies at him. It is only afterwards that she realises that she is holding a knife which she must have picked up in the kitchen. What was she going to do with it? Kill Michael? She knows that she would have done it too, to save her baby. But just as Emily, propelled by mother fury, lunges at her one-time boyfriend, the front door bursts open and first Totti, trailing a broken rope, and then Raffaello fling themselves on the unsuspecting neurologist.

Michael falls to the floor and releases Charlie, who runs to Emily, clinging to her like a monkey with his arms and legs and anything else that he thinks might help. Sweet-tempered Totti is growling furiously as he attacks Michael's leg. Michael pushes him off and struggles to his feet, only to be knocked out cold by a punch from Raffaello.

Breathing heavily, Raffaello comes over to Emily. 'Are you all right, Mrs Robertson?'

In answer, Emily throws herself into his arms. Quite a difficult feat considering that she is still holding Charlie. Raffaello, though, shows no difficulty in enfolding them both in a fierce hug.

'It's OK,' he says. 'It's OK now.'

'Is he dead?' asks Charlie hopefully.

'No,' says Raffaello. 'Only knocked out. Who is he?'

'My ex-boyfriend,' says Emily with a shaky laugh.

'*Dio mio*,' says Raffaello. 'Have I interrupted a school reunion?'

'That's right,' says Emily. 'We were just having a little chat about old times.'

'You can drop the knife now,' says Raffaello.

Only a few hours later, Emily, Charlie and Raffaello are in the red restaurant celebrating Zio Virgilio's birthday. Charlie has refused to be parted from Emily and even Totti is with them, lying peacefully under the table. Michael, on the other hand, has been driven away in the charge of Tino the policeman.

'Do you want to press charges?' asks Raffaello.

'I don't know,' says Emily. On the one hand, she wants

Michael locked up, preferably somewhere a long way away from her, but on the other, she doesn't want all the publicity and hassle of going to court, of having to relive the whole nightmare: the terrifying sight of Michael appearing in her kitchen, dressed for a formal party, the realisation that he had been spying on her for months, the dreadful moment when she thought Charlie was in danger.

'I could just ask Tino to scare him a bit,' offers Raffaello.

'I want him to leave Italy. I never want to see him again. Could Tino scare him that much?'

Raffaello laughs grimly. 'Just leave it to me.'

One of the magic waiters appears to fill up their glasses. Emily takes a gulp of champagne but she doesn't feel drunk; she feels wonderfully alert, as if she is seeing everything for the first time. The long table with its glittering glasses, the restaurant with its antlers and photographs and single grinning skull, Raffaello's family, his great-uncle, resplendent in red velvet, his cousin Renato, sleek in a black dinner jacket, watching from the other end of the table.

'Raffaello,' says Emily, 'what made you come to the house this afternoon?'

'Renato told me that some Englishman had been hanging around asking lots of questions about you. Then Tino told me that his car had been spotted near your house. So I thought I'd better come and investigate. Besides,' Raffaello grins, his black eyes gleaming in the candlelight, 'I came to take you to the party.'

'But I said I wasn't going.'

'I thought I might be able to persuade you. I thought that maybe you wanted to come. Was I right?'

'Yes,' Emily admits. She realises now that she has been in love with Raffaello for a long time, possibly since that day in Badia Tedalda.

'Raffaello?' says Emily. 'What happened in Rome? Are you going to be able to save the dig?'

'Shh,' says Raffaello. 'Zio Virgilio is about to speak.'

Don Virgilio gets to his feet. He looks curiously regal in the sumptuous darkness of the restaurant, the red king in the red restaurant. Poised and elegant, he thanks everyone for coming, thanks his grandson Renato for organising this wonderful meal, thanks his dear great-nephew and his lovely lady friend for attending, wishes everyone good health and happiness.

'Just one more thing,' he says, 'before I sit down. Tonight, in this restaurant, which has seen so many good times and so many dangerous times, I would like officially to name my grandson Renato as my heir. He will inherit the restaurant when I am gone.'

There is a murmur of voices and a scattering of applause. Across the table, Renato looks at Raffaello with blazing triumph on his face. Raffaello lifts his glass to him.

'So Renato gets the restaurant,' says Emily. 'What do you get?'

Raffaello looks at her. 'I've got what I want,' he says, very seriously. 'I've got you. I could have done with a great archaeological find as well though,' he adds, more in his normal voice.

'Ah,' says Emily, I think I can help you there.' And, under the table, Totti wags his tail in agreement.

EPILOGUE

Summer and the grass grows high on Carlo Belotti's grave. The Villa Serena lies sleepily in the sun, shaded by the cypress trees. The only incongruous touch is an official-looking sign by the gate which points to the *Scavi*, the ruins. A few tourists brave the trek up the unmade road and stand and stare at the sunken road and the stone tombs but, without explanations, it is hard to bring the past to life and the tourists often turn away, disappointed, dreading the long, hot walk back.

The slab found by Totti did, after all, turn out to be the equivalent of the lost city of Atlantis. Barely twenty centimetres wide, the stone has only fifty words carved onto it but they are, literally, priceless. This is because Totti's Stone (as Raffaello insists it must be called) contains an Etruscan inscription with a Latin translation, the only word-for-word translation of the Etruscan language in existence. Raffaello's site is now world-famous and the Soprintendenza approved it the second she saw the stone, still covered with Totti's muddy footprints.

By leaving the stone in the ground, it turned out that Emily had done exactly the right thing. 'I left it because I wasn't sure if you were coming back,' said Emily, 'and I didn't want you to come back for the Etruscans and not for me.'

'Oh ye of little faith,' teased Raffaello. 'Didn't I tell you that I wouldn't give up without a fight?' And he did have a fight with Michael, reflects Emily, albeit a short-lived one. But, even if he hadn't been taken by surprise, Emily knows that Michael would have been no match for Raffaello.

Chad, contacted by Emily, says that Michael had a nervous breakdown last autumn, when his daughter suffered a relapse. He had come to Italy to try to recover. 'I'm surprised he didn't look you up,' said Chad. 'He seemed to have become a bit obsessed by you.' Emily said nothing. Thanks for the warning, Chad, she thought.

Michael, dutifully scared by Tino, has gone back to England. Emily discovers this in a letter from Gina who has sold her Bologna restaurant. 'There is no point in my staying here,' she wrote, 'without my darling boy.' It occurs to Emily that there was always something weird about that relationship, right from the beginning. Vittorio's has been bought by Renato, hell-bent on extending his empire. Emily thinks they deserve each other.

On the strength of the Totti Stone, Raffaello has been offered a job at (of course) Bologna University. Raffaello says that, when the children have left school, they should move to Bologna. They should get married, he says. Emily is not really too bothered about this. She likes things as they are; she likes having Raffaello's big, comforting pirate's body in her bed. She loves the moment when the empty space in front of her suddenly becomes filled with his presence, his dark hair and wicked black eyes, his familiar ironical grin. She even loves his noisiness, the way he always arrives when she is at a critical point in her book, bringing mud and cold air and loud requests for English breakfasts.

Emily is writing a book. She is at last writing the book she always wanted to write: about the dark side of life in a Tuscan town, about long-dead secrets, hidden loyalties, unspoken enmities. She doesn't know if anyone will want to read it but she thinks that, when it is finished, she will send it to Giles, whose partner works in publishing. He owes her a favour, she thinks.

Paris is still going out with Andrea. Emily is pleased but she doesn't make the mistake of assuming that it will last. Who knows what will happen? They still have all their lives ahead of them and who knows better than her the folly of attaching too much importance to your first love. Siena is going out with Camouflage Man, who turns out to be a second-year medical student at Bologna University. Emily is slightly worried that he is three years older than her and even more worried that he is a medical student, but she keeps these fears to herself. Siena also says that she wants to become a Catholic. It's restful, she says. Emily does not quite know what to make of this but she feels that Don Angelo would have approved.

Petra, too, is happy. She is living with Darren. The boys, especially Harry, adore him. As for Petra, she can never forget the moment when Darren swept Harry up into his arms and strode with him out of the supermarket, away from all the censorious faces and pointing fingers, a true modern-day knight in shining tracksuit. Unlike Emily, she quite likes the idea of getting married one day. 'It'll be something different,' she says. 'You can even do it on the pier these days.'

Emily still hasn't really spoken to Olimpia since that terrible day when the cross fell onto the floor and exposed Don Angelo's act of betrayal. Emily is convinced that it was Olimpia who put the skull on her doorstep. After all, her son is a doctor. She could easily have got hold of a medical school skull. But, despite everything, Emily feels that Olimpia deserves to know the truth about Don Angelo, to know why he felt that he had to betray her father, all those years ago. She feels that perhaps this is why Don Angelo unburdened his soul to her, an uncom-prehending foreigner, so that she can make sure his story is heard by those who need to hear it. So, eventually, she sits down and writes Olimpia a letter explaining things as best she can. Olimpia never acknowledges the letter but, one day, Emily comes home to find a present for Charlie on the doorstep, a beautiful, painted spinning top. 'For Carlito,' says the note. 'It was my father's.'

Charlie is climbing the mountain behind the olive groves. They say it's a hill but he knows that it's a mountain. It's one of the Mountains of the Moon, so high that when you get to the top you can see the moon and the stars and the sun. So high that sometimes it's all covered in mist and it looks like it's really joined on to the clouds.

It is hard work climbing in the sun but it is an expedition so he is determined. He and Edoardo are *partigiani* and this is going to be their lookout. The *partigiani* were here in the war and they were very brave and they hid things and took messages and climbed hills. Edoardo's great-great-grandfather was a *partigiano* and he was called Carlo, which is what Charlie's name is really, in Italian.

When he reaches the top, he can see for miles. He can see the town which is on the top of another mountain, it's like being on a ship, the kind with very high sails. A pirate ship. If he doesn't become a *partigiano* when he grows up, he's going to be a pirate. Or a man who digs things up, like Raffaello. Raffaello says that Totti's better at his job than he is but that's a joke, he thinks.

There are lots of stones on the hilltop, little shiny ones with sharp edges. They're sort of pink, which is a bit of a girly colour, but quite nice all the same. They're pirate's treasure. He'll collect them all up and bury them in a box somewhere and make a map with a big X on it so people will know where to dig. The map will be all brown like the one that Monica made at school; she stained it with tea and wrote on it with an inky red pen to make it look like blood.

Charlie sits down and plays with the stones for a while. And, for some reason, he thinks of that day on Brighton beach and the story that Siena told him.

Once there was a boy called Charlie (she'd said Harry too but he wouldn't have him in his story). One day they went to the beach and they found a magic stone. They didn't know it was magic at first but, when they held it up to the light, it started to shimmer and glow. Charlie started to rub the stone and he heard a little tiny voice saying, 'Throw me back into the sea and I will give you three wishes . . .'

So Charlie wished. He wished for lots of treasure and a pirate ship and a scooter like Edoardo's. No, first he wished for three more wishes and then he wished for treasure and a pirate ship and a scooter and a dog and a friend called Edoardo and a big house in Italy with shiny stones in the garden. One, two, three, four, five . . . how many is that? Then he wished for everyone to be happy and to live happily ever after. The end.

And Charlie begins to walk slowly back down the mountain.

ACKNOWLEDGEMENTS

With thanks to the tourist office at Badia Tedalda, especially to Fulvio. Badia Tedalda is a real place, as is the tourist office and the church of St Michael. It is a beautiful town, well worth visiting. Monte Albano, though, is fictional. I am particularly grateful to Fulvio for giving me a book called *Nonno, Nonna Raccontami* which details the experiences of the town's inhabitants during the war.

Thanks to Roberta Battman for correcting my Italian and to Patricia Tombolani for her advice on names. I should add that Michael Bartnicki in no way resembles any member of the Bartnicki family!

Thanks, as always, to my agent Tif Loenhis and my editor, Mary-Anne Harrington. Love and thanks always to my husband Andrew and our children Alexander and Juliet. Special thanks to Andrew, my favourite archaeologist, for his constant support.